Selected Praise for Kat Martin

"Drugs, lies, corruption, and long-held secrets are at the core of this hard-hitting romance and well-done series opener."
—*Library Journal* on *The Conspiracy*

"Both a suspenseful mystery to find a lost brother and a thrilling romance, Kat Martin's latest is an easy page-turner."
—*BookTrib* on *The Conspiracy*

"Martin keeps the twists and turns coming in the sensuous and spirited first Maximum Security romantic thriller.... Readers will find it hard to wait for the next book in this tantalizing series about detectives, bodyguards, and bounty hunters."
—*Publishers Weekly* on *The Conspiracy*

"Kat Martin is a fast gun when it comes to storytelling, and I love her books."
—#1 *New York Times* bestselling author Linda Lael Miller

"[Kat] Martin is a terrific storyteller."
—*Booklist*

"It doesn't matter what Martin's characters are up against—she dishes up romantic suspense, sizzling sex and international intrigue."
—*RT Book Reviews*

"[A] suspenseful, emotion-packed page-turner... This nonstop, high-stakes adventure stands on its own."
—*Library Journal*, starred review, on *Against the Edge*

"Martin has a consummate skill for developing the most lovable and the most despicable characters."
—*Publishers Weekly*

Also available from Kat Martin

*Don't miss The Deception, the next book
in the Maximum Security series from HQN Books!*

KAT
MARTIN

THE
CONSPIRACY

HQN™

ISBN-13: 978-1-335-04575-1

The Conspiracy

Copyright © 2019 by Kat Martin

The publisher acknowledges the copyright holder of the individual work as follows:

Wait Until Dark
Copyright © 2018 by Kat Martin

Recycling programs
for this product may
not exist in your area.

www.HQNBooks.com

Printed in U.S.A.

CONTENTS

To my husband, Larry, for all your years of love and support. Thanks for a wild, wonderful ride.

THE CONSPIRACY

CHAPTER ONE

Dallas, Texas

She knew who he was. The only man at the gala in a black tuxedo and shiny black alligator cowboy boots. Chase Garrett. The man she intended to hire to help her find her missing brother.

Harper Winston had known Chase since the day her father had thrown an obnoxiously extravagant party in honor of her sixteenth birthday.

Chase had attended with her older brother, Michael. She had spotted Chase in a swimsuit standing next to the pool, tall, with a lean, hard-muscled body, whiskey-brown eyes and thick, dark blond hair. In the sun, it had gleamed like pirate's gold.

Aside from the close-trimmed beard along a jaw that had hardened with maturity, Chase hadn't changed. He still had the perfectly symmetrical features of a movie star combined with a toughness that appealed to a legion of women.

Now that she was thirty, Chase thirty-five, Harper still found him ridiculously attractive, though he'd never given her more than a passing glance.

He didn't notice her tonight, though she wore an elegant black strapless gown that hugged her slender curves and set off the pale blond hair she wore long and slightly turned under, framing her face. She glanced over to where he stood next to a stunning brunette, a successful lawyer in Dallas, the typical sort of woman Chase dated. Self-made career women, professors, bankers, stockbrokers. Not someone like her, the daughter of a wealthy Texas businessman, a woman who had attended Sarah Lawrence along with a bevy of other rich socialites from around the country.

It didn't matter that she was nothing like they were. That she hadn't the least interest in society. Her interests lay in the business world, in Elemental Chic, the company she had started, a line of affordable, stylish and well-made casual clothing and accessories.

She wasn't cut out for teaching or social work, she had discovered during a year of volunteer work in South America, an adventure she had undertaken mostly because her father disapproved.

Harvard Business School was where she was meant to be, she had grudgingly conceded. As her father had insisted and was eager to pay for—business being one of the few interests she and Knox Winston, a self-made multimillionaire, had in common.

Unlike her father, Chase Garrett came from old money, which he disdained, though he and his two brothers had inherited a not-so-small fortune from Bass Garrett, Chase's dad.

Harper lifted a champagne flute off a passing waiter's tray and took a sip. Chase might not notice her tonight, but he was the reason she was there. She hadn't seen him in years, but when she had read in the newspaper that he would be attending the gala, she'd seized the opportunity. She wanted to see the man he had become, the man she would be facing tomorrow.

It didn't matter what he thought of her as a woman. She needed his professional assistance. Her brother was in trouble. She knew it deep in her soul. Mikey had disappeared, and Chase was among the few people she trusted to help her find him.

Chase owned Maximum Security, a firm that specialized in private investigation, bail enforcement, personal protection, business and residential security. She had done her homework, knew he had offices in Phoenix and San Diego as well as here in Dallas. Chase was wildly successful, his reputation impeccable.

No matter his opinion of her, he had once been a close friend of her brother's, a man Michael trusted completely. She needed Chase's help, and she was determined to convince him.

She wouldn't give up until she did.

Standing next to Chase, Marla Chambers, his date for the evening, took a drink of her martini. "You don't look like you're having a very good time," she said. "Should I be insulted?"

His mouth edged up. "Sorry. I was thinking about a case. I can't seem to get it off my mind."

"The missing teenage girl?"

He'd mentioned her earlier. He nodded. "Tammy Bennett. Her parents think she's been kidnapped. They've managed to convince the police, who are in the middle of an all-out search. I think she's a runaway."

"Are you working for the parents?"

"No. I just happened to hear something on the street today. I'd like to check it out."

She eyed him with speculation. "And you're wishing you were doing that now instead of being here with me."

He hated to admit she was right. His gaze ran over the attractive brunette he had been seeing for the past couple of weeks. He enjoyed Marla's company. Enjoyed her in bed. But it wasn't serious for either of them, and he kept thinking of the missing fourteen-year-old, a story that had been all over the news.

"She's just a kid. If my source is right, she's in very big trouble, and I might be able to find her."

"I don't suppose you could let the police handle it."

"I could. I need to check it out first, make sure the tip is real."

Marla shook her head, went up on her toes and kissed his cheek. "Then you'd better go."

"What about you? You don't look like you're ready to leave."

"I'm a big girl. I'll stay awhile longer, catch a cab when it's time to go home."

Chase set his scotch down on one of the linen-draped tables. "Thanks, Marla. I appreciate this."

"Call me tomorrow. Let me know what happens."

"If I'm right, you'll see it on the news." Chase left Marla chatting with a friend and headed for the door. As he made his way through the throng of elegantly dressed men and women, an attractive blonde caught his eye. Slender figure, porcelain skin, big blue eyes. She looked familiar.

As the puzzle pieces slid together, he recognized her, Harper Winston, the younger sister of his best friend in college. As a teenager, Harper had been pretty. Looking at her tonight, seeing her for the first time in years, he realized she had grown into a beautiful woman.

Unfortunately, she was a Winston. Her father, Knox Winston, was one of his least favorite people. Ruthless in business, his crooked dealings had made him a very wealthy man. But worse than his shady business enterprises was the mental abuse he'd heaped on his son, that had put Michael on a downward spiral into drugs. And effectively destroyed his friendship with Chase.

Chase had steered clear of the Winstons ever since. He remembered hearing Harper had moved to Houston some years back. After that, he'd lost track of her and Michael, and he intended to keep it that way.

Though he had to admit as he took in Harper's sleek curves and shiny silver-blond hair, he wouldn't mind taking her to bed.

Even if the lady was of a similar mind, renewing his connection with the Winstons was the last thing he wanted. Besides, as he thought back on it, Harper had a reputation for being as cool and remote as she looked.

On his way out the door, he passed her. For an instant, her gorgeous blue eyes slid over him, and Chase felt a jolt of heat he hadn't expected. He wouldn't pursue it. Sleeping with Harper Winston, no matter how good it might be, just wasn't worth it.

His thoughts returned to the task ahead, and Chase headed for the valet stand, a harsh October wind whipping against him on the way. He needed to get home and change. He couldn't go to the Double Eagle dressed in a tuxedo—the bar was in Old East Dallas, one of the meanest sections of the city.

Earlier that day as a favor to Jason Maddox, a PI in his office who was looking for a bail skip, he had contacted one of his sources. During the conversation, his informant had mentioned the missing girl. Bennie had figured the tip was worth money, and if it turned into anything, Chase would gladly pay him.

It didn't take long to reach the high-rise building on Pearl Street where he lived. He parked his silver Mercedes in the garage next to the brown Dodge Ram pickup he used for work.

Taking the elevator up to the seventeenth floor, he stepped into the entry and crossed the high-ceiling living room. An oversize sofa in a nubby cream fabric, dark brown throw pillows and lots of dark wood gave the condo a masculine tone that suited him. Stylized contemporary Western art hung on the walls.

With thirty-five hundred square feet of space, a spectacular view of the city, and a big terrace that opened off the living room and master bedroom, the condo was expensive and worth every dime.

Changing out of the tux, he pulled on a pair of worn jeans, a frayed blue denim shirt and a pair of scuffed cowboy boots. He retrieved the little .380 he carried when he wanted a weapon he could easily conceal, clipped the holster onto his belt behind his back and pulled his shirttail down over it.

It didn't take long to reach the bar. The Dodge was ten years old, a few dents here and there, the paint a little faded, which helped it blend in. But the tires were new, and under the hood, the rebuilt engine ran like a scalded dog. He parked it on the street half a block from the bar and hoped the truck wouldn't get jacked.

Looking at the trash on the sidewalk, broken beer bottles, used hypodermic needles and drunks asleep in the gutter, part of him hoped his information was wrong and the girl wasn't there.

The other half hoped like hell she was.

If he got lucky, maybe he could get her out of there.

CHAPTER TWO

The Double Eagle smelled like sour whiskey and stale beer, the inside as run-down as the outside, with sagging wood floors, holes in the plaster walls, battered wooden tables and rickety chairs filled with loudmouth drunks.

The neon beer sign behind the long bar didn't work quite right, reading Shiner Cock instead of Shiner Bock, which seemed to entertain the patrons no end.

There were women in the bar, some with men; a chunky older gal with a tattoo of a heart on her arm sat at the bar by herself. Looking for a customer, he suspected, without much luck.

Chase spotted the teenage girl right away from the photos he'd seen on TV, Tammy Bennett, a petite blonde in a short, tight skirt sitting on a barstool next to a thick-necked dude with greasy shoulder-length black hair. The fear in her eyes was almost tangible, her body folded in on itself as if she were trying to disappear.

Occasionally her glance darted toward the door, then

shifted back to the big dark man beside her. She'd stumbled into some bad company with that one. The girl was clearly his latest money earner. No way was she going anywhere unless he said so.

Chase walked up to the bar and ordered a Lone Star, took the bottle and sat down at an empty table. It was time to call the police, but the minute the guy pimping Tammy out heard the sirens, he would grab the girl and disappear.

A chair scraped against the floor, and a fat man with sweaty armpits walked up to the man and the girl.

"I got an itch, Martinez. How much for twenty minutes?"

A guy down the bar said something about it being a quickie and disparaging the fat guy's manhood. The fat guy grunted and Martinez laughed.

Chase silently cursed.

The men haggled, settled on a price and the fat guy handed Martinez a couple of folded bills, which got stuffed into the pocket of the pimp's dirty shirt. When Martinez tipped his head toward the stairs, indicating the deal had been struck, Chase rose and walked up to the bar, blocking the fat man's way.

"I want the girl," he said to Martinez. "I'll pay for the whole night—whatever she's worth. But I don't take sloppy seconds."

Martinez looked him over. Clearly Chase wasn't one of the locals. "You're not a cop, are you? You look like a cop."

"Not a cop." He let his gaze wander salaciously over the girl, ignored the poor kid's cringe. "I just have a taste for something a little more…tender, shall we say."

Martinez pulled the fat man's money out of his

pocket and handed it back. "Sorry, Bud. Gotta make a living."

"Wait a minute! I seen her first."

"Come back tomorrow night." Martinez gripped the girl's slim arm and hauled her over to Chase. "You better have the cash."

"I can pay. Name your price." Martinez rattled off an exorbitant sum, and Chase handed the money over.

Taking the girl's arm, he led her toward the stairs. Tammy pulled back, clearly reluctant, but one glance at Martinez and she kept walking, her legs shaking with every step. Chase hadn't missed the bruise on her cheek.

He tugged her up the stairs, didn't pause until they reached the landing out of sight. "Don't be afraid. I know who you are. I'm here to help you."

She looked up at him with wide, doe-brown eyes that flooded with tears. "You mean it?"

"You can trust me, Tammy." He could tell she wasn't sure she should believe him, but he was her only hope.

As soon as they got into the cheesy bedroom, he pulled out his cell and called 9-1-1, identified himself and gave the police his location, told them he had found the missing girl.

"I made a mistake," Tammy said tearfully when he ended the call. "That man downstairs…he found me and made me go with him. He made me do things…" She swallowed and wiped the wetness from her cheeks. "I just… I want to go home."

"My name's Chase Garrett. I'm a private detective. I'm going to get you back to your parents, Tammy. We just need to sit tight till the police get here." He glanced at the sagging mattress, the orange bedspread covered with cigarette burns. He didn't want to think what Martinez had made her do.

Tammy wrapped her arms around herself and shivered as if she were freezing, though the room was overly warm. "Thank you for helping me."

He nodded, glad he had found her.

But, of course, it wasn't that easy. Only a few minutes had passed before heavy footsteps pounded up the stairs. The door flew open, and Martinez walked into the room. The bed was still made and Tammy wasn't naked, which pretty much told the story.

"I figured you were a cop."

"I'm not a cop. I bought the whole night. I didn't figure there was any need to hurry. And I'd appreciate a little privacy. For the money I paid, I don't think that's too much to ask."

"Bullshit. Give me your wallet."

"Not gonna happen," Chase said, shaking his head. "We made a deal. You got paid. I get the girl."

Martinez laughed and lunged forward like a pit bull entering the ring. He wasn't laughing when Chase's boot shot up and landed hard between his legs, lifting him clear off the floor.

Gasping and howling, Martinez dropped to his knees, fell over and rolled on the dirty brown carpet, clutching his balls and groaning, his face a weird bluish red.

Chase grabbed Tammy's hand and tugged her toward the door. They raced down the dimly lit hall and tore down the stairs at breakneck speed. Unfortunately, when they reached the landing, what looked like half the bar waited for them at the bottom of the stairs. In this part of town, the bad guys had a habit of sticking together.

Chase jerked the little .380 out of the holster behind his back, and fired two shots into the ceiling, choosing a spot he hoped wouldn't kill someone on the second floor. Plaster rained down and the crowd scattered, giving them a clear path to the door. Gun in hand, Chase pulled Tammy out the door onto the sidewalk.

"This way!" he shouted, keeping his gun aimed toward the front door as he headed for his truck. Police sirens wailed in the distance. Red and blue lights flashed and patrol cars roared around the corner, sliding to a stop in front of the bar. Car doors flew open and uniformed officers poured out, guns drawn.

Chase leaned down and set his pistol on the sidewalk in front of him, lifted his hands in the air. "Over here!" Officers spotted him, turned and ran in his direction.

"I'm Chase Garrett," he said. "I'm a private detective. I'm the one who called you."

A big redheaded cop used his foot to move the pistol a little farther down the sidewalk. "You're Garrett?"

"That's right. The girl's Tammy Bennett."

The officer patted him down in search of other weapons, which for once he didn't have.

"He saved me," Tammy said, tears running down her cheeks. "Please… I'm sorry I ran away. I just want to go home."

A female officer hurried over. "It's okay, honey. We've already called your parents. Everything's going to be okay." The woman took Tammy's arm and led her away. The two of them talked for a moment, then the officer opened the back door of a patrol car and settled the girl inside.

Chase followed them, leaned down and handed Tammy a business card. "Next time you think about running away, you call me, okay?"

She studied the card and looked up at him. "Thank you." She wiped tears from her cheeks. "I'll never forget what you did."

The red-haired cop returned. O'Kelley his name tag read. "We're going to need a statement."

"No problem."

O'Kelley's gaze moved off toward the bar. "The guy in there? That's Ray Martinez. He's one tough hombre. You made a bad enemy with that one."

"With any luck he's on his way to jail for a good long while. But thanks for the warning."

It didn't take long for Chase to give his version of events, and he was finally able to head on home. It was a long day, but a good one. He just hoped Tammy and her parents could find their way back to each other.

CHAPTER THREE

She hadn't thought she would be this nervous. But as an ominous fall wind whipped her pale hair and dark clouds threatened rain, Harper's mouth felt dry and her palms were sweating. Crossing the sidewalk, she paused to take a deep breath, then pushed through the glass front door into the single-story brick building that housed the offices of Maximum Security.

For her meeting with Chase, she had dressed with care in a navy blue cotton pencil skirt, a crisp print blouse, tucked in and belted, and high-heeled navy pumps. Simple, classic pieces, moderately priced, from the latest Elemental Chic collection.

"May I help you?" A perky little receptionist, pretty and dark haired, with big blue eyes behind round tortoiseshell glasses, sat at the front desk.

"I'm Harper Winston. We spoke on the phone yesterday. You made an appointment for me with Chase Garrett."

"Yes, I remember. Chase saw it when he checked his calendar this morning. I'll let him know you're here." She buzzed him and announced Harper's arrival. Harper had no idea what sort of greeting she would receive.

The petite brunette smiled. "You can go on back. His office is just through that door."

Harper crossed the room, paused for a moment to steady herself and pulled open the door. She walked into an airy corner office furnished with a big oak desk, a brown leather sofa and photos on the walls of the Hill Country ranch Chase owned with his brothers, Reese and Brandon.

Seated behind the desk, Chase rose, walked around and took the hand she extended in greeting. "Hello, Harper. It's been a while."

"Hello, Chase." She managed to come up with a smile. "Actually, I saw you last night at the gala."

His mouth curved. He'd always had the sexiest smile. She wished she hadn't remembered.

"Now that you mention it, I saw you there, too."

She withdrew her hand, ignoring the little tingle that raced up her arm. "You must have left early. I saw the article about your daring rescue in the newspaper this morning. You found that missing girl, Tammy Bennett."

He shrugged as if it meant nothing. "I followed a lead. I got lucky."

"You did a good thing."

"At least she's back home. It's going to take some time for her to heal after what happened. I hope it works out for her." He walked back behind his desk. "Why don't you sit down and tell me why you're here?"

She took a seat on the opposite side of the desk in

one of two dark brown leather chairs, and Chase sat back down.

"Can I have Mindy get you something? Coffee? Soft drink?"

"No, I'm fine." Her nerves returned. He had always had that effect on her. She crossed her legs. Chase's whiskey-brown eyes followed the movement of her skirt hem, his gaze sliding over her bare thighs. She tugged the skirt down, surprised he had noticed.

"What can I do for you, Harper?"

She steeled herself. She had to convince him. Her brother's life could very well depend on it.

"I need your help, Chase. Mikey's missing. I'm afraid something terrible has happened to him."

"Missing? Are you sure? How long has he been gone?"

"Today's the fifth day. Almost a week without a word."

"As I recall, it wasn't unlike Michael to disappear for several weeks at a time. He always turned up sooner or later."

"He isn't the same man he used to be. Michael doesn't do drugs anymore. He hasn't for nearly five years. He turned his life around, moved to Houston and started his own tech company. He was doing really well before he disappeared."

"What happened?"

"Remember how he loved to sail?"

"I remember. We went out on your dad's yacht a few times when we were in college."

"Michael always loved the ocean. Last year he bought a forty-two-foot Beneteau. This year, he took a month off to sail the Caribbean."

"That's where he was the last time you heard from him?"

"That's right. He would email or text every day or two, letting me know where he was and where he was going. He had a satellite phone and internet on the boat." Her chest was beginning to ache. She was so worried about him.

"Everything was fine. He was having a wonderful time. Then five days ago, I stopped hearing from him. No emails, no texts. Nothing. I've called his cell phone over and over, but the calls go straight to voice mail." She swallowed past the lump that was forming in her throat. "I know he's in trouble. I can feel it."

"You could be wrong, Harper."

She pulled herself back under control. "I'm not wrong. I know my brother. After he moved to Houston, we got really close. We made a deal before he left. I was worried about him going on a trip like that by himself. He promised he would get in touch every few days so I wouldn't worry. He would never go this long without letting me know he was okay."

"You think he could have had some kind of trouble at sea? Some problem with the boat?"

"No. He is a fantastic sailor. I think it's something else. But I called the authorities in Aruba and reported him missing. I called the US Coast Guard and asked them to look for the boat. Apparently, they weren't able to make radio contact, but they said sometimes that happens."

"What about the hospitals? Maybe he was in a car accident onshore or something."

"I called everywhere. Even the morgue." A chill swept through her at the memory of the dreaded phone call she had forced herself to make.

Chase shifted forward in his chair. "Aruba? That's where he was the last time you heard from him?"

"That's right. So far no one's found any sign of the boat or my brother."

His dark gaze never wavered. "So you're here because you want me to find him."

Not exactly, but close. "I want you to go with me. I'm leaving for Aruba in the morning. I won't be back till I know for sure Michael is safe."

Chase eyed her with speculation, then leaned back in his chair, giving himself some time, she figured.

He didn't want anything to do with the Winstons. He'd never approved of her father's business tactics. And he believed Knox Winston's emotional abuse had been the cause of Michael's addiction.

Chase had done his best to help her brother, but it hadn't been enough. Not back then. But Michael had finally found the courage to defeat his addiction. Harper prayed Chase would be willing to help him again.

"All right, I'll go after him," Chase finally agreed. "But I go alone, Harper. I'm a private investigator. That's what I do for a living. I'll find Michael for you. There's no reason for you to get involved."

She shook her head. "I knew that's what you'd say, and I understand your feelings. But I won't sit here and do nothing. Not when I know Michael is in trouble." She had only one brother. Her mother was dead. She and her father rarely spoke. She couldn't lose Michael, too.

"I don't know what you think of me," she continued, "but I'm not that naive young girl you knew all those years ago. There are ways I may be able to help. I'm going, Chase—with or without you."

The words hung in the air, and she silently prayed he would agree. She needed his help, and both of them knew it. She prayed his past affection for Michael would be enough to sway him.

She swallowed, felt the sting of tears. "Please, Chase…" She couldn't believe she was pleading, but she was desperate. "There isn't anyone else I trust. I need your help."

His jaw clenched. He swore a soft curse. "Fine, I'll help you find him. With any luck he's just back to his old tricks. He's hooked up with some girl and both of them are binge drinking—or worse."

Harper stood up from her chair. "You're wrong. He isn't like that anymore. And if you can't at least give him the benefit of the doubt, then I don't need you." She stormed toward the door, but Chase was out of his chair and moving, blocking her escape.

"I'm sorry. That wasn't fair. I haven't seen your brother in years. The Caribbean can be a dangerous place. If something's happened to him, we'll figure it out and we'll find him. Okay?"

She swallowed and nodded, relief pouring through her. "Okay."

"You said he was in Aruba when you last heard from him."

"That's right. He had just sailed into the marina in Oranjestad. That was five days ago. When I didn't hear from him, I called the harbormaster to see if the boat was still there, but the slip he'd been using was empty. He had some fancy GPS tracking system on his sat phone, but I have no idea how it works."

She dug into her purse, pulled out two first-class airline tickets. "The flight to Oranjestad leaves at seven ten in the morning."

Chase's dark blond eyebrows went up. "You were that sure I'd agree?"

"I wasn't sure at all. But I was hoping and praying you would."

Amusement touched his lips, then it was gone. "International flight. We'll need to be at the airport early. I'll pick you up at four thirty. What's your address?"

When she rattled off a number on Armstrong Avenue, he seemed surprised. It was a nice neighborhood but not overly expensive. She didn't take money from her father. She had a substantial inheritance from her mother, but she rarely used it, preferring to make her own way in the world, as she had done since she'd graduated from college.

She had only recently moved back to Dallas, following a decision to relocate Elemental Chic's company headquarters. There were opportunities here that she and her business partner, Shana Davis, wanted to explore.

The company's success was far more important to her than living in a fancy condo she rarely spent time in. Instead she owned a modest town house that suited her just fine.

Chase walked her back to the reception area.

"Thank you for doing this," she said.

"Michael was once my best friend."

She nodded. "He still talks about you, you know. I'll see you in the morning."

Chase pulled open the door. "Let's hope you hear from your brother before it's time to leave, and we won't have to worry about going."

But Harper believed soul-deep that if she didn't find Michael before it was too late, he wouldn't be coming back at all.

CHAPTER FOUR

Chase watched the willowy blonde walk out of his office to her car. With her sleek pale blond hair, delicate features and perfect complexion, she wasn't just pretty, she was lovely in the extreme. He clamped down on a thread of sexual heat as she disappeared from view.

It surprised him. He remembered hearing talk at the country club before she moved to Houston. Rumor had it Harper Winston was an ice queen. Her ex-boyfriend had made jokes about taking a dead fish to bed. Aside from being slightly irritated on her behalf as a former friend of her brother's, he hadn't paid much attention.

Seeing her today, he wondered. The woman who had come into his office to help her brother was passionately determined, willing to put herself in danger to find the brother she obviously loved.

He couldn't help but admire her. And it made him doubt what her ex and the country-club crowd had said.

All that fire had come from somewhere deep inside. Maybe it just took the right man to stir the flames.

The thought didn't sit well. The pull of attraction he had felt last night had only grown stronger today, reminding him of the first time he had seen her all those years ago.

She'd just turned sixteen that day. He'd let Michael drag him to her birthday party, both of them twenty-one, just graduated from Yale. He'd thought Harper looked like an angel.

Unfortunately, an angel who was his best friend's sister, way too young and completely out of his reach.

Over the years he and Michael had gone their separate ways, Chase ending up in law enforcement, a lifelong passion, Michael sliding deeper and deeper into drugs and alcohol—thanks to his no-good father.

Knox Winston was a gangster in expensively tailored business clothes. His ruthless, shady dealings had made him obscenely rich, but at a tremendous cost. His wife had committed suicide. His son had overdosed more than once.

How the man had escaped prosecution for so many years was something Chase could not comprehend.

After his friendship with Michael had ended, Chase had stayed away from the family and until this morning, had every intention of keeping it that way. Now a pair of big blue eyes clouded with worry and memories of a man he had once loved like a brother were dragging him back into the fold.

Chase silently cursed. Grabbing his navy blazer off the back of the chair, he shrugged it on over his jeans and shirt and walked out into the open area the guys called the bull pen.

Nine oak desks arranged in rows of three were occupied by the independent contractors who worked at Maximum Security. Antique farming tools decorated the walls, along with framed photos of the ranch Chase owned with his brothers.

Across the room, Jason Hawkins Maddox, a bail enforcement agent and one of his best friends, was heading out the door. They called him Hawk because he swooped down on his prey like a raptor and always came back with his man.

At a desk a few feet away, Dante Romero and Lissa Blayne, both PIs, were arguing over a case, not unusual for the pair who did everything in their power to ignore the attraction between them. Chase shook his head and kept walking, making his way to the reception desk.

"Mindy, I need you to cancel my appointments for the next three days. I may be gone longer. If I am, I'll call and let you know."

"I'll take care of it, boss." Mindy was a temp who had been working at The Max less than three weeks, replacing a longtime employee who had retired to spend time with her grandkids.

Mindy was good. He was thinking of bringing her aboard full-time.

"If a problem comes up, go to Bran or Jason. They should be able to handle it."

"Okay."

Turning, he walked over to his youngest brother, who had just gotten off the phone. Bran was a PI who specialized in personal protection, law enforcement being a tradition on their mother's side of the family. The Devlins, including Chase's grandfather, great-grandfather and a handful of uncles, had all worked as cops, FBI or been career military men.

His younger brothers were two very different people, Bran a former special ops soldier turned bodyguard, Reese the extremely successful businessman, CEO of Garrett Resources, the Texas-based oil company founded by their great-grandfather. Both brothers had blue eyes, but Reese's hair was black, Bran's dark brown. Both were an inch taller than Chase's six-foot-two-inch frame.

"Something's come up," Chase told Bran. "I'm leaving the country for a few days, maybe longer. I need you to keep an eye on things while I'm gone."

"No problem. What's up?"

"Missing-persons case. Michael Winston's disappeared. His sister needs help finding him."

Bran grunted. "Guy's probably off drunk somewhere or loaded on drugs."

"According to Harper, he's turned his life around. Been clean five years."

Bran sat up a little straighter. "Well, that's good to hear. He was a great guy before he went haywire."

"For his sister's sake, I hope he hasn't fallen off the wagon."

One of Bran's dark eyebrows went up. "His sister? I thought I recognized the luscious little blonde who was in here earlier. Seems to me you had a yen for her way back when."

"She was Michael's sister and way too young. Plus she's a Winston. That family's nothing but trouble."

"So why'd you take the case?"

"Moment of weakness, I guess. Or maybe for old

times' sake. Mike was once my best friend. Worst of it is Harper's going with me."

Brandon laughed. "Jeez, big brother, you must have a masochistic streak."

Chase grunted. "With any luck, we'll find Michael and be home in a couple of days. Harper Winston is trouble I don't need."

And no matter how much he'd like to find out if she was the cold fish people believed or the passionate woman he had glimpsed, it wasn't going to happen.

Harper had picked the right guy to go with her. She was definitely safe from him.

It was still dark when Harper heard the knock on her door early the next morning and hurried to open it. Chase stood on the porch in a pair of light blue denim jeans and a yellow knit polo shirt, looking as perfectly groomed as he always did.

She wasn't surprised at the brown lizard cowboy boots on his feet. Except for her birthday party when he had been barefoot and wearing a swimsuit, she couldn't remember seeing him in anything other than boots.

"You ready?" he asked.

She yawned. She preferred to work late rather than get up early. "More or less. I'm packed, at any rate."

He didn't crack a smile. "Good, let's go." Spotting her carry-on, he grabbed the handle and headed out the door.

Harper caught the rope handle of her striped, multicolored, oversize canvas bag, part of EC's accessories line, slung the rope over her shoulder and followed him out to the long black stretch limo parked at the curb.

The driver held the door as they slid into the plush red leather interior.

This early, the thirty-minute drive to the Dallas–Fort Worth airport went off without a hitch, though it felt strange sitting in the car next to Chase, his elbow occasionally brushing hers. She tried not to notice the impressive biceps stretching the sleeve of his yellow knit shirt.

They went through precheck and boarded an American Airlines A320 for the seven-hour trip to Aruba, putting them on the island late afternoon. Chase told her he'd made contact through a friend with a man in Oranjestad who would pick them up at the airport and be their guide while they were on the island.

"He's the kind of guy who knows what's happening and can get you whatever you need."

She cocked an eyebrow in his direction. "Including weapons?"

He just shrugged. "If necessary. Too much hassle getting guns through customs. With luck, I won't need to be armed."

But Harper wondered. If Mikey could have called, he would have. He wouldn't want her to worry. If something had happened to him, it wasn't going to be good.

They settled back in their first-class seats and Harper took out her sketchbook. She was working on next year's clothing designs. Although her partner, Shana Davis, was the primary designer, the idea for the type of clothing the company would market had been hers, a concept developed during the year she had spent doing volunteer social work in Ecuador.

She had recognized a need for versatile, durable

women's sportswear and accessories. But she believed it should also be stylish and not too expensive.

She'd spent the following year at the Harvard Business School, then gone in search of a designer. She'd met Shana, a beautiful African American two years her senior, through a friend of Michael's.

Shana had immediately grasped the concept Harper had envisioned and was wildly excited about it. As luck would have it, her designs were exactly what Harper was looking for, practical fabrics trimmed with bright, colorful accents that made the designs unique.

Using a portion of her inheritance to fund the company, Harper had formulated a business plan and she and Shana had gone to work.

Harper hadn't expected to be steaming garments at two in the morning, dealing with suppliers who demanded to be paid far too soon, poring over receipts that didn't add up while trying to manage production and get fabric and trim to manufacturers on time. But she was committed, willing to do whatever the job called for.

Amazingly, the company had succeeded beyond her expectations. Little by little she had discovered her own design abilities and began to contribute ideas each year. Fortunately, Shana had also learned to handle both sides of the business, and as soon as she'd learned of Michael's disappearance, had taken over so Harper could focus on finding him.

But there was always work to do. Flipping open her drawing pad to a clean page, she began to sketch a design for culottes. The knee-length pants were slightly gathered at the waist, fashioned in a bell shape, a modification of last year's design, which was fitted in the hips and flared in an A-line. Both garments were stylish yet allowed maximum freedom of movement. She had a wrinkle-free khaki version of the A-line in her suitcase.

Harper glanced up to see Chase watching her. He didn't ask what she was doing, but she could tell he was curious.

"I own a company called Elemental Chic. We specialize in women's sportswear. I started the company in Houston, but recently we relocated to Dallas."

"So you're a businesswoman?"

"That's right." She smiled. "You seem surprised."

"I guess I figured you had enough money you wouldn't need to work."

Or be interested in doing anything productive, she figured. She was a Winston after all. "You thought I'd just marry some man my father picked out and have babies?"

His mouth curved. "To tell you the truth, I probably made that assumption. I suppose I mostly just hoped you wouldn't end up like your brother."

"I told you, he isn't—"

Chase held up a hand, stopping her words. "I know what you said. I hope you're right."

But Harper didn't have the slightest doubt. She remembered all too well the agony her brother had endured as he fought to conquer his heroin addiction. He would never go back to drugs again. He didn't even drink anymore.

She glanced up at Chase. "I'm not the least surprised at what *you* do for a living. Michael always said law enforcement was in your blood."

Chase's wealthy father, Bass Garrett, had married down, or so it was said—an Irishwoman named Margaret Devlin, a beautiful dark-haired, blue-eyed secretary in his office.

When they'd divorced years later, Maggie had taken Chase and Brandon to live with her while Reese had remained with his dad. According to Michael, Maggie Devlin Garrett was close to her family, many of whom had law enforcement backgrounds. Police work, in some form or other, was all Chase had ever wanted to do.

Even after Bass died and Chase inherited a third of the family fortune, that hadn't changed.

"I remember Michael telling me your grandfather was a sheriff."

"That's right. Sam Devlin was sheriff of Titus County for fifteen years." He settled back in his seat. "I guess you could say I've found my calling. I'm good at what I do, and I like the challenge. I like making sure people have the kind of protection they need, or helping them get justice."

Harper just hoped Chase would be able to help her find her brother.

She went back to her drawing, but every once in a while she could feel those penetrating golden-brown eyes on her. Just sitting this close made her stomach quiver.

She was glad he didn't find her attractive. Chase was a definite temptation, the first man to make her think of sex in months. She was too busy to date very often, and she wasn't the type for one-night hookups. She hadn't had a serious boyfriend since she had broken up with Stephen Larsen last year, well before she had moved to Dallas.

She hadn't really missed the sex. She told herself it was just that she hadn't met the right guy, but she had heard what people said about her. She had a reputation for being cold and unresponsive.

She almost believed it. Except that when she looked at Chase Garrett, she felt warm all over. Last night she had dreamed about him. She remembered the way he had kissed her in the dream, the feel of his mouth on her breasts, and her skin flushed.

It was a fantasy, she reminded herself, though even now she felt a tug low in her belly.

Harper forced herself to ignore him, pretend he wasn't sitting right beside her and was finally able to concentrate on her work.

But it wasn't that easy to do.

CHAPTER FIVE

Chase pulled his MacBook out of his carry-on, opened it and went to work. He'd spent yesterday afternoon and most of the night digging up information on Michael Winston and setting up contacts he might need in Aruba.

According to everything he'd read, Michael had done exactly what his sister claimed, rebuilt his life. He was the owner of BUZZ, a successful tech solutions company that dealt in problem solving and computer programming. A happy-faced, buzzing bee was the company logo.

As Chase thought back on it, Michael had always been fascinated with anything digital, from cell phones to computer games. As he read articles describing Michael's successes, something loosened in his chest.

He'd never really stopped caring about his friend, never completely given up on him. It felt good to know Michael had finally been able to overcome his demons.

Which meant his sister might be right and something bad actually had happened to him.

Where are you, Mikey? It was the nickname Michael had acquired as a kid, one Chase hadn't used in years. Not since the last time he had found his friend passed out in his apartment, overdosed on heroin—for the third time in six months. The wild ride to the hospital had saved Michael's life but ended their friendship.

Chase couldn't deal with it any longer. It was just too painful to watch a man who meant so much to him destroy himself. In a way it had destroyed Chase, too.

After that night at the hospital, Chase had finally come to believe the only person who could save Michael Winston was himself. According to Harper, that had happened. Chase could only hope it was true.

Chase spent the next hour digging around on the internet: Facebook, LinkedIn, Twitter, all Michael's social media connections. His last Facebook post was a week ago, photos of a trim, athletic-looking, brown-haired man, lightly muscled, tanned and smiling. Nothing since then and nothing that hinted at any reason for him to disappear.

It was too soon to think about the yacht going down. As Harper had said, Michael was an expert sailor, and she had alerted the authorities to be on the lookout for the boat. In that regard, at the moment, there was nothing else they could do.

Chase turned to Harper. "What about enemies?" The words interrupted the quiet hum of the engines. "Anyone you can think of who might want to do your brother harm?"

She shook her head. "Everyone loves Michael. You know how he is. People are just naturally drawn to him."

He remembered the popular young man Michael had been, outgoing and always smiling. Though both of them were from Dallas, they hadn't met until college. Determined to compete with the Garrett family money, Knox had sent his son to Yale, where Chase was enrolled. He hadn't expected Michael and Chase to become best friends.

Michael had been a happy kid back then—before his mother's suicide and his father's constant verbal abuse had begun to whittle away his confidence.

"You said he texted or emailed as often as he could."

"That's right."

"Did he mention meeting anyone? Someone in one of the ports he sailed into? Maybe someone he took on the boat with him?"

"No. He wanted to make the trip on his own. Captain the yacht by himself. It was a lifelong dream."

"What was the name of the boat?"

"*BUZZ Word.* For his company."

Chase settled back in his seat. He dug around on Google a little longer, but didn't find anything useful.

With a glance at Harper, he typed in *Elemental Chic.* On the webpage, he discovered the company was five years old, a partnership between Harper and a woman named Shana Davis. According to the articles he read, the business was amazingly successful.

Chase had always been attracted to successful women. Harper's business acumen only made the pull he felt toward her increase.

It didn't matter. The last thing he needed was to be sucked into a family that ran a criminal enterprise, no matter how attractive the daughter might be.

Chase forced himself to focus on work. He would

find Michael—hopefully unharmed. Then head back to Dallas, where he would put Harper Winston out of his mind. He'd call Marla Chambers and invite her over for the weekend.

Sex was always good between them. And their relationship was far from exclusive. He'd spend some time with Marla, enjoy some mutually satisfying sex and forget the woman he wanted but couldn't have.

After a brief stopover in Miami, the plane landed right on time, 3:30 p.m. at Queen Beatrix International Airport. The contact Chase had hired was waiting when they walked out the departure gate, pulling their carry-on bags.

The hot Caribbean sun shone down from a cloudless blue sky. The temperature stood at eighty-five degrees, and a dry wind sifted through the fronds on a row of palm trees along the side of the road.

Aruba was part of the Netherlands, its capital city Oranjestad, with an arid climate and sixty-nine square miles of cactus-strewed hills and white-sand beaches. The total population, a little over a hundred thousand, was a mix of Spanish, European, Black and Indian. It was one of the most popular tourist destinations in the Caribbean.

Chase walked up to the big, sandy-haired Dutchman he had hired, a guy named—what else—Dutch, who stuck out a wide, meaty hand in welcome.

"It is a pleasure to meet you, Mr. Garrett. I am Dutch van Noord. You can count on me to take care of whatever you need."

"It's just Chase. Good to meet you, Dutch. The lady is Harper Winston."

"Please call me Harper," she said. "Nice to meet you."

"My car is parked in the lot. If you will please follow me." He took the handles of both bags and started tugging them across the asphalt parking lot. When he reached a white Suburban, he paused to unlock the doors, loaded their bags into the rear and reached down to help Harper into the front passenger seat.

"I'm fine in the back," she said and climbed in without assistance.

She was letting Chase take the lead, for which he was grateful. Just having her along was trouble enough. It took considerable willpower to ignore the faint arousal that hummed through him whenever he looked at her. Just the scent of her perfume, a soft, fragrant jasmine, turned him on.

They settled themselves and put on their seat belts. Dutch climbed in and started the engine, pulled the SUV out of the parking lot.

"You are staying at the Renaissance Resort and Casino, yes? At the marina?"

Harper had made the arrangements in Oranjestad. The hotel was at the harbor where *BUZZ Word* had been docked, the last place Harper had heard from Michael before his disappearance. Chase knew the hotel. He had been to Aruba, but only once, and for pleasure not business.

"That's the place," he said.

As the SUV traveled along Lloyd Smith Boulevard from the airport to the hotel, Harper sat quietly in the seat behind him. Chase turned to look at her, found her staring out the window, her eyes full of worry.

"We'll check in and get settled," he said. "Then see what we can find out down at the marina."

She just nodded, her gaze still glued to the arid landscape passing by outside, various forms of cacti and thorny shrubs, Aruba being desert, not tropics. Harper's face looked pale, and tension formed lines across her forehead. It was the first time he had seen her succumb to uncertainty. Chase didn't like the way it made him feel.

"Look at me."

She blinked, slowly turned away from the window, and her troubled gaze found his.

"We're going to find him, okay?"

She just nodded.

"Say it."

She swallowed. For an instant, her eyes shimmered. "We're going to find Michael."

"That's right, we are. It might take a little time, but sooner or later we're going to figure out where he is."

Her lips trembled for a moment, then she relaxed back in her seat, the color returning to her cheeks. "Thank you for saying that."

"Just keep believing it. Do it for Michael."

A soft smile touched her lips, the first he had seen. She sat a little straighter in the seat, her eyes brighter than before. "I need a shower after all that flying. Then I'll be ready to start our search."

"Good idea." He smiled in return, and at her renewed resolve, felt an odd sense of relief. No matter the animosities of the past, he was going to help Harper find her brother. He wouldn't give up until he did.

CHAPTER SIX

Dutch dropped them off at the hotel with a promise to make himself available twenty-four hours a day for anything they might need. Harper thought the big Dutchman had an air of confidence that would be impossible to fake.

It didn't take long for them to get situated. The Renaissance Hotel at the marina wasn't ridiculously expensive or overly luxurious, but the two-bedroom suite she had booked faced the ocean, with a balcony that ran the length of the living room outside the sliding glass doors. The view of the turquoise sea stretching endlessly in front of her was magnificent.

Harper showered and changed into a pair of lightweight capri-length khaki pants with embroidered multicolored seashells on the pockets, and an orange-and-white cap-sleeved boatneck T-shirt from the EC collection, her feet in the same comfortable white canvas deck shoes she had put on very early that morning.

A wide-brimmed straw hat lay on the dining table, sun protection for their trip to the marina, which was a short walk from the hotel. She plucked it up as she walked into the living room.

Chase wandered in a few minutes later, buttoning a light blue flowered, short-sleeved tropical shirt, his pirate's-gold hair still damp from the shower. The shirt gaped open and she got a look at his chest, all tanned skin and solid sinew. Lean muscle formed a ladder down his stomach.

Heat washed over her. Her pulse beat faster. It was ridiculous. Chase had no interest in her, and Harper needed his help, not his sexual attentions. She thanked God he hadn't noticed her reaction.

She allowed herself to quietly finish her perusal, her gaze traveling down his long legs. She blinked at the leather boat shoes that had replaced his usual boots. Classy and sophisticated, that was Chase, but now that he was older, there was a dark edge about him, an air of danger Chase hadn't had as a young man in college.

She remembered that he had joined the army as soon as he had graduated from Yale—much to his father's chagrin—signing up for the military police. Bass Garrett had been furious, but Chase had always been his own man. And though she had lost track of him years ago, she didn't think that had changed.

She knew a little about Brandon and Reese, had met Bran a couple of times when Michael and Chase were friends, but she hadn't kept track of the brothers in the years since then. After she'd moved to Dallas, she had read articles in the *Morning News* about Reese, who was CEO of the family-owned company and a well-known figure in the community.

"I need to follow up on that GPS tracker you mentioned," Chase said, returning her thoughts to the moment.

"Oh, I meant to tell you. After we talked about it yesterday, I remembered Michael had me write down the information about it. With packing and having to get up so early, I forgot."

She ran back into the bedroom and dug it out of her suitcase, hurried back into the living room. "'Iridium 9575 Extreme Satellite Phone GPS Tracking System.' The phone number is written below."

Chase took the note from her hand, pulled out his cell and hit one of his contact buttons. He pressed the phone against his ear.

"Morning, Tabby, it's Chase. I need your help."

Harper ignored a pang. She wondered which of his lady friends he was calling, couldn't imagine one of Chase's usual sophisticated women having a name that sounded like a cat.

"His name's Michael Winston," Chase continued. "He was last seen in Aruba. I need to find him."

They talked awhile longer, Chase giving the woman more details, including Michael's satellite phone information, then finally ending the call.

"You ready to go?" he asked.

"Who was that?"

"Tabitha Love. She's a computer specialist. Tabby's a genius at digging up information off the internet."

"She works for you?"

"She works for anyone in the office who needs her help."

"So she isn't one of your girlfriends."

He laughed and shook his head. "Tabby? No. We

have a business relationship. Besides, Tabby has a boyfriend."

It was ridiculous to feel relieved. Hat in hand, Harper headed out the door and they took the elevator down to the first floor. The hotel was modern, with rattan and teakwood furniture in the lobby, and turquoise accents the color of the sea.

This time of year it wouldn't be long before sunset. As they walked down the sidewalk, a warm, dry breeze toyed with strands of her hair beneath the brim of her wide straw hat. Chase was wearing a straw hat, too, a flat-brimmed panama that made him look way too sexy, and more like a local than a tourist, which she figured was his intent.

But the hard jaw and dark eyes, the close-cropped, edgy beard along his jaw hinted at the man he had become, one capable of taking on a bar full of dangerous criminals and coming out on top, as he had done to save the teenage girl.

The marina, a U-shaped enclosure that opened directly into the sea, wasn't full, but Harper counted forty yachts of various shapes and sizes, mostly sailboats but a few powerboats as well, bobbing at their tethers along the dock. Chase headed for the marina office, a small, flat-roofed, freestanding structure. A bell chimed as he opened the door and led her inside.

A slightly built, cocoa-skinned man with neatly trimmed black hair slicked back from a high forehead stood behind the counter.

He smiled, flashing very white teeth. "May I help you?" A name plaque reading Len Wadadli sat on the counter next to a computer screen. Probably an Arawak name or some other indigenous island surname.

"We're looking for Michael Winston," Chase said. "His boat, *BUZZ Word*, was moored here last week."

"Yes, I remember the boat. It was very nice. I handled the paperwork for the mooring." The little man turned to study the computer screen and began clicking through pages of information. "I was off for a while after the boat arrived. I came back the day it sailed."

"How long ago was that?" Chase asked.

"Four days, counting today."

So he had actually been missing only four days. It should have relieved her. But she hadn't heard from Michael in six days. He wouldn't have gone that long without contacting her. He was in trouble, or else she would have heard from him.

"I'm Michael's sister," Harper said. "Do you have any idea where my brother might have been going when he sailed?"

"No, I am sorry. But before he left, he told me he would be back. He said he planned to do some island-hopping. He was not sure how long he would be gone."

"Was he alone?" Chase asked.

"I do not believe so. I remember seeing two people aboard as *BUZZ Word* sailed out of the harbor."

Harper's worry cranked up. He was with someone. He didn't have friends in Aruba, so who was it? Her head began to throb, a slight ache forming behind her eyes.

"Man or woman?" Chase asked.

"I am sorry. I could not say. I only noticed there were two aboard the yacht as it sailed."

"What about the weather?" Chase asked. "Any unexpected storms in the area? Anything that could account for a boat having unforeseen problems?"

"The weather has been very good. Nothing out of the ordinary."

Chase gave a brief nod. "Thank you, Len. You've been very helpful."

They left the marina office, Harper even more convinced the problem wasn't boat trouble, but in a different way, more worried than she had been before.

"We need to find out who was with him." She looked up at Chase, her headache building. She didn't have them often, but today had been long, tiring and filled with worry she fought not to show. "Mikey was always so trusting. Anything could have happened out there if he was with someone he didn't know."

"You need to stay positive. We have no reason to suspect foul play. Not yet. He may have just sailed off somewhere with someone he met and his communications went out. Now we know he was here four days ago. We'll know more when we hear from Tabby. Which should be very soon."

Chase was right. Michael was an adult, not a reckless kid anymore, and there was no point in worrying until they had more information. Michael had warned her unexpected things could happen. There was nothing foolproof when you went on an adventure like the one he was undertaking.

"You're right. I'm sorry. Michael told me not to panic if I couldn't reach him, but—"

"But you love him and it's been almost a week. You did the right thing, Harper."

She relaxed at his words. "I won't stop worrying until we find him."

"Which we will. Come on." He reached down and

took hold of her hand, and a tingle raced up her arm. Chase must have felt it, too, because he let go.

"Michael's a single man, and he came here to enjoy the island," Chase said. "We'll start at the hotel, show his photo around."

He pulled out a picture she recognized as the one on Michael's Facebook page. He was standing on the deck of his sailboat in a swimsuit, holding a red plastic cup and laughing. Seeing him so happy made her heart hurt.

"There are a couple of bars in the hotel—"

"Michael doesn't drink."

"Doesn't mean he can't enjoy meeting people and relaxing. It's the closest place to the marina to get a soda or something to eat."

She shook her head, mad at herself for overreacting. "You're right. I'm sorry. I guess I've been defending him for so long it's gotten to be a habit."

Chase caught her shoulders. "Michael was always a good person. He just took a wrong turn. You don't have to keep defending him to me. I'm more than willing to forgive whatever transgressions he might have committed. We all make mistakes. At any rate, the person he hurt most was himself."

She nodded, though that wasn't completely true. Michael's addiction had hurt everyone who had cared about him.

"Michael would be happy to hear you say that. He missed your friendship terribly. After he got himself straightened out, he wanted to call you. He just couldn't work up the nerve."

Chase made no reply, but something shifted in his features.

Dusk had settled in by the time they headed back to

the hotel, and Chase led her to an outside bar that over-looked the ocean, now just a shiny dark mirror disappearing in the distance.

"I'd appreciate if you'd follow my lead on this," Chase said as they walked into a circular, thatch-roofed, open-air structure that looked out over the water. "Getting people to talk, no matter the subject, isn't always easy."

"Of course."

She let him help her up onto a bamboo stool in a row in front of a long counter. Around them, people chatted at tables scattered across the floor. A black Aruban man in a short white jacket flashed a silver-toothed smile as he walked up behind the bar to greet them.

"Welcome to Papagayo's." He mopped the counter in front of them with a white terry dish towel. "I am Kosmo. It is my pleasure to serve you. The special of the day is a pineapple piña colada. Would you like to try one?"

Kosmo had the deepest voice Harper had ever heard. "No, I don't think—"

"That sounds great," Chase said. "We'd love one. We just got in from the States. Long day of flying, you know."

"Where in the US are you from?" Kosmo set two piña colada glasses in front of him and began to concoct the drinks with obvious expertise.

"We're from Texas," Chase said.

"A very long way," said Kosmo. "I hate air-o-planes."

Chase smiled. "Who doesn't?" He took a breath, making a point of filling his lungs with fresh ocean air. The sound of a steel drum drifted over the hotel grounds. "Sometimes it's worth it."

Kosmo smiled. "Oh, yes, that is true."

Though Harper was eager to question the man, Chase waited patiently for the bartender to finish making their drinks and set them on the bar in front of them. The delicious aroma of pineapple and coconut made her stomach rumble, reminding her how long it had been since she had eaten.

"We're looking for a friend," Chase said casually, toying with the straw protruding from his drink. "An American named Michael Winston. He's the lady's brother. Anything you could tell us about him would be helpful."

Kosmo hesitated, continued to mop the bar as he sized the up the two of them.

"He was here last week," Harper added, sipping her drink, which tasted delicious. She began to relax as she hadn't all day. "He was staying in the marina on a boat called *BUZZ Word*."

Chase slid a folded-up twenty across the bar and drew Michael's photo out of his shirt pocket. Harper had one in her purse and several more in her suitcase back in the hotel room.

The big, thick-shouldered bartender took the picture, held it up and studied it, then shook his head.

"I am sorry. He does not look familiar." But he turned and called to a waitress. "Perhaps Marty will remember him."

Marty walked over, carrying a drink tray on the flat of her hand. She had creamy cocoa skin, was small and very pretty. When her dark eyes landed on Chase, she smiled.

"How may I help you?" she asked.

The words sounded no more than friendly, but

Harper recognized the interest in Marty's face as purely feminine.

"We're looking for the man in this photo." Chase showed her the picture. "He was here last week, staying on a boat called *BUZZ Word*. This lady is his sister. We're trying to find him."

At the news Harper was Michael's sister and not necessarily Chase's girlfriend, Marty's face lit up. "Oh, yes, I remember him. Very handsome. He drank diet sodas. I recall because he liked the little umbrella I put in his glass. He said it made the drink look more festive. He came in several times and always ordered the same thing."

Harper's pulse began to pound.

"Do you remember if he was with someone?" Chase asked.

"The first time he was here, he came in by himself. But the next time he came in, he was with a woman. Small, long dark hair. Very beautiful. She came with him the next day, too."

"Did he leave with the woman?" Harper asked.

"I think so but I am not sure. I looked up and their table was empty. I haven't seen them since."

"Thank you, Marty." Chase tossed a bill onto Marty's tray and helped Harper down from the barstool.

"Are you staying at the hotel?" the waitress asked with a smile directed at Chase.

"For the time being. My name's Chase Garrett. If you think of anything more that might help us find him, you can reach me by calling the front desk."

"Yes, all right. Have a nice day, Chase."

Harper felt his hand at her back as he escorted her out of the bar. She wondered if the pretty little waitress interested him as much as he interested her, but whatever he was thinking didn't show.

"Let's go upstairs. I need to get on my computer. Len said Michael was planning to do some island-hopping. Let's figure out the most likely places he would go."

"Yes, good idea."

"Len also said the boat sailed with two people. Now we know there's a good chance he was with a woman."

"We don't know that for sure."

"Private investigation is always a matter of guesswork, angel. Lining up the information you've collected and making the most logical assumptions. That gives you a working theory. If it doesn't pan out, you reevaluate, come up with something new. You keep doing it until you get the answers you need."

"I see," Harper said, still reeling from the endearment. Calling her angel probably meant nothing, just something he said to women all the time, or maybe just to blondes.

She took a calming breath. "So right now, with the information we have so far, it looks like Michael met a woman and may have taken her somewhere with him on the boat."

"That's right. We need to figure out his most likely destinations. And since he isn't back yet, he may have made more than one stop."

CHAPTER SEVEN

Chase set up his laptop on the dining table in the suite, which was roomy and had magnificent views of the ocean.

"I'm starving," Harper said. "I'm going to order us something from room service."

"Good idea. A sandwich, anything works for me." He opened the laptop, sat down in one of the dining chairs, brought up Google Maps and typed in *Aruba*. The island popped up. He located the Renaissance Marina, then zoomed out to study the ocean around them.

The living room sliders were open, letting in a soft evening breeze. He could hear the ocean lapping against the shore somewhere below. Finished with her phone call, Harper stood behind him to look over his shoulder, eager to get on with their search.

Chase did his best to ignore her, but as he typed, the faint scent of jasmine drifted over him. His pulse began to pound and his lower body stirred to life. "I could use a little breathing room," he said gruffly, leaning back in his chair.

"Oh. Sorry." Harper took a couple of steps back—as if that would do any good.

Chase blew out a breath, resigned to the constant state of arousal she left him in, which, no matter how he tried to ignore her, didn't seem to lessen.

He pointed to the map. "See this protrusion of land at the end of the peninsula off the coast of Venezuela?"

"I see it."

"That beach is Piedras Negras, the closest place Michael could have sailed."

She leaned down to look at the computer, and fine blond hair feathered across his cheek. Chase inwardly groaned. When she backed away, he blew out a breath and started typing, checking the distance between Piedras Negras and Oranjestad.

"Thirty-nine kilometers," he said. "That's about twenty-four miles. He could have made an easy day sail there." He looked back at the map. "Curaçao is farther, about a hundred seventeen kilometers. Roughly just under eighty miles. Cruising at eight or so knots, it's a long day sail. They would probably opt to stay overnight. Bonaire is another little Dutch island about forty miles farther away."

He turned in the chair to look at Harper and saw her shoulders slump. "How will we figure it out?" she asked.

"If we have to, we'll go there and start looking for answers. With any luck, I'll get a call from Tabby. I should have heard from her by now."

As if saying her name had somehow made his cell ring, his iPhone signaled. He pulled it out of his jeans pocket and checked the caller ID.

He pressed the phone against his ear. "Talk to me, Tab." In his mind's eye, he could see her, very short black hair, razor cut on the sides and moussed on top, a little silver hoop in one of her sleek black eyebrows. A row of tiny hoops curled around the side of her left ear. She had several tattoos and a tongue stud.

At twenty-seven, Tabitha Love was unlike any woman he had ever met. She hadn't gone to college, barely graduated high school and was basically a genius.

"I tracked down your guy's last location."

"Hold on. Let me put you on speaker." He set the phone on the table, looked over to see the relief in Harper's face that he was treating her as part of the investigation.

"GPS on his sat phone pinged him four days ago at the Zee Winden Marina in Curaçao," Tabby said. "That's in a bay on the south end of the island. I'll give you the coordinates."

"Great." *So not Piedras Negras.*

"There're some nice beaches in the area," Tabby said. "A few casinos. Good diving off the island."

He remembered Michael had loved anything to do with the sea. One spring break they had gone diving in Florida.

"That's great, Tab. We thought he might have been headed to Piedras Negras, closest landfall to the marina where he was moored. Looks like he went for a longer sail."

"The Iridium Extreme is a really great sat phone. It has an SOS button, but it wasn't used. It also allows you to send an SMS text message with your exact location to anyone, viewable on an online map from anywhere on the planet. Apparently, that didn't happen, either. Unfortunately, the phone hasn't moved from the last location, and it's no longer sending signals."

"You think the battery could just be dead?" Harper asked hopefully.

"Tabitha Love, meet Harper Winston," Chase injected into the conversation.

"It's possible, Harper. Or something could have happened to it. The phone got busted, fell into the water, something like that."

"At least we know where he was," Chase said. "Anything else, Tab?"

"I'll keep digging, see if I can pick up something else that might help us. I'll let you know if I stumble across anything useful."

"Thanks."

"Good luck." Tabby ended the call.

"We have to go there," Harper said. "We need to find out what happened to him."

"Tomorrow. I'll call Dutch tonight and have him arrange transportation. We might need someone local to take us around after we get there."

"That's a good idea."

"Remember, it could just be problems with Michael's communication system."

"Both his radio and his sat phone went dead. You really believe that?"

"No. But I've learned not to jump to conclusions. We'll find out more tomorrow." A light knock sounded at the door. "In the meantime, let's eat."

Harper took a bite or two of the food she had ordered from room service—coconut shrimp and conch soup—but after the phone call from Tabitha Love, her worry about Michael had resurfaced and she had lost most of her appetite.

Something had happened to her brother, and it wasn't a boating accident.

Tired but unable to sleep, she phoned Shana, just to check in. Shana assured her that so far everything was running smoothly. Calling from the Caribbean was expensive so Harper didn't talk long, just brought her partner up-to-date on the search, then ended the call. She was still sitting at the desk when the hotel phone rang.

Harper walked over to answer, and a woman's voice floated over the line. "Hello. I'm looking for Chase Garrett. I'm calling from a house phone. The front desk put me through."

It wasn't Marty. The female voice on the other end of the line was American. "I'll get him for you."

"No, wait. Are you Michael Winston's sister?"

"I'm Harper, yes."

"My name is Christy Riggs. I was wondering if I could come up and talk to you and Mr. Garrett. I talked to the bartender at Papagayo's. I have information about your brother."

Her heart jerked. She glanced at Chase, who had finished his sandwich and was back at work on the computer. When he saw the look on Harper's face, he was out of his chair and walking toward her.

"We're in suite 815," Harper said. "I'll see you soon."

"What's going on?"

"That was a woman named Christy Riggs. She talked to Kosmo down in the bar. She says she has information about Michael."

"That's great, angel, but next time we don't give out

our room number—we meet people downstairs. We don't know what's going on here, and until we do, we take precautions."

She wasn't sure which bothered her the most, being called out for revealing too much information or Chase calling her angel again.

A knock sounded at the door, ending the thought, and she hurried over to open it. Chase cut her off, stepping in front of her with a quick shake of his head. He checked the hallway through the peephole, then, apparently satisfied they weren't about to be attacked, pulled open the door.

A petite redhead walked into the room, and Chase closed the door. Dressed in cutoffs and a pink flowered T-shirt, she was in her late twenties, fair-skinned and cute, with a small nose and a freckled forehead.

"I'm Christy. The bartender gave me your names when I asked about Michael Winston."

"Why don't we sit down?" Chase suggested, and they took seats on the turquoise patterned sofa and chairs around the rattan coffee table.

"So you went to the bar looking for Michael?" Chase asked, picking up the line of conversation.

"Actually, I was looking for my friend Pia Santana. We were supposed to meet here for a weeklong vacation. Pia had ten days off, so she came early for a little me-time. When I got here and checked into our room, she wasn't there. She didn't show up last night, and I haven't been able to find her all day. I've been calling her cell, but it goes straight to voice mail. I've been emailing, but she hasn't replied."

Harper exchanged a glance with Chase, and worry

tightened her chest. If Pia was with Michael, maybe both of them were in trouble.

"How do you know she was with Michael Winston?" he asked.

"The last time we talked before I left Florida, she told me she had met this really terrific guy in the bar at the hotel. She said his name was Michael Winston, and he was sailing the Caribbean on his yacht."

"When did you hear from her last?" Harper asked.

"Four days ago. I was just about to call the police, but…"

"But…?" Chase pressed.

"Pia was spending a lot of time with Michael. She was going sailing with him that morning. They were going snorkeling."

"Did she say where they were headed?" Harper asked.

"She hadn't talked to Michael yet so she wasn't quite sure."

"When did you say she'd be back?" Chase asked.

"That's the thing. They were only supposed to be gone for the day, but she said if they were having fun, they might stay a little longer. I guess she really liked him. But she should have been back yesterday at the latest."

Christy turned to Harper. "Your brother, he wouldn't… He wouldn't hurt Pia, would he?"

Harper's throat constricted. "Michael wouldn't hurt anyone." She swallowed back the threat of tears. "He's one of the nicest people you could ever meet."

Christy's eyes filled. "Then where are they? Why didn't they come back or at least call to let me know they were okay?"

"That's what we're here to find out," Chase said. "I'm

a private investigator, Christy. We're going to find Michael and Pia. Give me her cell number. We'll find out where she was the last time she used it."

"You can do that?"

He just nodded.

"It's expensive, so she might not have made any more calls," Christy said.

"We'll find out."

Harper figured Chase's friend could find the location of the phone even if Pia hadn't made any more calls. He put both girls' numbers in his cell, then phoned Tabitha Love again. It was getting late, but it was an hour earlier in Dallas.

"I need one more thing, Tab, if you don't mind." He rattled off Pia's cell number, talked a little longer, then ended the call.

"It might take a while to get the information," Chase said. "Tabby's on a project for Jonah that has to take precedence—missing six-year-old girl."

"Jonah?" Harper asked.

"Jonah Wolfe. He's one of the PIs in my office. Finding the little girl has to come first, but she promised to call no later than tomorrow morning." He turned to the petite redhead. "In the meantime, Christy, why don't you get some sleep? We'll call you in the morning before we leave."

"Where are you going?"

"Unless we hear something that will change things, Curaçao. The GPS on Michael's satellite phone puts him there early evening four days ago. We're pretty sure he was with a woman."

"Oh, God, I hope they're okay."

"We're going to find them," Chase said. "I'm not

sure what's going on, but as soon as we figure it out, we'll let you know."

"Do you think I should report Pia missing?"

Once the police got involved, Harper and Chase would be sucked into the investigation, and precious time would be lost. Harper glanced over at Chase, knew by the look on his face his thoughts ran the same.

"Time is of the essence," he said. "I'd appreciate if you waited until we're out of here tomorrow morning."

"Oh, God—"

Harper rested her hand gently on Christy's shoulder. "My brother is a good man. If Pia is with him, he'll do everything in his power to protect her. I promise you that."

Christy nodded and wiped the wetness off her cheeks. "Thank you." She walked over to the door and pulled it open. "I'll be praying for both of them. Please let me know what you find out."

The door closed with an ominous click behind her. Harper looked up at Chase.

"We're making progress," he said. "Tomorrow we'll know more."

Harper drew in a shaky breath. "I wish I could turn back the clock. I wish he was safe back in Houston."

"There are a lot of things in life we'd like to change. Since that isn't an option, we just have to go forward. Get some sleep, Harper. We'll start again early tomorrow morning."

Harper turned and walked into her bedroom. She closed the door and began to get ready for bed, but she was fairly certain she wouldn't be able to sleep.

CHAPTER EIGHT

In the throes of erotic sex with Harper Winston, Chase awoke covered in a film of perspiration, an unwelcome erection throbbing beneath the sheet. Cursing, he sat up in bed and ran a hand over his face. *Only a dream.* Or in this case, a nightmare.

He shoved his fingers through his sweat-damp hair. Jesus God, he couldn't remember a dream that had felt more real. Or ever being more aroused.

Swearing foully, he rolled out of bed. His brother Bran would get an I-told-you-so laugh out of his misery, but Chase didn't find his unwanted attraction to Harper Winston the least bit funny.

Not when her father ran his world much like a Mafia don, a highly successful criminal enterprise that allowed him to get away with murder—literally. Everyone in the Dallas underworld knew that to cross Knox Winston might get you dead. The DA's office turned a blind eye, along with the dirty cops on Knox's payroll.

Aside from the legitimate businesses Knox now ran—from motels, restaurants and laundries, to larger enterprises like hotel chains—no one really seemed to know how Knox had actually amassed his fortune. Since his son had once been Chase's best friend, Chase didn't want to know, either.

He wondered how much Harper knew about her father's activities. Not much, he would guess, since Knox had gone to great lengths to keep his children under the illusion he was just a megasuccessful businessman. And Harper had been gone from Dallas for years.

Chase had a hunch Michael had suspected, that it was part of the reason he had turned to alcohol and drugs, but they had never talked about it.

Padding naked into the bathroom in his room, he reached into the shower and turned on the water, setting the temperature a little colder than he liked. He wanted to wash Harper's beautiful face out of his head, the memory of her small, perfect breasts that—thank God—he had never actually seen.

Pulling on his jeans and a blue short-sleeved Oxford shirt, he was ready to meet with Dutch, who had arranged a boat to Curaçao. They could have gone by plane, but he wanted the flexibility to check, if necessary, other spots around the island once they got there.

He wished he was going by himself instead of dragging a woman into what might turn out to be a bad situation. But as he walked into the living room, Harper came out of the other bedroom, straw hat in hand, dressed and ready to go. His mind flashed back to the hot, erotic dream, and a shot of lust hit him like a fist.

Chase dragged in a lungful of air and forced himself to think of something else. Palm trees might have worked if she hadn't walked close enough for him to catch a whiff of her soft perfume.

"Good morning," she said. "Sleep okay?"

Jesus God, help him. He didn't want to think of the dream, refused to allow his mind to slide back into the gutter. Chase had never been more grateful to hear his iPhone ring.

Pulling his cell out of his pocket, he recognized Tabby's number. "What have you got for me, Tab?"

"Pia's phone pinged at the Zee Winden Marina in Curaçao, same as Michael's. Both phones are now inactive."

Not good. He could contact the authorities in Curaçao, but he could probably be there before the investigation—such as it would likely be—actually got underway. And once he got the police involved, it would limit what he would be able to do.

"Anything else?"

"Not at the moment. If I get something, I'll call."

"Thanks, Tab. You're the best." Chase hung up the phone, his mind back on the case. In his business, the job had to come first. People's lives depended on it.

"What did she say?" Harper asked.

"Zee Winden Marina in Curaçao, same as your brother. Call Christy and tell her, then pack an overnight bag. We might not get back tonight."

So saying, he grabbed the duffel, now packed, he had brought empty in his carry-on, something smaller, a little easier to manage. Just a Dopp kit, clean underwear, a dress shirt and linen slacks, high-top boots and cargo pants, things that might be useful as they moved into uncharted territory, where his search for Michael might lead.

A few minutes later, Harper came back into the living room carrying the oversize canvas tote bag she had brought on the plane. It was stuffed full and zipped shut, ready to go. She had pulled her hair into a ponytail, but pale blond flyaway strands floated around her face, gleaming like pale spun gold.

The heat returned to his groin. Dammit, what was there about her?

"I told Christy where we were going, and said we'd keep her posted on whatever we found."

Chase nodded. "Dutch is meeting us at the marina. He's arranged for a guide in Curaçao, someone who can take us around the island." Not the usual sort of guide, but a man who knew the underbelly of the island, places to dig up the kind of information they might need. But he didn't tell Harper that. No use worrying her even more than she was already.

Harper slung the rope handle on the bright-colored tote over her shoulder and grabbed her hat; Chase grabbed his duffel and his laptop, and they headed out the door.

The boat was idling at the dock in front of the marina office when they arrived. Dutch stood on the deck next to a tall, bone-thin man with dark skin, fierce cheekbones and a shaved head.

Chase helped Harper climb onto the deck of the older-model thirty-five-foot Riviera sport fisher. The boat, *Island Runner*, had an enclosed cabin, two steering stations and looked to be in very good condition. Chase's respect for Dutch went up a notch.

"This is Captain Lupete," Dutch said in his faintly accented English. "He is from Cuba. He and the boat are yours for as long as you need them."

"Good to meet you, Captain."

"You and the lady, as well."

Dutch said his farewells, and Captain Lupete gave him and Harper a quick tour, showing them the main salon, where they left their gear, the galley and the compartment where the life jackets were stored. The captain gave Chase a rundown on how the boat was powered, showed him the radio, GPS and the rest of the equipment.

Chase owned a twin-engine Baron that he and his brothers flew down to the ranch, so he was familiar with how communication systems worked.

From the deck, they climbed the ladder to the bright blue canvas-covered flybridge. Harper sat down on a white vinyl bench while Chase sat in the chair next to Captain Lupete. As the captain shoved the throttle forward, twin Cummins diesels pushed them at a fast crawl out of the marina into the open sea.

At eighteen knots, roughly twenty miles an hour, the sail that would have taken Michael as much as ten hours would take *Island Runner* less than four.

Chase hoped they would find some sign of Michael Winston when they got there.

As the hours slipped past, Harper made her way down the ladder to the deck below, leaving Chase on the flybridge with the captain. Settling herself in one of the deck chairs, she leaned back and closed her eyes, enjoying the feel of the sun and wind in her face.

Though the boat was far nicer than the dirty trawler she'd half expected, she prayed they wouldn't need it after today, prayed they would find Michael and Pia holed up in the cabin of Michael's yacht, enjoying each other so much time had simply slipped away.

She knew it wasn't true. Michael would know how worried she was. He would have called or somehow gotten word to her.

Her chest clamped down. She felt like crying, but she wouldn't let it happen. She didn't have time for emotion—she could break down after she knew Michael was safe.

She took a fortifying breath. Michael was alive, and they were going to find him. Maybe he was injured and at the hospital in a port he had visited. Maybe—God forbid—he'd been arrested for breaking some little-known local law.

She didn't want to think Pia Santana had anything to do with Michael's disappearance, and after meeting Pia's friend Christy, she didn't really believe she had.

Earlier this morning, Chase had been on his computer, looking into Pia's background, but so far they hadn't had a chance to talk about what he had found.

The hours slipped past. She heard a sound, glanced up as Chase stepped down off the ladder. For an instant she forgot to breathe. He had taken off his shirt to catch some sun, exposing his wide shoulders, the ladder of muscle running down his stomach and a set of biceps that made her mouth water.

A dusting of dark golden hair spread over his hard-muscled chest, and arrowed out of sight below the light blue jeans that rode low on his narrow hips and outlined the long bones and sinews in his thighs. He looked amazing, his once-lanky young man's body matured into that of a powerful, virile male.

"We're about halfway there," he said. "You doing okay?"

She tried not to stare at all those tempting muscles

and concentrate on what he was saying. *Was she okay?* She hadn't been okay since Michael disappeared.

"I'm all right. I was wondering, though, what you found out about Pia Santana."

Chase sat down in the deck chair next to hers. Just having him so close made her pulse hammer. She wished he was wearing his shirt.

"I didn't find anything that would make me think Pia was somehow involved in Michael's disappearance," he said. "Pia's twenty-seven, very pretty if her Facebook photos are to be believed, with big brown eyes and wavy long brown hair. Looks like your brother's taste in women is as good as it always was."

Harper almost smiled. "Does she live in Florida like Christy?"

"Born and raised in Miami. Her dad's Hispanic. Parents still married. Pia's a CPA. Works for Thompson, Peters and Handel, a well-respected Miami accounting firm. No connections to this part of the world, at least that I found so far." He cast Harper a sympathetic glance. "Feel better?"

Relief trickled through her. "A lot better."

"My guess…whatever is going on with Michael, Pia was swept up in it, too."

"What do you think it could be?"

He hesitated just long enough for her to know he didn't want to tell her.

"Please. I really want to know."

"Could be some kind of piracy. Curaçao's just off the coast of Venezuela. People there live well below the poverty level. Some will do anything for money. The boat Michael owns is worth hundreds of thousands of dollars."

Chase didn't say more, and Harper was glad. She'd been worried about pirates from the start. It was the worst possible scenario.

"It could be something else, Harper," Chase said gently. "We know they made it as far as the marina in Curaçao, but we don't know what happened after they got there. I checked the hospitals last night before I went to bed. Nothing. But they could have had an accident in one of the ports they visited after they left the marina. They could have had boat trouble and gotten stranded somewhere. Maybe they haven't had a way to communicate."

She just nodded. Chase was trying to stay positive. She appreciated that more than he could know. Whatever had happened, she prayed Michael was alive and safe.

Chase returned upstairs to give the captain a break and coordinate their arrival at the destination Tabitha Love had given him.

Now that he was gone, Harper could finally breathe. She didn't want him to sense the attraction she felt for him, which only seemed to grow stronger the more she was around him. Chase was clearly a professional, capable and in control of the situation, a take-charge guy she felt she could rely on. He was honorable and determined. Add to that, the man was flat-out hot.

She was so tuned in to him she knew where he was without looking. Knew when he was watching her, though most of the time he ignored her.

Which, she told herself, was good. She was there to find her brother, not indulge in a brief affair with a man who barely knew she existed.

She glanced up as he came back down the ladder sometime later—wearing his shirt, thank God.

"Won't be much longer."

She followed his gaze out over the ocean, and spotted the island rising out of the sea like a mushroom cap, growing larger and larger as the boat drew near. Curaçao had a dry desert climate like Aruba, with more cacti than palm trees. A warm trade wind blew across the deck from the east.

Soon the harbor appeared ahead, tall masts swaying in the breeze, sailboats and powerboats lining each side of the inlet, which was several miles from the capital city of Willemstad. Captain Lupete cut the engines as the boat entered the Zee Winden Marina. Ocean swells shoved the boat forward, closer to shore, and Harper's anxiety grew.

Where are you, Mikey?

But as another day slid past without word, she was more and more afraid to find out.

CHAPTER NINE

Chase helped Captain Lupete secure the lines, then he and Harper left the boat to start their search, beginning at the marina office. Tabby had given them the exact location of Michael's phone before the battery had gone dead or the phone had been destroyed. Putting the coordinates into the GPS app on his cell, Chase tracked it to an open area in the center of the marina—underwater.

Pia's phone was in a spot not far away. If Chase had any more doubt that something was seriously wrong, he didn't now.

Harper stood beside him, her eyes fixed on the ocean where the phones had disappeared. Worry lines creased her forehead. "What could have happened?"

"They were purposely tossed into the water. Unless Michael and Pia didn't want to be found, someone took their phones and disposed of them so they couldn't be tracked."

Her features paled. Chase took Harper's arm and

turned her toward the office. "Come on. Let's go see what we can find out." A faint tremor ran through her and Chase forced himself to ignore it. Silently he cursed, wishing again he could have left her in Dallas.

In the office, a heavyset, gray-haired woman sitting behind the counter checked marina records.

"Here it is… *BUZZ Word.* Arrived October 3, owner Michael Winston. The yacht was assigned slip A-6."

"Did you talk to Michael or the girl who was with him when the boat arrived?" Chase asked.

"I signed them in so, yes, I talked to them. They were a good-looking couple, such a handsome young man, and the girl—beautiful long brown hair and so pretty. They couldn't take their eyes off each other. They seemed to be having a wonderful time."

"Did either of them mention what they planned to do while they were here?"

"They asked me for a casino recommendation and I said the Trade Winds was a nice place and close to the marina. The girl asked if there was dancing, and I told her there was a band there every evening."

"Anything else you can think of?" Chase asked.

"Just that they paid the fee for two days, but they must have changed their minds because the boat was gone when I got to work the following morning."

They changed their minds, Chase thought, *or someone changed it for them.* "Thanks. We appreciate your help." Ushering Harper out of the office, he closed the door behind them. He could tell she was upset but she was doing her best not show it, to concentrate instead on finding her brother.

"It makes sense that they went to the casino," she said.

"Michael loves to gamble. He likes to play blackjack and craps. He says everyone deserves a vice and that's his."

Chase's instincts went on alert. "Deep play?"

"No. Never. Michael says he works too hard for his money. He usually takes a couple thousand dollars. When he loses it, he stops."

"You sure? Gambling debts owed to the wrong people can be deadly."

"I met him in Vegas for a couple of days last year. We had fun, but we didn't lose more than we could afford."

Unless Michael was putting on an act for his sister, another possibility had just been shot to hell.

Harper glanced back toward the open water where the phones had disappeared. "If they changed their minds and sailed that night, something must have happened to them while they were here. We need to see what we can find out at the casino."

That was definitely the plan. "We'll go there later. It was a long sail from Aruba to get here. It would have been evening when they went to the club. Better to go there when they would have been there, speak to people who work the same shift."

"Good idea."

"Meanwhile, I need to make a phone call." Passing a couple of teenage girls in the skimpiest bikinis Chase had ever seen, he walked beside Harper along the dock back toward the boat. He wondered how he would feel if the girls were his daughters. Not good, he didn't think. He'd probably never know. Home and family had taken a backseat to his work years ago.

"Who are you going to call?" Harper asked, intruding on his thoughts.

"Dutch's Curaçao contact, a man who might be able

to help us get some answers. After I set things up, we'll do a little legwork, see if anyone on one of the boats in the marina heard anything that night."

Harper nodded. A warm sun shone down from a clear blue sky, the breeze soft, and scented with the clean, salty fragrance of the sea. It looked as if they would be spending the night aboard. Harper could take the cabin; Chase would take one of the bunks. Lupete would be staying with a friend.

Chase phoned Dutch's contact, a man named Jules St. Ange, and arranged for him to pick them up at eight. They would start their search at the Trade Winds, hit some of the other casinos in the area if they didn't have any luck there.

The rest of the afternoon, they wandered the marina, stopping to speak to people on their yachts or working in the area, asking questions and hoping to get some kind of break.

Had anyone heard anything out of the ordinary? Loud conversations, maybe an argument or altercation of some kind? Had they seen someone in the area who looked out of place or was behaving oddly?

But no one had heard or seen anything unusual when *BUZZ Word* had arrived or when the boat had sailed sometime that night.

Unfortunately, no one was aboard the forty-five-foot Hatteras in slip A-7, the boat docked closest to *BUZZ Word*. Chase hoped the owners would eventually show up. More than that, he hoped they had heard something that might help him figure out where *BUZZ Word* had sailed.

The hours slipped past, and darkness settled over the island. Disheartened at their lack of success, they returned to the boat to dress for the casino. While Harper changed in the cabin, Chase dressed in the linen slacks and dark green flowered, short-sleeved shirt he had brought.

He was standing in the salon, checking his wristwatch and beginning to get antsy, when the cabin door opened and Harper walked into the salon in a short black cocktail dress with a flirty little skirt that showed off her long smooth legs. Tiny black straps on the bodice left her back and shoulders bare, and silver heeled sandals pushed her up nearly as tall as he was.

A surge of heat hit him, slid into his groin. He managed to choke out a comment. "You had all that in your canvas bag?"

Harper smiled. "It's expandable. The bag is part of the EC line." She turned, the skirt flaring out as she showed him the back, giving him an even better view of her pretty legs. "So is my dress. We specialize in casual, easy-care clothing that is extremely versatile."

He'd always been a leg man. He looked away, fighting not to get hard. *Dammit.* She had swept her pale gold hair into a sophisticated twist, and a pair of small gold earrings dangled from her ears. She looked delectable.

Harper smoothed a hand over the front of the dress, mercifully unaware of the effect she had on him.

"The dress is made of a polyknit fabric that doesn't wrinkle. You can just stuff it in your suitcase, take it out and put it on and you're ready to go."

She was obviously proud of the business she had built and the products she sold. He liked that about her. But he didn't want to want her any more than he did already, and looking at her in that sexy black dress wasn't helping.

His mouth felt dry. He wanted to walk over there and haul her into his arms. He wanted to release that silky hair, grab a handful and drag her mouth up to his. He wanted to kiss her until she begged him to take her.

He prayed his thoughts didn't show. "You look beautiful, angel. But then you always do."

At the name he had secretly been calling her since he had first seen her the day she turned sixteen, color washed into her cheeks.

"Thank you," she said softly.

"Now, let's go find out what happened to your brother."

Some of her sparkle faded. She was worried about Michael, and she had every reason to be. Something had happened to him after his arrival in Curaçao. Chase prayed that wherever he was, he and Pia were still alive.

They left the boat and headed for the parking lot, where Jules St. Ange was waiting, a dark-skinned Haitian who spoke English with a French Creole accent. Chase shook his hand, but Harper greeted him in French, which seemed to please him.

"Enchanté, mademoiselle," he replied with a smile. *"Un plaisir de vous rencontrer."*

Harper smiled back, and St. Ange tipped his head toward Chase. "My vehicle is waiting. Shall we go?"

Though his tone was casual, the man possessed an intensity Chase recognized from his years in law enforcement. Jules St. Ange wasn't your typical friendly tour guide. Like Dutch, he knew the workings of the darker side of the island.

Chase hoped he would be able to help them come up with a lead on Michael and Pia's disappearance.

Harper felt Chase's hand at her waist as Jules St. Ange held open the door to the Trade Winds Casino and

Chase steered her inside. The whole time she had been riding in the backseat of St. Ange's blue Jeep Cherokee, she had been thinking about Chase calling her angel and saying how beautiful she looked.

For the first time, she had seen heat in his eyes, the unmistakable glint of desire. She thought she'd caught that look before, but it was gone so quickly she'd been sure she had imagined it.

Was it possible Chase wasn't as immune to her as he pretended to be? The thought made her abdomen clench the way it had when he had come down the ladder on the boat with his shirt off.

What would it mean if the desire she had glimpsed was real? This wasn't the time or place for an affair. She needed to concentrate on finding her brother.

Her thoughts returned to Michael as they walked farther into the casino and she was swept up in the familiar glitter of neon lights and loud conversations. Slot machines whirred and clanged around her, and patrons cheered and shouted when they won.

It looked a lot like Vegas, but the colors were brighter, the wild blues and greens of the Caribbean, hot crimson, bright pink and gold.

Chase paused to survey their surroundings, his gaze going to the dealers at the tables in their white shirts and black pants. "You said Michael liked to play blackjack and craps."

"That's right."

"Let's split up and do a little gambling ourselves, see what we can find out."

St. Ange moved up beside them. "I will do the same. I will find you later." He slipped off into the crowd as if he were never there.

"You need money?" Chase asked, reaching for his wallet.

Harper almost smiled. Chase was supposed to be working for her, not the other way around. She had a hunch that had changed the moment he'd discovered Michael's phone had been tossed. Or more likely she hadn't been in charge from the start.

Chase had once been Michael's friend. Apparently, that hadn't changed.

She smiled. "Thanks, but I'd rather use my own money. If I win, I get to keep it."

Chase smiled back. "I'll start over there." He headed for the craps table while Harper found an ATM, withdrew some cash, then sat down to play at one of the blackjack tables.

The dealer, a handsome Native man with long-lashed, chocolate-brown eyes, flirted with her outrageously. If Harper hadn't been so worried, she might have enjoyed the attention. As it was, she concentrated on not losing her money too quickly and used the dealer's interest to start a conversation about her brother and Pia Santana.

Unfortunately, the answers led nowhere.

Two hours later, she had played at half a dozen different tables and shown her brother's photo to the dealers and a few of the patrons, along with the one Chase had given her of Pia, printed at the hotel business office before they'd left Aruba.

She had come up empty-handed, prayed Chase or Jules would do better.

A little after midnight, Chase found her at one of the tables, a busted hand in front of her and only a small stack of chips. She had lost most of her money, which she wouldn't have minded if it had paid off with some kind of lead.

"Time to cash out," Chase said, urging her up from her chair. She collected the last of her chips, and he walked her back to the cashier's cage. Both of them cashed out, Chase's stack of chips a lot bigger than her own.

"You won?" she asked.

"Broke even." Which in gambling she considered a win. "Jules is waiting out front," he said. "He's got something for us."

"What is it?"

Chase just shook his head. "Not here."

They made their way back through the casino, weaving their way through the crowd, stepping out into the soft night air and heading for the parking lot, where Jules stood next to his Jeep.

"What did you find out?" Harper asked, unwilling to wait a moment more.

"Two men followed your brother and the woman out of the club. They spoke Spanish. According to my information, they were not locals. From their description, soldiers would be my guess."

"Soldiers?" Harper repeated, fear curling in her stomach. "Why would soldiers be following my brother?"

"Mercenaries, Harper," Chase said. "Men paid to do a job."

"What…what job?"

Chase's eyes met hers in the harsh white beam of the security light illuminating the parking lot. "It's time to phone your father, Harper. We need to find out if he's received a ransom call from whoever took your brother and Pia."

CHAPTER TEN

The sounds of the rain forest surrounded him, the hum of insects, the shrill cry of a monkey, the rustle of leaves as a wild animal moved through the undergrowth not far away.

In the blackness of night, Michael Winston leaned back against the thick trunk of an eighty-foot kapok rising up from the damp, mossy floor of the rain forest. His wrists burned from the plastic ties biding his hands behind his back. The white Bermuda shorts his captors had allowed him to put on when they had boarded *BUZZ Word* and found him sleeping naked next to Pia in the master cabin were gone, replaced by khaki fatigues more suitable for their trek into the jungle.

Huddled on the ground beside him, hands also bound, Pia rested her head on his shoulder, her long mahogany hair teasing his cheek. She was petite, no more than five foot three, with big brown eyes and smooth olive skin. Even with her makeup gone, her baggy fatigues damp from the afternoon rain and sticking to her lush curves, she was beautiful.

Every time he looked at her, guilt and fury washed over him. Fury that he was helpless to protect her from what might be in store for them. Guilt that if he hadn't convinced her to go sailing with him she would be safe back in Aruba.

He could only pray that their captors would continue to obey whatever orders had apparently come down from their leader, which seemed to be not to hurt them.

At least no more than had already happened during the fight to subdue them that night on the boat. His jaw and cheek were bruised, and his ribs ached from the blows he had taken. He would have kept fighting if one of the men hadn't pulled a gun and pressed it against Pia's head.

That had been days ago. What day was it now? He tried to count backward, remembered making incredible love to Pia for the first time after a night of gambling at the Trade Winds Casino. Both of them had won a little money, enough to have them smiling when they returned to the boat and ended up in bed.

He remembered Pia falling asleep in his arms. Remembered the deep, satisfied sleep he'd drifted into himself, a rarity with the heavy work schedule he'd been under.

Sometime later that night, two men—big, burly and tough—had boarded the yacht and taken control, forcing him to sail out of the marina into the open sea. For the next two days, Michael had been certain the men's intention was to pirate the yacht, kill them and dump their bodies in the ocean.

If it hadn't been for Pia, he would have made an attempt to overpower his captors, but the men were heavily armed and well trained, and he wasn't willing to risk Pia's life unless there was absolutely no other choice.

Eventually, the boat had sailed into a quiet cove on a deserted stretch of beach several hundred miles from Curaçao. If his mental calculations were correct, they'd arrived somewhere in Colombia.

They'd been imprisoned two more days before soldiers had arrived to take charge of them. By then, Michael had been certain the motive was ransom, a demand for millions from his megarich father in return for his son's release. But he was no longer sure.

Not since the soldiers had forced him and Pia to begin this grueling trek into the rain forest that covered the steep sides of the mountains. They had hiked all day in ill-fitting boots provided by their captors that rubbed blisters on their feet.

At dusk, the soldiers had stopped the march and began making camp. Exhausted, Michael had slumped against the tree and Pia had eased down beside him. He had no idea how long they'd sat there while the men ate and drank between raucous bursts of laughter.

They'd been given water and a little food, which they'd been released just long enough to eat, given a bathroom break, then been tied up again and left beneath the tree.

Equally as wet, numb and cold as he was, Pia shifted and raised her head to look at him. "How many more days, do you think, till we reach wherever they're taking us?"

They hadn't arrived at their final destination—he was sure of that. "I heard some of them talking. My Spanish sucks, but if I got at least some of it right, they're planning to reach the main camp by tomorrow night."

Which meant another long day of hiking through the harsh, wet, mountainous tropical landscape. Pia spoke far better Spanish than he did, but she'd been careful not to let them know. She was extremely smart, which was one of the reasons he'd been attracted to her in the first place.

"Do you think they've sent word to your father?"

He had told her his ransom theory mostly to keep her spirits up, told her his father was worth millions of dollars and that he would surely pay for the safe return of his only son and the girl who was with him.

Though Michael had never been able to live up to his father's expectations and they rarely spoke these days, it didn't change the fact they were blood. His father would pay the ransom demand and Pia would be part of the bargain—Michael wasn't leaving without her.

"They've probably sent word by now," he said. "They'll want to be paid in cash. It might take my father a while to get the money together and get it down here."

And his sister would be looking for them; he was sure of that. He hadn't called her in days, as she had made him promise to do. Harper would know something was wrong, and she would be doing her best to find him.

Next to him, Pia shivered. Darkness surrounded them. This high in the mountains, the temperature had dropped from the seventies in the afternoon into the high fifties after dark. Heavy rainfall left the leaves and grass soaked, the air chilly and damp. Though the fatigues they wore offered some protection against the elements, neither of them were dressed for the colder weather.

He couldn't resist a glance at her pretty face, or noticing the soft swells beneath her drab cotton shirt. After the unplanned but glorious night he had spent with her on the boat, he remembered the exact shape of her lush breasts, the way her nipples hardened in his hands. He remembered her desire for him, the way she cried out his name when she lost control.

As battered and bruised as he was, as worried as he was, a trickle of heat slid through him.

He thought of how bravely Pia had fought their abductors, scratching and clawing, twisting and kicking, a naked hellion who refused to give up.

That the men hadn't tried to rape her was a clue of some sort, because clearly they wanted her. If he was right and he was being ransomed, maybe the soldiers were keeping them alive and unharmed so that they could get paid.

Michael looked into her big brown eyes. "I know I've said this before, but I'm really sorry I got you into this. If I could go back in time, I would never have bought you that drink in Aruba."

Pia leaned up and pressed a kiss on his beard-stubbled jaw. "My grandmother used to say that fate was a hunter. She believed everything happened for a reason, that ultimately it was God's will. If you hadn't bought me that drink, I never would have met you and I am very glad that I did."

He swallowed. "Pia…"

"If we are meant to survive, we will. What happened is not your fault."

Maybe not, but Michael wasn't so sure. How had the men found them in Curaçao? If it was ransom money they were after, how had they known who he was? Who his father was?

Michael looked into Pia's beautiful face, his gaze running over the bruise on her cheek and her puffy bottom lip, and another shot of guilt slid through him.

He would get her out of this, he vowed. No matter what it took, he would find a way to protect her and get her safely home.

It was one in the morning Dallas time when Harper phoned her father. His sleep-groggy voice boomed over the line in an unfriendly "Hello."

"Dad, it's me."

"Harper. It's the middle of the night. What's going on?"

Standing in the salon aboard *Island Runner* with the phone pressed to her ear, Harper felt a rush of fear. Clearly her father hadn't received a ransom call.

"I'm in the Caribbean, Dad. Michael's missing. We think he's been kidnapped." She could hear him moving around, his heavy frame shifting as he sat up in bed.

"Kidnapped? What are you talking about?"

"He's been missing for more than a week, Dad. We tracked him to Aruba, then on to Curaçao. We think men came aboard his yacht in the middle of the night and took control of the boat. We think they forced him to sail out of the harbor, but we don't know where."

Her father grunted. "I told him it was a stupid thing to do, going down there by himself. The world's a dangerous place. He should have known better."

"We thought by now you would have received a call demanding money for his release."

"No one's called." He moved the phone to his other ear. "You said *we*. Who's with you?"

She hated to tell him. She knew about the feud between her father and Bass Garrett when he'd been alive, though she had no idea the cause. Knox Winston didn't like Chase and his brothers any better than he had their father.

"Chase Garrett. He's a private detective now. I hired him to help me look for Michael."

"I know what he does for a living. Garrett's with you? Are you telling me you're down there alone with him?"

"It's business, Dad. We're trying to find Michael. Don't you care about what might have happened to him?"

"Of course I care. He's my son."

"But you haven't received a ransom demand."

"No. He's probably just off on another bender. A leopard doesn't change his spots."

Harper stiffened. "Michael doesn't do that anymore. You should be proud of him."

He just grunted.

"He's in trouble, Dad. I need you to let me know immediately if someone calls. In the meantime, we're going to keep looking."

"Stay away from Garrett. I'm warning you."

"Good night, Dad." Harper hung up the phone. Her hands were shaking. She loved her father, but sometimes she didn't like him. She'd never really forgiven him for the way he'd treated her brother, the constant verbal abuse, the relentless chipping away at Michael's self-esteem, the humiliation. It was no surprise her brother had turned to drugs.

She glanced over at Chase, who leaned against the cabin wall a few feet away, his arms folded over his impressive chest, his eyes hooded and unreadable. "No one's contacted him," Harper said.

Chase shoved away from the wall and walked toward her, his dark eyes intense. "So he wasn't kidnapped for ransom."

Her throat felt tight. "Maybe they just haven't called yet."

Some of the tension eased from Chase's wide shoulders. He reached out and touched her cheek. "There's always the possibility. We'll start again in the morning, figure out where they were taken. In the meantime, you need to get some sleep."

She swallowed. He was standing close enough for her to inhale his scent: fresh air, sun and sea, combined with a sexy masculinity that belonged exclusively to Chase. She wished she could just lean into him, rest her head on his shoulder, feel those hard arms around her.

Instead she took a step back, fighting a feeling of loss. Turning, she walked into the cabin and closed the door. After another fruitless day and tonight's crushing disappointment, she was exhausted. But no way would she get to sleep.

CHAPTER ELEVEN

Chase awoke to the buzzing of his cell phone. Rubbing a hand over his night's growth of beard, he grabbed the phone off the floor next to the bottom bunk and swung his legs over the side of the bed.

Looking down, he recognized Tabby's number. "Hey, Tab. What's up?"

"You are so going to love me."

"Yeah?" He almost smiled. "What have you got?"

"So after we talked yesterday, I got an idea. I thought I might try a different angle, see if I could find something that would help us track the boat instead of the people."

"I'm listening."

"I took a look at Michael Winston's credit card, started searching for equipment he might have purchased before he left on his voyage. A few months back, he bought a GPS device called a NAV Tracker, an upscale model 2.0. It's used to locate a boat that's been stolen. The device tracks the vessel's speed, heading, latitude and longitude every thirty minutes."

Chase felt a rush of excitement. "Tell me you found the boat."

Tabby laughed. "Yup, I did. The device reports to your cell phone, which in Michael's case is disabled, but I was able to tap into the information that is still being sent to that number. Key this into your phone." Tabby rattled off the longitude and latitude of the yacht, which Chase entered into the notepad on his cell.

"Got it. You're right, darlin', I love you."

"The yacht hasn't moved since it arrived at that location a couple of days ago. I looked at the satellite photos. It's a cove off a beach in Colombia."

"Colombia? What the hell?"

"If you're planning to fly down there, Santa Marta is the closest airport. The cove is about ninety kilometers north and east. There's a tiny village nearby called Punta Gato."

"I'm giving you a raise. You're the best, darlin'." Chase ended the call. He looked up as Harper came in, wearing jeans and a white V-necked shirt embroidered with bright flowers, a tiny EC logo on the front.

She stopped a few feet away from where he sat on the bunk, dark smudges beneath her big blue eyes, which were glued to his naked chest. When he shifted on the bunk, her gaze went to the bulge at the front of his briefs, and her cheeks flushed pink.

Harper turned around, which was good because the way she was looking at him had made him hard. "Give me a minute and I'll tell you what we just got."

Back straight, she headed for the galley. Coffee

was brewing by the time he had pulled on jeans and a T-shirt and joined her.

"Coffee?" She poured him a cup before he even had time to answer, then poured one for herself. She handed him a mug, and both of them took a shot of badly needed caffeine.

"Who was it?" Harper asked, careful to keep her eyes on his face. Freshly washed, her ponytail gleamed silver gold.

Chase ignored the heat still pulsing through his lower body. "Good news. That was Tabby. She found the boat."

Harper's eyes widened. "She found the boat? Oh, my God, where is it?"

This was where it got sticky. He hoped she wouldn't guess the most likely scenario—that the yacht had been stolen, Michael and Pia murdered, their bodies dumped in the sea.

"That's the thing," he said carefully. "*BUZZ Word*'s in Colombia."

She frowned. "Colombia? Why would Michael go to… Colombia?" Her pretty face paled. "Oh, God. You think…think those men were pirates. You think they forced Michael to sail out to sea, then they…they killed him and Pia and stole the boat."

He forced himself to stay where he was, to ignore the fear in her face and the urge to comfort her. "Take it easy, okay? We don't know that's what happened."

But her eyes welled with tears. The hand holding the mug started to tremble, sloshing hot coffee over the sides. Chase grabbed the mug and set it down on the counter. The next thing he knew he was pulling her into his arms.

"It's all right, angel, don't cry. We don't know what happened. It's too soon to give up. We can't do that until we know for sure."

Harper's arms went around his waist and she rested her head on his shoulder. He could feel her trembling. He drew her a little closer, the heat of his body relaxing her muscles and he hoped easing some of her fear.

"You hear me, Harper? We aren't giving up. Okay?" He felt her faint nod of agreement, but she didn't let go, and Chase didn't want her to. He wanted to keep her right there. He wanted to tip her face up, bend his head and very softly kiss her. He wanted to tell her everything was going to be okay, that they would find her brother and Pia, and they would both be alive and safe.

Since he couldn't make that promise and there could never be anything more than friendship between them, he was glad when she took a deep breath and stepped away.

"I'm sorry." She wiped tears off her cheeks. "It's just… I was worried about pirates even before Michael left."

"There's still a chance he was kidnapped. If that's what happened, sooner or later the kidnappers will get in touch with your dad. In the meantime, I'm going to Santa Marta. I'll find the boat and figure out what happened to your brother and the girl. I won't come back to Texas until I know for sure."

Harper's head came up and her spine went stiff. "Wait a minute. You think I'm going back to Texas while you go to Colombia? No way. That isn't going to happen, Chase."

"Listen to me. Colombia isn't the Caribbean. Bad stuff happens down there. You need to go home and let me handle this. If I need help, I'll call my brother and ask him to fly down. Bran was army Special Forces, spent a lot of time in South America. He knows his way around down there."

"You can do whatever you want. I'm going to Santa Marta. I'm going to find out what happened to Michael. I hope you'll take me with you, but if you won't, I'll go by myself."

Chase fought to hold on to his temper. "Dammit, Harper. If I take you with me, you'll only get in the way."

"I don't think so. I'm fluent in Spanish—are you?"

"No, but—"

"I spent a year doing volunteer work in Ecuador. I understand the culture. I know what it's like down there. I'm going." She cocked a sleek blond eyebrow. "Should I buy one plane ticket or two?"

She looked like a tiger ready to fight for her cub. He didn't want to admire her. Another curse slipped out, this one under his breath.

"Fine. But I'll make the arrangements. We'll fly private. I want to stay under the radar as much as we can."

Harper relaxed. "All right. I'll go pack my things."

Chase watched her walk away, wishing there was something he could say to convince her, knowing there wasn't. Harper was a lot stronger than her brother, or at least the man Michael used to be when he was young.

Mikey was lucky to have a sister who cared about him as much as Harper did.

With a sigh, he picked up his phone and punched the contact number for Jules St. Ange. "It's Garrett. I need to charter a plane to Santa Marta, Colombia. I want to leave as soon as possible. Can you handle it?"

"Bien sûr. Absolutely. I will call you back." The phone went dead, and Chase walked back to the bunk to collect his gear. When he finished, he went to speak to Lupete, who was up on the flybridge, checking equipment.

Chase climbed the ladder to join him, let him know they wouldn't be needing the boat any longer and paid him the balance of what he owed. His phone buzzed as he walked back into the salon. St. Ange had made the arrangements and would pick them up in twenty minutes for the trip to the Curaçao airport.

As the call ended, he looked up to see Harper walking into the salon, gripping her canvas bag. Harper seemed to gravitate toward bright colors. Another indicator she wasn't as cool as her persona seemed to suggest.

"Looks like you're ready," he said. "St. Ange is coming to take us to the airport. We'll make a stop in Aruba to collect the rest of our gear and check out of the hotel. I've got some arrangements to make before he gets here."

Harper looked up at him, her features strained. "Do you really think there's a chance they're still alive?"

A slim one, maybe. But there was always a chance. "Knox Winston is worth a lot of money. Whatever my feelings about him, I don't think he'd hesitate to pay his son's ransom, no matter how much it was. If people found out, it might affect his reputation and he wouldn't want that."

Harper frowned at the remark.

Clearly Knox's daughter had no idea the man he really was, a reminder to Chase to keep his distance.

"I know you and Michael both received substantial

inheritances from your mother," he continued. "So I assume Michael's worth plenty of money on his own."

"He's also a very successful businessman," Harper added.

"Money's everything down there. Your brother's smart. He'll try to work that angle. So yes, I think there's a good chance they're still alive."

Some of the tension seeped out of her shoulders. "I know you don't want me to go, but thank you for taking me with you."

Chase felt a pang in his chest. It was followed by a trickle of irritation. "The last thing I want is for you to thank me for putting your life in danger. Now, check your bag and finish getting ready to go."

Harper sat in the seat behind Chase in the chartered Piper Twin Comanche that St. Ange had arranged for their flight to Colombia.

Before the pilot took off, Chase had done a thorough inspection of the aircraft to be sure it was in satisfactory condition. Apparently, he was a pilot himself, Harper had learned, the owner of a twin-engine Baron he and his brothers flew down to their Hill Country ranch.

As she'd waited on the tarmac for the plane to be loaded, Harper had phoned Christy Riggs. She'd told Christy that Pia and Michael had sailed from Curaçao, and that she and Chase were still looking for them. Christy was going to update Pia's worried parents, who would undoubtedly phone the Aruba police, but Chase had cautioned Harper not to mention their trip to Colombia.

Chase, she had learned, was a very cautious man.

The engine hummed as the plane winged over the

open sea where miles of ocean glittered in the sun below them. Harper found her tired muscles relaxing, her head nodding, her eyelids drooping. She hadn't slept much last night.

When she had, she'd dreamed about Michael, little things she remembered from when they were kids. Michael teaching her to play blackjack, which their mother disapproved of, staying home on the weekend to help with her homework.

Five years older, he had always been protective, had often taken the blame for things she had done. He had paid the price with their father, who had never approved of Michael's more sensitive nature. He wanted a son tough enough to take over his business empire. Michael's gentle disposition was more like their mother's.

Their mother's suicide had hit him hard, perhaps the initial push toward drugs and alcohol. After recovering from his addiction, Michael had become a stronger man, one who dealt with adversity instead of becoming a victim of its whims. He would fight to live, she believed. And he would do his best to protect the young woman who was with him.

Her last thought before she drifted into sleep was that if Michael could be strong, so could she.

It wasn't much later that the wheels touching down on the runway jolted her awake. Dutch was waiting when the plane rolled up to the executive terminal for their brief stop in Aruba to pick up their gear. At Chase's instruction, the big Dutchman had gone to the hotel earlier that morning, packed their bags and checked them out of the suite.

Harper didn't like to think of a stranger rummaging through the silk thong panties and push-up bras in the dresser drawers, but it was faster than doing it themselves, wasting time when there was no time to waste.

In less than thirty minutes, they were back in the air, the engines humming as the plane soared over the turquoise sea toward Santa Marta, three hundred miles away. The pilot, a thin man with course black hair, seemed to be competent, and Chase could fly the plane if he had to.

Chase. Harper could still remember the way he had held her when she had cried that morning. When she was younger, she'd had an unwanted crush on Chase Garrett for years. Before her move back to Dallas, she had stupidly believed she had outgrown her infatuation, only to discover it had actually gotten worse.

Maybe when this was over and Michael was safe, she would act on the desire for him she worked so hard to ignore. Maybe she would seduce him, prey on the hunger she had begun to recognize in his eyes. Maybe she could satisfy her ridiculous fascination and put an end to the hopeless attraction she felt for him.

The idea was tempting, particularly after she had seen him nearly naked that morning, looking spectacularly good in nothing but a pair of small white briefs. She flushed to remember that he had been aroused, and wondered if it was possible she had been the cause. It was something to think about instead of her constant fear for her brother.

As the engines droned on and her body relaxed once more into sleep, she thought that her idea of seducing him might actually work. As soon as they found Michael, she might even work up the courage to try it.

CHAPTER TWELVE

Sprawling white-sand beaches, an ocean that bled into jungle, and rain forests that climbed to incredible twelve-thousand-foot, snow-covered peaks made Santa Marta a fascinating place.

Fascinating, yes. But this part of Colombia could also be deadly.

Before they'd left Curaçao, Chase had done some research on what turned out to be the oldest existing Spanish city in South America, dating back to 1525. While he was digging, he'd run across a State Department travel advisory for Santa Marta and all of Colombia. Travelers were warned against domestic insurgency, narcotrafficking, crime, extortion and kidnapping.

US government employees weren't allowed to travel outside urban areas at night, were restricted from entering the coastal Caribbean area at all—exactly where *BUZZ Word* had ended up.

In a way, Chase figured the propensity for kidnapping in the region was a reason to be hopeful. Maybe Knox Winston would get a ransom call yet—and a fat payoff would save the lives of his son and the young woman who was with him.

Since that hadn't happened yet, Chase had phoned his brother. Bran never talked about his special ops missions, but Chase knew he'd been deployed to a number of South American countries.

After he'd been wounded and left the army, Bran had worked protection in Venezuela, specializing in corporate personnel, mostly bigwigs and their families. But he'd also worked in Colombia. Nestlé, Kellogg, Pepsi, Coca-Cola and Dole all had enterprises in the country.

Bran still had contacts, former military who worked freelance for big dollars, mercenaries who knew Colombia and could get just about anything, including information.

The hum of the engine shifted as the plane began its descent. Chase looked out the window to see Santa Marta below, a sprawling city overflowing with humanity spilling out on a horseshoe bay.

The landing went smoothly. It didn't take long to clear customs, then Chase hit the currency exchange. Information didn't come cheap, even in a third-world country. With a conversion rate of sixteen pesos for every US dollar, he wound up stuffing his canvas satchel with Colombian banknotes.

As they made their way toward the exit, the airport seethed with humanity, people of every color, shape and size, speaking everything from Spanish to Japanese. Pushing through the door into the humid heat, Chase spotted the taxi line and guided Harper in that direction.

After a forty-minute ride in a cramped yellow Hyundai cab that wound its way through traffic to the east side of the city, the driver drove toward a motel a few kilometers off the highway that led to their destination, Punta Gato.

They were meeting a man named Killian Dawson, who had chosen the motel as their rendezvous point. According to Bran, whatever they might need, Kil Dawson could provide, including his help locating Michael Winston.

"You ready for this?" Chase asked Harper as the taxi pulled up in front of the Puesta Del Sol Motel, an L-shaped, flat-roofed, single-story structure painted an ugly mustard yellow.

Before she could answer, the driver opened her door and both of them got out. The driver popped the trunk and started unloading their bags onto the cracked sidewalk in front of the motel.

"You've had time to think things over," Chase said. "It's not too late to get back in the cab and head back to the airport. I'll keep you posted on whatever's going on down here."

She just looked at him as if he'd lost his mind, slung the strap of her canvas bag over her shoulder, grabbed the handle of her carry-on and started walking. He couldn't stop a grin as he watched those long shapely legs and very fine ass moving so determinedly toward the motel office, her carry-on bouncing along a concrete path with weeds growing up between the cracks. The shrubs beneath the office windows badly needed a trim.

Chase grabbed his carry-on and caught up with her. "Looks like you've made up your mind."

She didn't bother to answer, just paused as he opened the office door, then continued past him into a small room. The clerk, a tiny woman with long black hair streaked with gray, stood at the counter behind an ancient computer. She was expecting them.

"Senor Dawson, he is waiting for you," she said in broken English. "You will find him in room fourteen."

Harper smiled. *"Gracias, senora."* She said something more in Spanish, which led to a brief conversation that seemed to put the older woman at ease. Chase had to admit, Harper's ability to communicate was a definite asset.

Towing their luggage, they crossed the parking lot and Chase knocked on the door to room fourteen. Heavy footfalls sounded on the opposite side, and the door opened as far as the chain would allow.

"Chase Garrett," he said. "You Killian Dawson?"

"Kil Dawson. That's me." Dawson unlocked the door and stepped aside, inviting them into a shabby room with worn avocado shag carpet and a sagging mattress covered by a threadbare gold bedspread.

He was a big man, as tall as Chase's six-two but more heavily built, with a powerful chest and arms the size of Christmas hams. A deep scar bisected one dark eyebrow, another ran from the corner of his mouth down to his jaw.

"The lady is Harper Winston," Chase said as Dawson closed the door behind them. "She's here to find her brother."

Dawson's gaze swung to Harper, slid over her body, taking in her taller-than-average height and slender build, the blond hair she'd pulled into a ponytail. Since Harper was a beautiful woman any man with a dick would notice, Chase didn't take offense—as long as Dawson kept his distance.

Dawson turned a hard look in Chase's direction. "Bran said you were with a woman. I didn't think you'd be dumb enough to bring her here."

Chase didn't take offense because bringing her was dumb. He returned the stare. "She was coming—with or without me. Didn't leave me much choice."

Dawson's eyebrows went up when he caught the stubborn tilt of Harper's chin, a trait Chase had noticed the first time she'd walked into his office.

When Dawson continued to look at her like some kind of lab specimen, Harper got right in his face. "I speak fluent Spanish. I lived in the Ecuadorean jungle for a year. I won't be a liability if that's what you're thinking."

For an instant, the scar at the corner of Dawson's mouth twitched, tipped into what might have passed for a smile, then turned hard again. "Long as you do what I tell you, you can stay. You don't, you'll be on your way home."

For once Harper didn't argue.

Since Chase pretty much agreed, he didn't, either. The hard truth was this was rough, dangerous country, even more so for a beautiful woman. Sex trafficking was a major problem—women being kidnapped and forced into prostitution. Chase wished for the tenth time since they had left Dallas that she had stayed home.

Dawson gestured toward the round Formica table in the corner. "Let's sit. You can bring me up to speed, and we'll figure out our next move."

"You get the weapons I asked for?"

Dawson grinned, softening his hard features. "And then some."

Chase relaxed. This man was a close friend of his brother's. If Bran trusted him, so did Chase.

"All right, let's get to it." Dawson seated himself at the table, waited while they both took seats. He glanced at their surroundings, then looked at Harper. "I know this place isn't the Ritz, but the motel's a safe place to meet. Senora Aguayo and her husband are good people, and using their motel as a meeting place makes them a little money."

"It's fine," Harper said. "Wherever my brother is, it's bound to be a lot worse than this."

Kil nodded. "We won't be staying, anyway. We'll be moving out as soon as we're finished here." He turned to Chase. "Bran told me you located the boat in a cove near Punta Gato. There're a few low-rent motels in the area. We can stay there if we need to."

"You got transportation?" Chase asked.

"My Land Cruiser's parked in the lot. We'll take that."

For the next twenty minutes, Chase filled Dawson in on what they had so far: that Michael Winston had been with a woman named Pia Santana when two men followed him from a casino in Curaçao back to his boat, docked in the marina.

"Working theory is the men boarded the boat in the middle of the night and forced Michael to sail into open water. Yacht wound up in Colombia."

"*Yacht,*" Dawson repeated. "Sounds expensive. How much is it worth?"

"Beneteau forty-two foot?" He turned to Harper. "Best guess?"

"Michael paid around two hundred fifty thousand for the boat, but he added a lot of extras."

"So three hundred grand out the door," Killian said. "That's a helluva lot of money down here. Piracy, most likely."

Piracy meant a death sentence for Michael, and maybe something far worse for Pia. Harper's face went pale.

"Could also be kidnapping," Chase countered. "That's the assumption we're working on. Michael's father is worth half a billion dollars or damned close. The son's worth way more than the boat if his kidnappers are smart enough to figure it out."

Killian shoved up from his chair and stalked over to the closet. Pulling out a big black canvas duffel, he tossed it on the bed, unzipped it and started tossing weapons onto the worn gold spread.

"Browning 9 mil, Ruger SR9, a couple of Beretta M9s. Nighthawk .45." He pulled out a long-barreled weapon. "M40 sniper rifle." Kil reached back into the bag, pulled out another weapon. "Eighteen-inch, short-barreled tactical shotgun and—last but definitely not least—a relatively new AK-47." He grinned. "Pick your poison."

Chase eyed the weaponry. "It looks like we're going to war."

"If Winston and the girl are still alive, it may come to that. The area around Punta Gato is rebel territory. Los Proscritos runs the show along the coast and into the Sierra Nevada mountains."

Killian finished emptying the bag: holsters, extra magazines, a sound suppressor for the rifle, two Ka-Bar knives in thigh sheaths, flash-bang grenades and door-breaching charges.

Chase picked up one of the Berettas, standard for

army MPs and still one of his preferred weapons. It felt good in his hand. At home he carried a Glock, but the Beretta felt familiar, like a trusted old friend.

He dropped the magazine, found it fully loaded, the gun freshly cleaned, shoved the mag back in. "I'll take this one. Should do for now." Slipping it into a clip holster, he attached the weapon to his belt, pulled his shirt loose to cover it. He grabbed an extra mag, which he slid into the pocket of his jeans.

Killian picked up the Nighthawk, slid the holstered weapon onto his belt, let his denim shirt fall over it. "I've got bottled water, energy bars and MREs already loaded. I've got a couple of backpacks in there, too."

Chase glanced over at Harper, whose features were set in a determined line. She walked to the bed, reached down and picked up the Ruger, looked it over, then tested the grip and the weight in her hand. She dropped the mag to check the load and shoved it back in.

"I'll take this one." She gripped the pistol in two hands and sighted down the barrel, sending Killian's eyebrows up again.

"Where'd you learn to shoot?" Chase asked.

"Ecuador. Our village sat at the edge of the bush. Learning how to handle a gun seemed like a good idea."

Chase was still trying to wrap his head around it. He had imagined her in some Ecuadorean preschool taking care of little kids, not working in a remote village with no toilets or running water.

Harper was a far different woman from the one he had imagined. There was no way the woman standing in front of him ready to fight a rebel army to rescue her brother was the cold fish her ex-boyfriend and half the men at the country club believed.

This was a woman of courage and passion. Chase felt a rush of heat just looking at her. He wanted to unlock that passion, taste the fire, feel the heat. He turned away before his hunger became obvious, didn't miss the faint tilt of Kil Dawson's lips or the knowing look in his eyes.

"What about personal gear?" Dawson asked. "It's rain forest. Gets wet and muddy, cold at night up in the mountains. We'll need to be prepared if we have to go in."

"I've got gear in my bag," Chase said. "Harper, what about you?"

"I'm all set."

This time he wasn't surprised. He'd been underestimating Harper from the start. He wouldn't do it again. "Let's load up," he said, and Killian nodded.

They grabbed their bags and headed out the door, following Dawson to a newer-model white Toyota Land Cruiser that looked like it hadn't been washed in years. Stowing their gear in the back, which had WASH ME drawn on the windows, Chase climbed up in front with Dawson while Harper slid into the seat behind him.

It was ninety kilometers to Punta Gato. As Kil fired up the engine, Chase settled back in his seat. They were on their way.

He had no idea what they were going to find when they got there.

He hoped to hell it wasn't two dead bodies.

CHAPTER THIRTEEN

As the Land Cruiser rolled along the highway, Harper tried to relax, but worry nagged her. She didn't like the big, dark-haired man with the obsidian eyes and scarred face. With his hard features and powerful, muscular body, Killian Dawson made her more than a little uneasy.

Even his name set her on edge. Killian. *Kil*, he called himself. She wondered if he spelled it with two *l*'s.

She couldn't imagine how a man who hadn't cut his hair in months, hadn't shaved in days, could possibly be handsome, but somehow Dawson was. She thought that a man who exuded that kind of masculinity wouldn't have any trouble attracting women, though his crude brand of sexuality didn't appeal to her and only made her dislike him more.

It didn't matter what she thought of him. They needed his help to find Michael, and Dawson clearly knew what he was doing. She would follow his orders, do whatever she had to.

Besides, she was armed and so was Chase. In a different but equally masculine way, Chase was Dawson's equal. He was smart, his body hard, all lean-muscled power and strength. She could count on Chase to protect her, believed that in every cell of her body.

Maybe it was because she was Michael's sister, or that she was a woman, but she didn't think so. Something was happening between them. She had begun to see it in Chase's eyes whenever he looked at her and thought she wouldn't notice.

Something hot and sexual that neither of them wanted—Harper revised the thought—or at least something Chase didn't want. Harper was growing more and more certain having sex with Chase Garrett was exactly what she wanted.

Whatever the truth, at least for now both of them were doing their best to ignore it. They were there to save Michael and Pia. That was all that mattered.

An hour and a half after they left Santa Marta following the GPS coordinates Tabitha Love had given to Chase, Kil Dawson pulled the Land Cruiser off the Mingueo–Santa Marta highway onto a two-lane road headed directly toward the ocean. The road quickly narrowed to a single dirt track, and a few miles later, the sea appeared in front of them, an endless expanse of blue.

The road turned slightly south and ran along the edge of a cove. Farther on, a few weary structures appeared, a gas station with only a single pump, and what passed for a restaurant with rooms above. A permanent vacancy sign swung in the breeze on a pole outside the entrance. Next to it, the door to Las Palmaras cantina stood open.

The village was mostly deserted, just a kid on a rusty

bicycle and a couple of older women in ankle-length gathered skirts walking along the dirt street. A black-and-white mongrel sniffed a trash can in the alley beside the restaurant, looking for something to eat.

It was the sleek white sailboat bobbing at a long wooden dock on the west side of the cove that captured Harper's attention. Her heart leaped as she recognized her brother's beautiful yacht, *BUZZ Word*.

"There it is!" She pointed excitedly over Chase's shoulder. "Michael's boat. That's it!"

Dawson pulled the vehicle off the main road onto an even narrower dirt track that wound into deep green foliage, traveling north on the west side of the U-shaped bay. Reaching beneath his seat, he pulled out a pair of binoculars and began to scan the dock, the village and the area around it for what seemed the longest time.

"Looks deserted," he finally said. "No way to know for sure till we check it out."

Harper's gaze remained fixed on the boat, her heart throbbing. They'd found the yacht, but what had happened to Michael and Pia? She didn't see anyone aboard the vessel. Had they been murdered for the money the valuable yacht would bring? She shoved the grim thought out of her head. Her brother was alive somewhere and being held for ransom. Chase had said it was still a possibility.

Putting the cruiser into Four-Wheel Drive, Dawson drove farther down the muddy trail until they were completely hidden from view. He cut the engine and stepped out of the vehicle. At the same time, so did Chase.

Silently, the men walked around to the back of the cruiser and opened the tailgate to the cargo area. They both started unzipping gear bags and pulling out clothes and equipment.

When the men began to peel off their shirts and jeans, Harper looked away. By the time she looked back, both men were dressed in camo pants and T-shirts. Chase's olive drab T-shirt outlined the muscles across his chest and abdomen, and stretched around his amazing biceps. He'd strapped one of Dawson's long-bladed knives to his thigh, and a second pistol hung from a belt around his waist.

He looked like a man she had never seen before. Tall, hard-edged, hard-bodied and determined. He hadn't shaved since they'd left Aruba, and the dark gold beard along his jaw now joined the rough stubble on his cheeks, making him appear rugged and dangerous. He looked like a man who could handle whatever he faced, exactly the right man for the job ahead of him.

It was exactly the wrong time for her to feel a shot of lust.

Kil Dawson closed the hatch while Chase walked around and opened her door. "You need to stay here," he said. "You've got a gun. If you get in trouble, fire off a shot. We won't be far away."

Harper just nodded. She didn't demand to go with them this time. She was smart enough to know when she was an asset and when she was a liability. The men clearly knew what they were doing. If they got into trouble, she didn't want them handicapped by feeling they had to protect her.

She watched them disappear into the jungle. She took the Ruger out of her bag and laid it on the seat beside her. She had told them she knew how to shoot, but she had conveniently forgotten to mention she had fired a pistol on only one occasion. She grimaced at the small white lie. She'd only had a single lesson from one of the villagers and hadn't picked up a weapon since.

Harper studied the gun on the seat, remembering the handsome young Ecuadorean who had spent the afternoon showing her how to handle the pistol, showing her the safety features, telling her that a pistol should always be treated as if it were loaded.

She picked up the Ruger and wrapped her hands around the grip, lifted it and aimed down the barrel, remembering how to brace herself against the recoil. Then she set the gun down and sat back to wait, her gaze on the spot where the men had disappeared.

The boat dock floated in the water on the west side of the cove at the edge of a dense tropical jungle. Tall kapoks grew next to palm trees, some willowy and elegant, others short and stout, and a profusion of banana plants. The jungle grew right down to the water. Which meant the men could stay out of sight, moving through cover till they reached the yacht.

If the boat was as empty as it appeared, the most Harper could hope for was finding something that would prove Michael and Pia were still alive, something that might provide a clue as to where they'd been taken.

Harper kept her eyes on the spot where the men had disappeared, and said a silent prayer for all of them.

Moving quietly through the lush, wet tropical landscape, Chase caught the movement of Kil's raised hand, signaling to split up and circle, come at the boat from two different angles.

Gripping the Beretta, he moved off to the left, deeper into the jungle, placing each step carefully, making as little noise as possible. He didn't want to run into a guard posted to protect the boat or, if someone was aboard, give them any kind of warning they were coming. So far, he hadn't seen a soul.

There was probably no need for a guard. Chase figured whoever had stolen the yacht and brought it to this location was probably well-known in the area. They were dealing with tough, ruthless men, the sort that the locals would be afraid to challenge.

He reached the edge of the jungle where it spilled onto the white-sand beach, and saw the sailboat bobbing placidly alongside the dock. There was no sign of anyone aboard. Farther down the beach, Kil stepped out of the leafy foliage and Chase followed his lead, both of them moving toward the boat with cautious, determined strides.

Kil went ahead of him, the AK-47 across his chest as he stepped onto the deck. Chase covered him, stepping onto the boat behind him.

Kil signaled he was going below, and Chase took up a position in front of the open hatch, out of sight. Nothing moved in the jungle. The village in the distance remained quiet, just a couple of people on the street, no one going into or out of the restaurant or cantina. It was late afternoon, hot and humid, time for a siesta.

"Clear," Kil called up to him. "Nobody here. Come on down."

Chase ducked through the hatch and descended the ladder to the main salon. "What have we got?"

"Traces of blood on the floor in the master cabin, a smudge of red on the sheets, some on the built-in dressers. Looks like he fought, maybe they both did. But I don't think they were killed on the boat."

"That's something, I guess."

"Could have killed them once they were at sea and dumped their bodies overboard."

Chase wasn't ready to believe it. "Michael was a first-class sailor. They could have used his skills to help them get here."

Kil nodded. Chase was already beginning to fall into sync with him, beginning to know how he thought. They were both ex-military. There was a certain rhythm, an unspoken link between men who had endured the same training, learned to work together to form a cohesive team.

But Chase had been military police while Kil, like Brandon, had been a Special Forces soldier, the most highly trained men in the army. Chase had no problem letting him take the lead.

"For the moment we'll assume they're still alive," Kil said. "Let's look around, see if we can find something that'll tell us where they might have been taken."

Kil took the sleeping quarters while Chase headed for the galley. He searched the counter, the tiny sink full of dirty dishes, the floor, anyplace that might hold a clue. He found what he was looking for in one of the cupboards—a coffee mug with a message written in lipstick.

"Rebels," it said in a precise, likely feminine hand that didn't belong to Michael. Had to have been put there right before they left the boat or the kidnappers would have found it. Apparently, Pia Santana wasn't anybody's fool.

"Got something," Chase called to Kil, who was busy searching the salon. He held up the mug, showing the message in bright red lipstick.

"Rebels. Shit, I was afraid of that. Fucking Los Pro-scritos."

"You said they controlled this area. You think they could be holding them in the village?"

Kil scrubbed a hand over his face. "I doubt it. They've probably taken them to one of their camps in the mountains. Nobody bothers them there."

"Ransom, then?"

"Most likely. If Winston's old man is as rich as you say."

"How the hell did they know Michael was his son? And why haven't they made any demands?"

"Maybe by now they have. Let's get out of here and go find some answers."

Chase dropped the mug into a plastic bag he found beneath the galley counter and stuffed it into one of the pockets in his cargo pants. At least he had some hope-ful news for Harper.

Checking the area around the dock to be sure they didn't have any unwanted company, they left the boat and crossed the beach into the jungle, heading back to the Land Cruiser.

When Harper spotted them, she opened the door and stepped out of the car, and he could read the fear in her face. Chase pulled the plastic bag out of his pocket, took out the mug and held it up so she could read the message on the side.

Harper saw the lipstick, knew it meant they must have been alive when they reached Colombia and burst into tears.

CHAPTER FOURTEEN

"Women," Kil grumbled. "Last thing you need on a goddamn mission."

"Leave her alone," Chase warned sharply, drawing the bigger man's glare. "Michael's her brother, for chrissake. At least now she knows he and the girl were alive when they got here."

Embarrassed, Harper wiped tears from her cheeks. She was determined to hold her own with the men. Crying wasn't the way to show them she was equal to the task. "I'm sorry. I just... I was so afraid you'd come back and say they were dead."

The scar at the corner of Kil's hard mouth eased. Kil Dawson looked tough enough to eat nails for breakfast, but he didn't say anything more. Harper had a feeling Chase had just gained a notch of respect for not being afraid to stand up to him.

"Looks like your brother and the woman made it this far," Kil said. "Unfortunately, they'll be facing more trouble ahead. A forced march into those steep mountains is gonna take everything they've got."

"My brother won't give up," she said. "He works out. He's in excellent physical condition. He'll make it."

No one mentioned what might happen to Pia. From her pictures, she was a beautiful girl with a lovely figure. Harper shuddered to think what a rebel army might do to a woman like that.

"Where do we start looking?" she asked.

"We'll head into the village," Kil said as he and Chase stashed their weapons in the back of the Land Cruiser, all but the big semiautomatic pistols on their belts beneath their T-shirts. "We'll see what the locals have to say."

Harper stashed her gun in the EC woven leather purse she'd taken out of her carry-on.

"Might not be easy getting someone to talk," Chase said.

"You got money, right? Show them a stack of fifty-thousand-peso banknotes. Somebody will talk."

It sounded like a lot of money, but the rate of exchange was so low fifty thousand pesos was worth less than twenty dollars. Harper didn't care what the information cost. Chase had a satchel full of Colombian money in the back of the cruiser for just such a situation.

They climbed into the cruiser. Kil put the vehicle in Reverse and backed up, then turned and drove down the road into the village, heading straight for the Las Palmaras cantina. He parked the cruiser in front.

The sun was beginning to slip behind the mountains. It was still hot and humid, but darkness came early this time of year. As they climbed out of the vehicle and walked up on the covered wooden porch in front of the cantina, the smell of mildew and rotting fruit drifted out of the narrow alley that ran beside the building.

Kil shoved the front door open a little wider and they stepped into the stark interior, began to weave their way across the wooden floor between the few tables scattered around the room. At a round table in the corner, three rough-looking men played cards. A half-full bottle of tequila and three shot glasses sat within arm's reach.

Harper could feel the men's eyes sliding over her skinny jeans, the blouse she'd tied up around her waist, and could almost hear their crude thoughts. She should have changed into the T-shirt and loose-fitting jeans in her bag while the men went to scout the boat. Lesson learned—a mistake she wouldn't make again.

As she approached the long wooden bar, she felt Chase's hand settle protectively at her waist. Kil's heavy footfalls sounded just a few steps behind. The men at the table cut their eyes and settled back in their chairs.

A bartender, whose girth barely allowed him to move around in the space behind, stepped up to take their orders.

"¿Qué les gustaria beber?" the man asked. What would you like to drink?

Kil replied in perfect Spanish, *"Tres Aquilas, por favor. Y un poco de informacion."* Three beers, please. And a little information.

The bartender reached into a cold box and brought out the beers. He set them on the counter, popped the tops and shoved them over. Each of them grabbed a bottle and took a long swallow. Harper felt the slow burn and the welcome easing of the tension in her shoulders.

Kil went on to talk to the man about the boat, asking questions about when it had arrived and who it belonged to. Chase shoved a stack of banknotes across the bar, but the bartender just shook his head.

He pointed to the men playing cards. Apparently, they were the ones with the answers.

"Stay here," Chase said. "We'll be right back."

Harper adjusted the woven leather strap on her shoulder. Knowing the pistol was in her purse helped bolster her courage. She refused to be anything but an asset to the men putting themselves in harm's way to save her brother.

She listened to what was being said, Kil repeating the questions he'd asked the bartender, Chase setting the stack of banknotes on the table.

"Los Proscritos," the largest of the three men answered, naming the rebels who called themselves *The Outlaws*. In a sweat-stained T-shirt, with his shaggy black hair and small black eyes, the man was as big and muscular as Kil.

In rapid Spanish, he went on to say that three men and a woman had been aboard the boat that had sailed into the cove. One of the men was American. When the man stopped speaking and picked up the money, Chase laid another stack down.

"Rebels met them when they arrived," the man said. "Money was exchanged, and the American and the woman were handed over to Los Proscritos. The rebels took them into the mountains."

Kil translated for Chase.

"We need to find them," Chase said. "We need someone who can lead us to their camp."

Silence fell over the table. "It will cost *mucho dinero*." Much money, the man with the beady eyes said, speaking mostly English.

"He'll be well paid for his help," Chase said.

One of the other men, this one tall and bone-thin, got to his feet. "I know someone who will take you."

They bartered back and forth, settled on a price. "His name is Francisco. He is my cousin. He will meet you here tomorrow morning. Be ready to leave at first light."

Kil nodded, and Chase handed the skinny man a wad of money. Chase and Kil walked back to the bar, upended their beers and set their empty bottles on the counter.

"May I take mine with me?" Harper asked the bartender.

The fat man grinned. *"Sí, senorita."*

Harper turned and walked ahead of the men out of the bar.

"You need to call your father, Harper," Chase said. "By now the rebels should have demanded a ransom."

She upended her beer and drained it, tossed the empty bottle into the rusted metal barrel at the mouth of the alley, then pulled her cell phone out of her purse and held it up to check the bars. "No signal."

"We'll use the sat phone," Kil said. "It's in the cruiser."

Chase retrieved the satellite phone out of a duffel in the back, and they walked across the dirt street to an aging picnic table on the grass facing the ocean. The sun sank behind an outcropping of land to the west, a golden dome disappearing into the shadows, the long day coming to an end. A humid breeze cooled the hot white sand along the beach.

"What's the number?" Chase asked. Harper rattled off her father's personal cell number. Chase punched it in and handed her the sat phone, which she pressed against her ear.

Her father picked up on the second ring. "Who is this?" he answered harshly, wary of his privacy and not recognizing the caller's number.

"It's me, Dad. I need to know if you've been contacted by Michael's kidnappers."

"Harper. Where are you? Whose number is this?"

"It's a satellite phone, Dad. I'm in Colombia. We think Colombian rebels are holding Michael and the girl who was with him, Pia Santana. We think they're planning to demand some kind of ransom. Are you saying they haven't called?"

Silence fell on the other end of the phone.

"Dad? Have you been contacted by the men who have Michael? Have they demanded money for his release?"

"I'm sorry, Harper. I haven't heard from anyone."

Fresh worry filtered through her, and Harper's throat tightened. "They're going to call, I know it. Sooner or later. Please, Dad, when they contact you, tell them you'll pay whatever they ask."

"Don't be ridiculous, girl. Of course I'll pay. Michael's my son. If they call, I'll pay whatever they want."

She felt a rush of relief. He was going to pay. Michael and Pia would be released. "This number will show up on your phone. Call me the minute you hear from them. Promise me, Dad."

"You need to come home, Harper. Colombia can be a very dangerous place. Anything could happen. Whatever trouble Michael has gotten himself into, it's his problem not yours. Now, get yourself on the next plane out of there and back to the States, where you belong."

Harper swallowed. "I have to go, Dad. Please call

me if you hear anything." She disconnected the call, blinked back tears as she returned the phone to Chase.

"No call yet?" he asked.

"Not yet."

"We'll go in tomorrow," he said. "Find out where they're holding your brother and the girl, try to negotiate their release."

Hope rose inside her. "You think we can?"

It was Kil who answered. "If the rebels won't release them, we'll find another way to get them out."

She looked into Killian Dawson's hard, handsome features and felt the first softening toward him. "Thank you" was all she said.

Knox Winston tossed his cell phone onto the massive mahogany desk in his wood-paneled study and swore a foul oath.

"I take it that was your daughter." Simon Graves, ten years younger than Knox's sixty years, an inch taller and twenty pounds lighter, lounged in a chair across from him. He was the closest thing Knox had to a friend.

A very loose term, since Simon wouldn't be there if Knox weren't paying him an obscene amount of money for the job he did.

But Knox trusted Simon. And he needed him.

"I couldn't very well tell her the goddamned rebels are being paid to keep him. That has to be what's going on. Montoya wants revenge for the move we made against him."

Simon swirled the expensive single malt in his glass. "We took a risk. Bringing in another player to take over one of the man's most productive coca fields was a ballsy move to say the least."

Knox just grunted. He despised failure.

"We took a risk," Simon continued, "but it was a calculated one. If Hernandez had succeeded in taking those fields, we would have controlled a large percentage of production. In the long run, the dividends would have been huge."

"Unfortunately, we failed. Hernandez is dead, and now Montoya's men have my son. How the hell did they know he was down there?"

"Had to be monitoring his phone."

"Must have heard him talking about his trip. Harper said he planned to call her every day or two, keep her updated on where he was. Those calls would have given them exactly what they wanted."

Simon shifted in his chair. "Like you said—revenge. The question is, what do you want to do about it?"

Knox took a drink of his scotch. "I'll call Montoya, try to smooth things over. He still needs us for US distribution. I'll tell him Hernandez was the one behind the move. We just went along with it."

"You think he'll buy it?"

"No, but it lets him save face. It gives him an excuse, keeps him from looking weak to his men when he goes back to working with us. As soon as that happens, we all go back to making money."

"What about Michael?" Simon asked.

"Montoya wants some kind of payback. Holding my son sends a message, but I don't think he'll kill him. It would just escalate the trouble between us."

"You think he'll let him go?"

"Hard to say. Long as he has Michael, he has leverage." Knox took another drink, giving himself time to think. "Harper's in Colombia with Chase Garrett. Much as I dislike the SOB, he's good. If there's a way to find Michael and get him out of this mess, Garrett will find it."

"So we just sit back and wait?"

"We'll make a few overtures, then wait for Montoya's next move."

"Shall I let our people down there know what's going on?"

"Not yet," Knox said. "We don't want to make things worse than they are already."

Simon crossed one long, lean leg over the other. Unlike Knox, who admittedly had a volatile temper, nothing ever ruffled Simon's sophisticated feathers. "I guess time will tell."

"Always does," Knox said. "One way or another."

CHAPTER FIFTEEN

Harper couldn't get the phone call out of her head, her father's seeming lack of concern. Surely he was as worried as she was. That he and Michael hadn't gotten along these past few years—never really—didn't change the fact that Michael was his only son.

"Been a long day," Chase said. "Before we head for the motel, we need to fill the cruiser, then get something to eat. After tonight, we'll be living on MREs till this is over." *Meals Ready to Eat*. Rations supplied to soldiers. She'd heard the guys talking about the packaged food on the road—and not in a good way.

"I could definitely use some grub," Kil said. "I'll fill up and meet you there."

Chase waved to Kil as he fired up the cruiser and headed for the only gas pump in town, then Chase and Harper crossed the street, heading for the only restaurant—La Paloma, The Dove—in the run-down building next to the cantina.

The owner, a stout older Colombian woman recommended *sancocho de bocachico*, a fish and chicken dish served with Colombian cheese bread. One of only three items on the menu. Considering how worried she was, Harper was surprised to discover she was hungry, and the food was delicious.

It was dark by the time they finished their meal and climbed into the cruiser, ignoring the heat that had built up inside. Kil started the engine, and they drove off toward the motel a mile and a half down the road.

El Palacio. *The Palace.* What a laugh. The run-down pink stucco two-story building had a total of eight small rooms and an office. Surrounded by palm trees, it sat on the ocean, just off the beach. Kil parked the cruiser next to a pothole in the asphalt lot and went into the office. He came out with keys to a pair of adjoining rooms on the second floor and one to a room downstairs.

Kil tossed an upstairs room key to Chase and one to Harper, then grabbed his duffel out of the back of the cruiser and crossed the lot toward the room downstairs. He stopped when he reached his door and turned back.

"By the way…did I forget to mention your brother'll be here in the morning?"

"Bran? What the hell?" Chase asked.

"We made a deal when he called me in on this mission, said I had to keep him posted. I phoned and told what we'd found on the boat and he said he was coming down, said something about your brother Reese and using the company jet. With a fuel stop, it's about five hours."

Kil stuck the key into the lock, turned the knob and pushed open the door. "He'll bunk with me when he gets here." Kil disappeared into the room and closed the door behind him.

Chase rubbed the back of his neck. "Looks like we're going to have extra backup."

Harper stared up at him. "So your brother's coming to Colombia?"

"That's right. Can't really say I'm sorry."

"You said he was Special Forces. If he's coming, he must think things could get bad."

"They could, Harper. I won't lie to you. We have no idea what we're going to be facing when we get up there. If I thought you'd be safer here—"

"I'm not staying here."

Chase's dark eyes met hers. There was something in them she couldn't read. Resigned, he reached for her bag, but Harper shook her head. "I've got it." From now on, she needed to carry her own weight in every way, and all of them knew it.

Hauling her carry-on up the stairs, she went into her room to repack what she would need for their trek into the mountains. Tossing the suitcase up onto the bed, she began to go through the items she had brought. From the start, she'd believed that Michael was in very serious trouble. She'd packed accordingly.

Setting the slinky little black dress she had worn to the casino aside, ignoring the silver heeled sandals, she took out a canvas backpack and a pair of comfortable hiking boots. Socks and underwear followed, a medium-weight jacket, lightweight waterproof poncho, long-sleeved T-shirts, a pair of khaki cargo pants, black jeans, bug spray and a first-aid kit.

Separating the clothes she'd be wearing tomorrow, she tossed a few more personal items into the pack and zipped it shut. In the morning, before they set off on their trek, she'd add the pistol, Kil's bottled water and energy bars.

When she finished, she went into the bathroom and turned on the shower, climbed under the warm spray, probably the last time for a while.

She quickly washed her hair but, afraid she'd use up all the hot water in the run-down motel, she didn't stay in as long as she would have liked. She blow-dried her hair and pulled on a sleep T-shirt that came to midthigh and had an orange-and-green parrot on the front.

Satisfied she was ready for their trip in the morning, she flopped down on the saggy full-size bed. After another exhausting day, she was tired. The hum of the window air conditioner should have been relaxing, but instead it set her nerves on edge.

In the room next door, she could hear Chase moving around, checking his gear, same as she had done. For a while she lay there listening to his movements, remembering the way she had seen him earlier that day, dressed in camo pants and military gear, armed to the teeth.

Her stomach clenched the way it had then, and she found herself swinging her legs to the side of the bed, moving toward the door between the rooms and knocking lightly.

The door immediately swung open. Harper gasped at the sight of Chase in only a pair of jeans, the top button undone, his T-shirt gone, a fine spray of dark gold covering his bare chest. Still damp from the shower, strands of dark gold curled against the nape of his neck.

She stared at him and couldn't seem to look away, and suddenly she felt like a fool. "I'm… I'm sorry. I didn't mean to bother you. I just… I thought I'd check, see if there was anything last-minute you needed me to do."

Chase's intense gaze swept her from head to foot, and though the long T-shirt protected her modesty, the gleam she saw in his eyes was hotter and fiercer than ever before.

He looked as if he were trying to decide whether or not to haul her into the room and ravish her, and in a moment of clarity, she realized exactly how much she wanted him to.

"Come on in," he finally said, though his mask of control had fallen back into place. "We'll go over what you've got, see if there's anything else you need."

With all those beautiful muscles on display, her mouth went dry. "Okay." He must have noticed her staring because he grabbed a short-sleeved shirt and slipped it on, but didn't bother with the buttons.

Those hot, dark eyes settled on her breasts, braless under the T-shirt, her nipples peaked beneath the cotton fabric. Chase glanced away.

"Let's make a quick run-through," he said a little gruffly. "Then we both need to get some sleep. Tell me what you're planning to take."

She tried not to notice the bed, which suddenly seemed to dominate the room, and forced herself to concentrate. She did a quick rundown, listing everything in her pack, finishing with the first-aid kit.

"Sounds like you've done this before."

She hadn't done anything remotely like it, never even camped overnight. Her dad was a businessman. He was gone a lot, and the great outdoors weren't high on his list of priorities. She'd day hiked, though, seen some spectacular scenery in Ecuador and also in Europe.

And having lived in a jungle village with no indoor plumbing or running water, she at least understood the conditions she would be facing.

"I already had most of what I needed. I did some research on the internet before we left Dallas to see what else I should take. I wanted to be ready for whatever might come up."

"Smart girl." His gaze came to rest on the peaks of her breasts. The gold in his eyes seemed to glitter, and she felt her cheeks flush. She could swear both of them were thinking about the bed just a few feet away, wondering what it would be like to be lying there together, wearing nothing at all.

She didn't realize she had taken a step closer until she felt his hand at her waist, drawing her the last few inches to where their bodies touched.

Insanity struck. Harper went up on her toes and lightly pressed her lips to his. For a moment she was actually surprised when Chase gently returned the kiss. Then her lips softened, parted, and she opened for him, inviting him in.

Chase groaned. The next thing she knew he was roughly backing her up against the wall, his tongue in her mouth, hers in his, the kiss deep and erotic, the sexiest kiss she had ever known.

"Harper…"

"Oh, God, Chase…" She felt his mouth at the side of her neck and tipped her head back to give him better access. Hot, damp kisses trailed over her throat and shoulders. One of his big hands palmed her breast, rubbed her nipple through the cotton fabric, and the feeling was so erotic she moaned.

"We can't do this," he whispered, kissing her again. He nibbled her bottom lip and sank in, his lips melding perfectly with hers. He returned to her throat, nipped the side of her neck.

"Chase, please…" Was she actually begging? She didn't recognize her own voice.

"Jesus God." Another kiss, this one deep and endless. His hands circled her waist, slid down over the T-shirt to cup her bottom, and he drew her against his erection, thick and hard and pulsing.

A growl came from his throat, and for a moment the kiss went deeper, wilder, hotter. Then he groaned as if he were in pain, and the kiss came to an end. Chase's hands tightened around her waist as he set her away.

"We can't do this, Harper." Troubled dark eyes bored into her. "Your family and mine. It would be a disaster."

She barely heard him. Her body was on fire, her breasts tingling, her heart speeding out of control. She had never felt anything like it. "Do you want me, Chase?"

He moved even farther away. She could still recall the imprint of the hard ridge at the front of his jeans.

"Any man would want you, angel. Me more than most. It doesn't matter. I don't want you getting hurt, and the way things are, sooner or later that's what would happen."

Color washed into her face. She was making a fool of herself. She had never thrown herself at a man before. She wouldn't do it again.

"I'm sorry. I don't know what I was thinking. We're here for Michael. That's all that matters."

There was something in his eyes. She had seen it before, still didn't understand what it meant.

He took a step toward her, stopped himself. "If I touch you again, I won't be able to stop. Go to bed, Harper. Get some sleep. Things will look different in the morning."

She swallowed. "It's just the stress," she said, perhaps the biggest lie she had ever told. "I hope you'll forget this happened."

A corner of his sexy mouth edged up. "That, angel, is a promise I can't make. Now, get some sleep. Dawn is going to come early."

Turning, she went back to her room, quietly closed the door and leaned against it. Chase wouldn't forget what had happened? He wouldn't forget their burning kiss or the feel of her breast in his hand?

One thing Harper knew—she would never forget it. And as foolish as it was, she wanted it to happen again.

CHAPTER SIXTEEN

Scattered campfires blazed in the darkness at the crest of the mountain. Tents dotted a flat plateau circled by the heavy jungle rain forest controlled by Los Proscritos, a force of rebel soldiers numbering somewhere near fifty.

Michael sat next to Pia in front of the canvas tent they had been assigned for sleeping. Both of them were damp and cold after the day's long march, but at least their hands were now bound in front of them instead of behind their backs.

So far the men had left Pia unmolested, though the heat in the soldiers' eyes was easy enough to read. They believed she belonged to him, that she was his woman. And from the moment the men had taken her from his bed in the middle of the night, Michael had thought of her exactly that way. She was his to protect, his to keep safe no matter what.

Michael prayed the men had contacted his father,

that his father had agreed to pay whatever ransom the kidnappers wanted, but there was no way to know. Asking might only make things worse.

The sound of approaching footsteps snared his attention. Michael looked up to see a tall, black-haired, broad-shouldered man in a dark green uniform piped in red and dripping with medals. The commandant of the camp, Benito Velasquez.

"Senor Winston," the commandant addressed him in passable English. "You have endured a great deal since your capture. I admit I am surprised. An educated man of your social stature… I had expected you to break long before now. Perhaps somewhere in your lineage, you have the blood of a soldier, no?"

Michael didn't answer. Knox Winston had never served in the military, nor Michael's grandfather, who was reputed to have been a con artist of some renown, nor had anyone he knew of on his mother's side of the family.

The commandant pulled a folding knife from his uniform pocket, and Michael stiffened. "Hold out your hands."

He hesitated a moment, then did as he was told and was relieved when the commandant sliced through the plastic ties that bound his wrists. He stifled a groan as feeling rushed back into his fingers.

The commandant cut through Pia's bonds and she rubbed her wrists, the red marks around them making Michael want to smash a fist into the commandant's long, angular face. He wore his thick black hair slicked back with some kind of shiny pomade, and a coarse black mustache curled beneath a sharp, pointed nose.

"Tomorrow," Velasquez said, "if you continue to follow orders and keep your woman in line, I will allow you to move freely around the camp."

A moment of relief filtered through him. He glanced over at Pia, read the same emotion in her beautiful brown eyes.

"You will have a measure of freedom," the commandant continued. "But as you can see, the camp is extremely well guarded. Should either of you disobey my orders, the punishment will be severe. If you try to escape, you will be shot. Do you understand?"

He understood perfectly. Still, if he got the chance, he would find a way to get them away from the camp. "I understand."

The commandant's attention swung to Pia. "You will do as your man tells you. You will not leave the camp or you will deal with me—personally. Is that understood?" There was no mistaking how Velasquez would deal with Pia. Lust burned in the depths of the man's black eyes. It matched the blackness in his heart.

Pia nodded. "I understand."

"Good. I suggest you get some sleep. Starting tomorrow, there will be work assignments for both of you." Turning, the commandant strode off toward the big tent on the opposite side of the camp, his own personal quarters.

"Now that we're free," Pia said softly, "we can find a way to get out of here."

He thought of what the commandant would do to her if she tried to leave, and a shudder moved through him. Unless there was a ransom demand and his father paid what was asked, they would have to try to escape.

"We'll take our time," he said. "Make plans, figure

out our best chance. In the meantime, we need to get some rest."

Pia nodded and ducked into the tent, and Michael followed. Inside, they found two sleeping mats rolled out on the canvas floor side by side to form a single pallet. Clean clothes were neatly folded on top, a pair of brown twill pants and a long-sleeved plain cotton shirt for him, a yellow gathered skirt and peasant blouse and a pair of flat leather sandals for Pia.

Pia looked at him and began to strip off her damp, baggy fatigues. Insane as it was, desire burned through him.

"I wish we could make love," she whispered, her naked body so sweetly curved his breath caught. "I wish you could make me feel the way you did on the boat so I could forget we're in this place."

He cupped her face in his palm, ran his thumb over her cheek. "Pia…honey, I want you so much. But more than anything, I want you safe." Which she wouldn't be if the soldiers outside heard them in the tent making love.

A sad smile touched her lips. "I know." Pia helped him strip off his damp clothes, her hands running gently over his chest and down his flat stomach. She smiled impishly when she realized she was making him hard.

Michael kissed her. "Be a good girl and get in bed before I lose my mind and do something I shouldn't."

She grinned. He loved that she could find something to smile about under such terrible conditions. They spread their damp fatigues out to dry, put on the clean clothes and lay down on the sleeping palette. Michael pulled the thin blanket over them and curled Pia spoon-fashion against him.

With nothing beneath her skirt and blouse, he could feel the roundness of her bottom against his groin. One of his hands brushed a soft, full breast, and need burned through him. Michael ruthlessly tamped it down.

Exhausted, Pia fell almost instantly asleep, and his hold tightened protectively. He felt things for Pia he had never felt for another woman. Along with the lust she stirred without the least effort, he admired her courage. He respected the way she so bravely accepted the grim situation fate had handed her.

A situation that would likely get worse.

Michael kissed the top of her head, lay back and closed his eyes. He dozed but always kept an ear cocked for danger. One thing he had learned about himself. He wasn't a coward. He would give his life to protect the woman who slept so trustingly in his arms.

Half an hour before dawn, Chase knocked on the door between his and Harper's motel rooms. When the door swung open, Chase barely recognized the female in front of him as the woman who had fired his blood the night before, whose soft curves had filled his hands, whose warm lips had tempted him nearly to the breaking point.

This Harper wore olive drab cargo pants and a black T-shirt, her feet encased in a pair of high-top hiking boots. Long pale hair, plaited into a single braid, hung down her back.

She looked fit and strong, ready to face whatever challenge lay ahead. She looked determined and beautiful and sexy as hell. Chase's groin tightened so fiercely he had to grit his teeth and look away.

"I'm ready when you are," she said.

Hell, yes. As if he hadn't noticed. He dragged in a calming breath, angry at himself for his momentary loss of control, grabbed her backpack and slung it over his shoulder before she could protest, walked back and grabbed his own, and they headed downstairs.

When he reached the concrete path at the bottom, the door to Kil Dawson's room swung open and his youngest brother, Brandon, appeared.

"Hey, bro." Bran was dressed in full camo, same as Chase, but a Glock 19 9 mil, modified with Bran's custom grip, was strapped to his hip. Bringing his personal weapons was one of the advantages of flying private. For a few hundred thousand pesos, getting weapons through customs wasn't that hard.

Chase found himself smiling. "Guess you couldn't stand to miss all the fun."

Bran grinned. "Never could resist crashing a party."

Chase dropped the packs and the men leaned in to grip each other's shoulders. "Glad you're here, little brother," Chase said. "The way it looks, things could get pretty dicey." No way around it. Having his brother there was a tremendous asset. Three men instead of two—all former military, Bran and Kil both special operators—greatly increased their chances for success.

"You remember Harper," Chase said.

Bran surprised him by leaning over and hugging her. Chase wasn't sure how he felt about that, especially when Harper softened and hugged him back.

"Sorry about Michael," Bran said. "We're going to do our best to bring him home." Bran had met Harper a few times when Chase and Michael were in college.

Her eyes glistened. "Thank you for coming."

His brother nodded. With his dark hair and blue eyes,

Bran had always been the pretty boy of the Garrett clan. Now, after his years in the military, there was a hard edge to his features, a darkness in his eyes that hadn't been there before.

Chase looked up as Kil Dawson walked out of the motel room, duffel over one thick shoulder. "There's some arepas in there—that's corncakes with eggs and cheese. I got the *senora* whose husband owns the motel to whip us up some for breakfast. Bran and I've already eaten. We'll load up while you and Harper grab a bite. As soon as Francisco gets here, we'll hit the road."

They stowed their gear in the back of the cruiser, left everything they didn't need in Kil's room and paid the motel owner two weeks in advance. If they weren't back by then, Chase figured they would likely be dead.

"Don't leave anything important behind," Kil said. "No way to know for sure we'll be coming back this way."

"Yeah, about that..." Bran said. "I made a few calls, got hold of a pilot friend of mine. Flies helos. He's on standby if this whole bargaining-for-their-release thing goes FUBAR and we have to get the fuck out of Dodge."

"Sounds good," Chase said. By now, Kil would have filled Bran in on everything they knew and what they had planned, depending on what they found at the rebel camp.

Depending on if Michael and Pia were actually still alive.

Chase glanced over at Harper and worry slid through him. The good news was, with Bran and Kil in charge of the mission, he could focus his attention on Harper and keep her safe.

He tipped his head in her direction and, she walked

ahead of him into Kil's motel room. The warm aroma of corn, cheese and coffee drifted toward them, and his stomach grumbled.

"Eat up," he said. "Long day ahead."

They each grabbed a couple of arepas, which were delicious, and polished off the thermos of coffee Kil had managed to commandeer along with the food. By the time they were finished, dawn grayed the landscape, and the thin, dark Colombian guide they had hired joined them where they stood next to the cruiser.

"I am Francisco," he said in heavily accented English. "I will take you up the mountain as far as it is safe. I will show you the route from there. But once we reach rebel territory, you must go the rest of the way on your own."

Kil nodded. "Fair enough." Reaching out a hand, he and Francisco shook. Money passed between them. Half now, half when they got up the mountain. "I'm Kil," he said. "That's Bran. The guy over there, that's Chase, and the *senorita* is Harper. Let's go."

The plan was to drive as far as the rutted dirt road would allow, then walk in from there. There were miles of deep jungle and forest ahead of them. They wouldn't have to worry about being spotted until they got closer to the rebel camp.

The plan would evolve as they went along, collected information, figured out the best way to achieve their goal—bringing Michael and Pia out safely. Getting all of them safely back home.

They settled themselves in the cruiser, Kil and Francisco up front, Chase, Harper and Brandon in back. It was a snug fit, but no one complained. Riding beat walking—and plenty of that lay ahead of them.

Even with the windows rolled down, it was warm in

the car, especially with Harper pressed snuggly against Chase's side. He did his best not to think of last night, of Harper's feminine curves filling his hands, the way she had tasted, the soft womanly scent of her, fresh from the shower. But every now and then, he felt himself begin to get hard.

Son of a bitch. Kil was right—a woman on a mission was the last thing they needed.

Nothing he could do but grin and bear it. Chase inwardly groaned at the picture in his mind that phrase conjured, even if the spelling wasn't the same.

The ride went on much of the day, the going slow as the road dropped into ravines, changed from dry ruts to deep muddy puddles and crawled through dense jungle as it wound its way deeper into the vast Sierra Nevadas.

It was afternoon when the road finally came to an end at the base of a steep, jungle-covered mountain, but with four-wheel drive and Kil behind the wheel, they had gotten farther than the guide had expected.

"We go now on foot," Francisco said, his long face as narrow as the rest of him. Though he hadn't smoked all day, he smelled of tobacco and his fingers were nicotine stained.

They grabbed their gear out of the rear of the cruiser, and Chase helped Harper slide her backpack across her shoulders. It was heavier than he had first thought, but Harper didn't seem to mind. Later, if necessary, he could load some of her stuff into his own pack.

Chase glanced at his brother, who was strapping a long, lethal-looking, serrated Ka-Bar knife to his thigh. Chase did the same, and so did Kil. They checked their weapons and ammunition. Kil carried the AK across his back. Brandon carried an HK416 assault rifle, along with his Glock and God only knew what else.

The assault rifle, Bran had once told him, had been specifically designed for Delta operators, a subject they officially never discussed.

Chase grabbed a canvas slouch hat out of the duffel and slapped it on Harper's head, settled another one on his own.

"Sun protection," he said. "Once we get deeper into the rain forest, it'll be shady and you won't need it."

She adjusted the hat, which made her look like the teenage girl who'd been far too young for him all those years ago. Chase found himself smiling. Harper smiled back and he felt the kick. *Dammit.* He forced himself to ignore it.

"Let's move out," Bran said, and it was clear in the tone of his voice that his brother had assumed command of the mission.

Bran flicked a glance at Harper that slid to Chase, and an unspoken look passed between them. Harper was Chase's problem, his to look after and protect.

Chase wouldn't have it any other way.

CHAPTER SEVENTEEN

Every bone in Harper's body ached. Inside her boots her ankles were swollen and her feet were sore. She hadn't hiked like this in years. *Correction.* She had never hiked like this.

But she had known trying to keep up with battle-hardened soldiers wouldn't be easy, not even Chase, whose veneer of sophisticated civility had disappeared when they'd landed in Colombia.

From the start, the going hadn't been easy. After the first few miles, the trail had narrowed to a thin, winding path through thick vegetation. In some places, the men had to hack their way through vines and downed trees, dense leafy roots and thick shrubs.

Twice they had run across snakes, one a simple ground snake Harper had stepped across in the trail. The other, some kind of South American rattlesnake, which she'd heard rattle only an instant before Chase swung the long serrated blade of his survival knife and severed the creature's head. The memory still made her shiver.

All afternoon the men had pressed hard, and though they were pushing her, she had a feeling they were stopping more often because of her, trying not to make the trek any more difficult than it had to be.

At a signal from Bran, the men paused in the trail and swung their packs to the ground. Chase eased Harper's pack off her shoulders and set it down next to his beside a fallen log.

"Thanks." Harper checked the log for any unwanted creatures, then dropped down on top of it, grateful for the break. They had pressed forward all day, but Harper had pushed herself even harder. She needed to reach her brother. If he and Pia were in the rebel camp, they were in terrible danger. The sooner the men reached them, the better the chance for their release.

"You doing okay?" Chase asked.

She managed a weary nod.

He took the lid off his canteen and handed it over, and Harper took a long, cooling drink. Instead of the broiling heat on the beach below, up here it was a pleasant seventy degrees and it hadn't rained all day. The weather had turned out to be the one plus on a very difficult journey.

"Thanks." She capped the canteen and handed it back to him, stretched her legs out in front of her, trying to work out some of the kinks. She took a deep breath, determined to ignore her aching feet. "You don't have to wait for me. I'm ready whenever you are."

"We're done for the day," Chase said. "The sun's about to set, and in this kind of country, it'll take a while to make camp. We need to build sleeping platforms off the ground and round up something to eat."

Relief filtered through her. They were finished hiking for the day! Her legs and feet would do a silent happy dance if they could manage to move.

"Bran and Kil are scouting the area," Chase said. "Making sure we're secure. We should be okay. Francisco isn't expecting any rebel activity until we're higher up in the mountains, but we need to be certain."

That sounded good, but there was still work to be done before the camp was ready for the night. She forced the muscles in her legs to shove her up from the log. "What can I do to help?"

Chase's dark gaze ran over her, taking in her exhausted features.

"What?" she asked, slightly defensive. She wasn't a special ops soldier. She was doing the best she could, and if that wasn't enough, by God she'd do more.

Chase just shook his head. "You're amazing. You know that?"

Amazing? Did Chase just say that? Warmth filtered through her, easing the soreness in her muscles and bones.

"Rest for a while," he said. "Get back some of your strength. That's the most important thing you can do. Tomorrow's going to be another long day."

"Are you sure?"

"You did great today. I was proud of you."

Her cheeks warmed.

"Francisco and I are going to get started on those platforms. Sleeping on the ground in this kind of country is asking for trouble. If you need me, I won't be far away."

She nodded, watched his long, confident strides carry him across the area at the base of a cluster of trees Kil and Bran had chosen as a campsite. Chase stopped to speak to Francisco, who held up his long-bladed machete. Chase pulled out his survival knife, and they both began to hack away at dense patches of green.

As Harper sat on the log, sounds of the rain forest reached her, the caw of a large bird somewhere in the trees, the chatter of monkeys. A small, bright green parrot perched in the branches of a palm tree, though Kil told her it was actually an overgrown parakeet.

She'd had an interesting conversation with him earlier, when he had pulled her aside at the beginning of the journey.

"I know you don't trust me, Harper." He'd held up a big hand before she could contradict him, which would have been a lie.

"You don't know me," he'd said, "so it's only natural for you to feel that way. But there could be a time when our lives depend on your trust in me. I want you to know that when we were in Afghanistan, Brandon Garrett saved my life. I owe him for every breath I take. Clearly you belong to his brother—"

"I don't belong to—"

He'd held up his hand, silencing her once more. "Doesn't matter. You're under Chase's protection and he's Bran's older brother. I would give my life before I let anything happen to you or to him. You believe me?"

She'd looked into those hard, dark eyes and something eased inside her. She had jumped to conclusions about this man, which wasn't usually her way. "I believe you."

He'd nodded. "Good. You're safe with me in every

way, but if I ask you to do something, you need to do it without question. That goes for whatever Bran and Chase say, too. You do exactly what they say, and we'll all get out of this alive. Are you all right with that?"

Was she all right with it? She was now. "Yes. I'll follow your orders without question."

His hard look had softened into a smile, and she caught a glimmer of the man women undoubtedly fell all over.

"Good," he'd said. "Now, let's get going before I have to defend myself against the dagger looks Chase is sending my way."

Harper had laughed. The last of her misgivings about Killian Dawson had evaporated as the men began to head up the trail. Francisco had led the way and Bran took a place behind him. She'd felt Chase's hand on her waist, urging her to the next place in line. Chase had followed and Kil Dawson fell in behind, guarding the rear.

That had been this morning. The memory slipped away as the faint smell of tobacco smoke reached them, drawing her back to the present. Francisco puffed on a hand-rolled cigarette as he knelt to light a campfire in the clearing. Off to the side, pallets for each of them had been completed, some suspended among the low branches of the trees, others built with pieces of wood, a few feet off the ground.

She noticed a platform a little away from the others, big enough for two, and relief slipped through her. Chase had stayed close to her all day. Apparently that wasn't going to change. She thought of the snake and suppressed a shudder. She was glad he would be sleeping beside her.

Her thoughts turned to Pia and Michael, and she

wondered about their sleeping arrangements. She hoped Michael had been able to protect Pia from the rebel soldiers.

She hoped Chase and the men would reach them soon.

Chase sat next to Harper on a log he'd pulled over in front of the campfire. Back from their scouting expedition, Bran and Kil had seen no sign of rebel forces, and the fire was snugged away amid the foliage where it wouldn't be seen. Bran had returned with a plastic bag filled with the meat from a peccary, a small boar he'd killed, skinned and cut into pieces.

Francisco had the meat roasting on sticks braced over the campfire, the succulent aroma making Chase's stomach grumble.

"Is it... Is it snake?" Harper asked, eyeing the meat with obvious distaste and making him smile.

"Nothing so dramatic. It's wild pig. You like roast pork, don't you?"

She looked up at him, and her lips tilted up at the corners. "I love it. And now that I know I'm not eating a reptile, I'm starving."

He laughed. "There're wild onions in the skillet, fresh guavas, bananas and cherimoyas. We won't have to eat MREs tonight."

They grabbed broad green leaves to use as plates and sat down to eat. No one talked much. They were all too tired.

When they finished, Chase dumped his leftover bones into the campfire, which had dwindled to a tiny blaze providing minimal light. While Harper helped

Francisco pack up, Chase caught a motion from Bran and walked over to join him.

"Francisco says we'll enter rebel territory around midday tomorrow," Bran said. "He won't go farther. He's mapped out the rest of the route, thinks we'll reach the plateau where the rebels are camped by dark tomorrow night."

"He got any idea what kind of force we'll be facing?"

The tightening of Brandon's jaw was not a good sign. "He figures forty or fifty men, but there could be more."

"Jesus."

"Yeah. And still no call from Winston. Kil's got the sat phone. If Winston got a ransom demand, he would have phoned Harper, right?"

"Michael and his father never got along, but Knox has always been protective of his daughter. He knows she's in Colombia searching for her brother. If there'd been a ransom demand, he would have offered to pay the money and called Harper to let her know."

"Los Proscritos...those guys are bad news, bro. Not much more than bandits masquerading as soldiers. If Michael and Pia are in the camp, we can't risk trying to negotiate a deal. With that many men, they'll take whatever we offer and slit our throats without the slightest hesitation. We have to figure the best approach for a snatch and grab."

Chase glanced across the camp to where Harper once more sat on the log. "We do that, we could have fifty soldiers sweeping down on us. No way we can make it all the way down the mountain to the Land Cruiser."

"We need to locate our targets and find out what we're up against. Once we've got the intel we need, we'll figure how to get them out." Bran's gaze went to Harper, who was leaning back against a tree trunk, her eyes closed, half-asleep. "How's she holding up?"

"Helluva lot better than I ever would have guessed." Bran smiled. "You always thought she was special. Looks like you were right."

He'd been right about Harper. And he wanted her the way he had never wanted a woman before. "Looks like" was all he said.

Bran walked over and raked his boot through the dirt around the campfire, extinguishing the last of the flames, leaving the camp in darkness except for a sliver of moonlight that passed in and out between the clouds.

"Let's get some sleep," Bran said. "We should be okay tonight, but you can't be too careful. Two-hour shifts. Kil first, you, then me."

Chase nodded. A ray of moonlight lit the jungle long enough for him to make his way over to Harper. He crouched in front of her, tipped up her chin with his fingers and watched her eyes slowly flutter open.

"Come on, angel. Time for bed." Inwardly he groaned as the words slipped off his tongue. *Dammit.* He needed to keep his mind out of the gutter.

"'Kay." Harper rose sleepily from the log. Digging a flashlight out of his pocket, Chase scanned the area around the clearing and they climbed up on the pallet, where he had laid out their bedrolls.

He took off his boots, stretched his socks over the tops to keep out unwanted visitors and set them aside.

Harper watched and did the same. "You seem to know a lot about this stuff," she said, a little more awake than she had been. "Have you been in the jungle before?"

"I spent a lot of time camping out on the ranch when

I was a kid. Still go as often as I can, but I don't think the jungles of Texas count. That and military survival training. Under these conditions, it all comes back pretty fast."

"You definitely handled that snake. I'm just glad we didn't have to eat it."

He chuckled as he slid into his bedroll, and Harper lay down beside him. He could no longer see her, but she was close enough he could hear her breathing and feel the heat of her body.

He thought she had fallen asleep until she shifted on the pallet. "What happened between you and my father?" she asked softly.

"He never told you?"

"I asked him, but he said it was none of my business."

"My dad wouldn't talk about it, either. But your father's animosity extends to the whole Garrett clan. When I was younger, he tolerated me for Michael's sake. After your brother got involved in drugs, I confronted your dad. Michael had overdosed for the third time and nearly died. I told your father the way he had treated his son made him at least partly responsible. We argued. It was bad. After that, things went downhill."

"And your friendship with Michael ended."

"By then I believed no one could save Michael but himself. Maybe that was wrong. At the time, I felt I had no choice."

"Something turned him around. Losing his best friend, one of the few people who really cared about him, may have been at least partly responsible."

"Whatever it was, I'm glad it worked."

"Me, too," she said softly. She shifted again in the darkness. "So what do Bran and Kil think about you sleeping with me?" she asked, beginning to sound sleepy again.

Chase blocked the image that popped into his head. "I'm not sleeping with you. I'm lying next to you on a bedroll in the jungle. You hired me. I brought you here. That makes you my responsibility. That's what they think."

"Oh."

He didn't say he wouldn't have let any other man near her. In some strange way, she was his. Maybe it wouldn't be for longer than these few days, but for now she belonged to him. He wouldn't let anyone or anything hurt her.

"Go to sleep, angel. I'm taking the second shift. I need to get some rest."

"Sorry," she mumbled, yawning.

"None of this is your fault, honey. Your brother is lucky to have someone who cares about him the way you do."

She made no reply, thank Christ. Just the sound of her voice was making him hard. Fortunately, his military training kicked in and in several slow breaths he was asleep. He didn't wake up until two hours later when Harper released a bloodcurdling scream.

CHAPTER EIGHTEEN

The spider was huge. The weight of its massive legs and thick body crawling over her chest slowly awoke her. Enough moonlight shone down through the tall trees and leafy foliage to outline its enormous, fuzzy, hideously ugly body right in front of her face.

The high-pitched shriek erupted before she could pull it in, and suddenly Chase's hand was shooting out, knocking the spider away, sending it flying into the air. It landed in the forest below with a heavy thud that made her skin crawl.

"She all right?" Kil called out, on watch somewhere in the darkness.

"Spider," Chase answered. "Big as a dinner plate. It didn't bite her. Just scared her." He turned toward her. "Right?"

"I-it didn't bite me."

"Motherfuck…" Bran grumbled sleepily from his pallet, then rolled over and went back to sleep.

Harper kept shaking, couldn't seem to stop.

Chase eased her into his arms. "Adrenaline rush. You're okay. It'll be over in a minute."

Chase continued to hold her, his arms like steel bands around her. She wanted to just curl into him, forget she was in the middle of a Colombian mountain jungle, pretend Michael was safe and that she was in bed with Chase for real.

He eased away. "About time for my shift. Will you be okay?"

"I'm… I'm okay." Reluctantly, she let him go. "Thanks for…umm…the spider."

"I don't mind spiders so much, but I hate the hell out of a snake. As you may have noticed earlier today."

A soft laugh escaped. It felt good under the circumstances.

"Go back to sleep." Chase slid out of his bedroll and pulled on his boots, climbed down from the pallet and disappeared into the darkness below. She heard soft whispers as the men changed places, then nothing but silence.

She needed sleep but finding it wouldn't be easy, not with Chase gone and the night so black and impenetrable around her. For the next half hour, she listened to sounds in the darkness, the growl of a big cat—jaguar or puma—somewhere higher in the forest; the hoot of an owl; something slithering through the foliage below.

She must have fallen into an exhausted slumber. When her eyes cracked open, purple light streamed through the lush green leaves and the rich aroma of coffee drifted up from the tiny campfire in the clearing below. It was enough to get her moving.

Chase's bedroll was already gone. She packed her

own, climbed down and checked the rest of her gear, then took a bathroom break, privacy being fairly easy with the dense forest around them.

At the campfire, Chase handed her a tin mug of coffee and a broad green leaf-plate filled with the corncakes and cheese that Francisco had prepared, cooking over what Bran told her was the last campfire they would have until their mission was complete.

A thread of worry slipped through her. From now on they needed to be careful. They couldn't risk alerting the rebels who lurked in the higher elevations of the mountains.

Chase scraped dirt into the fire with his boot, erased any other sign of the camp, and they set out behind Francisco as they had the day before, though the trail seemed steeper today. Narrower and even more overgrown, winding relentlessly upward, it strained her tired muscles even more.

When a rainstorm blew in, they put on their slickers and kept walking. Her feet still ached, but the overnight rest had helped, and without the heat, her ankles were no longer swollen. The sun had crested overhead and tipped a little to the west when Francisco called a halt to the march.

"I am sorry, *senores y senorita*, but this is as far as I go. If you follow the trail, you will find the plateau where the rebels are camped. It is in the flat spot before the mountain begins its final rise to the peak."

The peak being more than seventeen thousand feet, Kil had told her. Fortunately, they wouldn't be going that far.

"You should be there before nightfall." Francisco stuck out a dark, calloused hand and all three men shook. Kil handed him the balance of the money they owed for his services, plus a little extra, and Francisco tucked the money into his shirt.

"*Vaya con Dios*, my friends. God go with you." Turning, he started back down the mountain, his thin legs moving like well-oiled pistons, lean body disappearing into the leafy foliage as the trail wound around the bend, out of sight.

Silence descended in his absence.

"A couple of things before we go," Bran said, regaining their attention. "First, I'll be moving out ahead of you. I want to scout the area, see if I can locate an LZ that will work for a helo extract. I'll meet up with you before you reach the plateau. Second, you're in rebel territory now. Keep your eyes open. Stay quiet and out of sight as much as possible. You don't want them to spot you."

Harper figured the warning was probably more for her than the men, but she didn't really need a reminder. If she were any more worried, she'd be turning around and heading back with Francisco.

"I'll see you up the trail." Bran moved off the path and disappeared into the bush. Harper had heard the men talking enough to understand that Bran was heading off to find a landing zone for a helicopter to pick them up if it became necessary. Sounded darn good to her.

Kil slung his backpack across his powerful shoulders. "You heard what Francisco said. We'll be there before nightfall. Let's move out."

They started up the trail, Kil in the lead, Harper, then Chase. Three men and a woman against an entire rebel army. Harper thought of her brother and Pia and just kept putting one foot in front of the other.

They reached the farthest edge of the rebel camp at dusk. Bran had joined them on the trail a couple of miles back, satisfied with a spot he had found that was large enough for a chopper landing. It was far enough away from the rebel camp the chopper wouldn't be seen, close enough for them to reach with what might be injured civilians in tow.

Chase prayed that wouldn't be the case, that they would find Michael and Pia alive and well enough to travel. They would know the answer later tonight.

The plan was for Chase to stay with Harper while Bran and Kil reconned the area around the camp and located the targets—if they were actually there. If they were, they would lay out a rescue operation, grab the hostages and get the hell out of Dodge.

He almost smiled at how easily he slid back into military thinking. Almost. Smiling wasn't easy, sitting in the jungle next to Harper, listening for the sound of enemy soldiers on the move.

So far nothing. Before the guys had set out, they'd all filled up on MREs, meatballs in marinara for Bran and Kil, shredded barbecued beef for Chase, chicken and noodles for Harper. Though he could tell Harper hadn't been enthusiastic, she had finished the meal without complaint.

In the small clearing, darkness surrounded them. He could feel the warmth of her slender body close beside him, but tonight he was more concerned with her safety than taking her to bed.

Well, mostly.

They hadn't spoken for hours. He hadn't expected the silence to be as easy between them as it was. Aside from the chirp of bugs and the rustle of nocturnal creatures, the only sound was the babble of water running along a stream coming down from the peak.

A soft birdcall came from the woods, and he felt Harper stiffen. Chase cupped his hands around his mouth and returned the sound, a Texas birdcall he and his brother had used to communicate as kids when they were out at the ranch. He hoped to hell none of the rebels were ornithologists.

Brandon appeared like a ghost out of the deep green foliage, full camo, his face covered with black greasepaint. Kil popped out, looking much the same. Apparently not satisfied that their present position was safe, Bran grabbed the pack he'd left behind, indicated they should all do the same and motioned for them to follow.

Chase and Harper grabbed their gear and moved out, following the men half a mile back down the trail the way they had come to an area they deemed safe.

"Found them," Bran said softly as he dropped his pack on the ground. A sound of relief slipped from Harper's throat.

"Condition?" Chase asked.

"Mobile. They're sleeping in a private tent, which is good. Lots of soldiers in camp, which is bad."

"How many?" Chase asked.

"Counted forty. Could be a few more sentries around." He'd hoped for better odds.

"Can we get them out tonight?" Harper asked anxiously.

"Negative," Kil said. "With that many men, we definitely need the chopper for extract. Which means we'll need a day to do more recon and set things up."

"It's late," Bran said. "We're far enough away to get some sleep. Tomorrow we observe the camp, study their schedules, learn their timelines. We got some of that info tonight, but we'll finalize plans tomorrow. Go in late tomorrow night."

"Sounds good," Chase said.

Bran's gaze zeroed in on him. "It's going to take all of us to get them out of there."

Chase's head came up, a thread of tension slipping through him. "You aren't talking about Harper?"

"We're going to need a diversion. The three of us are going to have our hands full. Distracting them has to be her job."

Chase just shook his head. "No way."

"Sorry, man," Kil said. "No other choice. She brought us here. She wants her brother out, she'll have to help."

"Of course I'll help," Harper said.

"No," Chase said flatly. "She could wind up getting killed."

Harper's chin went up. "Just tell me what you need me to do."

Chase softly cursed.

Bran's grin flashed white against his black face paint. "We'll figure it out tomorrow. In the meantime, find a spot and grab some z's. We'll talk again in the morning."

When Chase reached for his pack, Bran caught his arm and tipped his head to the side, a gesture he recognized as the need for a private conversation.

Chase nodded. He'd be there as soon as he got Harper settled.

Using his flashlight, he grabbed his pack and scoured the area for a safe place to rest for what little of the night remained. Harper grabbed her pack and joined him. He never offered to help with her load—by now knew better than to ask.

She carried her own weight, just the way she'd said.

He located a small open area where he didn't see any snakes, spiders or poisonous frogs, and made a place for the two of them on his bedroll.

"I'll be back in a minute," he told her, then slipped off into the darkness to speak to his brother.

"What's going on?" Chase asked once they were out of hearing.

"Picked up some intel while I was scouting the camp and the area around it. The head of Los Proscritos, the commandant, is a guy named Benito Velasquez. Got ties to a powerful coca grower in the region, not sure which one. Apparently, as a favor, Velasquez is holding Michael and his girlfriend in the camp. It's some kind of payback for a business deal gone wrong."

"How's Michael involved?"

"I don't think he is."

"Someone went to a lot of trouble to track him down and bring him to Colombia." Chase swore softly. "You're thinking this has something to do with his father."

"Not that much of a stretch, is it? I'm going out on a limb and guess the guy behind the crooked business deal is Knox Winston."

"And they're holding Michael for revenge. Son of a bitch."

"It's been rumored for years Knox is up to his sleazy eyeballs in the drug trade."

Chase grunted. "I should have figured that from the start."

"I think your attraction to Harper might have clouded your vision. Makes anything happening between you two a whole lot tougher."

The situation wasn't just tough, it was impossible. As Chase had known from the start.

Bran reached out and squeezed his shoulder. "We don't know for sure that's what's going on."

Chase made no reply. Knox Winston was involved. He could feel it in his bones.

"Get some sleep," Bran said. "You'll be taking the second rotation, same as last night."

His brother went in search of a place of his own, and Chase made his way over to his bedroll to join Harper. Thinking about Knox's likely involvement, he was glad she was already asleep.

He sighed as he sat down next to her and propped his back against the trunk of a tree. He had known from the start a relationship between them was hopeless.

Tomorrow they would make final plans to rescue Michael and Pia, do their best to get everyone out safely, then return to their lives in Texas.

Chase chose not to think about Knox Winston and his criminal empire and what might happen when he got home.

CHAPTER NINETEEN

Dawn arrived and with it another grueling day, hours where Pia worked with the women doing chores for the men and Michael built battlements, digging trenches around the camp perimeter for use in combat.

Who Velasquez's men would be fighting, Michael had no idea. Another group of rebel soldiers, perhaps, or maybe the Colombian army. He had no clue what would happen to him and Pia if the camp were invaded. They might end up in a worse situation than they were in now.

Which was the reason they had to escape.

And they had a plan. Tomorrow night the commandant was planning a celebration, a party in honor of the three-year anniversary of the formation of Los Proscritos. Any excuse to get drunk and whore was good enough for men like these.

According to what Pia had heard while she'd been standing around the fire boiling laundry, there would be feasting and drinking. *Big-time.* The commandant was even bringing in "fresh women" to entertain the men. The soldiers were excited, the sentries already growing less watchful, more relaxed as the big event grew near.

It would be the perfect time to escape.

Michael dug his shovel into the soil and tossed the heavy load of dirt over his shoulder. The sun beat down, but at least the temperature this high in the mountains was cool.

It was late afternoon when he looked up to see one of the rebels, a burly, flat-faced soldier in a dark green uniform, Captain Alvarez, who worked closely with the commandant. Alvarez motioned for him to stop work and join him.

Tossing his shovel aside, Michael followed the man off the hill, down into the camp. It had rained earlier, but the sun was shining as the day moved toward an end. Alvarez led him to the tent he and Pia were sharing and motioned him inside. As he ducked beneath the flap, the burly soldier followed him in.

Michael was surprised to find Pia waiting. Even more surprised to find the commandant sitting in a carved high-back chair upholstered in purple velvet that had been brought in and set up like a throne. Next to it, an upended barrel served as a table.

Benito Velasquez rose elegantly to his feet. "Mr. Winston. Good of you to join us. Would you care for a refreshment, something cool to drink?" A cut-crystal water pitcher and a crystal decanter sat on a silver tray next to three crystal tumblers. For a soldier, Velasquez lived the high life.

"No, thank you," he said, though he could use a glass of water after his hours in the sun. He didn't trust Velasquez.

He looked over at Pia in her yellow embroidered skirt and white peasant blouse. She had unbraided her hair and spread it around her shoulders. His pulse kicked up when he noticed the pallor of her face. When her eyes met his, he could read the fear in them.

If Velasquez has touched her—

The commandant smiled. It was a wolf's smile, cold and calculating, the smile of a predator. A few feet away, Captain Alvarez stood guard next to the entrance.

"I have a special favor to ask of you," Velasquez said. "You see, when I agreed to entertain you here in the camp as my guest, I made a promise that I would leave you unharmed. As a man of honor, that promise must extend to your woman. As you know, I have kept my word."

Michael said nothing. A tremor ran through Pia's small frame.

"I am an extremely virile man, Mr. Winston, a man of great and varied appetites. Aside from enjoying the pleasures of a woman's body, I also enjoy watching another man enjoy that same pleasure."

Michael's stomach twisted.

"The favor I am asking is a small one, and you will both be rewarded. Clean clothes, larger portions of food and drink."

Michael swallowed past the dryness in his throat. "And in return?"

"I watch the two of you together, there on your sleeping mats. It would give me great pleasure to watch, and it would give you pleasure, as well."

Pia made a soft sound of distress. Michael wanted to rip Velasquez's head off his shoulders and stuff it down his throat. *One more day*, he told himself. One more day and they would be gone.

"I'm afraid I'll have to decline your generous offer, Commandant Velasquez. The lady and I prefer our love-making to remain private, a personal affair just between the two of us. You understand."

Velasquez's smile went from wolfish to cruel, almost demonic. He was enjoying himself, relishing every moment.

"Perhaps I did not explain myself well enough. You will take the woman there on the mat, use her for your pleasure. The two of you will engage in intercourse, and I will watch."

Michael looked at Pia, whose eyes filled with tears. They brimmed over and trickled down her cheeks. The burly captain drew a pistol from his holster and pressed the barrel against Michael's head.

"If you do not do as I say," Velasquez continued, seated once more on his throne, "I will order Captain Alvarez to pull the trigger. After you are dead, he will take your place on the mat, and I will watch him fornicate with your woman."

The bile rose at the back of Michael's throat. His hands balled into shaking fists. Black rage like nothing he had ever known descended on him. The cold steel barrel of the pistol pressed into his temple and yet he felt no fear, only the nearly uncontrollable urge to kill Benito Velasquez with his bare hands.

Pia stepped in front of him, blocking any move he might have made. She set her small hands on his chest, and he could feel them trembling. His whole body vibrated with the need to commit murder.

"Michael…" She swallowed. "Please, Michael. I don't…don't want anyone to touch me but you."

He looked into her tear-ravaged face. "Pia…" The

word felt torn from his throat. Alvarez stepped back, the gun just out of Michael's reach, but his aim didn't waver.

"Michael…please. You must do this for me."

He swallowed against the rage. If he didn't do this, he would be dead, and Pia would be left at the commandant's mercy.

But how could he violate her in this way?

She went up on her toes and pressed a trembling kiss on his lips. "Please, Michael. For me…"

"I would do anything for you, Pia." Michael kissed her softly, tenderly. He deepened the kiss, drawing it out, trying to let her know how much she meant to him. Telling her he would do whatever he had to in order to protect her. When he ended the kiss, the commandant began to smile his wolfish smile again.

"Perhaps some refreshment—a little *chicha* would help you relax," Velasquez said, referring to a drink made with fermented corn and honey. If they were going to do this, the potent concoction made by the locals was exactly what they needed.

"Yes…" Michael said. "A glass of *chicha* would be good."

The commandant poured a tumbler full and set it down on the upended barrel. Pia walked stiffly over to pick up the glass. Her hands trembled as she held it to her lips and took several long swallows. Michael knew how strong the brew was. He had seen its effects on the men and women in the camp.

Pia returned to Michael, pressed the glass into his hand. He took a drink but not too much, afraid he would lose control. He handed back the glass and Pia finished the drink, swallowing all of it. She returned it to the tray and turned back to him.

Taking his hand, she led him over to their sleeping mat. Michael looked across the room at Velasquez. There was no mercy in his black eyes, just pure, unmitigated lust.

Michael pointed to Captain Alvarez. "Not him. Just you."

Velasquez jerked his head toward the captain, who brought his pistol over and set it down on the barrel close to the commandant's hand. Silently he left the tent.

Michael looked at Velasquez, knew the commandant wouldn't hesitate to shoot him and take Pia himself, or have other men do it so he could watch.

A wave of nausea hit him. He felt Pia's small fingers working the buttons on the front of his shirt, centering him, returning his focus. Her hands were steadier now, after drinking the *chicha*. Michael leaned down and kissed her softly, trailed kisses along the side of her neck.

"Whatever happens, it's just you and me in here," he said. "No one else. Just you and me. Can you remember that?"

Fresh tears rolled down her cheeks. "Just you and me," she whispered.

Michael stripped away the rest of his clothes, then turned Pia's back to the commandant and stripped off her garments. He kissed her as they settled on the sleeping mat, leaning over her, covering her naked body with his as much as he could. He prayed he could manage to get aroused with a man he wanted to kill watching them from the other side of the tent.

His muscles began to relax, the strong drink beginning to do its work on both of them. Pia kissed him and Michael kissed her back. *We just have to make it till tomorrow night*, he told himself and prayed Pia would hang on to that thought, too.

Michael deepened the kiss, working to close off his mind and think only of the beautiful woman beneath him, the smooth curves of her body, the softness of her breasts.

He touched her, let himself love her, thought only of Pia and did his best to make her think only of him. Taking her with exquisite care, he moved gently inside her, began to hear her soft cries and prayed he was giving her at least some small degree of pleasure.

For an instant, long enough for his body to reach release, he battled down his rage and allowed himself to feel the heat of her beautiful body, the pleasure of having her glove him so sweetly, allowed himself to climax.

Velasquez groaned and Michael's fury returned, so strong his chest clamped down, locking the air in his lungs. He looked up to see Velasquez disappearing out of the tent, and closed his eyes. The last rays of sunlight burned through the canvas walls.

His throat tightened, and his eyes stung as he eased himself away. "He's gone." Emotion tightened his chest. "I'm sorry. So sorry." Pia sobbed and clung to him as he settled himself beside her, pulled her into his arms.

"It's over," he said. "You're safe. Everything's going to be okay."

She curled even closer against him.

"Tomorrow night, no matter what happens, we leave."

She nodded, and he could feel the wetness of her tears.

I love you, he thought. *I've fallen so in love with you.* But after what had happened, he couldn't tell her. He didn't deserve a woman like Pia. He should have done something. Surely there was some way he could have protected her.

He would give his life for Pia. But if he'd been killed, he couldn't stand to think what Velasquez might have done.

Velasquez. A viper in a man's body.

Though darkness had only just fallen, he pulled the thin blanket over them, his arms still tight around her. The strong liquor would help both of them sleep. They only had to make it one more day.

He didn't tell Pia that tomorrow night, before they left camp, he was going to find a way to kill Benito Velasquez.

CHAPTER TWENTY

It was three in the morning. The plan was set. Almost time to go. Harper glanced over at Chase, busy making a last-minute check of his gear. In full camouflage and tactical gear, he looked terrifying—and amazing.

The damp air put a slight curl in his hair. With his face streaked with black paint, and those warm brown eyes, she thought he was the sexiest man on planet Earth. Desire clenched low and hard in her belly, which was completely out of line.

Harper glanced away and, returning her focus to the mission, mentally began running through the details one last time. In order to create the diversion, she and the men would have to split up, Harper staying in a designated spot above the camp on one side while the men went in from the opposite direction.

Once she'd completed her task, she would meet up with all of them, including Michael and Pia, and they would make their way to the landing zone, where the helicopter would be arriving just before dawn.

A faint shiver ran through her. She would be on her own tonight. The men would be counting on her, all of them would. Fortunately this high up in the mountains, the area around the plateau wasn't dense jungle terrain. Rocks and boulders littered the ground around thick mountain scrub.

She wouldn't have to worry about fighting her way through heavy vegetation, reptiles and bugs, but she'd have to stay low and out of sight. She had dressed for the mission in black jeans and a black long-sleeved T-shirt.

Standing beneath the faint rays of moonlight streaming down through the clouds, she stuffed her pale hair beneath a black knit cap.

"Hold still." Chase turned her to face him, reached out and caught her chin. Using his fingers, he striped black greasepaint over her cheeks and forehead. She could read the worry in his eyes. He checked her gear, straightening the camo vest she was wearing that Killian had managed to jury-rig to fit her.

Half a dozen flash-bang grenades were clipped to the front. Her Ruger rode in the holster on the belt at her waist. Her first day on the trail, she had learned to tuck her pants into the tops of her hiking boots to keep out unwanted creatures.

"You know what you have to do, right? You don't have any questions?"

She shook her head. They'd been over it a dozen times. "I toss a flash grenade into the camp and move. Toss another grenade and move again. I don't look at the flash and I keep going. I don't stay in one place. The grenades confuse the guards and cause general havoc, enough for you to reach Michael and Pia's tent, get inside and get them out of there."

"That's right."

She managed to smile. "Don't look so nervous. I was the pitcher on my high school softball team. We won the championship that year."

His mouth curved a little, not much. "Good to know."

She checked the flash grenades for the umpteenth time. Apparently, they erupted in a blinding light and made a helluva lot of noise. Chase had shown her how to pull the pin and hold the grenade before she made the toss.

"You ready for this?" he asked.

"More than ready." Brandon and Killian would be clearing the path ahead of them, taking out any guards who might pose a threat. She hadn't asked what that meant. She didn't want to know.

"Remember, when we reach the spot on the east side of the camp, Killian will stop and turn and tap you on the shoulder. That'll mean you're in position, ready to lob the first grenade."

They had spent all day observing the camp, timing the guards, working out exactly how to implement the extraction.

"Count to three hundred," Chase said. "One thousand one, one thousand two—like that—before you make the first throw. We should be in position by then."

"Got it." The idea was for the distraction to lure the soldiers in the opposite direction, away from Michael's tent. The trick was to toss the grenades and get away safely.

"The minute you lob the last grenade, make your way up the mountain to the rendezvous point."

"That big boulder that stands out up on the ridge."

"That's the place." Chase reached out and cupped her face between his hands. "Damn, I wish you didn't have to do this." He surprised her with a brief hard kiss. "Promise me you'll be careful, angel."

"I—I'll be careful." She looked up at him. "Just find my brother and Pia, and get them out safely."

He nodded. "Let's go."

They moved out, heading up a trail that wound its way around the perimeter of the camp, Killian and Brandon in front, Harper, then Chase. On the plateau below, the embers of dying campfires glowed in the night. She couldn't see Michael's tent, but she knew it was among those on the opposite side of the wide, open clearing.

She kept moving along behind Kil. A ways farther, he stopped and turned, tapped her on the shoulder, then disappeared on down the trail. Harper hunkered down among the stiff mountain scrub, getting into position. Chase squeezed her shoulder as he passed and continued down the trail.

She was already counting by the time he was out of sight. Her heart beat hard as she readied the first grenade, gripping the flash bang tightly in her hand, her palm a little sweaty. She took a deep breath. She was ready for this. She had a job to do and so did the men.

Harper kept counting, repeating a silent prayer that all of them would make it out safely.

Michael lay in the darkness, Pia cocooned spoon-fashion against him. After the commandant had left, she had succumbed to a heavy alcohol-induced sleep. It wasn't until several hours later that she had awoken. Silently, she had left the mat, used the washbasin to cleanse herself, then pulled on her baggy fatigues instead of her yellow skirt and blouse.

It made his chest hurt to think she was hiding herself from him.

Quietly, Michael pulled on his twill pants and work shirt and walked up behind her. He hadn't used a condom. He hadn't had one.

He settled his hands on her shoulders, gently turned her to face him. "If...something happens because of today...you don't have to worry. I'll be there for you, Pia. No matter what."

She eased away from him. "It's all right. It wasn't the right time of month. I should be okay."

"We," he corrected. "Whatever happens, we're in this together."

Pia made no reply.

"We just have to make it one more day," he said. "Tomorrow night we're leaving."

She looked up at him, and some of the dullness faded from her eyes. She nodded. Her resiliency was one of the reasons he had fallen in love with her.

The hours slowly passed. Michael had worried that Velasquez might return with some of his men, but no one had come. A tray had been brought to the tent and left for them. They shared a portion of meat and fruit, and eventually returned to the woven mat and went back to sleep.

Now, as he lay in the darkness, Pia sleeping beside him, he listened to the sounds of the camp, mostly quiet this late. For hours he had gone over the escape plan for tomorrow night during the celebration, imagined ways he could slip into the commandant's tent, how he would find Velasquez drunk, passed out with one of his whores. Imagined stealing his knife and using it to cut his throat.

Imagined the heady feel of revenge.

He must have drifted to sleep. It took a moment for him to identify the faint noise that awoke him, someone moving around behind the tent. His instincts went on alert as a long serrated blade poked through the canvas and began to slice upward.

Rolling off the mat, he quietly hurried to the barrel, grabbed the handle of the cut-crystal water pitcher, hurried back and raised the pitcher over his head, prepared to strike whoever broke into the tent.

A soldier in full camo and tactical gear ducked through the opening, his hand shooting up to blocking the blow.

"Take it easy, Mikey," a familiar voice said, a voice he hadn't heard in years. "We're going to get you out of here."

The water pitcher trembled in his hand. "My God. Chase?"

Chase gripped his shoulder as a second soldier entered the tent through the flap in front, as tall as Chase, maybe taller. The soldier grinned, a flash of white against a black-painted face. "Good to see you, dude."

"Brandon! Man, you have no idea." Bran slapped him on the back and the solid contact felt amazingly good. "I can't believe you two are here."

Pia stirred on the mat. "What's happening?" She jumped up and ran to Michael, who caught her against him.

"It's okay, honey. Chase and Bran are friends. They're going to get us out of here."

She sagged in his arms.

"We need to move," Chase said. "Put some shoes on and get ready to leave."

Michael grabbed his boots and herded Pia over to hers.

They hurriedly put them on, and Chase motioned them toward the opening he'd sliced in the back of the tent.

Chase held up his hand in a signal to wait. He must have been counting the whole time because he said, "One thousand two hundred ninety-nine. One thousand three hundred." An explosion rocked the camp, and Michael's eyes shot to Chase's.

"Time to go," Chase said.

Michael urged Pia forward, following Chase out through the hole in the tent, Brandon right behind them. But as they started along the trail, Michael thought of Benito Velasquez.

"I'll catch up with you," he said. "There's something I have to do."

Brandon blocked his way. "There isn't time. You need to keep moving."

"I'm not leaving until Benito Velasquez is dead. It's personal. Take care of Pia."

"Michael, please," Pia begged.

Brandon just shook his head. "Sorry, bro. Not gonna happen."

Michael swallowed. Bran was right. He couldn't risk Pia's safety, couldn't put all of them in danger. Burying his hatred, he nodded, turned and started up the trail behind Chase, the man who was, apparently, still his best friend.

The path skirted the perimeter of the camp, winding farther and farther away from the soldiers scurrying like mice out of their tents at the brilliant flash of light and explosive roar of another grenade.

Chase kept moving, Pia and Michael behind him. Bran silently veered off the path, heading into the darkness to provide cover while Chase led the way along the narrow game trail they had scouted earlier in the day. Staying low and out of sight, he pressed forward, edging up the hill, making his way toward the huge granite outcropping at the top of the ridge.

More grenades flashed and exploded, each tossed from a different location, landing where they were least expected, the soldiers swarming, running haphazardly into each other, certain they were under attack.

Chase fought down his worry for Harper. She was doing her job. She was smart and determined. He had to trust that she would be okay. Grenade number four exploded. Number five. A few seconds later, number six. Just the way they'd planned. Chase felt a surge of pride.

Spotting Killian up ahead signaling for them to continue on past him, Chase urged Pia and Michael up the steepest section of the trail toward the rendezvous point. Harper should be moving that way, too. Chase prayed she would be waiting for them when they got there.

Instead, when they reached the giant boulder at the top of the ridge, there was no sign of her.

Worry sank into his chest. Leaving Michael and Pia with Killian, he angled back down the hill toward the spot where the last grenade had been tossed. He spotted her in the darkness, fighting two rebel soldiers, one of them shorter than she was, both of them muscular, powerful and ruthless.

With her cap gone, her hair gleamed silver gold in the moonlight. She was a prize any man would want, and those two were determined to have her. Chase's protective instincts kicked in, goading him to rush in and deal with the men, but he couldn't afford to make a mistake. If he did, all of them would be dead.

Clamping hard on his fury, he slowed and circled,

watched as Harper's hiking boot shot out and smashed into a soldier's face, felt a rush of satisfaction at the spray of blood erupting from the man's broken nose. The second soldier viciously slapped her, grabbed a handful of hair and dragged her down on the ground.

Chase fought a fresh rush of fury. The soldier used his body to pin Harper to the ground while the first man unbuckled his belt, unzipped the fly of his uniform pants and freed himself.

Chase stepped up and drove his Ka-Bar knife hard into the soldier's torso. He was dead before he hit the ground. Moving behind the other man, Chase wrapped an arm around his neck and squeezed, cutting off his air supply and any sound he might make. Dragging him off Harper, he let the man's lifeless body sag to the dirt.

He couldn't leave the man alive. Couldn't let him live to tell which escape route the prisoners had taken. If they did, the entire Los Proscritos army would be on their tail.

Harper scrambled to her feet, her eyes locked on the two dead bodies on the ground. Chase gripped her arm and spun her around, gave her a nudge up the trail. "We need to go, baby. Now."

She stumbled, righted herself, took a long, shuddering breath, then fixed her gaze ahead and started up the nearly invisible game trail that led into the trees at the edge of the plateau.

"Keep going," he commanded once they were out of sight, taking the lead on the path. "Don't look back."

Harper took a deep breath and settled into her usual steady pace, keeping up with Chase's long strides. Below them, he could hear the sound of gunfire, soldiers shooting at whatever unknown enemy they imagined.

He almost smiled.

He paused for a moment out of sight behind a tree, gently wiped a trickle of blood off Harper's lip. The man who'd hit her was lucky he was already dead.

"You okay?"

She nodded.

By now, Kil would have Michael and Pia farther up the mountain toward the landing zone, where, with any luck, the helicopter would be arriving very soon. Brandon would stay behind, waiting for them at the rendezvous point to provide cover.

Chase stiffened as a shadow moved into the trail up ahead. He signaled Harper to drop down out of sight and was about to move into position to eliminate the threat when he recognized the flash of white that was his brother's infamous grin.

"You two okay?" Bran asked.

"You were supposed to wait at the rendezvous point."

Bran just shrugged. "So sue me. Let's go."

Chase's lips curved. He wasn't really surprised. Family meant everything to the Garrett brothers. Any one of them would trade his life to protect the other. Bran needed to be sure Chase was safe. Which also went for Harper, since she was under Chase's protection.

They didn't encounter any more trouble the rest of the way to the LZ, a spot in a clearing wide enough for the chopper to land. Once they got there, all they had to do was stay alive till the helicopter showed up at dawn, half an hour away.

Which, with an army of rebel soldiers searching the woods to find them, might not be that easy.

CHAPTER TWENTY-ONE

Standing out of sight at the edge of the clearing, Harper hugged her brother hard. "I've been so worried. I was afraid we'd be too late."

Michael hugged her back. "I can't believe you're really here."

"Someone had to find you, so Chase and I came."

Michael reached over and gripped Chase's shoulder. "I could always count on you. I can see that hasn't changed. No matter what happened, you were always my best friend."

"It's good to see you," Chase said, drawing him in and clamping him on the shoulder. "I'm glad you're both safe."

Michael introduced Chase and Harper to Pia, who hugged them both and wiped away tears. "Thank you for coming to find us."

Harper smiled. "It was a group effort." She introduced Killian and Bran, not pointing out that they weren't out of danger yet.

They spent the remaining time out of sight in the forest. As dawn approached, they grouped together, Harper crouched next to Chase, waiting out the final minutes, straining to hear the sound of the chopper on its way to pick them up.

Unfortunately, as gray light began to slide through the trees, the sound that reached them was an army of men moving through the woods, getting closer and closer, the soldiers relentlessly making their way up the side of the hill.

Harper searched the sky. "Where is it?" she whispered.

"Should be here any minute," Chase said. But the minutes ticked past and the soldiers kept coming.

Then, just as the *whop whop whop* of a chopper cut through the crisp mountain air, a barrage of gunfire erupted as the soldiers spotted the helo and realized their quarry was about to escape.

"Get down!" Chase shouted, pushing Harper to the ground while he ducked down beside her, aimed his pistol and began to fire. The first two soldiers cresting the rise went down.

"Give me a pistol!" Michael demanded, and Killian pressed a gun into her brother's hand. Michael fired, wounding one of the rebels. Kil laid down a stream of bullets from his automatic weapon, taking out the entire front line of the rebel force.

Blazing away with his carbine, Brandon took out three soldiers running toward them, scattering the rest of the men, who began to retreat back down the hill. Behind them the helicopter was dropping into position, blades spinning, ready to pick them up.

"Go!" Chase commanded. "Get your brother and Pia aboard the chopper!"

Staying low, Harper urged them into the clearing, and the three of them raced for the helicopter. Michael loaded Pia aboard and turned to help Harper, but she noticed a soldier in a dark green uniform rushing toward them, firing in their direction.

Ignoring a rush of fear, Harper jerked her Ruger, braced, gripped the gun in both hands and began pulling the trigger. Her eyes widened when blood erupted on the soldier's chest and he went down. Dear God, she had actually hit him!

"That was Velasquez!" Michael shouted. "That bastard deserves to be dead! I owe you, sis!"

There wasn't time to think about the man she had killed. She took a deep breath, aimed her pistol at the line of advancing soldiers, steadied her shaking hands, and she and Michael began firing together, providing cover for Killian, Chase and Brandon, who backed their way across the clearing.

Sporadic rifle fire pinged around the fuselage as Chase helped Harper aboard. She heard a shot and saw Michael go down, and fear tore through her. Then Chase was shoving him into the helo and following him inside, Kil and Bran leaping in behind him as the chopper lifted away.

Bullets pinged off the metal wheel struts, but the helicopter rapidly gained ground. It swept down into a ravine out of sight, then rose again over the mountains, gaining altitude and distance, soon flying too far away for rebel bullets to reach.

Harper grabbed Chase's shoulder. "Michael's hit!"

she yelled above the roar of the engine. But Kil was already working over him.

"Flesh wound," Kil said nonchalantly, cutting away the leg of Michael's dirty twill pants. *Flesh wound? Seriously? He actually said that?*

"Took one in the thigh," Kil continued. "Doesn't look too bad. Don't think it hit anything vital." Meaning not the deadly femoral artery, thank God.

Grabbing a set of headphones, Chase spoke to the pilot, then turned to Harper. "Chopper's taking Michael directly to the Santa Marta hospital. It won't take long to get there."

Harper relaxed against Chase's hard body, felt his arm go around her. "We made it, angel. You were amazing out there."

She looked at him and thought how dear he had become. She thought of how close they had all come to dying. She thought about the man she had shot and that her brother and Pia were safe, and emotion welled in her chest.

"I think I'm going to cry," she said, resting her head on Chase's shoulder. "I'm sorry."

She sniffed, and he eased her more fully into his arms. "Cry all you want, sweetheart. You've earned it."

Which was all she needed to steel herself, drag in a shaky breath and suck up her courage. She swallowed past the lump in her throat. "I'm okay."

"That you are, angel," Chase said, laughing. "That you are." Catching her chin, he leaned in and kissed her, not a soft, sweet, friendly little kiss, but a deep, demanding, grateful-to-be-alive kiss that had her toes curling in her boots and her arms going around Chase's neck.

They were safe. And they were going home. The danger was over. But so was her time with Chase.

Her brother was going to be all right. Michael's injury had required minimal surgery, and he had been released from Hospital Universitario late in the afternoon. Harper was finally able to stop worrying about him.

She had called her father as soon as the helicopter landed on the roof of the hospital in Santa Marta. Most of their gear had been left in the mountains, but all of them, except Michael and Pia, had managed to end up with their cell phones, their personal lifelines.

"Hi, Dad, it's me."

"Where are you, Harper?"

"I'm still in Colombia, Dad, but we found Michael. Rebel soldiers were holding him captive at their camp in the mountains. He was shot as we were escaping, but he's going to be okay."

"I never got a ransom call, Harper. If I had, you know I would have paid."

"I know, Dad. I'm just so grateful Michael's safe."

"We all are. You know that, Harper. You've always been there for your brother. I hope he appreciates what you've done."

"Of course he does." She wished her father would show a little more concern, but it just wasn't his way. "I'll call you when I get back to Dallas."

"You'll be there for my birthday party, won't you?"

It seemed like the wrong time to mention it, but it was always important to him. The party next week was a glamorous, no-expense-spared yearly event attended by the who's who of Dallas, a way to bolster Knox Winston's all-important social status. At least it was good for Harper's business.

"I'll be there. Bye, Dad."

She hung up without promising her father that Michael would call him. The two had been estranged for years. Apparently that wasn't going to change.

Her next call went to Shana. Her friend was relieved that the rescue mission was successful, that Harper was safe and on her way back home. Afterward, Pia used Harper's phone to call Christy. Pia had cried on the phone when she talked to her friend, and Harper had a hunch Christy was crying on the other end of the line.

Pia kept her emotions in check when she spoke to her parents. Harper guessed she didn't want them to know how bad it had really been.

While they were at the hospital, Reese Garrett had called for an update on events. The good news was the Garrett Resources jet would be arriving to pick them up first thing in the morning, returning them to Dallas after a brief stop in Miami to drop Pia off, and one in Houston for Michael.

Her brother hadn't said much. He seemed torn between gratitude that Pia was safe and despair that she would be returning to Miami. Pia was a beautiful girl, amazingly strong and very sweet. Harper had a feeling her brother had fallen hard for the petite little brunette.

Harper had hoped Michael might stay with her in Dallas a couple of days, give his leg a chance to heal, but he declined, saying he needed to get back to work.

At the hospital, while Michael was being treated, they'd taken a cab to a department store a few blocks away to pick up some clothes and a few necessities. They planned to shower and change as soon as they reached the place Reese had arranged for them to stay, a cluster of oceanfront two-bedroom bungalows at what Santa Marta called a luxury resort on Zuana Beach.

For their last night together, Pia and Michael would be sharing the bungalow next to the one Harper was sharing with Chase. She could read the questions in her brother's eyes when he heard the news. Since she had no idea how to answer them, no idea what sort of relationship she and Chase actually had, she was grateful he didn't ask.

Even Killian would be staying the night, bunking with Brandon, glad for the chance to clean up and get some badly needed rest before heading back to whatever part of Colombia he had magically popped out of.

"You don't think he'll go after his Land Cruiser, do you?" Harper asked as she and Chase walked up on the porch of bungalow number ten, the thatch-roofed cottage they had been assigned. "If he does, the rebels might be waiting."

Chase turned the lock and held the door while she walked past him across the red tile entry into a living room decorated in a tropical motif. Ceiling fans stirred a gentle breeze, and a blue ocean lapped at the shore of the bay outside the windows.

"Don't worry about Kil," Chase said. "When Dawson walks out in the morning, he's going to find a shiny new Land Cruiser waiting in the parking lot."

"Oh, I should have thought of buying him one. You can add the cost to your bill, and I'll gladly pay for it." She could afford it. She rarely touched her inheritance. And she owed Kil Dawson so much. Owed all of the men so much, especially Chase.

"It's already taken care of," Chase said, tossing their

shopping bags up on the beige-and-white floral-print sofa. A tray of snacks and a bottle of wine sat on the white wicker coffee table. "There's not going to be any bill, angel. It's been my honor to help you find your brother."

Her throat tightened. "Chase…" She knew the money wasn't important to him—he had more than enough of his own. She just wished there was some way to repay him for what he had done. Chase had helped her find Michael, and he had protected her. She hadn't the slightest doubt he would have given his life before he would have let anyone hurt her.

He was exactly the hero she had imagined him to be all those years ago. Tonight was their last night together. She had no idea whether she would see him after they got back to Dallas, no idea if Chase felt any of the things she felt for him.

Tonight, she didn't care. Not if he wanted her, too.

"I need to take a shower," she said softly, her eyes on his face.

Chase didn't look away. "Me, too." The heat was there, simmering between them, yet he made no move to touch her. He was leaving it up to her…if she had the courage to take what she wanted.

"These older hotels," she said softly. "There isn't always enough hot water. Maybe we should…share."

Hunger rose like a dark cloud moving across his features, and the gold in his eyes seemed to glitter. He tipped his head back and drew in a deep breath, as if he wanted to make sure he got it right before speaking.

"I want you, angel. More than I've ever wanted a woman. But once we're back in Dallas, things are going to get…complicated. Your family and mine. There's no way it could ever work."

She didn't believe it. If he cared enough, they could find a way. It didn't matter. Not tonight. She couldn't make him fall in love with her, but she could have this night with him, a single night to remember.

"I don't care. I've never felt this way about a man before. I've never felt this kind of need."

"Harper…baby…" His hand stroked her cheek. She was tall, but Chase was taller. Going up on her toes, she leaned in and pressed her lips to his. Strong arms came around her, hauling her against a hard-muscled chest, and his mouth crushed down over hers.

She knew the taste of him, remembered it from the last time he had kissed her, remembered the feel of his lips, soft yet determined, taking what he wanted, giving her pleasure in return.

He kissed the side of her neck, nipped an earlobe, kissed her again. "Are you sure, honey? I'd cut off my arm before I hurt you."

She wasn't sure about anything but this clawing need unlike anything she had ever known. "I want you, Chase. Please…"

He slid his hands into her hair and tilted her head back, kissed her long and deep, kissed her until she could barely breathe. She could feel the rough edge of beard along his jaw, and a slice of hunger burned through her.

Scooping her into his arms, Chase carried her down the hall into the bathroom. The minute her feet hit the floor, Harper reached for the hem of his camouflage T-shirt and stripped it off over his head, leaving his gorgeous chest bare. Beneath the ladder of muscle across his flat stomach, his camo pants hung low on his hips. Hard muscle rippled every time he moved.

Chase pulled her back into his arms and kissed her, a hot, wet, saturating kiss that seemed to have no end. His tongue slid over hers, hers tangled with his, and heat rolled through her. Desire unfolded low in her belly, and moisture collected between her legs. Chase pulled her black long-sleeved T-shirt over her head and tossed it away, unhooked her bra and slid it off her shoulders.

Filling his hands with her breasts, he bent his head and took a hard tip into his mouth and bit the end, suckled and tasted until her knees went weak.

Harper moaned.

Still, as he reached for the snap on her jeans, nerves suddenly struck and uncertainty trembled through her body.

Chase paused. "What is it, baby?"

"I'm just… I want you to like the way I look." She was a slender woman, her breasts not that big.

Chase caught her chin, bent his head and kissed her. "I like everything about you, angel. Everything." And then he was stripping away her clothes, cupping the back of her head to hold her in place as he ravished her mouth.

He paused long enough to turn on the shower and strip off his own clothes, then stepped into the warm spray and pulled her in beside him. Chase soaped his hands and they began to roamed slickly over her body— her breasts, her belly, her hips—sliding into forbidden places, making her hot all over.

Her hands moved over his amazing body, fingertips slipping wetly over sinew, dipping into muscular valleys, down his flat belly. She loved touching him. She could touch him for hours.

Chase shampooed her hair and his own. They rinsed beneath the warm spray and then he was kissing her again, lifting her as if she weighed nothing, wrapping her long legs around his waist. He was thick and hard, nudging the entrance to her passage.

"I've dreamed of this," he said, kissing her as he slid himself deeply inside. "It seems like I've wanted you forever."

Harper moaned. Her arms went around his neck and she clung to him as he started to move, gripping her bottom to hold her in place as he surged into her.

Fierce, determined thrusts went faster, deeper, harder, and a soft moan escaped. Her skin felt slick and tight. Her body burned. She felt a hot, deep pull low in her belly, like strings being drawn tight, then pleasure erupted. Heat roared through her as she flashed into climax, crying out his name.

Chase didn't stop, not until she reached a second powerful explosion. With a low, guttural growl deep in his throat, he let himself go, his muscles going rigid as he followed her to release.

Long seconds passed, their hearts pounding, their skin slick and wet. The water began to cool. Chase set her back on her feet and turned off the faucet. He stepped out of the shower and helped her out, handed her a towel while he dried himself and dealt with the condom she hadn't realized he had put on.

With towels wrapped around them, he led her over to the stool in front of the dressing table. She was only a little surprised when he took out the brush she had purchased in town and began to pull it through her hair.

They didn't talk, didn't say a word. She wondered

if he would sleep in her room or spend the night in the room next door, but when she looked into his eyes, she knew.

The heat was back, hotter than before. "You look surprised. You didn't think I'd want you again?"

"I wasn't... I wasn't sure."

She gasped as he lifted her into his arms, carried her into the nearest bedroom and settled her in the big king-size bed. "So you're sleeping in here?" she asked softly, just to be sure.

He ran a finger down her cheek. "I don't think we'll be doing much sleeping. If tonight's all I've got, I'm going to make it one we both remember."

The next hour passed in a haze of heat and pleasure. Afterward they dozed for a while. The clock said midnight when they stirred. Under the gentle breeze created by the soft whir of the ceiling fan, her hair was almost dry. Chase slid his fingers through it.

"Like silk," he said. Leaning over, he kissed her. "I want you, angel. I can't seem to get enough."

Exhausted as they both were after their grueling days in the mountains, they made love two more times before morning.

As Chase had promised, it was a night Harper would never forget.

CHAPTER TWENTY-TWO

It didn't feel right, saying goodbye to Pia at the airport. Not after all they had been through together. But the jet was waiting on the tarmac, and Pia's friend Christy had driven in to pick her up. The tearful reunion between the two friends only made Michael feel worse.

"Give me a minute, Christy," Pia said to her friend. "I'll meet you inside."

"No problem." Christy smiled. "Bye, Michael. Thank you for keeping Pia safe. I'm so glad you're both okay."

He was mostly okay. His leg hurt like bloody blazes, but he'd left his crutches on the plane. He didn't want Pia remembering him as an invalid.

He waited till Christy was on her way to the executive terminal and he and Pia were alone on the tarmac. A warm wind whipped the simple pink blouse and jeans Pia had bought in Santa Marta. She looked beautiful.

Last night they had slept in the same bed, but they

hadn't made love. "I can't, Michael," she'd said. "Please understand."

He understood completely. At least she had let him hold her.

He glanced down at the gauze bandage around his thigh, saw a hint of red seeping through. Harper had tried to get him to stay on the plane, but he had refused. He needed to do this, wanted to be with Pia a little longer.

"I'm sorry for everything," he said to her. "If I could change what happened, I would."

"I know that. It wasn't your fault."

"I don't want us to be over, Pia. Tell me you want to see me again."

Her big brown eyes filled with tears. "I need some time, Michael. I just… I want to forget everything that happened. I want it to all be in the past, but when I look at you, I remember."

She didn't resist when Michael drew her into his arms and buried his face in her warm dark hair. "Pia…"

She cried against his shoulder and clung to him as if she didn't want to leave him, but then she broke away.

"Please don't call me. Not for a while. I just… I need to figure things out."

He swallowed. "If that's what you want."

"Christy's waiting. I have to go. I'm sorry."

He caught her face between his hands and very gently kissed her. For a moment, Pia kissed him back. Then she pulled away. "Take care of yourself, Michael."

He wanted to tell her he loved her, but he couldn't. Not when looking at him made her remember all the horror she had suffered, all the pain and fear during the days they'd been held captive. Made her remember

Benito Velasquez's sick attentions and how Michael had failed her.

"Goodbye, Pia."

Tears rolled down her cheeks as she turned and hurried across the tarmac to her friend. Michael watched her disappear inside the terminal, a crushing pain in his chest.

The throbbing in his leg grew worse as he climbed the steps to the Garrett jet. His sister was waiting.

"You okay?" Harper asked.

"No." He looked at her. There were shadows in her eyes, just like the ones that darkened his own. When he glanced over at Chase, he knew what had caused them. "How about you?"

She smiled at him sadly. "I'll be okay. As long as we have each other, we'll both be okay."

Michael managed to come up with a smile. So did Harper. He returned to his seat, and Harper sat back down next to Chase. He didn't know what was going on between the two, but neither of them looked happy.

He thought about talking to his sister, trying to help her figure things out, but Harper wasn't a kid anymore. Whatever was happening between her and Chase was none of his business. He just hoped neither of them would get hurt.

Halfway through the flight, Chase came over and sat down beside him. Michael had been hoping they would have a chance to talk.

"How are you holding up?" Chase asked. "You're bleeding a little. How bad are you hurting?"

Michael scoffed. "My leg hurts like hell. I'll take a couple of pain pills and be okay." He rested a hand over his heart. "I feel worse in here. I really messed things up with Pia."

"It was a bad situation for both of you. Give her some time. Maybe things will work out."

"I'm not giving up. I love her, Chase."

"Yeah, I could see that every time you looked at her."

"I'll give her some space, let her sort things out, then I'm going after her."

Chase smiled. "I like the new you. You're not a quitter."

"I learned that lesson when I got clean and sober. Even if things don't work out with Pia, I'll never go down that road again."

Chase nodded his approval. "Harper tells me your company is doing really well. I'm glad for you, Michael."

"Thanks. I've thought about our friendship over the years. I want you to know I regret what I did to destroy it."

"Those days are over. You've changed your life, become the man you were meant to be. That's all any of us ever wanted for you."

Michael's eyes misted. "Thanks for saying that." He smiled. "I hear you've got your own security business, doing exactly what you always wanted."

"That's right. Maximum Security. We've got branches in Phoenix and San Diego."

"Sounds like a lot of work."

"The employees are all independent contractors. The way it's set up, each office is pretty much self-sufficient."

"You always did have a head for business."

"And you had a knack for computers."

"I miss our friendship, Chase. I hope we can stay in touch."

"We'll make a point of it. When things settle down, we'll pick a date, spend a few days out at the ranch."

"That'd be great." Michael didn't ask Chase's intentions toward his sister. He wasn't sure he approved. Chase had always had a legion of women. Until now, he'd kept his distance from Harper. But they had spent last night together, and he didn't think they had slept in separate rooms.

Time would tell.

In the meantime, Michael had problems of his own.

Night settled around the sprawling Spanish-style villa on forty acres of tropical hillside overlooking Santa Marta and the sea.

In his huge oak-paneled study, Luis Montoya sat in front of the hearth, drinking a glass of Napoleon brandy from a Baccarat crystal snifter. So far the expensive alcohol had done nothing to improve his mood.

"I'll find him." Joining him in the drink, his *segundo*, Eduardo Ramos, shifted in the burgundy wingback chair across from him. "I'll have Michael Winston brought back for you to deal with as you wish."

Ramos was the man he relied on for everything from flowers for his mistress to disciplining an insubordinate employee. What Ramos didn't handle personally, he delegated with ultimate authority, and there was nothing he wouldn't do.

Luis set the snifter down on the ornate table next to his chair. "I don't want him back. It's clear Winston's son means little or nothing to him. It's the girl I want.

She killed my cousin." His hand slammed down on the rolled arm of the chair. "I want Benito avenged!"

Luis calmed himself. He had a volatile temper. He was a solid man, not obese but at least thirty pounds overweight. It wasn't good for his heart to get too excited. "Once we have her, we'll find out if the girl is worth something to Winston."

"Ransom?"

"Perhaps. According to the information I received from our friends in Punta Gato, the girl is quite a beauty. Perhaps I'll enjoy her myself. If Winston meets our terms, we'll return her—broken and dishonored. That should send a message and tell him what will happen should he try to go against me again."

The edge of a smile curved Eduardo's thin lips. With his pockmarked complexion and hawklike nose, he was not a handsome man. But he was smart, cunning and ruthless, perfect for Luis's needs.

"As always, *mi jefe*, you have devised the perfect plan."

Luis took a sip of his brandy. "In the meantime, we'll resume our business relationship. Winston wishes to continue as we were before, and I see no reason not to. We will make money, and once we have the girl, we will also have control."

Ramos smiled. He took a last drink of brandy, finishing off his glass, and set the snifter down. "I shall begin making inquiries. It may take a while, but in time, my men and I will succeed and the girl will be yours."

Luis watched Ramos walk out of his study. Luis wasn't usually a patient man, but some things were worth the wait. In the meantime, he would return to business as usual—at least for a while. Luis never wasted an opportunity to make money.

But sooner or later, Winston would pay—of that there was no doubt.

Rising from the chair, he walked over to his oak desk, sat down and turned on the computer resting on the credenza behind it. It didn't take long to find his quarry. Harper Winston, co-owner of Elemental Chic, some kind of clothing company. There was a photo of the girl on the webpage. Tall and slender, with long blond hair and big blue eyes.

His shaft thickened as he began to go hard. He stroked a hand over the zipper of his slacks. Pulling out his cell, he phoned his mistress. Lupita would do for now, relieve some of the frustration he'd been feeling since news of Michael Winston's escape and his cousin's death had reached him.

Soon he would have the girl. He would take her, use her a dozen different ways.

He found himself smiling. Yes…there were times Luis could be a very patient man.

CHAPTER TWENTY-THREE

Two days had passed since Chase's return to Dallas. Two days since he had last seen Harper or had any contact. When the Garrett Resources Citation CJ4 had touched down at Dallas Executive Airport, Chase's insanely efficient brother Reese had a black stretch limousine waiting.

Reggie Porter had sat behind the wheel, a big, beefy African American former army ranger who owned the car and often drove for one Garrett brother or another. Since Brandon's black hardtop Jeep Wrangler waited in the parking lot where he had left it, he hadn't needed a ride.

Harper had walked over to Bran to say goodbye. "Thank you for everything." Sliding her arms around his neck, she'd hugged him. Bran had hugged her back a little longer than necessary, winked at Chase and grinned.

"It was my pleasure," Bran had said. With a final

wave at Chase, he turned and sauntered off toward the parking lot.

"Let's get you home." Chase had settled Harper in the backseat of the limo, slid in beside her and closed the door. Reggie started the engine and pushed the button to put up the partition, giving them privacy, and drove the limo out of the terminal, heading for Harper's town house.

She'd shifted on the deep red leather seat to look up at him. "I can't thank you enough, Chase. I'll never be able to repay you for—"

"You don't have to thank me, Harper. You and Michael needed help. I helped. We're friends. That's what friends do."

She'd swallowed and glanced away. "Will I see you again?"

His chest had tightened. He wanted to see her again. He wanted her back in his bed. After the previous night, he'd felt as if she belonged to him, that he had claimed her in some way. It made him feel sick inside to know he would have to give her up.

He'd reached down and caught her hand where it rested on the seat. "It's a bad idea, honey. You know it and so do I."

"I'm a grown woman, Chase. I don't care if my father approves of the men I sleep with or not. It's my decision, not his."

He'd almost smiled. "You make it sound like there's an army of them."

Color had risen in her cheeks. It had made him want to kiss her. "You know what I mean."

There hadn't been an army of men. From what he could tell, not even a handful. She was a novice of sorts. Which only made the hours he had spent with her sweeter.

He'd wanted to say he would call her. He wasn't nearly ready to give her up. But after what Brandon had discovered in Colombia—information his brother would feel obligated to pass on to the authorities—things were going to get dicey.

As if to prove it, when the limo had rounded the corner, a dark green Bentley sat in front of Harper's two-story brick town house.

"Oh, no. My father's here." She'd looked at him with those big blue eyes, and everything inside him clenched. "He knows where I hide the key. He'll be inside waiting for me."

And just that fast, he'd known it was over. As Reggie pulled the limo up to the curb, he'd cupped her face in his hands and very softly kissed her.

"Maybe someday things will be different, but right now…" *I may have a hand in putting your father in prison.*

But he couldn't say that. Harper had no idea the sort of criminal activities her father was involved in, no idea what the future might hold.

Reggie had gotten out and opened the limo door. Chase had exited the vehicle and helped Harper out. "If you ever need me, just call and I'll be there. I promise you that. No matter what it is, I'll be there."

She straightened, steeling herself as she had during those difficult days in the jungle. "Goodbye, Chase."

"Goodbye, angel."

Turning, she'd started up the concrete path to the door of her town house. Chase had watched her till she disappeared inside, then climbed back into the car. As the limo rolled off down the street, it was impossible to be missing her already, but he did.

Over the next few days, he thought of her a dozen times. At night, he remembered the way it had felt to touch her, kiss her, be inside her, and an ache rose hot and hard in his loins. He wasn't sleeping well, was going to work tired and out of sorts, the way he was today.

At least Jason Maddox and the temp receptionist, Mindy Stewart, had kept the place running smoothly while he and his brother were gone. He wanted to talk to Mindy, offer her a permanent position. He was reaching for the intercom to call her into his office when the speaker buzzed and her voice came over the line.

"Brandon's here with a friend, Chase. He asked me to let you know they need to speak to you."

"Tell them to come on back." Even before he'd completed the sentence, the door swung open and his brother walked in. So much for office protocol.

A tall, good-looking guy dressed in jeans and a scuffed leather bomber jacket walked in behind Bran and closed the door. Well built, dark hair buzzed short and dark eyes.

"Chase, this is DEA Special Agent Zach Tanner," Bran said. "Zach and I served together in the army." Bran was thirty-two. Chase put Tanner around the same age. "I gave him the info I ran across in Colombia, including Knox Winston's involvement with one of the major cocaine dealers in the country. We kicked around some ideas. Zach's hoping you can help."

Chase rose from behind his desk, reached over and shook Tanner's hand. "Good to meet you, Agent Tanner."

"You're Brandon's brother—that makes it just Zach whenever possible."

Chase nodded. He'd been expecting something like this. Bran had been deployed in South America. He hated drug smugglers and the lowlifes who dealt drugs on the street. He'd seen firsthand the evil it could do.

Chase thought of Michael and the years his friend had suffered from addiction. He thought of the sad people his work brought him in contact with in the alleys and drug dens of Dallas. Chase had seen the evil, too.

"Why don't you two sit down and tell me what I can do for you?"

The men sat in the brown leather chairs opposite Chase, Bran stretching out his long legs. "Knox Winston's been on our watch list for years," Zach Tanner began. "Unfortunately, we've never been able to connect him directly to smuggling, or gather enough evidence to end his distribution network. If we can find out who he's connected with in Colombia, we might be able to bring him down."

"No one deserves it more," Chase said.

"The DEA needs proof," Bran said. "The question is would you be willing to help?"

"Winston belongs in prison. Anything I can do to make that happen works for me."

Tanner smiled, but his brother's grin was missing, which put Chase on alert. "What are you two not telling me?"

"Zach thinks Harper could be the key to bringing Winston down," Bran said.

"I understand Winston's daughter came to you for help finding her brother."

"That's right."

"The two of you traveled to Colombia together. You

found Michael and helped his sister bring him home. That puts her in your debt."

He didn't like the direction the conversation was taking. "And you want me to do…what, exactly?"

"Continue your…friendship," Tanner said. "Use her to get close to Winston."

Chase shook his head. "No way. I'm not dragging Harper into this. As far as I can tell, she has no idea the kind of enterprise her father runs. She's got her own life, her own career. Aside from Winston being her sire, she has very little to do with him."

"Just hear me out," Zach said.

"I'm sorry. I'll do what I can, but leave Harper out of it."

Bran rose from his chair, leaned forward and braced his hands on the desk. "I know you have feelings for Harper, but you got into law enforcement to catch bad guys. I know that hasn't changed." He straightened. "You remember that guy you busted down in Old East Dallas, Ray Martinez? The guy pimping the underage girl?"

"I remember him. Far as I know, he's still in jail. What's Martinez got to do with this?"

"Martinez isn't just a pimp, he's a dealer," Zach said. "He gets his product from a guy named Perry Speers. Speers is part of a supply chain with links all over Texas and Louisiana. We think the man smuggling the drugs into the country and selling them to Speers is Knox Winston."

Chase swore softly.

Bran sat back down in his chair. "Winston's annual birthday gala is coming up on Saturday. Harper's father will undoubtedly expect her to be there. If you could get her to invite you—"

"First, Harper and I aren't seeing each other anymore," Chase said. "And even if we were, how does my going to the party solve your problem?"

Tanner stood up. "Give me a second and I'll show you." He left the office and came back a few minutes later carrying a brown paper sack. Reaching into the bag, he pulled out a tall silver box.

"Winston drinks single malt scotch," Tanner said. "He won't be able to resist this." He opened the cardboard lid, took out the contents and held it up. "This is twenty-five-year-old Dalmore single malt." He set the beautiful glass bottle on the desk. "Retails for nine hundred dollars."

"It's your birthday gift," Brandon explained. "You're there with his daughter, right? For Harper's sake, you're making a conciliatory gesture, trying to smooth things over between you and her dad."

"What's so special about this particular bottle?"

"It's bugged," Tanner said. "See that silver stag's head on the front? It's been hollowed out. There's a minuscule transmitter inside. Extremely powerful. Once the bottle is sitting on the bar in Winston's study, we can listen to every phone conversation, anything he says during meetings he might have. We'll know exactly who he's talking to and what's being said, and be able to record it all."

Chase mulled it over, feeling like a traitor for even considering it.

Brandon rose again, paced away from the desk and back. "We can nail the bastard, Chase. After all these years. You get that bug into his study, the DEA can find out who he's working with. They'll have enough proof for a search warrant. That could turn up something even more useful."

"We get evidence on one of his subordinates," Tanner added, "we can get them to roll on Winston."

He didn't want to do it. In the back of his mind, he still imagined spending time with Harper, exploring their relationship to see where it might lead. If he used her to go after her father, it would be over for good.

Chase walked around his desk to join the other two men. "This isn't an easy decision. I need time to think about it."

"You don't have time," Tanner said. "The birthday party is Saturday night. That's only a few days away."

"You're going to have to convince Harper to take you with her, bro, and that might not be as easy as you think."

Bran was right. He had cut his ties to Harper as cleanly as possible. Putting them back together wouldn't be easy. He didn't want to think of the lies he would have to tell.

Bran set a hand on his shoulder. "I know you don't want to do this, but you don't have any choice. It's what we do."

His chest tightened. *It's what we do.* His brother was right. Justice was the reason he got up in the morning. Knox Winston and his criminal associates had been dodging justice for years.

"All right, I'll try, but that's all I can promise. At this point, I'm not sure I can convince Harper to invite me, but I'll do my best."

"Oh, she'll invite you," Bran said. "If the sounds the

two of you were making in that bungalow was any indication, she'll invite you for sure."

Chase shot his brother a look.

Agent Tanner leaned over and slid his business
card under the edge of the bottle of scotch on the desk.
"Call me if you have any questions. Otherwise, I'll be
in touch." He stuck out his hand, and he and Chase
shook. "Good luck."

Chase watched his brother and the DEA agent leave
the office, heard the click of the door closing softly behind them and felt sick to his stomach. He cared about
Harper. He didn't want to hurt her. But he had agreed
to help.

He sat back down at his desk. Convincing Harper
might not be easy. He needed a few minutes to think
things through, figure out what to say. He'd tell Harper
the truth as much as he dared—tell her he couldn't stop
thinking about her. That much was sure as hell true.
He'd tell her he wanted to see her. Definitely the truth.

He ignored the part of his brain that was secretly glad
he had an excuse to call her. Another part that hoped
she would agree to see him.

Chase took a deep breath and pulled out his cell
phone. Still, it was an hour before he worked up the
courage to make the call. He wished he wasn't so eager
to hear the sound of her voice.

CHAPTER TWENTY-FOUR

Harper stood at the cutting table in the production room at the warehouse offices of Elemental Chic. Bolts of fabric in colors from tangerine to fuchsia, textures from denim to silk, covered every surface.

"It's really good to have you back," Shana said. "I managed to hold the fort while you were gone, but I didn't get much of my own work done." She was a beautiful woman, with high cheekbones and full lips, skin as dark and smooth as ebony. Shoulder-length black curls formed a halo around her face.

"I appreciate all the extra work," Harper said. "If Chase and I hadn't gone after Michael, I don't think he would have made it home alive."

"So…speaking of the infamous Chase Garrett, when do I get to meet him?"

Harper felt a pang in her heart. "Unless you run into him at a charity event or need him to investigate some-thing, the answer is never. He went to Colombia with me as a friend. We rescued Michael. Now we're back in Dallas and that's the end of it."

Shana frowned. "So you aren't seeing him anymore? Seems like you told me you used to crush on him big-time. I've seen his photo in the newspaper—the guy is hot. Are you saying he didn't live up to your expectations?"

Harper reached out and examined a length of neon-pink silk. "Chase was everything I imagined him to be and more."

Shana's black eyes widened, her all-too-perceptive gaze zeroing in on Harper. "Oh, my God, you slept with him! That's the reason you've been moping around ever since you got home. You don't think he's going to call you."

"He isn't. He doesn't think it's a good idea."

"Why not?"

"Because he and my father hate each other. My father and Chase's father were mortal enemies. Chase blames my dad for Michael's drug addiction. They fought about it. According to Chase, it wasn't pleasant. I have no idea what else there is between them, but the list seems long on both sides. To put it bluntly, Chase doesn't think I'm worth the trouble."

Shana huffed out a breath. "Then he's a fool. The man was lucky you gave him the time of day."

Harper smiled. "Thanks. I'll tell him that if I ever see him again." She sighed. "I should have been prepared for it to happen, and in a way I was. Chase has more women than he can count. I'm just another in a long list of conquests."

"Screw him. If he doesn't want to see you, it's his loss."

Letting the conversation drop, Harper returned her focus to the table. "We better get back to work. These fabrics aren't going to choose themselves."

"No, I guess not. Let's start with the denim. Which shade do you think we should go for? I kind of like the faded blue for a change. It's got some fresh possibilities."

Harper started to agree when her cell phone rang. She pulled it out of her jeans pocket and checked the caller ID. Her stomach knotted when she read Chase's name.

"It's him," she said to Shana, finding it ridiculously hard to breathe.

Shana grinned. "Guess the man isn't as big a fool as I thought."

Harper rolled her eyes. With a steadying breath, she pressed the phone against her ear. "Hello, Chase."

"Hello, angel. It's good to hear your voice."

It was good to hear his, too. "I didn't think you were going to call. You said it wasn't a good idea."

"I didn't think I was, and it isn't. But I can't seem to get you out of my mind."

"I've…umm…been thinking about you, too." Since Shana was still grinning, Harper walked over to the window, where her friend couldn't hear.

"I was wondering if maybe we could get together and talk," Chase said. "Maybe start all over again. You know, go out on a date or something. We could take our time, get to know each other."

"A date? You want to take me out on a date?"

"Yeah, angel, I do. I was thinking maybe tonight. We could go to the movies or dinner, do something normal."

Something normal. Oh, my God! She wanted to see

him in the worst way but, dammit, she had plans she couldn't change. "I can't go tonight. I have a business dinner."

"How about tomorrow night?"

"I've got clients in town." Silence fell. *Oh, God.* "What about Friday night?" She held her breath. Was she really this desperate to see him? Yes, she was.

"Friday would be great. The show or dinner?"

How about you take me straight to bed? But she didn't say that. "Dinner sounds good."

"Seven okay?"

"Perfect."

"Good, I'll see you then."

Harper still held the phone when Chase hung up. She was going to see him again. He wanted them to talk, get to know each other. Funny thing was, she felt as if she knew him better than any man she had ever met. He was honest and brave, he was a successful business-man, unbelievably sexy and amazing in bed. What else did she need to know?

She walked back to the cutting table. Shana was still grinning. "So you're seeing him again."

She nodded. "Friday night. He wants us to get to know each other."

"All right, Harper!"

For the first time since her return to Dallas, it was Harper's turn to grin.

It was Thursday, the office humming with activity. Chase had spoken to Mindy Stewart about working as a full-time receptionist, and she had happily accepted. One task completed.

He walked over to Maddox, who leaned back in the

chair behind his desk, his scuffed brown cowboy boots propped on top. At Chase's raised eyebrows, he swung his feet to the floor and flashed an unapologetic grin.

Jason was a big guy, six-four, two-hundred-plus pounds of solid muscle, with dark hair and blue eyes. He was a former spec ops marine and a notorious bounty hunter, the best in Texas. He was smart and reliable and way too reckless. But one way or another, Hawk Maddox always got his man.

"So what's up?" Jason asked.

"Just wanted to thank you for taking over while Bran was gone. Looks like you did a damn fine job."

"Yeah, well, I did my best. Running an office ain't exactly my cup of tea. I hate bein' cooped up." Maddox was a footloose kind of guy, which was one of the reasons he was good at his job. He'd bird-dog a bail skip to the end of the earth if that was what it took to make an arrest.

"Appreciate it," Chase said.

Maddox smiled. "Happy to help. Glad you were able to bring your friend back. Bran said he took a bullet but otherwise he's okay."

"He's healing. Nothing too serious. Unfortunately, he fell madly in love with the woman he was with down there. They're having some problems. He's trying to work things out."

Maddox grunted. "Woman trouble. I don't envy him that."

Chase thought of his upcoming date with Harper. He was about to have woman trouble of his own.

"Anything happen while I was gone I should know about?" Chase asked.

"Wolfe's been working a big case. Something to do

with a local politician. Got his hands full, I guess."
Jonah Wolfe was a former homicide detective, one of
the best PIs in Dallas.

"If anyone can handle it, Wolfe can," Chase said.
"Anything else?"

"Nah, just the usual."

Grateful nothing catastrophic had happened, Chase
waved over his shoulder as he headed back to his office.
He spent the most of the afternoon catching up on paperwork, trying not to think of Harper and pretty much
failing. Frustrated, he left his office for the back room
he'd had converted to a gym and changed into running
shorts and a T-shirt. He worked out for an hour, but it
didn't improve his mood.

Late in the day, a call came in from a guy named
Errol Dickerson, a referral from a former client.

"What can I do for you, Mr. Dickerson?" Chase said,
seated once more behind his desk.

"I think my son's wife murdered him," Dickerson
said. "I want you to find out the truth."

Chase sat up a little straighter. "What do the police
have to say?"

"They're calling it a heart attack. His wife had my
son's remains cremated just days after he died. There
was no autopsy. Things just don't add up."

"And you want me to look into it."

"That's right. I'm not a wealthy man, Mr. Garrett.
But I can afford to pay whatever you charge. Please.
I think there's a chance this woman is getting away
with murder."

"Can you come in first thing in the morning? We
open at eight."

"I'm out of town. I can be there first thing Monday."

"In a case like this, the sooner the better. I'll see you then." Evidence had a habit of slipping away. If the man's son had really been murdered, Chase wanted to find his killer.

Friday stretched endlessly but closing time finally arrived. He was taking Harper to supper, and he had come up with a plan. Unfortunately, it meant he wouldn't be sleeping with her anytime soon.

One thing he refused to do was take Harper to bed under false pretenses. He wanted her badly, but no way was he seducing her with lies.

He told himself when this was over, he'd find a way to make it up to her. He'd explain things, make her understand why he'd had to do what he'd done. If she still wanted to see him—sleep with him—he'd like nothing better than to take up where they'd left off in Colombia.

Unfortunately, as much as he wanted to believe it would all work out, the hard truth was, he didn't think he could ever convince her that using her to get to her father was something he had to do.

And he was pretty sure Harper would never forgive him.

Harper dressed with care for her date with Chase that Friday night. He was taking her to supper. He wanted to see her. She smiled. Lord knew she wanted to see him.

In a little black dress reminiscent of the one she had worn in Curaçao, she was surprised when instead of candlelight and expensive wine in a gourmet setting, the restaurant Chase chose was a lively Italian spot with red-checked tablecloths and heaping platters of pasta. Chianti jugs and bread baskets hung on the walls.

The food was good, though, terrific, in fact. And the

hearty red wine relaxed her. For the first half of the meal they made small talk, a case Chase had just taken that involved the possible murder of a man by his wife. He didn't name names, of course, but clearly he felt obligated to find out the truth.

They talked a little about fashion, the designs she and Shana were working on for the upcoming season. Chase was interested in business, so they talked about that angle and he didn't seem bored.

At the end of the meal, he reached across the table and took hold of her hand, laced his fingers with hers. "I brought you here for a reason, Harper."

"I like this place. It's fun and the food is great—and, of course, the company is top-notch." She flashed him a flirty smile and Chase smiled back.

"I would have taken you to Abacus or the Mansion at Turtle Creek, someplace like that, but I didn't want you to think I was trying to seduce you."

One of her eyebrows went up. "Really? You didn't think I'd want to be seduced?"

For a moment, heat glittered in his dark eyes. He let go of her hand as if touching her was too much of a temptation.

"There's nothing I want more than to take you to bed," he said. "Believe me, angel, one night with you wasn't nearly enough. But there are things that need to happen first."

"Like what?"

"If we're going to see each other, I don't want to lie about it. I'm not willing to sneak around so your father won't find out. It isn't fair to either one of us."

"I told you before, my father doesn't run my life."

"No? What do you think he'd say if he found out you were seeing me?"

She glanced away. Her dad would go ballistic.

"Listen, honey, this thing with your father needs to be resolved before we can move forward. Once that happens, our relationship can take its natural course."

She mulled that over. Chase seemed really serious. She knew her feelings for him ran deep, but she had no idea he felt the same way. Her heart swelled. Maybe there was hope for them yet.

"I've got an idea," she said, not sure it was a good one. "My father's birthday party is tomorrow night. He expects me to bring a date. I was trying to decide who to invite, but there wasn't anyone special I wanted to take, so I've been putting it off. Why don't you come with me? I mean, if...if you're serious about resolving this thing with my dad."

Something moved across his features, then it was gone. "You'd be willing to do that?"

"If you think it's a good idea."

He took hold of her hand once more. "All right. Let's do it. Since it's your dad's birthday, I'll bring him something special, some kind of peace offering. Maybe he'll at least be willing to accept the idea of us seeing each other."

Harper's mind spun. She could hardly believe it. Chase wanted her father to accept their relationship. He was willing to try to make peace. They could see each other openly. Her heart soared. She wanted that so badly.

"It's black-tie," she said. "It's always quite an event. A place on the guest list is highly prized."

His mouth curved into a smile. "There's a good chance he'll have me thrown out."

"He won't do that. You're Bass Garrett's son. You and your brothers own Garrett Resources. You're members of the Dallas elite. Having you at the party enhances his social status. That means everything to my father."

Chase nodded. "All right, then." He brought her hand to his lips and kissed the back. Goose bumps feathered over her skin. "What time shall I pick you up?"

"The party starts at eight. We don't want to get there too early." *Just in case.* She didn't believe her father would make a scene, but it would be safer if the guests were already there before they arrived.

"I'll be at your place at eight thirty. It'll take us a while to get there." He rose from his chair, walked around and helped her up. "Since seducing you tonight isn't an option, I'd better take you home. You, angel, are one helluva temptation."

And then he was walking her outside to the valet stand, holding open the door to his silver Mercedes and helping her slide into the passenger seat. At her town house, he walked her up on the porch.

"Are you sure you don't want to come in for a nightcap?"

Chase pulled her into his arms, bent his head and kissed her deeply. "Baby, if you had any idea how much I want to spend the night with you, you wouldn't need to ask. Let's get through this and get things settled. After that, you'll be lucky if I let you out of bed."

Harper laughed. She leaned up and kissed him. "I'll see you tomorrow night."

Chase looked at her for several long seconds. "Good

night, angel," he said softly, then waited for her to close and lock the door before he headed back to his car.

Harper grinned as she walked into her bedroom. She had tried to convince herself she wasn't in love with Chase Garrett, but it wasn't the truth.

For the first time since her return to Dallas, she was beginning to think there was a chance he might be falling in love with her, too.

Harper couldn't remember ever being so happy.

Sitting in his living room with the lights off, Chase took a sip of the whiskey in his glass and stared out through the plate-glass windows. The lights of Dallas flickered in the streets below him, a beautiful sight that, tonight, did nothing to lift his mood.

Harper had looked so beautiful tonight, and so happy. She wanted to be with him, and, goddammit, he wanted to be with her.

And not just to get evidence against her father.

He enjoyed her company, liked just talking to her. He admired her strength and her intelligence. Admired her courage. And Jesus, he wanted her. Turning down her invitation had taken every ounce of his will.

He wanted way more from Harper than a nightcap, wanted to spend the night in her bed, wanted her in his.

Chase tipped his head back on the sofa. He was taking advantage of Harper, lying about his intensions, abusing her trust. He was more than half-tempted to call Zach Tanner and tell him he had failed, that he hadn't been able to get Harper to invite him to the party.

He couldn't believe it had happened so easily, without him saying a word. That she wasn't afraid to confront her father on his behalf only made him feel worse.

Chase swore foully. Harper was sweet and trusting. Too damn trusting, especially of him.

But Knox Winston and his minions had ruined too many lives already. They needed to face justice, and this was a chance to make that happen.

As his brother had said, *It's what we do.* He really had no choice.

Chase drained the last of the whiskey in his glass and rose from the sofa. He needed a good night's rest, needed to be at his best when he faced Knox Winston. But his mind was churning, and guilt weighed heavily on his shoulders.

Add to that, after seeing Harper tonight, his desire burned hotter than ever, a deep, primal need unlike anything he had felt for a woman before.

He sighed as he started down the hall toward his bedroom. It looked like another night of very little sleep.

CHAPTER TWENTY-FIVE

Harper swept her hair into a twist, but left a few strands to fall loose. She wanted to look her best for Chase. She had chosen a forest green V-necked, off-the-shoulder gown of her own design. The bodice was lightly beaded while the skirt hugged her waist and hips, then flared softly to the floor.

She hurried out of the bedroom and descended the stairs, wanting to do a last-minute check of the town house in case he wanted to come in—now or later. Her stomach fluttered. She forced herself not to remember what it had been like when they made love.

She glanced around. The versatile cream walls were accented throughout with the same bright oranges, reds and yellows used by Elemental Chic. She straightened the abstract painting of a bright plumed parrot over the sofa and the orange and red throw pillows and took a deep breath. Chase would be there any minute.

Harper didn't delude herself. It was going to be a difficult evening. She was fairly sure her father wouldn't make a scene, but there was a chance he would ask both of them to leave.

Fortunately, the society editor for the *Morning News* was certain to be there, along with several other media outlets. If any sort of scandal occurred, the press would find out. Not something Knox Winston would want.

A firm knock sounded at the door. Harper grabbed her dark green beaded bag and opened the door. In a perfectly fitted black Armani tux, Chase looked gorgeous.

He leaned over and brushed a kiss on her cheek. "You look beautiful, angel."

She didn't expect the single white orchid he handed her. "Oh…thank you. I love orchids. It's lovely."

"It suits you." He smiled at her softly. "You deserve orchids every day, sweetheart."

Her cheeks flushed. She had seen this side of him only from a distance, the gallant, charming Chase Garrett that half the women in Dallas adored. She liked this side of him, but no more than the rugged, protective male he had been in Colombia. She took the orchid into the kitchen, put it in water, carried it back out and set it on the coffee table.

They headed for the same black stretch limo that had picked them up at the airport. The driver stood next to the open rear door. Tonight he was wearing a white dinner jacket.

"You remember Reggie," Chase said.

The driver grinned and tipped his cap. "Good evening, Ms. Winston."

"It's nice to see you again, Reggie."

He helped her into the back, and Chase slid onto the

red leather seat beside her. Reggie climbed in behind
the wheel and fired the engine. She settled back as he
pulled the limo out onto the road for the thirty-minute
ride to her father's palatial sixteen-thousand-square-
foot residence in Westlake, the most expensive neighborhood in Dallas.

Chase reached for the chilled bottle of Taittinger in
the built-in ice bucket and held the champagne up in
silent question.

"I'd love a glass," Harper said, hoping it would help
calm her nerves.

Chase poured champagne into a crystal flute and
handed her the glass, poured one for himself and settled
back in the seat beside her.

"You ready for this?" he asked, taking a sip of his
drink.

Was she ready to face her father's wrath? Hell, no.
"I want to see you. If this is what it takes, then yes."

Something flickered in his eyes, something she
didn't recognize and had never seen before.

He lifted his champagne flute. "To success tonight
and happier days ahead."

Harper lifted her glass and clinked it to his. "Happy
days," she said.

The party was in full swing by the time Chase
walked Harper up to the carved front doors of the house,
a sprawling Italian-style villa with red tile roofs, twin
square towers, a water fountain with a sculpture of Bot-
ticelli's *Venus* in the front yard and an Olympic-size
swimming pool in back, as well as a man-made lake.

Chase had been to the house with Michael when they
were students at Yale. It wasn't a place you ever forgot.

So far they had passed the first test, the guest list that included Harper's name at the kiosk next to the wrought-iron front gates. From there, Reggie had driven the limo up the winding drive to the mansion.

A white-coated valet opened the car door. Chase slid out of the back and helped Harper out. Reaching back inside, he grabbed the gift wrapped box of scotch, and the valet closed the door.

Setting a hand at Harper's waist, Chase walked her up a path inlaid with mosaic tiles in colorful patterns into a towering entry beneath a massive Venetian crystal chandelier.

The house, which should have been garish, somehow wasn't. Whoever had done the interior design had read Knox Winston perfectly. Not gaudy, but close—and somehow intimidating.

A woman with silver-streaked black hair elegantly dressed in white chiffon sat at a table in the entry checking names. She recognized Harper and smiled.

"Good evening, Harper. Your father will be pleased to see you. He was beginning to worry you weren't going to make it."

"Marybeth, this is Chase Garrett. Marybeth is Father's personal assistant."

"Pleasure, ma'am," he said.

"Nice to meet you, Chase."

He wondered if she knew who he was, knew Knox would be far from pleased to see him there with his daughter.

"Where is he?" Harper asked.

"He's been outside greeting guests around the pool, but he just came in. I saw him heading down the hall to his study."

"Thanks, Marybeth." Harper led Chase across the sienna marble floors, farther into the house. "We might as well talk to him now. Better to get the shock over with as soon as possible."

"Good idea. We can take him his gift. Maybe when he sees it, it'll help."

"What is it?"

"Bottle of twenty-five-year-old Dalmore scotch. I understand your father's a connoisseur. I think he'll appreciate the gift if not the giver." So far things were going even better than he'd hoped. The gift was going straight to Knox's study, and he hadn't been tossed out yet.

Harper smiled, but he could tell she was nervous. Hell, so was he. If the evening went south and Winston figured out what he was doing there, he might leave the estate in a body bag.

Their steps echoed in the cavernous interior. He wished he could leave Harper out of this, but she was crucial to the plan.

She knocked on the door to the study and opened it. "Hi, Dad. Happy birthday!"

Winston was talking to a tall man with dark hair threaded with gray, fifties, attractive, perfectly tailored tuxedo.

"Give me a minute, Simon," Knox Winston said, rising behind his massive desk, which didn't look massive at all in the enormous two-story study. A gallery lined with books looked down from the second floor, which could be reached by a wrought-iron spiral staircase.

"Harper." Simon nodded a greeting as he walked out of the room, but didn't bother to stop for introductions.

Winston rounded his desk toward his daughter. "Harper. I thought you'd decided not to come."

"You know I wouldn't miss your birthday."

Knox came to a shuddering halt when he recognized Chase. He was a tall man and powerfully built, with thick shoulders and a barrel chest. "What the hell are you doing here?"

Chase managed to smile. "Your daughter was kind enough to bring me as her date." He handed Winston the beautiful foil-wrapped gift. "Happy birthday."

Winston snatched it out of his hand and raised it up as if he meant to smash it on the red tile floor.

"Don't, Dad! Chase picked it out especially for you. It's twenty-five-year-old Dalmore scotch. He knows you appreciate a good bottle of whiskey. He thought you would like it."

Winston ripped the silver foil off the box, opened the lid and pulled out the bottle. Clearly he knew the value.

"Chase and I are seeing each other, Dad. We wanted to be up front with you about it. We didn't want to sneak around behind your back."

Winston drilled Chase with a glare. "I can't believe you have the nerve to come here—"

"I know we've had our disagreements," Chase said smoothly. "I know you and my father didn't get along, but for Harper's sake, I'm hoping you'll be willing to set the past aside and accept things as they are."

"Get out!"

Harper moved between them, a hand on her father's thick chest. He was vibrating with anger. "Chase and I are involved, Dad. I don't need your approval, but I'd like to at least have your acceptance. I'm asking you to give him a chance."

Winston's jaw looked ready to crack. He took a deep breath, looked at the ridiculously expensive bottle of

"...going to change."

"Dad, please."

Winston set the bottle on his desk. "For Harper's sake, I'm not going to have you thrown out. You're welcome here for the rest of the evening, but don't come back again."

"I hope you won't hold this against your daughter," Chase said, meaning it. "She was just trying to do what she felt was right."

Knox seemed to pull himself under control. "Like I said, enjoy the evening, but you won't be welcome here again."

Chase nodded curtly. "Happy Birthday. Enjoy the scotch." Chase led Harper out the door into the hall. "I'm sorry that didn't go better, but at least we tried."

Her eyes glistened. "I think we should go."

At the sight of her tears, Chase's chest clamped down. "Maybe he'll come around."

"Maybe." But both of them knew it wasn't going to happen.

Harper led Chase out a side door so they wouldn't run into the press or anyone they might know. He texted Reggie and had the limo waiting as they rounded the house and made their way across the lawn.

His job was done. The bottle of scotch would likely find its way to the built-in bar in Winston's study. From here on out, it was up to the DEA to get the information they needed.

It was a quiet ride back to Harper's town house. They each drank another glass of champagne, which helped

ease th_____
it's early. Please ___
you don't want, but… I… I'd rather _he limo drove up
ning alone."

He shouldn't. It wasn't fair to Harper. But instead of refusing, he found himself nodding. Harper was still holding his hand as she led him up the walkway. He told himself he'd just have the nightcap she had offered him the night before, then he would leave.

He signaled for Reggie to go on home, telling himself he could catch a cab when he was ready to head back to his condo, but the moment he stepped into the entry and closed the door, Harper was in his arms.

"I need you, Chase," she said, pressing soft butterfly kisses to the corners of his mouth. "Please stay."

He wasn't a saint, and this woman was his weakness. When she went up on her toes and kissed him full on the lips, his whole body clenched.

"Do you want me, Chase?"

Jesus God. Did he want her? He felt her slender curves melding with his harder frame, felt her soft breasts pillowing his chest. "I've never wanted a woman more."

Framing her face between his hands, Chase kissed her, long, deep, wet kisses that Harper returned full measure. She tasted like expensive champagne and beautiful, sexy woman, and he couldn't get enough.

Heat crackled in the air between them, seemed to burn him from the inside out. The bedroom was too damned far away. He had to have her now, had to make up for the days he'd been without her.

It wasn't fair. It wasn't honorable. It wasn't like him

to take advantage, yet he couldn't make himself stop. Nothing mattered but Harper and his raging desire for her. Nothing mattered but claiming her as he had done before.

He took her mouth, kissing her softly then fiercely, tasting her, delving deep.

"I need you," he said, nipping the side of her neck. "Here. Now. I don't want to wait."

"Chase…" she whispered, sliding his tuxedo jacket off his shoulders, letting it fall to the floor. "I don't want to wait, either."

He groaned low in his throat. Tomorrow he would regret this. Tonight, with Harper demanding exactly what he wanted to give her, he refused to listen to his conscience.

Chase took her mouth in a savage kiss, his tongue sweeping in, tangling with hers, hers sliding over his. Her fingers worked the buttons down the front of his white tuxedo shirt while he hurriedly unfastened his cuff links. He stripped the shirt off and tossed it away and Harper ran her hands over his chest.

"I love touching you," she said. "I love the way your beautiful muscles flex and tighten."

"Harper…baby…" He kissed her again, deeper, even more demanding. Reaching behind her, he buzzed down her zipper, slid the dark green beaded gown off her shoulders to pool at her feet.

She stepped out of the fabric, naked except for a tiny silver thong, and his mouth went dry. He stepped back to admire her, the sweet curve of her waist, the way her small breasts tilted slightly upward, the feminine triangle of silver gold at the juncture of her legs.

"So damned beautiful."

"Chase…"

He groaned. Harper pressed her hand against the heavy erection beneath the fly of his slacks, and he could feel her trembling.

Reaching up, he pulled the clip from her hair, freeing the long silky mass to slide down around her shoulders. "I need you, baby." His hand slid over her body, palming her breasts, sliding beneath the tiny elastic band on her thong to stroke her.

Harper made a sound and arched against his hand. She was wet and ready, eager for him. Desire, thick and hot, slid through his veins, and his blood pounded.

He walked her backward till she came up against the wall, gripped the silver thong and tore it away, heard her soft whimper. He carried a condom in his wallet. He took it out, freed himself and took care of protection. Lifting her up, he wrapped her long, pretty legs around his waist and buried himself deep.

Harper moaned. For several long seconds he just held her, propped against the wall, fighting to stay in control. But when she whispered his name, when she started to move against him, making her own silent demands, everything inside him broke loose.

Gripping her hips to hold her in place, he surged into her, began to drive hard and deep, Harper clinging to him, her arms around his neck, moaning as he took her. Took her and took her and took her. Her inner walls pulsed around him, and he knew she was close to release.

He kissed her hot and deep. "Come for me, angel…"

A soft sound slipped from her throat. Her body tightened and Harper tumbled into climax, her sweetly feminine cries driving him over the edge. Thick, saturating pleasure burned through him and his own release struck hard. Chase groaned, the harsh sound cutting through the silence in the living room.

Long seconds passed.

Harper rested her head on his shoulder, and the fragrance of jasmine drifted over him. "That was so… You were amazing."

Smiling, he kissed the side of her neck. "You were pretty amazing yourself, sweetheart." Her legs still snuggly around his waist, he carried her up the stairs and down the hall, found the master bedroom and settled her in the middle of the bed.

He returned from the bathroom to join her. Brushing silvery hair away from her cheek, he kissed her. A stack of foil packets glittered on the nightstand. Harper wanted him, and Chase had never wanted her more.

For an instant, his thoughts strayed to the listening device in her father's study, and guilt washed over him. But even if he left her alone, he wasn't going to like himself in the morning.

Fortunately, morning was still hours away.

CHAPTER TWENTY-SIX

Though Chase seemed unusually quiet Sunday morning—probably because of her father's hostile reaction to their relationship—Harper managed to coax him into spending the day with her.

After the ham-and-cheese omelets and toast she made for their breakfast, they drove her Beemer over to Chase's condo so he could change out of his now-wrinkled tux. Deciding to spend a lazy afternoon prowling the museums and exhibits in the Arts District, they spotted a local artists' sidewalk show, picked up a few small pieces, then stopped in at the Tex-Mex for nachos and beer.

It was fun just being together—without worrying about someone shooting at them, or even just thinking about work. Harper couldn't remember a day she had felt so relaxed.

Inwardly, she grinned. Maybe it was the amazing sex she'd had last night and again this morning. Maybe it was the multiple orgasms she had once been sure didn't actually exist.

She was a little worried about her relationship with her father. She knew he was angry, but they had been living separate lives since the day she'd left for college. In time, he would get over it.

They spent Sunday night at Chase's, ordered Chinese food and ate while they watched an old John Wayne movie—or at least watched part of it—before they wound up in bed.

Chase was everything she had ever wanted in a man. Now that she knew he returned her feelings, she could let down her guard and be completely open with him.

Monday morning she drove back to her town house, showered and went to work. All day she was like a teenager, waiting for Chase to phone, ridiculously excited to see him again.

She must have begun to look anxious because by afternoon, Shana was casting her worried glances. Little by little, her stomach balled into a knot.

By nine o'clock that night, Harper realized Chase wasn't going to call.

After Harper left early Monday morning, Chase drove to his office. Their weekend together had been incredible, better than he could have imagined.

He was worried about Knox Winston and the case the DEA was pursuing, but there was a good chance, even if the bug worked and the DEA got the evidence they needed, the way the information had been collected might never come to light.

Harper would never know the role he had played, and though his conscience nagged him, he wouldn't have to give her up. He didn't like the idea of a lie standing between them, but in time, he'd find a way to tell her the truth.

Setting the problem aside, Chase shoved open the glass front door of Maximum Security, his gaze going to Mindy, who sat at the receptionist desk going over office ledgers, her background in bookkeeping part of the reason he had hired her.

"Morning, boss." The cheerful way she said it always made him smile.

"Morning, Mindy."

She shoved her round tortoiseshell glasses up on her nose. "You've had a couple of calls. I put them through to your voice mail. Oh, and Mr. Dickerson called to confirm your appointment. He should be here any minute."

"Thanks, Mindy." He wandered into his office, played the messages on his voice mail, returned a couple of phone calls and thought about calling Harper, which was ridiculous since he had just left her.

His intercom buzzed. "Mr. Dickerson is here," Mindy announced.

"Send him in."

The door opened, and a thin, gray-haired man with a narrow, lined face and slightly stooped posture walked into the office.

"Errol Dickerson," the man said. "Thank you for seeing me."

"Chase Garrett." He shook Dickerson's age-spotted hand. "Why don't you have a seat and tell me what I can do for you?"

Dickerson sat down and immediately began spinning a tale of greed that ended with what he believed was the murder of his son.

"My wife and I were on a cruise when it happened. By the time we got home, James was dead. His body had already been cremated, which we would have opposed."

"You told me the cause of death was a heart attack," Chase said.

"That's what the doctor said. Since he was in attendance when James died, there was no autopsy. James was only forty years old and extremely healthy. I believe he was murdered. I'm not sure how his wife accomplished it, but I'm convinced she did."

The appointment took longer than Chase expected, but after hearing what Dickerson had to say, it sounded as if there were plenty of unanswered questions that deserved to be pursued.

The bottom line was Errol Dickerson's very successful son, James, was dead under somewhat suspicious circumstances, leaving his wife a wealthy widow.

"I'll get a copy of the police report," Chase said. "I'll know more after I take a look."

"I brought you a copy." Dickerson set a manila folder on the desk, along with a flash drive. "This is everything I've been able to dig up. I'm hoping, after you've had a chance to read what's inside and in the digital file, you'll find something that can tell us the truth."

"I'll do my best, Mr. Dickerson, though I can't guarantee the outcome."

"Find out what you can. That's all I ask."

Chase rose and walked Dickerson to the door. By the time he had returned to his desk, the intercom was buzzing.

It seemed like one problem followed another, old cases where something new cropped up, new cases where one of his PIs needed help.

He thought about calling Harper but something held him back. He had never been good at deceiving a person he cared about. He didn't like doing it now.

It was well after dark by the time he left the office and headed home. By 10:00 p.m. he still hadn't texted or phoned Harper. Instead he sat in his living room staring out at the familiar sparkling lights, thinking of Harper and wishing she were there with him.

Thinking of his role in bringing her father to justice.

Thinking of the lies he had told her. Wondering how the hell things had gotten so balled up.

Whatever happened, he refused to let Harper believe he didn't care. With a fortifying breath, he picked up the phone and punched in her number.

She answered on the first ring. "Chase...?"

"Hi, baby. I'm sorry it's so late. Long day. Lots of problems."

"I...umm...didn't think you were going to call."

"I meant to call sooner. Time just slipped away."

"It doesn't matter." Relief softened her voice. "You're calling me now."

Guilt swept over him. He couldn't go on like this. It wasn't fair to either one of them. He had to tell her the truth or put their relationship on hold, as he had meant to do from the start. It wasn't what he wanted, but it was the only thing his conscience would allow.

"There's something we need to talk about, baby."

"That's not a problem," Harper said, a smile in her voice. "I'm just walking up to your front door."

Chase swore softly. He tried to pretend he didn't feel a leap in his heart, but he would be lying. Striding down the hall, he pulled open the front door, and Harper stepped into his arms.

"When I didn't hear from you, I thought you didn't want to see me." She leaned into him, her arms around his neck. "I thought a few nights in bed and you'd had enough of me. I figured if that was all you wanted, I deserved a goodbye in person."

"Harper…angel…" He looked into her beautiful face and longing swelled inside him. His hand slid into her silky hair, fisted, and he pulled her mouth up to his for a deep, burning kiss.

He wasn't sure what happened next, how they started tearing each other's clothes off as they stumbled down the hall to his bedroom.

He wasn't sure how they ended up naked in his big bed, both wildly aroused, mouths and bodies fused, both of them reaching a mind-blowing climax. How afterward they drifted down, covered in perspiration, utterly sated and barely able to move.

He wasn't sure how it had happened, but he knew one thing for certain. He wasn't tired of Harper Winston. He wasn't sure he ever would be. And giving her up was out of the question. He'd work things out, find another solution.

Curling her into his side, he draped an arm possessively around her. As he drifted to sleep, he was still trying to figure out what the hell he was going to do.

Knox Winston sat at the desk in his study, staring at the expensive Dalmore single malt. The bottle had sat in the same spot every night since Chase Garrett had brought it, a gift meant to buy his daughter like a high-priced whore.

Every time he looked at it, his fury swelled. Tonight, he'd finally had enough. Balling his hand into a fist,

Knox looked over at Simon Graves, who sat with one leg crossed over the other, the epitome of cool.

"Get Angelo and Carlos in here. Now."

Simon didn't ask why, just rose and left the study. Only a few minutes passed before he returned with two of Knox's top enforcers. Angelo Pierucci was lean, tough and wiry. Carlos Escobar was thick-muscled and stout.

"You got a problem, boss?" Angelo asked.

"Yeah, I got a problem. Chase Garrett. That's my problem. He thinks he can buy the right to fuck my daughter with a fancy bottle of scotch. It isn't going to work. As of now, he and Harper are finished. I want you to deliver that message loud and clear. Make sure he knows he'll get far worse than a beating if he tries to see her again."

"We got it, boss," Carlos said. "After we're done with Garrett, he won't even remember your daughter's name."

"Take a couple of guys with you. Garrett won't go down easy."

"Oh, he's going down, boss," Angelo said. "One way or another."

"Don't kill him. I don't need the aggravation."

Angelo nodded. "We'll need a couple of days to figure his schedule, get him alone."

"Two days. That's it. Now, get out of here."

"Anything else?" Simon asked Knox as the men left the study.

"Not at the moment."

Simon followed them out, and Knox returned his attention to the bottle of vintage scotch. Lifting the bottle, he cracked the seal and poured three fingers into the crystal tumbler sitting on the desk beside it.

Now that things were settled, he could relax and enjoy a drink. No use letting a good bottle of single malt go to waste.

Knox lifted the crystal glass and took a long, satisfying swallow.

Early Tuesday morning, Chase left Harper asleep in his bed, her silky hair spread over his pillow. The sight he had once only imagined was, in reality, even more arousing.

He sighed as pulled on a pair of lightweight sweats and padded down the hall into the kitchen to brew himself a cup of coffee. He had work to do this morning, and he still hadn't decided what to do about Harper.

The Keurig machine on the granite counter bubbled, and his mug slowly filled. He took his coffee and started for the study to check his email when a knock sounded on the front door.

Way too early for company. Wary from his years in law enforcement, Chase checked the peephole, then relaxed when he saw his brother standing in the hall. Bran had a key and security clearance. No need for a heads-up from the guard in the lobby.

When he opened the door and spotted Special Agent Zach Tanner next to his brother, Chase's unease returned. "From the scowl on your faces, whatever brought you here isn't good news. Come on in."

He had talked to Tanner Sunday morning while Harper was in the shower, and brought him up to speed on Winston's party and his success in planting the bug. He had also called his brother.

"You guys want a cup of coffee?" Chase asked.

"I could use a cup," Bran said, yawning, scratching his chest through the dark blue Henley he wore with his jeans.

Chase wondered what he would tell Harper if she saw the men, but it was barely dawn and she was still sound asleep in his bedroom. He led them into the kitchen, set out a couple of coffee pods and brewed them each a cup.

"Nice work with the bug," Tanner said, taking a seat next to Bran on a barstool at the kitchen counter.

Chase stood on the opposite side. "Thanks."

Zach sipped his coffee. "The device is working great, even better than we expected."

"How long will the battery last?"

"Couple of weeks," Zach said. "Maybe a little longer. Unfortunately, a problem's come up."

"Yeah, what problem is that?" Chase took a drink of his coffee.

"Apparently, Winston isn't happy about you dating his daughter," Zach said.

"No kidding."

Bran sat forward. "He's a little more than just unhappy."

Zach's hand tightened on the handle of his cup. "Last night Winston called a couple of his thugs into the study and told them he wanted them to deliver a message. He wants you out of Harper's life."

"He's sending his goons after you, Chase," Bran said. "Winston won't be satisfied until they pound you into the dirt. They mean to convince you to leave Harper alone."

"Christ."

"We can put a tail on you," Tanner said. "Give you some protection."

Chase shook his head. "I can handle Winston's goons. Security is what I do for a living, remember?"

"Plus you'll have me bird-dogging you," Bran drawled. "Personal protection is what *I* do for a living—remember?"

Chase grunted.

"You need to end this thing with Harper before it goes any further," Tanner said.

"No," Chase said flatly. "I'm not letting Knox Winston run my life."

"What about Harper?" Bran asked softly. "You don't want her getting caught up in this any more than she is already. If you're with her, she could get hurt."

Chase had a sinking feeling in the pit of his stomach. Bran was right. He never should have gotten Harper involved in the first place. But God, he didn't want to let her go.

"Now that the DEA's got a bug in his study," Bran continued, "they can get what they need to bring Winston down. Once he's cooling his ass in jail, he won't give a fuck who his daughter sleeps with."

Chase clenched his jaw. He was trying to think, running over his options, when a sound caught his attention. Dressed and ready to leave, Harper stood in the doorway, her face pale as glass.

"So that's what this was all about. You're using me to get information on my father. I can't believe it. Your birthday gift was just a way to plant some kind of listening device in his study."

"We need to talk, Harper," Chase said. "This isn't the way it seems."

The DEA agent rose from his barstool. "I'm Special Agent Zach Tanner, Ms. Winston. I need to inform you the Drug Enforcement Administration had a warrant for the placement of that device. If you inform your father of its existence, you'll be interfering in a criminal investigation. You could very well end up in jail."

Her gaze zeroed in on Zach. "You're DEA? You... you think my father is involved in drugs?"

"I'm not at liberty to discuss the case," Tanner said.

Chase crossed the room and took Harper's hand. It was cold as ice, he noticed, the instant before she jerked it away.

"What's going on between us has nothing to do with this," Chase said.

Harper just shook her head. Tears welled in her big blue eyes and slipped down her cheeks. "I was falling in love with you, Chase. How stupid is that?" She turned to leave but Chase caught her arm.

"Harper, please—one thing has nothing to do with the other. Give me a chance to explain."

She just shook her head and wiped tears from her cheeks. "I trusted you. I guess my father was right about you all along." She turned to leave, but Bran moved to block her way.

"Before you go, Harper, you need to know that last night your father ordered a brutal attack on Chase to stop him from seeing you. His men won't quit till they find a way to get to him. I know my brother well enough to know his feelings for you are real. He doesn't deserve a beating—or worse."

She looked at Chase, wetness glistening on her cheeks. Her chin went up. "You don't have to worry.

I'll talk to my father, tell him we're through. It'll be my great pleasure to do so. Goodbye, Chase."

"Remember what I said, Ms. Winston," Zach called out. "You need to tread very carefully."

Bran caught her arm. "If your father finds out about the bug in his study, he'll know Chase put it there. There's a very good chance my brother will end up dead."

Harper looked at Chase, emotion clouding her features. Bran cast her a sympathetic glance and stepped out of her way, and Harper walked out of the kitchen. The front door slammed hard enough to rattle the cups on the kitchen counter.

Chase felt sick to his stomach.

CHAPTER TWENTY-SEVEN

Through a glaze of tears, Harper drove back to her town house. How could she have actually believed Chase was falling in love with her? How could she have been such a fool?

As she thought back on it, every time she'd been with him, she had been the initiator, the seducer. No virile male turned down sex when it was offered, and Chase was an extremely virile male.

A sob caught in her throat. All Chase had ever wanted was a connection to her father. A way to get information that would put Knox Winston in jail.

Her heart twisted, her despair so great her whole body ached with it. She'd had a thing for Chase Garrett since she was sixteen. As a woman, that attraction had grown far beyond infatuation.

On their perilous journey into the jungle, she had come to admire him—his skills, his instincts, his protectiveness. Her attraction had turned into a powerful sexual desire, then deepened into love.

A shudder rippled through her. Stupidly, those feelings had allowed him to manipulate her, use her to get to her father.

She never would have guessed his animosity ran so deep.

Harper wiped a fresh rush of tears from her cheeks. Was her father actually a criminal?

DEA. Drug Enforcement Administration. They had to believe Knox Winston was involved in drug smuggling or some other heinous crime. As she parked the car in her garage and went into her town house, a dozen thoughts swarmed through her head.

Her father did business with people in South America. After her mother had died, in the years before Harper had left for college, she had helped her dad entertain foreign business associates at the house. She spoke Spanish, which he was extremely proud of. She was a real asset, he had said.

But any business discussions were held behind closed doors, and she was never included.

She thought back to what Agent Tanner had said. What if he and Bran Garrett were telling the truth? What if her father had ordered an attack on Chase to keep him away from her?

She no longer trusted Chase but she trusted Bran. He wouldn't lie about something like that. *I know my brother well enough to know his feelings for you are real.*

Her heart squeezed. Was it true? It wouldn't change what Chase had done, but Harper desperately wanted to believe she was more than just a pawn in a scheme to get back at her father.

One thing was certain. No matter what Chase did or didn't feel for her, she didn't want to see him hurt. Add to that, she owed him for saving her brother. She didn't want him injured—or God forbid, even killed!

Since she couldn't face her father looking as if she had spent the night in Chase's bed—exactly where she had been—she hurried upstairs to her bedroom to shower and put on something presentable.

Choosing a conservative dark brown pencil skirt, she added a rust-colored silk blouse and heels, the sort of outfit she knew would please her dad. She pulled her hair into a twist, dabbed on enough makeup to hide the pallor of her face, grabbed her purse and headed back out to the BMW.

Pausing long enough to text Shana that she would be late getting to work, she backed the Beemer out of her garage and headed for Highway 114 for the half hour drive to Westlake.

All the way there, she tried to figure out what she could possibly say to ensure Chase's safety without letting her dad know his conversation last night had been overheard.

Which brought her to another problem.

Could she actually stand by and allow the federal authorities to collect enough evidence to put her father in prison? She couldn't let it happen, yet if she told him about the device in the bottle of scotch, she might be the one going to prison.

Worse yet, he would know Chase was responsible for putting it there. Would he actually order him killed?

Her stomach roiled and doubt prickled her skin. She

had witnessed her father's ruthlessness on more than one occasion, heard the brutal way he spoke to anyone who displeased him. More than once, she had actually seen him strike one of his employees.

She thought of her mother's suicide. At the time, she'd been too young to wonder what had caused her mother's depression, but as she'd grown older, she had begun to believe it was more than partly her father's fault.

She remembered his abusive language, the disdain he had shown Amelia Winston. The abusive way he had treated her brother.

Michael. Suspicion crawled through her. Michael had been kidnapped in Curaçao and taken to Colombia. He had been purposely singled out, yet no ransom had been demanded. Who was responsible? What was their motive? Was it something to do with drugs? Was her father somehow involved?

She pulled up to the gate and the guard let her pass. Following the winding road, she drove up in front of the sprawling Italian villa, pulled to a stop in front of the house. Harper took a deep breath. She had to be careful, handle her dad just right.

She rang the bell, and her father's latest butler opened the door.

"Good morning, Giuseppe. I need to see my dad."

Giuseppe Bonaventure was in his midthirties, with black hair and dark eyes. As with the villa, her father was fascinated by anything and everything Italian. *Like some kind of Mafia don?* she now wondered.

Giuseppe made a slight bow. "He is in his study, Ms. Winston. I will let him know you are here."

"Thank you." Her dad spent less and less time at his

office in the high-rise building he owned. He left most of the work up to the CEOs of his numerous companies or his right-hand man, Simon Graves. Most of his own work, he handled in the house.

Giuseppe returned. "He is waiting. You may go on back."

She headed down the hall and found him seated behind his massive, ornately carved desk, forced herself not to look for the expensive bottle of scotch. He had put on a little weight, she noticed, and there were fine strands of gray in his hair.

Harper managed to smile. "Hi, Dad. I had an errand to run out this way, and I wanted to talk to you. Have you got a second?"

He leaned back in his leather wingback chair. "I've always got time for my daughter. What is it?"

She sat down in a chair across from him. "After I left the party Saturday night, I got to thinking. There are lots of good-looking men in Dallas. I mean, Chase is all right, you know, but the two of you don't get along, and I respect your opinion. And I'm not ready to settle down yet, anyway. I wanted you to know I've decided not to see him again."

He father stood up from behind his desk, a slow smile making its way across his blunt face. Harper had her mother's fine features and pale blond hair. Michael had their father's dark hair but didn't look much like either one of them.

"I'm not surprised," her dad said, obviously pleased. "You always were a smart girl."

"The truth is guys like Chase are a dime a dozen. Now that I'm back in Dallas, maybe you can introduce me to someone interesting."

His smile broadened. "Now you're thinking like a Winston. Might as well find someone who can be an asset to the family."

She managed to smile in return. "That's right. I made it clear to Chase that we were over and he was okay with it, so there's no problem there."

She thought about walking around the desk and giving him a hug to make sure she had convinced him, but her dad wasn't a hugging kind of guy and she didn't want him to get suspicious.

"So we're good?" she asked, keeping her fake smile in place.

"Everything's fine. I'm glad you came by."

"Me, too." She glanced at the door, her gaze skimming the built-in bar along the way, spotting the bottle of scotch with the silver stag's head on the front. No way could she get to it, at least not today. "I'm afraid I've got to run. I've got a dozen things to do. Take care, Dad."

"You, too, sweetheart." He returned his attention to the paperwork on his desk as if she were already gone.

As she left the office, Harper prayed she'd done enough to get Chase off her father's hit list.

Bad choice of words, she thought, the notion sending a chill down her spine. By the time she had reached her car, she was drained. Lying took a lot out of a person. Though it hadn't been much of a problem for Chase.

Sitting in his rental car down the road from the mansion, Roberto Chavez watched the white BMW drive past and started his engine. Bobby had been watching the Winston girl for days, keeping track of her schedule, looking for vulnerabilities, weaknesses he could use.

His orders had come straight from Eduardo Ramos,

second in command of the Montoya empire. Ramos had made it clear what his *jefe* expected. Montoya wanted the girl, and it was Bobby's job to get her. Once he was ready, his plan laid out, he would bring in the help he needed to get the task done.

What he didn't want to do was make a mistake. He couldn't afford to fail. Luis Montoya didn't tolerate failure.

As the BMW headed back toward Dallas, Bobby kept his car a safe distance behind her. He didn't want to be spotted, though he didn't think there was much chance of that. He had time, not a lot, but enough to carefully go over and finalize his plans.

He followed the car back to the girl's warehouse office. He had already discarded the idea of taking her there. Too many people around, too many opportunities to screw up.

He pulled into the back of the parking lot to watch and wait, see what other info he could pick up. She usually came out after dark. An after-hours abduction might be a possibility, as long as she was by herself, but often she was with someone, the black girl who was her business partner or one of the other employees.

Her town house was a possibility. Just a quick in and out after dark—except for her fancy alarm system, which appeared to be highly complex. Bobby didn't like the look of that.

Another day or two, he'd figure it out, be ready to lay out the plan to his men. Once he had the girl, she'd be loaded aboard a private jet and taken out of the country. Montoya would be pleased, and Bobby would be well rewarded.

Montoya didn't tolerate failure. But he was more than generous when it came to success.

Chase sat behind his desk at The Max, trying to concentrate on work. So far without much success. His top priority was the Dickerson case. He'd managed to get through the police report and Dickerson's personal commentary on the flash drive.

But staying focused hadn't been easy. Not when every time he closed his eyes, he saw Harper's stricken face. *So that's what this was all about. You're using me to get information on my father.*

Harper was way more important to him than just a means to an end. Important enough that he would force himself to stay away from her. That he would give her up in order to protect her.

He leaned back in his chair and rubbed his eyes. At the sound of a solid knock, he opened them to see Bran striding up to the desk, his expression grim.

His brother frowned. "You look like crap."

"Thanks."

"Dammit, I know how rough this has been on you. How are you holding up?"

"I've been better. What's going on?"

"Zach just called. Harper went to see her dad. She told him the two of you were finished. Zach said it was a very convincing performance."

"It's easy to be convincing when you're telling the truth."

Bran ran a hand along his hard jaw. "You knew from the start seeing Harper would likely be a problem."

"Yeah, just not the kind of problem it turned out to

be. What about the device? Did she tell Winston about the bottle of scotch?"

"No. At least not yet."

"I wouldn't blame her if she did."

"She still might. The thing is, bro, Harper cares about you. She doesn't want anything to happen to you. She's trying to work things out, figure out what to do."

"I know."

"I said you should stay away from her, but I'm thinking maybe I was wrong. Maybe you should talk to her, try to explain."

Chase leaned back in his chair. "She won't see me. I used her. She won't be able to get past that."

Bran didn't argue. They both knew it was true.

"You think Winston will call off his dogs?" Bran asked.

"Hell, I don't have any idea. I'll keep an eye out, just in case."

"I'll stay close for a couple of days. You never know what a guy like that will do."

"I don't need a babysitter."

"Too bad," Bran shot over his shoulder as he headed back out the door.

Chase didn't see him for the rest of the day, but his brother had an uncanny ability to be around and at the same time invisible.

The afternoon dragged. Chase had a meeting with Jonah Wolfe about the homicide case he was working, listened to a funny story about Maddox wearing his white shirt backward, pretending to be a preacher to go in for an arrest on a bail skip he'd been tracking.

Late in the afternoon, Chase went back to work on

the Dickerson file, then drove his Dodge pickup out to Richardson to see Tabitha Love. Mostly an excuse to get out of the office.

Parking in front of her small redbrick house, he walked up and knocked on the door. He had phoned ahead so Tabby was expecting him.

"Hey, Chase, come on in." The small silver hoop in her eyebrow winked as she stepped back to invite him in. Today her nose ring was missing.

He wiped his boots before stepping onto the brown shag carpet in a living room decorated with thrift store furniture that had seen better days. Tabby wasn't much on interior design.

Chase followed her down the hall into her home office, where she spent every dollar she earned. Floor-to-ceiling computers and high-tech equipment lined the walls, lights flashing, screens lit up.

"What can I do for you, boss?"

Chase handed her a flash drive that held the scanned pages of the Dickerson file.

"I need info on a possible murder victim named James Monroe Dickerson. Forty years old, died of a heart attack. Wife's name is Betsy Marie Dickerson. James's father is convinced his son was murdered. No autopsy. Cremation three days postmortem. There was a big insurance policy." Which he'd discovered as he'd gone through the file. "Find me whatever you can."

"Your timing's good. I just finished running down a lead for Maddox. I can get right on this. Let me take a quick look, see if there's anything else I need."

Chase waited while Tabby plugged in the drive and made a quick scan of the information. "You've got quite a bit here. I'll go through it and get back to you."

"Thanks, Tab." Chase left the house and returned to the office. He finished up, made a few last-minute calls, then headed out the door.

He considered stopping to drown his sorrows at Clancy's, the Irish pub just down the block, a locals' joint The Max crew considered their second home. But he'd probably run into one of them, and he wasn't up for hanging out.

Stepping out into the darkness, he crossed the lot to where his pickup was parked, clicked the locks and pulled open the door. If his mind hadn't been a million miles away on Harper, he would have been ready. As it was, four men in ski masks were on him before he had time to react.

He took a hard punch to the jaw, spun around and took a deep blow to the stomach, doubling him over, damn near taking him to his knees.

"Stay away from Harper," the stout man said, which gave him a few seconds to recoup. Chase swung a punch that came from the ground up, knocking his opponent backward, then muscle memory kicked in, and he went to work.

An elbow to the face of the second guy, a kick to the groin of the third. A couple of solid punches to the stout guy, who was back on his feet; and a kidney shot to the fourth, a lean, tough guy with ropy muscles in his arms.

Fists flew. Men grunted. A knee to the groin took one of them down, groaning and clutching his privates. Chase threw a left-right combination, crunching bone, breaking the bastard's nose.

Then ski-masked men began flying backward as if they were on strings. Bran was in the fray, punching and kicking like a madman. Attackers rolled on the ground, groaning and cursing. One of them pulled a pistol that Bran kicked away, then the men scrambled to their feet and took off running.

Chase didn't follow. Neither did Bran. Just watched them disappear into the darkness at the edge of the parking lot.

Both he and Bran blew hard, fighting to catch their breath. Bran bent over, braced his hands on his thighs and looked up at him. In the glow of the parking lamps, Chase saw him grin.

"Fun times," his brother said.

"Yeah, a real laugh."

Bran turned serious. "Fucking scumbags. You can figure Winston for the attack."

"The question is did they get what they were after or will they be back?"

"Considering Harper told her dad she was finished with you, I'm guessing the old man'll let it go. Plus those guys are going to give him a far more colorful version of what happened." Bran grinned. "According to them, you got your ass kicked."

Chase laughed. "Let's hope you're right."

"Buy you a drink?" Bran asked, checking the abrasions on his knuckles.

Chase released a weary breath. Since the alternative was going home to face his empty condo, now filled with memories of Harper, he might as well.

"Why not? But considering your very timely arrival, I think I'm the one who ought to do the buying."

Bran chuckled and slapped him on the back. As they headed for Clancy's, Chase thought a drink had never sounded so good.

CHAPTER TWENTY-EIGHT

Though darkness had settled over the streets of Houston, computer techs in the BUZZ offices worked overtime to create new software programs, make repairs and implement changes to clients' computer systems.

The company was running smoothly. Michael was proud of the way his team had managed the business during his ordeal. He should be smiling. Under different circumstances, he would be. Instead he was thinking of Pia. Missing her with every beat of his heart.

He never would have guessed he could fall so hard so fast. But he had never met a woman like Pia Santana, and he didn't think he ever would again.

Sitting behind the sleek chrome-and-granite desk in his glass-enclosed office, he checked the time. The workday was over. Being an hour later in Miami, the day would also be over for Pia. Michael reached for the phone. He hadn't called her since he'd left her at the airport, had respected her wishes, given her time.

Agonizing days had passed. As far as Michael was concerned, he had waited long enough. He needed to talk to her, hear the sound of her voice.

Her cell rang, speeding up his heart rate. When Pia answered, his eyes closed for a moment, absorbing the simple warmth of her *hello*.

"Pia? It's Michael."

Her voice hitched. "Michael…"

"I just… I called to see how you're doing. I've missed you."

A pause. "I've missed you, too, Michael."

Hope swelled. "I've thought of you every day. Dreamed of you at night. I want to see you, honey. I'll come to Miami. Just tell me it's okay."

Silence descended.

"Pia…?"

"I'm sorry, Michael. I'm just not ready. I keep having flashbacks. What happened… I can't seem to get past it. All the fighting, men dying…other things. I'm seeing someone."

His chest clamped down. "A man?"

He finally heard a smile in her voice. "No, silly. A psychologist. She's helping me. She says I'll be fine. I just need some time to work things out."

Relief spilled through him. Time he could give her. Not that he wanted to. "I need to know, honey. Do you still have feelings for me? Or is it over?"

Pia sniffed and started crying. "I miss you, Michael. I tried to tell myself it was just a fling, but I… I miss you."

"I want to see you. I need to see you, Pia."

"Not yet. Please. It's too soon. I need time to put everything straight in my head. Will you… Will you wait for me to do that?"

His throat felt tight. He'd wait as long as it took. He thought of Benito Velasquez, and his hand unconsciously fisted. It was his fault she was having so much trouble. He should have found a way to protect her. He should have done something, anything.

"I'll wait, honey. You're worth waiting for, Pia."

She drew in a shaky breath. "I have to go now. Christy's here. We're going out to get something to eat. Take care of yourself, Michael."

Michael still gripped the phone. He wondered if Pia's feelings for him would last or if, little by little, they would slip away. His own remained strong. He could wait, he told himself.

But there was no way to know if Pia would do the same.

After leaving her father's house, Harper drove to work. Elemental Chic was still a young company. Harper and Shana held the staff to a minimum to keep expenses down, so there was always plenty to do. The warehouse office was noisy with activity and there were always decisions to make, but with everything that had been happening, it was hard to concentrate.

Shana had known immediately that something was wrong. They'd grown close over the years, sensitive to each other's problems.

"What's going on, girlfriend? You've been a million miles away all day."

Harper sighed. "I just… I've got a lot on my mind."

"It's more than that. Whatever it is, you can tell me, you know that. I'm your best friend. You can tell me anything."

Fighting back tears, Harper walked away from the

sketch she'd been studying on the worktable. "I know. We've always been able to trust each other." Through the big glass window in the second-story office, she could look out across the parking lot, into the warehouse district where the building was located.

She turned to her friend. "Chase and I... Something happened and I'm not seeing him anymore."

"Oh, honey."

Harper took a shaky breath. "He never really cared about me, Shana. He was just using me to get to my father."

Shana walked over and pulled her into a hug. "Men are such dicks. I don't know why we put up with them." She stepped back and smiled, hoping to lighten the mood. "Aside from the orgasms, I mean."

Harper actually laughed. "There is that." She thought of the nights she'd spent with Chase, and her laughter faded. "Maybe that's how he fooled me. Sidetracked me with amazing sex."

"Yeah, honey. Works every time."

Harper went back to work and as the afternoon progressed, she felt better. Then she came home to her empty house, which had never seemed empty until Chase had been there, and depression pulled at her again.

Tossing her purse on the coffee table, she sank down on the sofa. How could she miss him so much when she hadn't really known him?

She glanced at her watch, a preliminary production model of the watch Elemental Chic would be producing next year, affordable gold tone and stainless with colorful interchangeable leather bands.

It was 8:00 p.m. She pulled her cell phone out of her purse. It was still early enough to call her brother, and she really needed to talk to him. She hit his contact number and waited for him to pick up, then went for light and airy, figuring the call would turn grim soon enough.

"Hey, big brother. Got a minute for your little sis?"

"Sure. Glad you called. What's going on in your neck of the world?"

She sidetracked the answer for later. "How's Pia? Have you heard from her?"

"We…ah…just got off the phone. She says she isn't ready to see me. She needs a little more time."

Harper's heart went out to him. "She'll figure things out, Michael. Pia loves you. I really believe that."

"I don't know. Maybe. So how are you and Chase?"

Her throat constricted. There was so much to say, and nothing she really wanted to tell him. "We aren't seeing each other anymore. It's a long story. The thing is, Michael, there's something I need to talk to you about, and I need you keep it just between the two of us."

"You don't even have to ask. What's going on?"

"The DEA is investigating Dad. I assume they think he has some kind of involvement in the drug trade. Do you know anything about that?"

Silence fell.

"Michael?"

"You never suspected? You never guessed what was going on?"

"Oh, my God, it's true?"

"Knox Winston's been running all kinds of illegal activities for years. In the last four or five, he's managed to switch a lot of his money into legitimate businesses. I assume that's his goal—to legitimize his dealings completely, but I don't really know. I've stayed away from his business—and him—for years."

"You…you found out when you were in college?"

"I began to suspect in high school. I think Mom figured it out. She couldn't handle it. Neither could I."

"Oh, Michael."

"You need to stay out of it, Harper. Dad has gone to great lengths to keep you from knowing. You need to stay away from the investigation."

"The DEA put a bug in his study. I was planning to find a way to destroy it."

"Listen to me, sis. If Dad's gone legitimate, if he's no longer smuggling drugs, he'll be okay. If he's involved, he deserves what he gets. I know the terrible damage drugs can do. I know the pain of addiction. You need to let the DEA do its job."

Her eyes burned. This was their father they were talking about. "All these years… I never knew."

"Maybe not. But you must have had your suspicions. Just like I did."

It was true. She had seen things, overheard conversations she wasn't supposed to hear. "You're right. There were times I wondered what was going on. Some of the people who came to the house. Things I overheard. I guess I never really wanted to know the truth. It was easier to pretend."

"Is Dad the reason you and Chase broke up?"

Her throat ached and her eyes filled. "Yes."

"Don't let Dad destroy what you and Chase have, Harper."

"Chase used me, Michael. He was working with the DEA. I can't forgive that."

"He works with law enforcement, sis. That's his job. It's what he does."

"It was all a lie. There's no way I can forgive him."

"Chase forgave me for all the misery I put him through. He came when I needed him most. One thing I know about Chase, whatever happens, if you need him, he'll be there for you."

"I'll think about what you've told me. I'll think about everything. Bye, Mikey. Thanks." She swallowed, wiped tears from her cheeks. No matter what her brother said, it was over between them.

Chase awoke the follow morning with an anvil banging away in his head. Too much whiskey last night, a rare occurrence for him. After the fight in the parking lot, he'd been too wired to go home. At Clancy's, he and Bran had run into Wolfe and Maddox.

When Chase left the bar, Bran had insisted on following him home in case Winston's thugs were still around. His brother had come in for a nightcap. They'd both had a few more drinks. Bran had decided he shouldn't drive and wound up spending the night in the guest room.

At least the booze had helped Chase sleep instead of lying awake half the night thinking of Harper. According to Zach Tanner, the bug was still working, so Harper hadn't said anything about it to her father. That was something, he guessed.

But Chase was worried about her. He'd hurt her, as he had sworn he would never do. He wanted to call her, make sure she was okay. He wanted to tell her he cared about her. Hell, way more than cared.

Which, considering the situation with her father, was the reason he hadn't wanted to get involved with her in the first place. He'd always been attracted to Harper. Now that he'd spent time with her, slept with her, the attraction was over-the-top.

He told himself she was better off if he just left her alone, and somehow managed to convince himself.

Sitting behind his desk at the office, he slid open one of the desk drawers and took out a bottle of Advil and a bottle of Aquafina, popped a couple of pain pills and downed them with a slug of water.

The phone rang. Chase picked it up and Tabby's voice floated over the line. "I think Mr. Dickerson is onto something, Chase. This whole heart attack thing stinks."

"I thought you might say that."

"Did you know Betsy Dickerson took out a half-a-million-dollar life insurance policy on her husband forty-five days before he died?"

"Yeah, I saw that in the file. Could be coincidence."

"I don't think so. James had to have a checkup to qualify. Guess who did the checkup?"

Interest curled through him. "Don't tell me—the same doctor who was present when he died."

"Bingo. Dr. Bernard Atwood. Atwood is the Dickerson family physician. Forty-six years old, single, decent-looking, and my guess is he's plenty chummy with the widow."

"And you're guessing this…because?"

"I took a look at Atwood's credit cards. Until her husband died, Betsy Dickerson worked as a bank manager at Wells Fargo Bank. The branch is two doors down from the Copper Kettle Café. According to Atwood's Gold American Express, in the three weeks before Betsy quit her job, he had lunch seven times at the Copper Kettle."

"Very interesting."

"Yup. Especially since his office is a couple of miles away."

"So for some strange reason, Atwood drove downtown a couple of times a week to eat in the restaurant next to the bank where Betsy Dickerson just happened to work. Doesn't give us any actual proof, but it's a damn good start."

"You bet it is and believe me I'm on it."

"So am I. I'll make a trip to the Copper Kettle, see if I can confirm your guesses."

"Great. Back to you soon." Tabby hung up the phone.

The day slogged past. As lunchtime neared, he printed out a photo of Bernard Atwood he found on the internet and one of Betsy Dickerson, and drove down to the Copper Kettle. The place wasn't fancy, just booths and a counter, your average coffee shop with your average coffee shop food. Which made Atwood's trip there for lunch even more suspicious.

Chase talked to the owner, a heavyset Italian named Mario who spoke with an accent and wore a white apron tied around his impressive girth. Mario didn't know Atwood but he knew Betsy Dickerson, and he'd seen her eating more than once with the man in the photo Chase showed him.

One of the waitresses also confirmed that the bank manager had lunch several times with the attractive man in the photo.

By itself it wasn't enough, but Tabby had only started digging and she was good. The best. If there was something there, Tabby would find it.

In the meantime, Chase had an office to run. He headed back to Blackburn Street and had no more than walked through the door when Jax Ryker, one of his PIs, walked up with a problem. He worked with Jax to find a solution. Ryker left the office and a few minutes later, Maddox phoned.

"Chase, I'm outside the Boom Boom Club. There's a skip inside by the name of Harley Gibbons. He won't go down easy. Jax offered to back me up, but I just located the dude, and Mindy says Ryker got called away on a case. You think you could—"

"On my way." Chase opened the bottom drawer of his desk and took out his Glock. "I know where the club is. Just hang tight till I get there." Coming to his feet, he clipped the Glock to his belt, grabbed his jacket off the coatrack in the corner and headed for the door, grateful to Maddox for something to do besides worry about Harper.

It didn't take long to reach the Boom Boom Club out on Harry Hines Boulevard. As he pulled into the lot next to the club, Chase spotted Maddox's big black Yukon. Since half the drug dealers in Dallas drove similar cars, the vehicle blended right in. With the restraints welded into the back, the SUV provided a good means of transport for the bail skips Maddox arrested.

Chase got out of the pickup and caught up with him outside the back door of the club.

"Gibbons is inside," Maddox said. "He's a big bastard. He goes off in there, someone's going to get hurt. Let me see if I can get him outside."

"I'll be right here."

Maddox disappeared inside the club, and Chase took up a position beside the back door. It was noisy and dark inside, except for the colored spotlights flashing over the near-naked women onstage. From his vantage point, Chase could see Maddox moving through the crowd, heading for the table where his quarry sat next to a blowsy blonde.

Chase couldn't imagine what Maddox said to the

man, but the next thing he knew, Gibbons was out of his chair and charging after Maddox, who was running toward the door with just enough speed to keep from getting caught, but not enough for Gibbons to get discouraged.

The two men burst through the back door, out into the parking lot, Gibbons snagging Maddox's leather jacket and spinning him around, throwing a punch that Jason ducked. Maddox threw a roundhouse punch to Gibbons's jaw that had him staggering—Maddox was no little guy himself.

The two big men scuffled in the dirt parking lot. Maddox took a couple of punches and threw a few more. When Gibbons reached into the pocket of his jeans and pulled a small caliber pistol, Chase stepped in, back-kneeing Gibbons, who buckled and whirled toward the new threat. Chase grabbed Gibbons's wrist and wrenched the pistol out of his hand, and Hawk took him down.

It was over in a couple of minutes, Gibbons hand-cuffed, swearing and lying in the dirt.

"Nice work," Chase said. He waited till Maddox had his prey secured in the back of his SUV, then waved and headed back to his truck. Maddox would pick up a fat bounty, and a wanted fugitive would be taken off the streets. Not a bad night's work. Satisfied, Chase headed for home, worry about Harper not far from his thoughts.

CHAPTER TWENTY-NINE

Harper awoke the next morning, feeling listless, dull and depressed. Work didn't help, with a series of problems, one after another. First one of their suppliers filed bankruptcy without filling the Elemental Chic order. EC's deposit was gone, and the supplier was broke. Which meant they would have to find a new company and come up with more cash to pay for the product.

Two of her employees were out with the stomach flu. Harper didn't want the rest of the staff infected, so she asked them to stay home an extra day, just to be safe.

Shana had a flat tire in the parking lot, which put her in a bad mood. Add to that, Harper kept thinking of Chase's betrayal, going over everything that had happened and calling herself ten kinds of a fool.

Eventually, closing time arrived. At least by then Shana's mood had improved. She grinned as she headed for the door.

"Got me a hot date with a sexy new man and he is sooo delicious."

"What? Why is this the first I'm hearing about it? What's his name?"

"Alejandro Orlando. He's gorgeous and seriously ripped. Which I know from the magazine ads he does. I'll give you the gory details in the morning."

Harper grinned. "If he's that amazing, I don't mind if you come in late."

Shana laughed. "Depends if he's got anything upstairs to go with that sexy body. I'll give you the scoop tomorrow."

Harper stayed an extra hour before locking up and heading for her Beemer. It was dark, but the parking lot was fairly well lit and she was always careful, checking to be sure no one followed her out of the building or managed to break into her car and hide in the backseat.

With everything that had happened, she was ridiculously paranoid. She told herself, for the time being, at least, it was good she was watchful of her surroundings, constantly on the lookout for trouble.

Drug dealers. DEA agents. Colombian rebels. Her brother had been kidnapped. Her dad was under investigation for God only knew what. Anything could happen.

Which was the reason she noticed the car at the far end of the parking lot that pulled out behind her as she pulled out onto the street.

In her rearview mirror, she could see the car's headlights burning into the darkness, and something niggled at the back of her brain. The vehicle looked familiar. The same car or one very similar had been parked down the street the morning she had left her father's house in Westlake. A blue Buick sedan with Hertz rental plates.

She wouldn't have noticed the car except for her paranoia. Wouldn't have kept an eye on it a good deal of the way back to the city that morning. Thinking about it now, wondering if the car a few vehicles back could possibly be the same, should have been ridiculous, but somehow it didn't seem that way.

She reminded herself if a threat turned out to be real, it wasn't paranoia at all.

On a whim, careful to keep her speed the same so she wouldn't alert the driver if he really was following her, she made an unexpected turn onto a smaller, less traveled two-lane road that would take her in the same direction.

Headlights, several car lengths back, made the same turn. Her stomach tightened. She was pretty sure the headlights belonged to the same car, and her pulse kicked up.

Winding her way along the less traveled road, she continued on toward her town house as if nothing were wrong. The same car kept pace with her all the way, keeping its distance, just far enough back so she couldn't be sure what was going on.

If he'd followed her before, he would already know where she lived so there was no reason to avoid going home. Except she didn't want to be there by herself if the man came after her.

Her palms were sweating. Her grip tightened on the steering wheel. She needed to figure things out, needed to be sure she wasn't in danger. Where could she go that she would be safe? Oh, God, Chase was the last person she wanted to see and the first person she thought of.

Maybe Chase wouldn't be in the office but Bran would be there. If not, The Max was full of macho detectives, all armed and capable of handling whatever situation came up. She turned toward Maximum Security but didn't go too fast. The car stayed on her tail.

As she pulled into the parking lot, it occurred to her it was after closing. Her gaze shot to the window, and relief poured through her when she saw the lights were still on. Chase had told her the guys all worked late off and on.

As she parked in the lot, she looked for Chase's silver Mercedes, but it wasn't there. He usually drove his pickup, but there were no trucks in the lot, either. She breathed a little easier when she spotted Bran's black Jeep Wrangler. Since it was after hours, she walked around the building to the front door, and spotted the Buick pulling into a parking space a ways down the block across the street. When the headlights went off, a shiver ran down her spine.

Harper pulled open the front door and frantically glanced around the office, but the only person in sight was the little dark-haired receptionist, Mindy, a name she recalled from the plate on the desk the first time she had been there.

"May I help you?" Mindy smiled. "Oh, I'm sorry, I didn't recognize you. You're Chase's client Ms. Winston."

Harper felt an ache in her chest. *Chase's client.* Had she ever meant more to him than that? "I'm Harper Winston. I was hoping Brandon would be here. I saw his Jeep in the parking lot."

"Bran's down at Clancy's. Chase left to run an errand." Mindy frowned. "Are you all right? You're trembling." She rose and came out from behind the desk. "What's going on?"

Harper glanced toward the window, but all she could see was darkness. "I don't know. Maybe nothing. I think someone followed me from my office. I think maybe they followed me the other day, too."

"Sit down, Ms. Winston. I'm calling the police."

"No! I don't… I don't think that's a good idea. It might be nothing. I don't know. I'm not sure."

But Mindy was already hitting 9-1-1 on her cell phone. When the dispatcher answered, she reported a possible stalker lurking in a car out in front of the office. As she gave the police the information, she walked over and turned the lock on the front door.

Harper sank down on the tufted leather sofa in the reception area, and Mindy sat down beside her.

"I'm calling Chase," Mindy said. "He'll want to be here."

The knot in Harper's stomach went tighter. "Please don't do that. The cops are on the way. Listen. Do you hear that? Police sirens. They're almost here already."

Mindy looked uncertain. "You're Chase's client. If I don't call him, he's going to be very unhappy."

A police car rolled to a stop out front, siren wailing, red and blue lights flashing through the window. Harper jumped up as car doors flew open, and a pair of uniformed patrolmen ducked out of the patrol car.

Mindy unlocked the door and the officers streamed inside, one tall, black haired and wildly good-looking, the other older, heavier, with salt-and-pepper hair.

"You're the woman who called?" the handsome officer asked Harper.

"I'm the one who called," Mindy corrected, adjusting her tortoiseshell glasses. "I'm Mindy. This is Harper Winston. She thinks someone followed her down here. She thinks they've followed her before."

Harper looked out the window, but the space where

the Buick had been parked was empty. She took a deep breath, suddenly regretting her impulse to drive to the office. Her father was under federal investigation. Would a police report involving his daughter somehow make things worse for him?

"I'm sorry for the trouble, Officers. The car I saw is already gone. Things have been kind of unsettled lately. I was probably just overreacting."

"Did you get a plate number, Ms. Winston?" the heavyset officer asked.

"No. I got a look at the vehicle in the parking lot behind my office. It was a blue Buick sedan. I noticed the Hertz rental plates, but it stayed several car lengths back, and I didn't think to try to get a license number."

She should have. Would have if she weren't so new at this kind of intrigue. "I'm okay now. The car is long gone. I'll be fine."

"She'll be fine," a familiar voice said as Chase strode down the hall through the back door of the building. "You have my personal guarantee. From now on, Ms. Winston will be under my protection. She'll be safe, I promise you."

Harper's legs felt suddenly weak. As Chase spoke to the officers, she sank back down on the sofa, her insides tied in knots. Chase was the last person she wanted to see. And the person she wanted to see most in the world.

How had her life turned so completely upside down?

The cops took Harper's statement and left the office, and Mindy went home. Chase was thankful his receptionist had stayed after closing to catch up on some bookkeeping files she was reorganizing. Grateful she had been there when Harper arrived.

Chase had left to run an errand, but he had returned to review a couple of files before he headed home.

Or maybe he just hadn't been ready to face his empty condo tonight.

Now he wouldn't have to. Because as soon as he'd heard the reason Harper had driven to the office, there was no way he was letting her go anywhere alone.

"The cops are gone," he said. "It's just you and me, Harper. I want you to tell me exactly what happened. Start at the beginning."

Sitting next to him on the sofa, she sighed and leaned back. She looked pale and shaken. He wasn't sure if it was because she thought she was being followed or because he had shown up when she was hoping she would find Bran.

She looked nervous and upset, and she looked beautiful. And seeing her tonight, he knew one thing for sure.

He wasn't giving her up again. Not when she might be in even more trouble without him.

"There isn't that much to tell," Harper said. "I noticed the Buick parked in the lot behind my office. It pulled out behind me when I drove onto the street. I remembered a car like it, a blue Buick with Hertz rental car plates, parked on the street near my father's house the last time I was out there."

"The morning you told your father you weren't going to see me anymore."

Her head came up. "That's right. How did you…? Oh, I forgot. You were listening."

"I wasn't listening. The Feds were. Tanner sent word through Brandon. I appreciate what you did. I know you did it to protect me."

"Whatever happened between us, I owe you for saving my brother's life. I didn't want to see you get hurt."

He hoped it was more than that. And he hoped it wasn't too late to fix things. He didn't mention his encounter with her father's thugs, but apparently she noticed the bruise on his cheek.

Harper frowned. "What happened to your face?"

Chase managed to smile. "Nothing much. A little dustup. You ought to see the other guys."

Her hand curled in her lap. "Was it… Was it my father's men?"

He wasn't lying to her again. He wanted to hold her, comfort her. He forced himself not to touch her, sure she would pull back if he did.

"I'm not going to lie to you, Harper. I've done too much of that already. From now on you get the straight, unvarnished truth. It'll be up to you how you handle it."

"So it *was* him. My father ordered his men to attack you. How many of them were there?"

"Four. But Bran was there. The truth is, they wound up getting the worst of it."

"Oh, God." She pressed her fingers against her lips, sucked in a deep breath of air. "Will they come after you again?"

"You told your father we were no longer seeing each other." *True, at least for the moment.* "I don't think they'll come after me again."

She tipped her head back, then sat up a little straighter and looked him in the eye. "Is all of it true? My father is a drug smuggler?"

"Knox Winston has been involved in criminal activities for years. No one has ever been able to get the kind of evidence that would stand up in court. The DEA saw our relationship as an opportunity to bring your father to justice." He reached out and gently caught her chin. Harper turned away.

"Aiding law enforcement is what I do for a living, Harper. It doesn't matter who the bad guys are. The DEA asked for my help. I didn't want to hurt you, but I felt I had no choice."

She slowly rose from the sofa, exhaustion written all over her face. "I'm tired, Chase. I'm going home. Thanks for being honest."

"Do you have any idea who the guy who followed you is?"

She shook her head. "No. You don't think it could be DEA, some kind of federal agent?"

"In a rental car? Not likely. But I'll find out. In the meantime, you aren't safe by yourself, Harper. Your brother was kidnapped just a few weeks ago. We still aren't sure why. Which means you could be a target, too."

She trembled. "Do you really think so?"

"I think it's entirely possible. Until we know what's going on, you're going to need some kind of protection. I'm not leaving you alone, angel. I know you think the worst of me, but if you're honest with yourself, you know I'll protect you." With his life, if it came to that.

Her chin went up. "If you really think I need protection, I'll hire Brandon. He's a bodyguard. And I trust him."

Unlike you were the unspoken words.

"You can hire Bran if you want. You're still going to have to deal with me. I'm not letting you out of my sight, honey. Not until this thing is resolved one way or another."

"You can't do that! You can't just waltz back into my life and bully me into doing whatever you want!"

Amusement touched his lips. Damn, she was amazing. "Call it what you want, sweetheart. I'm coming home with you. Or you're coming home with me. What's it going to be?"

"Why? Why is it so important to you?"

Why? Because he couldn't stand the thought of something happening to her. Because he had finally realized how important she was to him.

"I'll tell you why. Because I made a mistake. I let you go when I should have fought for you. I'm not making the same mistake again. Now, let's go."

She stared at him as if snakes were growing out of his head, as if she couldn't believe what he had just said. He could hardly believe it himself. Then she picked up her purse, turned and started for the door.

Figuring she would be more at ease in her own place, Chase followed her to her car, then waited while she settled behind the wheel.

"I'll be right behind you," he said. "I'm driving my pickup."

Harper made no reply, just cranked the engine on the Beemer as he climbed into his truck. He relaxed a little when she braked at the edge of the lot, her taillights going on as she waited for him to pull up behind her. She drove into the street and he followed. Reaching over, he opened the glove box and took out his Glock, clipped the holster onto his belt.

From now on until this was over, he would be armed. No matter what happened, he'd make sure Harper was safe.

CHAPTER THIRTY

Harper couldn't believe it. Chase Garrett was not only back in her life, he was spending the night in her guest room.

I made a mistake, he had said. *I let you go when I should have fought for you.*

The words made no sense. Chase had betrayed her. Used her to get to her father. He had aided the men who wanted to put Knox Winston in prison. She would never be able to trust him again. Surely he knew that.

She heard the water running in the bathroom at the end of the upstairs hall. She didn't want to think of Chase in the shower. She didn't want to remember that steel-hard body, the wide shoulders and washboard abs, the feel of him pressing her down in the mattress, driving her to the most incredible climax she'd ever known.

The shower went off. She had almost escaped to her bedroom when the bathroom door opened and

Chase stood in the opening, a towel wrapped around his slim hips.

Her stomach clenched as Chase walked toward her, droplets of water clinging to the light dusting of dark gold hair on his chest. Muscle rippled across his flat belly. His biceps bulged as he towel-dried his hair.

Harper bit back a moan. Watching him approach, she began to feel light-headed. Who knew sexual desire could actually make a person dizzy?

Chase stopped right in front of her. "Everything's locked up tight. Even if somebody is dumb enough to try to break in, you don't have to worry. I'm a very light sleeper."

Remembering that from their days in the jungle, she managed to nod, forcing herself to keep her eyes on his face.

Chase reached out and touched her cheek. "Good night, angel."

Harper stiffened. "Don't call me that. We aren't together anymore. That's not going to change."

"I'm not a man who gives up easily, Harper. Not when there's something I want. I made a mistake. I'm going to find a way to fix it."

"You made a mistake when you used me to get to my father."

"That wasn't my mistake. My mistake was not trusting you with the truth. Making you understand the reason it had to be done."

She couldn't breathe. She didn't want his words to make sense. "He's still my father. He'll always be my father."

"I know. We'll have to find a way around it."

A way around it? "There is no way around it."

"I guess we'll see." Chase turned and walked away, his muscular back as enticing as his flat stomach and amazing chest. Disappearing into the guest room, he closed the door, and Harper breathed a sigh of relief.

It didn't matter that she was physically attracted to Chase. The man had broken her heart. She wasn't getting involved with him again.

Exhausted, she went to her bedroom. Chase had checked all the locks on the windows and doors. He had checked her security system and approved. There was nothing to do but try to get some sleep.

She knew Chase slept naked, and he was in the bedroom next to hers. He planned to stay until he knew for sure she was safe. God only knew how long that would be.

What in the world had possessed her to go to The Max for help? Harper sighed as she walked into the bathroom to brush her teeth. She didn't want Chase anywhere near her. But she couldn't deny she felt safer knowing he was staying in the guest room.

They finally agreed on a plan. They'd argued all morning, fought and even shouted, both of them equally determined. Chase liked that Harper was strong enough to stand up to him. He liked that she was also smart enough to understand the danger and back down when she realized he was right.

A reminder of her brother and Pia, kidnapped and force-marched through the jungle, had been his closing argument. Her protest had died on her lips. Harper's intelligence was one of the things he found so attractive.

In the end, they had decided that Chase would drive

Harper to work, then pick her up at the end of the day. Both could do their jobs and Harper would be safe.

She wasn't happy about the security guard he posted at the bottom of the stairs leading up to the Elemental Chic offices, but she understood it was important for the safety of her staff as well as herself.

Satisfied she was as secure as possible, Chase left her in her office and went to work. He made some phone calls, one to DEA Agent Tanner to be sure the blue Buick wasn't one of their undercover vehicles. He wasn't surprised to hear it was not.

It was midafternoon when an unexpected phone call came from Reese.

"Hey, bro," Chase answered. "Haven't heard from you in a while. What's up?"

"I need to see you. Bran called me this morning about what happened to Harper last night, that someone's been following her. He's been keeping me abreast of what's been going on since you two got back from Colombia."

"I should have called you myself. Sorry."

"You've been busy. I get that, believe me." As CEO of Garrett Resources, the billion-dollar oil and gas corporation his family owned, Reese ran one of the top-rated companies in Texas.

When Bass Garrett died, leaving the company and the millions Bass was worth to his three sons, Reese had taken over the business. Chase and Bran had no interest in running the company, but it had been Reese's dream.

Or at least had become his dream after he'd been released from juvenile detention and moved out of their father's house, where he had been getting into trouble since their parents' divorce. From the day he'd moved in with his mother and brothers, Reese's life had changed.

"There's something I need to talk to you about," Reese said. "You and Bran, both. Someplace besides your office or mine."

Chase frowned. "Sounds serious."

"It is."

"How about my place?" Chase suggested. "It's fairly central."

"That'll work."

"I'll phone Bran, ask him to meet us there."

"Say two o'clock?"

"I'll see you then." Chase hung up and punched in Bran's contact number. His brother picked up on the second ring. "Reese wants to see us. He says it's important. Can you be at my place at two?"

"Sure, no problem. I talked to him this morning, but he didn't say anything about it. Any idea what's going on?"

"Not a clue."

"I guess we'll find out when we get there."

"I'm not a fan of surprises," Chase said. "I'll see you there." He hung up the phone. Reese was separated from his wife, Sandra, and living in an apartment. Getting back together didn't look good. Maybe Reese was going to tell them he was getting a divorce—which wouldn't come as much of a surprise.

But from the tone of his brother's voice, Chase didn't think so. After the months Reese and Sandra had been apart, a phone call would have been enough.

By the time he grabbed his jacket off the coatrack in the corner and headed out the door, he'd come up with half a dozen different scenarios. Trouble with the family-owned company, a financial problem of some kind. A lawsuit. People were sue-crazy these days. He didn't want to think Reese might have some kind of illness.

Chase had no idea what the hell was going on.

A little before two, he parked the Dodge in its spot in the underground garage next to the Benz and took the elevator up to the seventeenth floor. Bran was standing in the hall in front of the door, using his key to get in.

"Hey, bro," Bran called out, turning the knob and stepping into the foyer. Chase followed him inside.

"You come up with any ideas?" Bran asked. "Nothing makes sense."

"We're about to find out. You want a beer or something?"

"I could use one. I got a bad feeling about this."

It wasn't like Reese to call a family meeting. Hell, it wasn't like any of them. They all got together on holidays or whenever they felt the urge, but the last time there had been an official meeting was when their mother got cancer. The memory made Chase's stomach burn.

They headed down the hall to the study, the place Chase spent most of his time. He walked over to the wet bar, opened the undercounter fridge and pulled out a couple of Lone Stars. Twisting off the cap, he handed one to Bran, opened another one and took a long swallow.

Reese's voice came from the doorway. "I could use one of those myself." His middle brother looked a lot like their grandfather, with Sam Devlin's black hair and blue eyes. Reese's good looks had been part of his problem in high school, too, too handsome, too many women and too much money, always a recipe for trouble.

"You might want to sit down for this," Reese said to both brothers, accepting the beer Chase handed him.

Bran didn't budge. Worry tightened his features. "Just tell us you aren't sick."

Reese's head came up. "No. God, no. It's nothing like that. I'm sorry. I should have told you that right off."

Chase locked eyes with Bran, and both of them breathed a sigh of relief.

"This is family business," Reese continued. "Something that happened in the past that you both need to know about."

At least they weren't going to lose another member of their family. Crossing the room, the men sat down on the brown leather sofa and chairs around the dark wood coffee table. A gas fireplace was built into the wall not far away, but it wasn't burning.

Chase took a drink of beer. Bran did the same. A little fortification. "Okay, we're listening."

"This is something Dad told me when he was in the hospital, the day before he died." Since Bass had mostly raised him, Reese had been closest to their father.

"Dad wanted someone to know. He made me promise I'd never tell anyone unless it was absolutely necessary. With everything that's going on, I think it's time you knew the truth."

Bran set his beer down sharply on the coffee table. "What the hell is it, Reese?"

"Michael Winston is our brother."

Stunned silence fell. "What the fuck...?" Bran said.

"Half brother, technically. Bass was his father. Amelia Winston was his mother."

Chase sat back in his chair, trying to wrap his head

around it. "So Dad was cheating on Mom with Knox's wife?"

"According to Dad, it was a one-night stand. Just an accident, really. He and Knox were attending some kind of business conference. He met Amelia there, then a week later he ran into her at a Christmas party at the Adolphus Hotel. He and Mom were fighting, as usual, so she wasn't with him. Knox was out of town."

"Convenient," Chase said.

"According to Dad, Amelia was upset about the way Knox was treating her. She cried on Dad's shoulder, and they ended getting a room upstairs. The next day, both of them regretted what happened and that was the end of it."

"Except that Amelia Winston got pregnant," Chase said.

"Yes."

"So all those years, Dad just ignored his son," Bran said darkly.

"Not exactly. Dad knew Amelia would suffer if Knox found out. He promised her he'd never tell, and he didn't."

"He should have helped Michael," Chase said. "Michael was his son."

"Actually, he did. How do you think Michael got the loan to start his business? With his drug history, it would have been a no go if it hadn't been for Dad. Dad hated the way Knox treated him."

Chase started nodding. "I remember Dad was always nice to Michael whenever he came over, interested in what he was doing, what he had to say."

"As I look back on it," Reese said, "I think Knox

knew Michael wasn't his. It was one of the reasons he hated Dad so much."

"And the reason he treated Michael so badly," Chase added.

"Probably," Reese said. "But it would have made things worse for Amelia—worse for Michael, too—if Dad had come out and told the truth."

Bran took a long swallow of beer. "I gotta say I didn't see this one coming."

"Neither did I," Chase said.

Bran's gaze swung in his direction. "Maybe that's why you and Michael became such good friends when you were in college. DNA's a funny thing."

Yes, it was.

Bran grinned. "Lucky for you, Harper's no relation. Different mother, different father."

Chase almost smiled.

"I'm glad she came to you for help after Michael disappeared," Reese said.

Chase nodded. "So am I." And thinking about it, he was beginning to understand why Reese had decided to call this meeting. "I'm guessing that's the reason we're here. You're worried Michael may still be in danger."

Reese sat forward. "Bran told me about the DEA investigation. I knew about Michael's kidnapping. Now Harper's being followed. It all revolves around Knox Winston. Michael's our brother. We need to make sure he's safe."

Bran shot up from the sofa. "I'll take care of Michael. I've got a problem I need to handle first, but I can be in Houston tomorrow. In the meantime, I've got a friend who can keep an eye on him till I get there."

Bran strode to the door, stopped and turned back. "You think I should tell him?"

Chase looked at Reese and silent agreement passed between them.

"I think it's time," Reese said.

Bran disappeared out the door, and Reese blew out a slow breath. "Man, it's a relief to get that off my chest after all these years."

"I'll bet," Chase said. "We should probably set up some kind of a trust fund or something."

"Dad took care of it. I'm the trustee. It's up to me to decide when to turn it over to Michael. I wanted to make sure he was…you know…okay."

"Clean and sober, you mean. Michael's doing great. I don't think we have to worry about that anymore."

"Good. As soon as all of this gets sorted, we'll talk to him about it."

Chase smiled. "Believe it or not, I think he'll be pleased. He and Knox were always viciously at odds. Like you said, DNA's a funny thing."

"What about Harper?" Reese asked. "You going to tell her?"

He'd promised her the truth. He wasn't going back on his word. "When the time is right."

Leaning over the table, Reese held up his bottle of beer. "Here's to family."

Chase clinked his bottle with Reese's. "To family."

He couldn't help wondering how all the pieces of the jigsaw puzzle would eventually fit together—and where it would leave him and Harper once they did.

CHAPTER THIRTY-ONE

Late in the afternoon, Chase took a call from Harper telling him she had to work late that night.

"No problem," he said. "I've got plenty to do here for a while."

"I should be done by seven…if that works for you."

"Fine. I'll see you then." He phoned the security guard, an ex-cop named Rich Mooney who'd been injured in the line of duty and now worked for Maximum Security part-time. He gave Mooney a heads-up, told him to end his shift at four instead of five, then call Pete Caruthers, another retired cop, to work the next three hours.

Better a shorter shift, followed by a guard who came in fresh, than one who was half-asleep on the job.

"I'll take care of it," Mooney said.

"No trouble so far?" Chase asked. "No sign of the blue Buick?"

"Not a trace."

Chase figured the guy had been scared off when the cops showed up at The Max. He would probably lie low for a while, which might turn into an even bigger problem. If that happened, they'd have no idea where or when he might pop up. Since there was nothing Chase could do about it, he ended the call and went back to work.

At five o'clock, Tabby called. "Got something for you, boss."

He'd been hoping to hear from her. He'd held off phoning Dickerson until he had something more concrete than an affair between his son's wife and the doctor who'd pronounced him dead. "Bad news or good?"

"Bad news for Errol Dickerson. Looks like his son was murdered."

"What have you got?"

"Betsy Dickerson had a credit card in her name only. Three weeks before he died, Betsy bought a can of rat poison over the internet and had it shipped to her at the bank. I checked it out. This particular poison contains thallium."

Anger filtered through him. "Banned in this country because it's so lethal."

"Exactly."

"It's tasteless and odorless. James wouldn't have even suspected."

"That's right. I did some digging. I found a case where a man killed his wife by adding rat poison to her tea. The woman went into a coma. Two days later, she suffered a cardiac arrest and died. The police were suspicious. They got an order for the body to be exhumed and found traces of thallium in her blood."

Chase's jaw felt tight. "Since we can't exhume

James's body, we'll have to find another way to prove it. Thanks, Tabby."

"I'll let you know if I come up with anything else." Tabby hung up the phone.

Sympathy for Errol Dickerson filtered through him, along with anger at the murder of his son. The question was how to prove it.

Picking up the phone, he dialed the Dallas Police Department and asked for Heath Ford. Heath was a homicide detective, best on the force as far as Chase was concerned.

The phone picked up. "Detective Ford."

"It's Chase Garrett, Heath. I've got a problem…a case I'm working that's looking more and more like a homicide. I'm hoping you can help."

"That's what I'm here for. What have you got?"

Chase filled his friend in on the possible thallium murder of James Dickerson by his wife, Betsy, and the man they suspected was her lover, Dr. Bernard Atwood, the motive primarily greed.

Heath promised to look into the case and get back to him.

At six thirty Chase drove his pickup out of the parking lot onto Blackburn Street, then took Highway 75 down to Harper's warehouse office on South 2nd Avenue, about a fifteen-minute trip.

When he walked through the main door of the building, Pete stood at the bottom of the stairs leading up to Harper's suite of offices, a tall, thin guy in a dark blue Maximum Security uniform, a pistol in the belt around his waist.

"How's it going?" Chase asked as he walked toward him.

"Been quiet. Same for Rich."

Chase nodded. "I'll take over from here. Have a good evening, Pete." Chase pounded up the stairs, saw the office door swing open and Harper step into the hallway. She spotted him and met him at the top of the landing.

Wearing brown leggings and a yellow knit sweater with a stand-up collar and the EC parrot on the front, she looked way better than good. But then she always did.

Chase ignored a slide of heat that went straight to his groin. "You ready to go?"

"More than ready. It's been a long day. I talked to your guy Rich a little earlier. He seemed very nice. He said he hadn't seen any sign of the Buick."

"Neither has Pete. He took over at four."

"Maybe the guy won't be back."

"Or maybe he's waiting for you to let down your guard—which we aren't going to do."

She made no comment, but her jaw looked a little tight. She wanted him out of the picture, wanted to keep him at arm's length. It wasn't going to happen. Not if he could help it.

When they reached the bottom of the stairs, he set a hand at her waist, which Harper shook off, and they walked to his pickup. From the warehouse, he drove toward her town house on Armstrong. It was Friday night, the streets busy, pedestrians strolling the sidewalks, couples walking in and out of local restaurants.

"I just realized how hungry I am," Harper said as the Dodge rolled along.

"You want to stop somewhere and eat?"

She sighed. "I'm tired. Let's just order some Chinese or something when we get to the house."

He knew she was thinking that after they ate, she'd be able to go upstairs and not have to spend time with him. "All right," he reluctantly agreed.

When they got to the town house, Chase checked for any sign of a break-in, found none and returned to the living room.

Harper looked up at him with those big blue eyes and a trace of vulnerability, and guilt trickled through him. He'd vowed to protect her and yet he had hurt her. He wondered if she had any idea how much she meant to him.

"So what should we order?" she asked. "Chinese or pizza?"

Chase knew exactly what he wanted. His gaze ran over her sleek curves, down those long legs in a pair of tight leggings and sexy high heels. Something shifted in the air between them, seemed to heat and thicken around them.

When he caught Harper looking at him with the same hungry need burning through him, Chase made a decision. Setting his hands at her waist, he drew her in front of him, close enough they were touching full length.

"Dinner can wait," he said, and bent his head to kiss her.

Harper shoved a hand against his chest and turned away. "This isn't going to happen, Chase."

"You don't think so?" He bent to nibble the side of her neck and felt her shiver.

"We can't... I don't want to do this. We need...to stop."

Chase tightened his hold. "If you mean that, I'll stop right now. Is that what you want?" He waited, let the seconds spin out.

When Harper made no reply, he kissed her again, a slow, deep melding of lips, a hot, deeply erotic kiss meant to arouse and seduce.

A faint sound seeped from her throat, and she swayed against him. When she trembled and slid her arms around his neck, Chase continued his assault, taking the kiss from slow and sensual to hot, hard and hungry, a kiss that sent his pulse racing and turned his erection to steel.

Harper moaned and kissed him back, her fingers winding into the hair at the nape of his neck as she gave herself up to him.

In the past, with the problems they were facing, he had let her set the pace. He hadn't wanted to push her into doing something that would wind up hurting her.

That was about to change.

Harper had been his since the night he had kissed her in the seedy motel in Punta Gato. It was time he made that clear.

Scooping her up in his arms, he climbed the stairs and strode down the hall to her bedroom. Her eyes widened as he set her on her feet, unclipped his pistol and set it on the dresser, and started stripping off her clothes.

"What…what about my father? It isn't right for us to—"

"Yes, it is." Chase kissed her, stroking deep into her mouth, staking his claim. Harper moaned. In minutes he had her naked, but he didn't stop, just lifted her and set her on the edge of the bed, pulled his shirt off over his head, spread her pretty legs and knelt between them. Her scent enticed him. Everything about her turned him on.

Harper was his. After tonight, she wouldn't doubt it.

Together they would find a way to solve the problems ahead of them.

Easing her back on the bed, he went to work, kissing the insides of her thighs, nipping and tasting, arousing her till she was begging him to take her. In minutes she had reached a powerful climax, her body quaking, his name a cry on her lips.

Chase didn't pause, just pulled off his boots and the rest of his clothes, and stretched out naked on the bed beside her. Lifting her astride him, he filled his hands with her pretty breasts and began arousing her all over again. Harper leaned over him, her breath coming in soft little gasps, her silky hair tumbling around them as he seated himself deep inside.

Gripping her hips, Chase surged upward, began to set up a rhythm, once more driving her toward the peak. Harper moaned. As release drew near, she took over and Chase let her, giving her the reins, making her part of the bond he was forging.

She was his. Somehow he would find a way to make things right between them.

Harper braced her hands on his shoulders as she rode him, challenging him, driving him to the brink. She was close. Chase used his skills to keep her there, right on the edge.

"Chase!" she cried out as a second climax struck, and the feel of her sheath tightening around him destroyed the last of his control. His release came swift and hard, more powerful with the deep feelings for Harper he had finally accepted.

Little by little they began to spiral down, Harper slumped over his chest.

He smoothed back her damp, silver-blond hair. "It's

all right, angel." Easing her down on the bed beside him, he cocooned her in his arms. "Everything's going to be okay."

He was determined to make things right, believed he would find a way.

But when he felt the wetness of her tears on his chest, Chase wasn't so sure.

Luis Montoya wasn't happy. Nearly two weeks had passed, and the Winston girl remained in Texas. Since he'd made his decision to have her, she had become an obsession. Half a dozen photos rested in his top desk drawer.

Later he would look at them, as he did each night before he left the study. He would pretend she was there with him and stroke himself to release. It didn't take long.

He looked up as the door opened and Eduardo Ramos walked into the study, his thick black hair gleaming in the lamplight. He reminded Luis of a predatory bird.

"You wished to see me, *jefe*?"

Luis leaned back in his chair. "Where is the girl? I told you to bring her to me! You said you would handle it."

"I have men working on it. There have been unforeseen problems."

"What kind of problems?"

"The girl is under the protection of the same *gringos* who were with her in Colombia. Security personnel. Former military. My men have assured me they have come up with a solution, a plan that will work."

"I'm tired of waiting. That *bastardo* Winston needs

to learn a lesson. Losing his daughter to me is one he will not soon forget."

"*Sí, jefe*. But vengeance will be costly. Since we resumed our business association, Winston has been distributing our product quite successfully. We have made a good deal of money."

Luis grunted. "I suppose that is some consolation." He thought of Winston's beautiful blonde daughter with her big eyes and soft pink lips, the ways he would use her, the things he would do.

"Once I am finished with the girl, I will return her to her father as a gesture of good faith, give Winston the opportunity to resume our business dealings."

Eduardo's thin lips curved. "That would certainly give him a clear understanding of who is in charge. But surely no man could forgive such an insult."

Luis reached across his desk to the glass humidor near the corner, lifted the lid and pulled out a thick cigar. The fragrant aroma of expensive tobacco filled the air.

"The use of the girl in exchange for the millions of dollars he makes with us? Hard to know what the American would do." Luis took a pair of silver clippers and snipped the end off the cigar. "I'll expect the girl here in no more than a week."

His *segundo* smiled. "If all goes as planned, *jefe*, you will not have to wait that long."

CHAPTER THIRTY-TWO

Harper rode in silence the following morning as Chase pulled his pickup into Elemental Chic's office parking lot and turned off the engine. By the time he came around to help her down, she was already out of the truck.

They had barely talked all morning. She was still upset about last night, angry mostly at herself. She had wanted him—yes. She always seemed to want him.

But surely the man wasn't completely irresistible.

She glanced over to where he walked beside her in snug jeans, a dark brown long-sleeved Henley and a pair of cowboy boots. Rays of sunlight turned his hair and the short-cropped beard along his jaw a dark shade of gold.

Feeling a tug of the same attraction she had succumbed to last night, she bit back a curse. Maybe *irresistible* wasn't a strong enough word.

Still, this morning when she had awakened beside

him, she had made it clear she wasn't in the mood to
continue where they had left off, which probably had
more to do with the multiple orgasms she'd had last
night than willpower.

Or maybe the man was just smart enough not to
push his luck.

Chase opened the glass front door, and they walked
into the building to find the Maximum Security guard
already at work. Rich Mooney was average height, late
forties, with sandy hair and a nice smile.

He seemed to have an easygoing disposition, but his
eyes moved constantly, always alert. Once a cop, always
a cop, she figured, probably why Chase had hired him.

"Morning, boss," he said. "Ms. Winston."

"Good morning, Rich," she said.

"No problems so far?" Chase asked.

"The parking lot was empty when I got here. No sign
of trouble since then."

"Stay alert. We still don't know what's going on
here."

"Will do."

They climbed the stairs together. Chase never left
without making sure she was safely inside the office.
When lunchtime came, she'd have Shana or Tony or
whoever was heading out for sandwiches pick her up
something to eat.

Chase opened the door to the Elemental Chic offices, and she stepped inside. She recognized the tall,
good-looking guy in the brown bomber jacket as Agent
Zach Tanner. He rose from a chair in the waiting area
to greet them.

"Agent Tanner," Chase said.

"Bran said you'd be bringing Harper to work," Tanner said. "I need to speak to both of you in private."

Harper's nerves shot up. She licked her lips. She thought of her father, worried what the DEA might have learned from the listening device in his study, and felt a sharp pang of worry.

"My office is this way." She led them in that direction, curious glances following their journey across the open room where members of her staff worked on various phases of projects.

Debbie Mayer, one of the EC models, gave Tanner a long, appraising glance. Even Shana took a good long look. Harper didn't really blame them.

Pausing next to a mannequin draped in bright yellow polished cotton, she pulled opened her office door and led the men inside.

"Would you like some coffee or something?" she asked Tanner.

"I'm fine," he said.

"Why don't you have a seat?" Harper sat down behind her desk, but Tanner and Chase both remained standing.

"What's going on?" Chase asked the agent.

"The DEA has acquired enough evidence against Knox Winston to obtain a search warrant. That warrant is being executed as we speak."

Nausea swirled in Harper's stomach. "Oh, God." She was glad she was sitting down.

"Whatever happens today, the agency won't make an arrest until they have enough evidence to be certain the charges will stick. I can tell you they've been working this case for months. So, depending on what they find during the search, an arrest may not be far away."

Harper's voice trembled. "I need to talk to him. Make sure he's all right." She wasn't close to her dad and never had been, but he was still her father.

"That would not be wise at this time," Tanner said. "You need to keep your involvement in this to a minimum. I can tell you that so far we have no reason to believe you have any connection to your father's affairs. That's the way you need to keep it."

Harper swallowed. "What about my brother? I can assure you he isn't involved. Michael and my father rarely speak. My brother doesn't even live in Dallas."

"Michael Winston recently made a trip to Colombia. We'll be looking at that very closely."

Harper shot up from her chair. "He was kidnapped on his boat and taken to Colombia by force! He was held against his will in the mountains by a rebel army!"

Chase strode around the desk and gently set his hands on her shoulders. She was surprised how much his touch eased her nerves.

"It's true," Chase told Tanner. "When Harper couldn't reach her brother, she reported him missing through numerous channels. She hired me to help her find him and bring him home, which we did. Bran was also there, which you must already know. We'll both be happy to give you any information you need to corroborate the story."

"As long as your brother cooperates, I don't think he'll have a problem," Tanner said to Harper.

As she sank back down in her chair, Chase's hands remained on her shoulders, and though she told herself to ignore him, silently she thanked him for his support.

Standing on the opposite side of the desk, Tanner's dark eyes drilled into her. "I want you to know you did the right thing in this. I know it may not seem like it right now. I know family is important, but there are other people's families to consider. I believe your brother would agree."

So he was aware of Michael's drug history.

"We talked about it," she admitted. "After I found out about the device, he convinced me not to interfere." When her hands started to tremble, she hid them in her lap. Her concern for Chase's safety had also been a factor, but she refused to say that.

"This is going to show up in the news," Tanner said. "I wanted to give you a heads-up so you would be prepared."

How was a person supposed to prepare for her father's arrest as a drug lord? "I appreciate you letting me know," Harper said. It wasn't the agent's fault. It was her father's.

Chase gently squeezed her shoulders. "Things happen we can't always control. As long as you do what's right, most of the time it turns out okay."

She had always believed that. Her father was his own person. He had made his choices. Now he'd have to deal with the consequences. Deep down Harper knew allowing justice to take its course was the right decision. Her brother would agree.

But even if Chase's reasons were the same, what he'd done was different. He had lied to her, preyed on her trust—her love. Knowing he was doing what he felt he had to didn't justify his actions.

Tanner pulled open the door to leave. "I owe you, Harper. The agency owes you and Chase both. If you need anything, call me." Agent Tanner walked out and closed the door.

Chase drew Harper up from her chair and into his arms. She should have refused the comfort, told herself to back away. Instead she slid her arms around his waist and leaned into him. Tears spilled onto his chest, and he ran his hands gently up and down her back. Some of her tension eased.

She wondered if he could be right, and someday she really would be able to forgive him. But she didn't think so.

Michael sat in the conference room at BUZZ. He had been there for nearly two hours, being grilled by the two drug enforcement agents sitting across from him. Answering questions about his father. Going over and over the details of his trip to Colombia.

As if he'd been there on vacation. As if he had enjoyed being marched at gunpoint, wet and freezing his ass off, into the jungles of the desolate Sierra Nevada mountains. Worried sick the whole time about the woman he had fallen in love with.

Leave it to his father to make his life miserable—again.

"Everything you've told us matches what we've learned so far," Special Agent Richmond said, a lean man with a receding hairline and piercing blue eyes. "Which means you should have nothing to worry about."

Yeah, nothing at all. Just a father who was a drug smuggler and a crime lord, among other things. "What about Pia Santana? She was with me—also against her will. Which you probably already know."

"We have agents speaking to Ms. Santana this morning." The second man, Special Agent Phifer, was young and a little too gung ho. He made Michael nervous. "If her story matches yours and the information we already have, she won't have a problem. On the other hand…" He let the sentence trail off, his meaning clear.

Michael's stomach knotted. He needed to talk to her, explain why she was being questioned, tell her what was going on. He had told her his father was rich. He hadn't mentioned how Knox Winston made his money.

"That should do it for now," Agent Richmond said, rising from his chair. "Be better if you kept yourself available in case we need anything more."

Michael nodded faintly.

Richmond and Phifer left the office, and Michael's brain began to function again. He needed to talk to Pia, but the conversation they needed to have wasn't something he could do over the phone.

Grabbing his cell off the desk, he headed out of the conference room, pausing long enough to speak to his office manager, tell him he had to go to Miami but he would be back in a couple of days.

If Pia agreed to see him at all.

He was on his way home to pack a bag when his phone started ringing. The caller ID popped up as Brandon Garrett.

Michael hit the hands-free. "Hey, Bran, good to hear from you."

"Where are you going, Michael?"

The serious note in Bran's voice put him on alert. And how did Brandon know he was going somewhere? "I just left my office. I'm on my way home. How'd you know?"

"A friend has been keeping an eye on you. He saw you walk out of the building."

He glanced around, looking for whoever was out there, but didn't see anyone. "Something's come up. I'm heading out of town for a couple of days. Who's watching me? What's going on, Bran?"

"I know your address. I'll meet you there. I'll explain when I see you."

Michael frowned. "You're in Houston?"

"That's right. Keep your eyes open and stay alert. We'll talk soon."

The knot returned to Michael's stomach. Considering he had been kidnapped only a few weeks ago and just left the company of two federal agents, God only knew what could be happening.

He drove home too fast and prayed he wouldn't be stopped, parked in his garage, went into his apartment and checked the place out. No one there. Nothing disturbed. He was definitely being paranoid, but still...

Since Bran hadn't arrived, he went into his bedroom and packed a carry-on for his Miami trip. A knock sounded on the door as he finished. Zipping the bag, he carried it out to the living room, checked the peephole, spotted Bran and breathed a sigh of relief.

When he opened the door, Brandon stepped into the living room and Michael noticed the bulge of a pistol in a shoulder harness beneath his leather jacket.

At Brandon's grim expression, Michael's senses went on alert. "What the hell, Bran?"

Brandon clamped a hand on his shoulder. "Sit down, Mikey. We need to talk."

CHAPTER THIRTY-THREE

Chase was still staying in Harper's town house instead of his condo. He wanted Harper to trust him again. He didn't want her to feel any more pressure than she did already.

Driving her home after work, he stopped to pick up takeout: pasta from Antonio's, the place he had taken her the night before her father's birthday party.

It seemed a lifetime ago.

As soon as he pulled into the parking lot, he wished he had chosen someplace else. Someplace that didn't remind him how happy Harper had been that night, remind them both of the lies he had told her.

She'd been quiet ever since, had barely touched the delicious lasagna he had dished up and served on colorful plates at her kitchen table. The candles he had lit for effect still lingered, though the wineglasses were empty.

"I'll clean up the dishes," she said, rising from her chair. "Why don't you watch TV or something?"

He shoved back his chair and stood up, caught her around the waist as she leaned over to pick up his plate.

"I know how hard this is for you, honey. I'll do everything in my power to make things right. I know you don't trust me right now, but I'm hoping in time I can convince you."

She rested her palms on his chest and looked up at him. "If you mean that, Chase, if you really think there's a chance we could make it work, then give me some time. We both know how strongly I'm attracted to you. When you touch me, make love to me, my world seems to turn upside down. I just... I need time to figure things out."

He could give her that, time to work things out. But giving her the space she believed she needed also meant giving her a chance to pull away from him, and that was the last thing he wanted.

He wanted her to know how important she was to him. He wanted her back in his bed. Even more than that, he wanted her to let him back into her heart.

"I can't leave you here alone," he said. "I won't leave you unprotected—you know that. But I'll go back to sleeping in the guest room if that's really what you want."

Relief eased the tension in her shoulders. "Okay."

He tipped up her chin. "I know how strong you are, angel. If you didn't want me, you'd never let me touch you."

A flicker of amusement touched her pretty lips. It was the first hint of a smile he'd seen.

"Wanting you has never been the problem, Chase."

At least he had that going for him.

Instead of bending his head to kiss her as he desperately wanted to do, he let her go. "I'll clear the dishes. You just relax."

She nodded. "Thanks. I think I'll go up and read for a while before I go to sleep. Good night, Chase."

"Good night, angel." He watched her walk away, a heavy weight pressing on his chest. No woman had ever made him feel the things he felt for Harper. No woman had made him want her the way she did.

He didn't think either of his brothers would have a clue what he was feeling, not even Reese, who was married. Always a planner, Reese had simply decided it was time for a wife and kids. Sandra fit the image he'd had in mind.

By the time they had learned she couldn't have children, the marriage was already on the skids and they separated shortly after.

Brandon had dated a score of different women, none of whom ever lasted more than a couple of weeks.

Finished in the kitchen, he went to the living room, unclipped the holster at his waist and set his Glock on an end table. A click of the remote turned on the TV. Chase sat down on the sofa, hoping he'd find something to distract his thoughts from the woman upstairs.

Nothing much on. He found an old cop show, *Hill Street Blues*, on Netflix, still felt restless when it was over. Deciding nothing was going to keep his mind off Harper, he grabbed his pistol and headed upstairs to the guest room.

He'd give reading a try, but he had a feeling it was going to be a damn long night.

Moonlight shone down on the thick Florida foliage along the roadway as Bran parked the rental car in front of Pia's apartment. "I'll wait out here."

Michael nodded, cracked open the car door and

started up the walkway. First the DEA had shown up that morning and interrogated him like a criminal—which he understood and was forced to accept since his father actually was one.

Then Bran had arrived with his stunning revelation that Bass Garrett, not Knox Winston, was his real father. That he had three brothers, all men he liked and admired.

Bran told him about the man who had been stalking Harper and that Chase was with her, protecting her. That until they understood what was going on, Bran would be acting as his bodyguard.

"Are you sure that's necessary?" Michael asked.

"You're the guy who marched at gunpoint through the jungle. You tell me."

Michael blew out a breath. "Okay, I get it."

He told Bran he was worried about Pia, that she had also been questioned by the Feds and Bran had agreed to accompany him to Miami.

Unfortunately, the plane had been delayed at the airport in Atlanta. By the time they landed in Miami, rented a car and located Pia's duplex apartment, it was approaching midnight.

He should have called, Michael knew, would have if he hadn't been afraid Pia would refuse to see him. But too much had happened. He needed to explain in person. He couldn't afford to wait.

Taking a breath for courage, Michael walked up on the porch and rang the doorbell, which chimed a merry little tune. He hadn't taken time to find a motel. He was too anxious to get there. Brandon was sure no one had followed them, but his brother—Michael felt a tug at his heart—*his brother* wasn't the kind of guy who took chances.

He pushed the bell again. An eye appeared in the peephole, then the door swung open. Before he had time to say her name, Pia threw her arms around his neck.

"Michael! Oh, God, Michael."

His throat tightened as his arms closed around her, and a shudder rippled through him. Michael breathed her in, the soft fragrance of flowers tinged with warm spice. "Pia… I've missed you so much."

She clung to him. "I've missed you, too, Michael. I'm so glad you're here."

"You are?"

She pulled him inside and closed the door. "I was coming to Houston tomorrow. I needed to see you, make sure you were okay."

"Pia…"

"Federal agents came to my office, Michael. They asked questions about you and your father. I kept thinking about you, worrying what might be happening to you. I wanted to be there for you—the way you've always been there for me."

She pressed soft kisses to the corners of his mouth. "I've been a fool, Michael. You're the best man I've ever known. I was an idiot to let someone as evil as Benito Velasquez ruin things for us."

He buried his face in her hair. "I love you, Pia. I love you so much."

Pia clung to him. "I love you, too, Michael."

He caught her face between his hands. "There are things I need to tell you. I want you to know I have nothing to do with my father or his business."

She went up on her toes and kissed him. "I know

the kind of person you are. I knew you would never do anything illegal. That's what I told those agents. I said I didn't even know your father. After a while I think they believed me."

"I'm sorry that happened. I've never been involved with my father's businesses. Illegal or otherwise. I came here to explain." Michael pulled Pia back into his arms and kissed her, soft and deep. "I've got so much to tell you." He kissed her again, then tugged her over to the sofa and pulled her down beside him, his arm firmly around her waist.

"What happened to us on the boat," he said. "The kidnapping? The DEA is investigating my father. They think the abduction may in some way be connected."

"I figured as much when men with badges showed up at my door and started asking questions."

"Bran Garrett came with me to Miami. He's out in the car. He's here to protect us in case there's trouble."

"You think there will be?"

"Bran doesn't think so, but he doesn't want to take any chances." He felt the goofiest smile tugging at his lips. "Turns out he's my brother."

Pia's big brown eyes went wide. "Brandon is your brother? How is that possible? Is Chase your brother, too?"

He nodded. "And Reese. I just found out today. You haven't met Reese, but he's great. I already have a terrific sister. Now, knowing I have three great brothers… You can't imagine the way that makes me feel."

Pia smiled up at him. "Like you're part of a real family."

He lifted her chin and looked into her pretty dark eyes. "When all of this is over and you're ready, I want you to be part of my family, too. Will you come back to Houston with me?"

Pia's eyes filled with tears. "I already took some time off. I really was coming to see you. I booked my ticket this afternoon."

"God, I love you."

"I'm so glad you're here." She pressed a soft kiss on his lips. "Take me to bed, Michael. Let's make a good memory tonight."

His heart squeezed. He felt so lucky, the luckiest man in the world. Michael flicked a glance at the door. His brother was sitting in a car out in front. He should at least invite him in.

But Pia was pulling him up from the sofa, tugging him down the hall toward the bedroom. Bran was his brother. Brothers understood situations like this. He would invite Brandon in after he and Pia had gotten… reacquainted.

Michael grinned. He was sure his brother would understand.

CHAPTER THIRTY-FOUR

The night sounds intruded, cicadas buzzing outside the guest bedroom windows. Only a sliver of moon lit the dark late-October night. The weather had turned cold, an icy breeze slicing through the branches of the trees.

Chase flicked a glance at the red numbers on the digital clock on the bedside table: 2:00 a.m. He had dozed for a while, but the sleep he needed remained elusive. He felt restless and edgy, worse knowing Harper lay in bed on the other side of the wall.

He could hear her, shifting on the mattress, awake, just as he was. It was all he could do not to go to her, give her what she needed to help her sleep, what both of them needed.

He knew it wouldn't take much to convince her— the physical attraction between them was stronger than ever. But he wouldn't break his word.

Instead he shoved his hands behind his head and

stared up at the ceiling, wishing dawn would arrive. Better to be at work than lying there, sorting through regrets.

The sound of glass shattering in the living room shot a jolt of adrenaline into his blood. Leaping out of bed, he pulled on his jeans, grabbed his pistol and his cell phone, and ran barefoot toward the door. The extra magazine in his pocket felt comforting as he bolted down the hall toward the stairs.

More glass shattered, a second window in the living room. Harper's door swung open as he raced past.

"Chase!"

"Stay in the bedroom!"

Pistol in hand, he ran down the stairs toward the red glow and crackling sound of flames. Fire engulfed the sofa, snaked across the carpet and climbed the curtains. Two homemade bombs filled with accelerant lay broken, spitting tendrils of flame across the floor.

"Oh, my God!" Harper stood at the bottom of the stairs in a pink shorty nightgown, her phone gripped in her hand.

"We've got to get out of here!" Chase shouted above the roar as more glass shattered and another firebomb crashed through the window of the dining room. The curtains erupted, billowing with hot streaks of red and orange. Thick black smoke made it difficult to see. "Head for the back door!"

The front of the town house was completely cut off. No chance of escape in that direction. Chase knew what he would be facing when they stepped out the back door, knew the fire was a means of forcing them into the hands of men waiting out back.

He pulled his cell from his pocket and punched Maddox's number, figuring half a dozen people had already seen the flames and called 9-1-1.

"I got trouble, Hawk," Chase said when Maddox answered. Honky-tonk music played in the background. "Shooters. I don't know how many." He rattled off Harper's address.

"I'm not far. Just hang on till I get there."

Maddox was close. They'd caught a break there. Now all they had to do was stay alive till Jason or the cops could reach them.

He spotted Harper in the kitchen, ending a call on her phone. "I called 9-1-1. They're on their way."

"Good girl." Trouble was the fire was closing in on them, burning on three sides, flames reaching closer every second they delayed. And the cops were still minutes away.

Chase took a quick glance out the window above the sink, spotted two men in the bushes an instant before a bullet shattered the glass next to his head. He jerked back out of sight and hauled Harper out of the way.

She was trembling. "The garage is on fire." Her BMW inside. "We can't get out that way, either. What... what are we going to do?" Her eyes looked bigger and bluer than Chase had ever seen them.

"Only one way out. I'll go first, try to lower the odds. Stay close beside me. If I go down, don't try to fight them. You're the reason they're here. If these men want you that badly, I don't think they'll risk hurting you."

Her face went even paler than it was already.

Chase reached for the doorknob, but Harper caught his arm. "There's a shed at the back of the property. The gate to the alley's behind it. If we could make it there—"

He nodded. "We'll head for the shed. You ready?"

She swallowed and nodded. Chase opened the back door and started firing, laying down a deadly line of cover. One man went down. Return fire peppered the back of the town house, three men, maybe more still out there. Spotting the shed, he started running toward it, keeping Harper on the other side of his body, gunfire swarming them.

He felt a sting in his calf, a bullet ricochet off the concrete walkway, but kept on running, firing as he made his way across the backyard. Another man popped up and Chase fired. The man cried out and went down, but more shots erupted.

Chase urged Harper behind the shed, pulled the fresh mag out of his pocket and shoved it into the Glock. "Run for the alley. Once you get there, head around front to my truck. I'll catch up with you there."

She looked as if she wanted to argue, but in the end, she ducked and ran. Chase fired a few more shots and started after her, felt the impact of a bullet slamming high into the left side of his chest. He grunted but kept moving toward the gate. His left arm went numb, but his gun hand still worked.

He fired off a couple of rounds, heard Harper scream and knew one or more men had been waiting for them in the alley. At the sound of a car engine behind the fence and the squeal of tires, he changed direction and ran for his truck. His calf was bleeding. So was his chest. His heart was hammering, his mouth bone-dry. He fought to keep his fear for Harper under control, but his hands were shaking.

When he reached the pickup, he felt beneath the bumper, grabbed the spare key and unlocked the door. Sliding in behind the wheel, he started the engine and slammed his foot down on the gas. The blue Buick roared out of the alley right in front of him, the driver and another man inside.

Chase raced up behind them and rammed the bumper of the Buick, jolting the vehicle forward. The man in the passenger seat shot out the rear window of the Buick and began firing at the pickup. Chase fought to control the truck, swerving side to side to avoid the barrage of gunfire.

Blood trickled down his side, but adrenaline helped numb the pain. He couldn't see Harper, but he was sure she was in the backseat of the car. *Stay down, baby. I'm coming.* He prayed he could get the vehicle stopped without hurting her.

The Buick was forced to slow as it careened around a corner, and Chase gunned the pickup, slamming into the side of the vehicle near the front passenger door, sending it spinning into a lamppost. By the time the car came to a halt, he was out of the pickup and running.

A second vehicle, an SUV, rolled up, guns blazing, forcing him to take cover behind a brick fence. Sirens screamed in the distance, police and fire, but they were going to be too late.

The driver of the second car, a tall guy wearing a hoodie, kept up a barrage of gunfire while a beefy man riding shotgun jumped out and ran to the rear door of the Buick, joining the Buick driver, who had climbed through the car window. As they dragged Harper's limp body out of the backseat, Chase fought to control his fear and rage.

If they'd hurt her... If he'd accidentally hurt her himself...

Chase shoved the anger and fear away. He couldn't

let his emotions get in the way. He had to stay focused if he was going to save her.

Unable to shoot with Harper in the line of fire, Chase swore foully as the beefy man tossed her over his shoulder, carried her a short distance and shoved her into the back of the big black SUV that looked a lot like the one that had just rounded the corner, driving hell-for-leather in Chase's direction.

Hawk had arrived. Tires smoked as Maddox's black Yukon screeched to a halt, and the passenger door flew open. Maddox laid down a stream of gunfire, and Chase ran for the Yukon. He jumped inside, Maddox hit the gas and the Yukon leaped forward like a panther in pursuit of its prey.

The driver of the Buick took off running, escaping around the corner, but Chase was focused on the other SUV. "Stay on them!" he shouted. "We can't afford to lose them!"

Maddox's concentration remained on the road, the supercharged engine in the big black Yukon rapidly gaining on the older Chevy Suburban, bringing them right up behind. Maddox yanked his T-shirt off over his head and tossed it to Chase, who pressed it against the bullet hole in his chest below his collarbone.

"How bad are you hit?" Jason asked calmly.

"Leg's a scratch. I'm losing a lot of blood from the chest wound. Not really sure how bad it is."

"They're all bad, brother."

Chase just grunted. The window was down, cold air streaming in, helping him stay alert. The good news was this time of night there wasn't much traffic.

Ignoring a wave of dizziness, Chase took aim at the vehicle blasting down the highway ahead of them, waited to pull the trigger till the SUV slowed to round a corner, then shot out one of the back tires.

The tire blew, making the SUV swerve, and Maddox moved in, bringing both vehicles side by side as they roared down the road.

Too dangerous to take out the driver. Chase shot the guy in the passenger seat, who slumped out of sight into the foot well. The driver fired a couple of shots that went wild. Maddox moved closer, waiting for exactly the right moment. Waiting... Waiting...

In an open area, Maddox cranked the Yukon into the side of the Chevy near the back wheels, forcing the car to spin around in a circle and slide to a stop. The driver was out of the car and running, disappearing around a corner out of sight.

Maddox ran toward the Suburban. So did Chase. Maddox got there first and jerked open the door. Hampered by his injured leg, pressing the T-shirt against the bullet hole leaking blood down his chest, Chase ran up behind him.

Harper lay on the backseat moaning, shifting on the seat. Maddox talked to her softly, shook her gently, trying to wake her up.

"I smell chloroform," Jason said. "I don't think they used too much. She's starting to come around."

Chase clamped down on a fresh jolt of rage.

"Chase..." Harper's eyes fluttered open and relief poured through him.

"Harper...angel..." He was reaching out to her, desperate to make sure she was okay, when the walls began to close in. He fought to stay on his feet, but his knees weakened, buckled, his vision narrowed, and everything went black.

CHAPTER THIRTY-FIVE

Still feeling sluggish and faintly nauseous, Harper sat next to Jason Maddox in the emergency room of Baylor Medical Center. Every time she closed her eyes, she saw Chase lying unconscious on the pavement, a pair of EMTs working over him, trying to stop the blood seeping out of a bullet hole in his chest.

After the crash, only a few minutes had passed before a swarm of police cars, red and blue lights flashing, screeched to a halt, hemming them in. Patrol car doors flew open and police officers poured out, guns drawn. Maddox raised his hands, his pistol hanging loosely from his fingers.

"On the ground! Now!" Three officers rushed forward, one of them snagging the pistol. Another whirled him around and shoved him to his knees, then facedown on the ground. Dragging Maddox's hands behind his back, the officer locked a pair of handcuffs on Jason's wrists.

"The men in that car tried to kidnap me!" Harper frantically explained, pointing toward the Suburban. "Chase Garrett and Jason Maddox saved me! Please, Chase has been shot! He needs help!"

Officers were already there, working to slow the bleeding. A few minutes later, an ambulance rolled up, and a pair of EMTs got out and took over.

She was shivering, Harper realized as she watched them, her short cotton nightgown little protection against the chill. A female officer walked over with a blanket, which she draped around Harper's shoulders.

"Thank you." She spotted a dark-haired man in a brown sport coat walking toward her.

"You're Harper Winston?" he asked. She noticed he wore wingtip shoes and had big feet.

"I'm Harper."

"Detective Heath Ford. I'm a friend of Chase's."

Relief filtered through her. Someone on their side. "Thank God."

He flicked a glance at Maddox, who was handcuffed on the ground a few feet away. "I'm a friend of his, too, though he can be a royal pain in the ass sometimes."

She was too upset to smile. "Jason and Chase saved my life tonight. If it hadn't been for them, I don't know what would have happened to me."

Ford turned to one of the patrolmen and tipped his head toward Maddox. "Uncuff him. Believe it or not, he's one of the good guys."

Jason cast Ford a dark look, but the officer chuckled as he unlocked the cuffs and Maddox rolled to his feet, rubbing his wrists.

"What about Chase?" she asked anxiously. "Is he going to be all right?"

"He's awake. Looks like the shot went all the way through, but he's lost a lot of blood. They're loading him into the ambulance now."

"I want to go with him."

"I've got some questions first," the detective said.

Maddox flashed her a glance. "I'll take you to the hospital. You don't need to worry."

She didn't want to wait. She wanted to be with Chase, make sure he was going to be all right.

Maddox leaned over and tipped up her chin, forcing her to look at him. "Chase's tough. He's had worse. He'll be okay."

Resigned, for the next half hour Harper explained what had happened, how men had started a fire in her town house to drive them outside. How they were waiting in back for them to come out. She told him how if it hadn't been for Chase and Jason Maddox, the men would have kidnapped her and taken her God only knew where.

She didn't tell them about her brother. She answered the questions she was asked but didn't expand on why she was being abducted or who might be behind it. Not a lie, since she didn't really know.

"You did good," Jason said as he drove toward the hospital after Detective Ford had finished his questions—at least for now. "Better to say as little as possible until we know what the hell is going on."

She glanced over to where he sat behind the wheel of his now-battered SUV. He'd found a T-shirt in the back and pulled it on, covering his powerful chest. Dark-haired and blue-eyed, Jason Maddox was a big, handsome man. With his two-day growth of beard and deep Texas drawl, he might seem a little rough around the edges, but he was also brave and loyal. She had learned that tonight.

"Until *we* know?" she said. "That includes you?"

His eyes remained on the road. "You're Chase's woman. Until he's back on his feet, I'll be looking after you. That's what friends do."

She started to tell him she wasn't "Chase's woman," never really had been, but she was too exhausted to argue. And she was grateful to have a man as obviously competent as Jason Maddox willing to protect her.

When they reached the hospital, Chase was being treated in a curtained-off area of the emergency room. A nurse brought her a set of scrubs to wear, and they were told to sit in an area out in front. While they were waiting for news, the fire captain phoned to explain the damages her town house had suffered. She wouldn't be moving back in anytime soon.

The thought depressed her, but it didn't compare to the worry she felt for Chase.

"He's gonna be okay," Maddox said, jolting her back to the present. "The medics arrived right away, and the ambulance got him here quickly."

Tonight was the first time she and Maddox had met, but he had been a rock, a true friend to Chase and to her.

She sighed. "I don't understand what's going on. Tonight men tried to abduct me. A few weeks back, my brother was kidnapped. Who's behind it? What do they want?"

Before Maddox could answer, a black-haired doctor in scrubs walked out of the back, where Chase had been taken.

"I'm Dr. Zamora. You're Mrs. Garrett?"

"I'm Harper Win—"

"She's Chase's wife," Jason interrupted, casting her a do-not-argue glance. "I'm his brother-in-law."

"Your husband is going to be fine, Mrs. Garrett. He lost some blood, but we're taking care of that. He was lucky. The bullet went into his chest just below his collarbone and traveled all the way through. We didn't need to operate, just clean the wound and stitch him up. There's always a chance of infection, but we're hoping that won't happen. If he does well tonight, he'll be released sometime tomorrow."

The tension ebbed from her body. "Thank you, Dr. Zamora. May I see him?"

"We've given him a sedative. He's been moved to a private room on the second floor. I'm afraid he's sleeping now."

"Is it all right if I sit with him?"

"I don't see why not." The doctor looked at Maddox.

"She wants to stay," he said. "That means I'll be staying, too."

Zamora nodded. "I'll let the nurses know." The doctor turned and walked back down the hall, his baggy green scrubs flapping around his legs.

Harper felt a little guilty keeping Maddox up all night, but mostly she was worried about Chase. She had known she loved him. Until tonight, she hadn't known how much.

It complicated everything. And considering what had just happened, things were already complicated enough.

CHAPTER THIRTY-SIX

After very little rest—thanks to the nurses checking on Chase's progress every few hours throughout what was left of the night—Harper finally fell asleep in the chair beside his hospital bed. She awoke to bright sun streaming through the windows and noises in the room that sounded oddly familiar.

When she opened her eyes, she saw Chase swinging his long legs to the side of the bed. A white bandage around his chest and shoulder showed where the hospital gown had slipped off. A faint groan escaped as he tried to sit up.

Harper leaped up and ran to him. "What on earth are you doing? You've been shot! You're going to hurt yourself!"

"I'm all right. It was a through and through. I'll be sore for a while, but I'll be okay."

She tried to push him back down, but it was like pressing against a wall. Beside the bed, an IV dripped fluid from a clear plastic bag into a needle taped to the inside of his arm. A heart monitor beeped rhythmically, a nice steady pattern on the screen she was relieved to see.

"You need to get back in bed," she argued, trying again to dissuade him. "You've lost a lot of blood. They're still putting fluids into you. You can't just leave!"

A faint smile tugged at his lips. "I'm glad you're so worried about me. I was beginning to wonder if you still cared."

"For heaven's sake, Chase. Of course I care! Please get back in bed and let the nurses take care of you."

"Not gonna happen, angel. Too much going on."

"Fine. I'm going to bring Maddox in here. Maybe he can talk some sense into you." Harper opened the door to find Jason sitting in a chair where he had spent the night in case there was more trouble. He rose as the door swung open.

"I need your help, Jason," she said. "This bullheaded idiot is trying to get out of bed."

Maddox just grunted. "This isn't his first rodeo. He knows what his body can take."

Maddox walked into the room as Chase finished disconnecting himself. "I gather you're feeling better," Jason said.

"Thanks for watching out for her. I need to get her somewhere safe till we can figure this out."

"The ranch?" Maddox asked calmly, as if Chase hadn't been shot two times last night.

"My condo for starters." He tipped his head toward the locker next to the bathroom. "Hand me my clothes."

"Dammit, Chase! Be reasonable."

Chase looked up at Maddox and grinned. "She's worried about me."

"Yeah, I figured that out last night." Maddox turned toward the door. "You don't have any clothes. They cut off your pants last night. Since you'd dressed commando, that's all you had on. I'll find you some scrubs."

Harper looked up at the ceiling. "Madmen. You're both insane."

Maddox unclipped his pistol from his belt beneath his T-shirt and handed it to Chase. "Kimber .40 cal. My backup piece. The cops took our weapons into evidence. The office isn't far. You can pick up something there before we head out."

Maddox disappeared into the hall, and the door swished closed behind him.

"All right," Harper said, both frustrated and resigned. "Obviously you have some kind of plan. I need to know what's going on."

The door swung open before Chase had time to answer, and a man with jet-black hair and ice-blue eyes walked in. He was even taller than Chase, and in an opposite, dark-versus-light sort of way, just as good-looking, with model-perfect features and a powerful, athletic build.

Harper knew who he was. She had seen Reese Garrett at a couple of fund-raisers, but Chase and Reese had been raised by different parents, so Harper had never met him.

Reese set a worried hand on his brother's uninjured shoulder. "I heard what happened. How are you doing?"

"I'm alive. That's always good."

Reese's mouth edged up but he didn't actually smile. He was worried and he didn't try to hide it. It was nice to see the affection the Garrett brothers felt for each other.

"I figured Maddox would call you and Bran," Chase said. "Harper, this is my brother Reese. Reese, meet Harper Winston."

Reese's features darkened, his eyes turning a cool, distant blue and pinning her where she stood. Clearly he felt the same animosity toward her father that Chase and Brandon felt.

She flushed to think what she must look like, with her hair a mess and dressed in ugly green scrubs. She forced herself not to step back at the hard look on his too-handsome face.

"She isn't her father," Chase warned, a note in his voice that had Reese's gaze swinging back in his direction. A look passed between them, but Harper had no idea what it meant.

"Nice to meet you," Reese said to her.

"You, too."

Reese frowned as he realized Chase was about to leave. "They're releasing you?"

"I'm leaving. There are things I need to do."

"Maddox filled me in on the fire and the shoot-out last night. You two need to be somewhere safe."

"I'm trying to work that out. My condo has round-the-clock security, and my unit has a top-of-the-line alarm system. Men died last night. Some got away, others didn't. Whoever these guys are, they're going to need time to regroup, figure a new strategy before they come after Harper again."

"You don't think they're going to quit," Reese said, not a question.

"No. They're being paid to do a job. They won't give

up until it gets done or we stop them. That said, we should be okay at the condo for a couple of days, time enough for me to get my strength back and Harper to get some sleep."

Chase gave her a smile. "Which, since she sat up all night watching over me like the angel she is, I know she needs."

Reese's blue eyes widened.

Harper's chin went up. "I owed you, that's all. You got shot trying to protect me."

Chase's smug smile faded. "We need time to figure this out, honey. We need to be someplace safe until we do."

"You're way less than a hundred percent," Reese said. "Until you're stronger, you need someone you can trust to protect you. Is Maddox staying with you?"

The door swung fully open and Jason walked in. "I'll be there—whether he likes it or not. He has Harper to think of, so he won't give me any trouble."

"Hey, you two, I'm right here in the room. But I accept your offer. Thanks, Hawk."

Harper felt a shot of irritation. "So I guess I don't get any say in this."

"'Fraid not, sweetheart," Chase said with a smile.

She wanted to argue, but after what had happened last night, she was clearly in danger. These men were tough, and they were determined. Harper was smart enough to know she needed them to protect her.

"I'll see what I can do to get you out of here," Reese offered. "Take care of yourself and if you need anything, call me." He cast a last glance at Harper. "That goes for you, too."

As Reese left the room, Maddox tossed Chase a set of scrubs. "Best I could do."

"They'll work."

A petite dark-haired nurse walked in—Joanne, Harper recalled. It was impossible to miss the hopeful smile Joanne cast in Maddox's direction.

She walked over to Chase. "If you're determined to leave, at least let me change your bandage before you go. I'll show Mrs. Garrett how to do it so she can take care of it next time."

Chase's eyebrows shot up before a smile touched his lips.

"It was his idea," Harper said defensively, casting a pointed glance at Maddox, whose lips twitched.

"I'll wait for you two outside," Jason said. Taking back his gun, he stepped out into the hall, the door swishing closed behind him.

Chase sat on the edge of the bed as the nurse showed Harper how to clean the bullet wound in his chest, how to pack it with gauze and replace the bandage. A bullet had sent a piece of concrete tearing into his calf. According to Joanne, if he kept it clean, in time the stitches would dissolve by themselves.

"Would you like some help getting dressed?" the nurse asked.

"My wife can handle it." His playful glance sent a rush of heat into Harper's cheeks as the nurse left the room.

Chase stripped off his hospital gown, leaving him naked, except for the bandages on his chest and calf. Smooth muscle rippled with every move and Harper's mouth went dry. Desired tugged low in her belly, followed by a rush of guilt. Considering the man was recovering from being shot, she couldn't believe she was thinking of sex.

"How about some help, Mrs. Garrett?" Chase teased, his dark eyes sparkling with humor.

"I told you it was Jason's idea. They might not have let me stay if they knew I was just a friend."

Chase's features softened. He looked as if he wanted to say something, but in the end, he didn't.

Harper was glad. Too much was going on, too much remained unsettled. No matter what she felt for Chase, she refused to let her thoughts stray from the problems at hand.

And there were plenty of them.

Ignoring the smell of antiseptic Chase had always hated, he leaned on Harper as she helped him put on the scrubs, then pull paper shoes onto his bare feet. He could probably do it himself, but it felt way too good having her pressed against him. He could feel her soft breasts, and strands of pale hair teased his cheek. He wished they were alone and he was feeling a whole lot better.

Across the room, the door swung open and Joanne rolled a wheelchair into the room. "The doctor's releasing you. I can't imagine why."

Chase figured it had something to do with Reese and the massive donation Garrett Resources made every year to Baylor Medical.

The nurse put Chase's arm in a sling to help immobilize his injury, then Harper and the nurse helped him into a wheelchair. They wheeled him out of the room and down the hall, stopping at the pharmacy to pick up the pain pills the doctor had prescribed. He wouldn't take them unless he had no choice, but he needed to get some rest in order to heal.

Maddox had his Yukon, which luckily still ran, waiting out in front. Harper helped Chase into the backseat, and they headed for the offices at The Max. Chase kept several changes of clothes there and a safe full of weapons.

Being Sunday, it was quiet. At the moment, none of the PIs were around. The meds were wearing off, his shoulder beginning to ache like bloody hell.

Harper helped him change into a pair of loose-fitting sweatpants and a baggy sweatshirt. Chase put the sling back on while he and Maddox armed themselves from the steel gun safe in the converted gym at the back of the office.

Chase chose the Nighthawk .45 he kept as a backup weapon. His little .380 S&W ankle gun was locked up in his condo. Maddox went for a SIG 220 .45 cal to use as backup. With the Kimber in the shoulder holster beneath his leather jacket, he shoved the SIG into the waistband of his jeans behind his back.

"I'll take the revolver," Harper said, which wasn't a bad idea. He'd seen her shoot in the jungle. The guy she had aimed at was dead.

While Maddox grabbed some extra ammunition, Chase handed Harper the .38, which she palmed and aimed. Then she flipped open the cylinder and checked to be sure the revolver was loaded. Since guns weren't much good if they were empty, she needn't worry.

"I've got to buy some clothes," Harper said, holstering the pistol. "Everything I owned was destroyed in the fire."

Chase preferred her naked, but he knew better than

to say so. "I want you close," he said. "We still don't know what's going on. I'll call Mindy, have her pick up whatever you need. Just give me a list of your sizes."

"I'll call Shana. She knows my size and what I like. I need to talk to her, anyway, tell her about the fire and ask her to cover for me until we get this sorted out."

Harper rested a hand on his cheek. "You need to rest. You shouldn't even be out of the hospital. Are you ready to go home?"

His chest wound was aching, his strength ebbing. Bullets had a way of doing that. "I'm ready." When she slid an arm around his waist to help him out the door, he didn't protest. He was smarter than that.

They climbed back into Maddox's battered SUV for the short ride to his condo. The Dodge pickup, part of a crime scene, had been towed. Even if he had it, after the crash it probably wasn't running. Chase figured if it hadn't been for Detective Ford, the Yukon would probably be in lockup, too.

He needed to talk to the detective, find out if the police had identified any of the attackers. He needed answers, hoped like hell Heath Ford had some.

When they reached the condo, Maddox parked in the underground lot next to Chase's silver Mercedes. Harper helped him over to the elevator for the ride to his unit on the seventeenth floor.

He checked the hall. No one around.

"I'll make a sweep," Jason said as soon as they entered the condo. He disappeared, made a brief search, then returned. "All clear."

Chase set the alarm and called down to the lobby to alert building security to be on the lookout for trouble.

"You need to get someplace you can lie down,"

Harper said when he ended the call. Figuring she had noticed the sheet-white color of his face, he didn't argue. He was amazed he was still on his feet.

"How are you feeling?" she asked, her pretty face lined with worry.

"Like I've got a bullet hole in my chest."

"And another in your leg."

He managed to smile. "Ricochets don't count."

Harper didn't look amused. "Which way is your bedroom?"

"Down the hall, but I need to make some calls first. Where's my cell phone?"

"I haven't seen it. You must have lost it last night."

No surprise there, considering. He'd deal with the problem later. "I can call from the study." Chase started in that direction, and Harper reluctantly hurried to help him.

Chase sat down behind his desk and picked up the phone, called Dallas PD and asked for Detective Heath Ford. He was hoping the police had been able to ID one of the victims. At least he'd have a place to start. Unfortunately, Ford wasn't in. Chase left a message and leaned back wearily in his chair.

"Okay, that's it. You're going to rest for a while—whether you like it or not. You won't be good to anyone if you wind up back in the hospital."

Knowing she was right, he blew out a breath as she urged him up from the chair. Harper helped him down the hall to the bedroom, turned back the covers on his bed, then helped him sit down on the edge. He tried not to wish she was joining him there naked.

She handed him a pain pill. Needing some rest in

order to heal, he took half instead of a whole, hoping to dull some of the ache throbbing through his body.

"Which room is mine?" Harper asked as he set the glass of water back down on the bedside table.

"This one."

"Wait a minute—"

"You don't have to worry, angel. I don't have the strength to attack you."

She looked even more worried. "You're injured. You need to rest."

"I need to keep you close, just in case."

"Jason's out there. Surely he can keep us safe until you're feeling better."

"I trust Jase. With my life if it came to it. I'm glad he's here." He sighed, scrubbed a hand tiredly over his face. "The truth is I almost lost you last night. It was a feeling I never want to have again. I need you to stay with me so I'll know you're okay. Will you do that for me, baby?"

She swallowed. Her eyes welled, cobalt blue and shimmering. She bent, cupped his face in her hands and gently kissed his lips. "I'll stay with you, Chase."

Something cracked open inside him. A truth he had known but refused to accept. His feelings for Harper ran deep and true. He had realized it as they'd marched through the jungle, had become even more certain last night.

There were obstacles between them that wouldn't be easy to overcome, but they had been there from the start. The attempted abduction had only made things worse.

It didn't matter. Whatever it took, Harper was worth it.

"Rest for a while," she said, easing him back on the

pillow. "I've got to call Shana and I need a shower. Get some sleep. I'll come back when I'm done."

Chase nodded, his eyes drifting closed. There were plans he needed to make, things he needed to do. It was past time he told Harper about Michael.

He shifted on the mattress and fresh pain rolled through him. Trusting Jason to look after Harper, he closed his eyes, hoping to get the rest he needed to regain some of his strength.

One thing he knew. He needed to talk to Harper's father. Knox Winston was the key. Chase had no idea if the man would be able to help him. Even if he could, Chase wasn't sure how far the guy would be willing to go to save his daughter.

His jaw hardened. Chase prayed he could unearth at least a shred of decency in a man who seemed to have none.

CHAPTER THIRTY-SEVEN

Harper showered and dressed in a pair of Chase's gray sweatpants and one of his colored T-shirts. She'd be glad when Shana got there with something that actually fit. She kept some extra clothes in the back room of the office, some EC samples, jeans, skirts, a few blouses and sweaters, sneakers, a couple pairs of heels. Shana would be shopping for the rest: makeup, underwear and anything else she thought Harper might need.

In the meantime, Maddox was in Chase's man cave, sprawled in a dark brown leather lounger that matched the sofa, watching ESPN on the big-screen TV. The room was equipped with the latest sound system. A poker table and chairs sat in one corner.

With Maddox occupied, Harper had a chance to prowl, see what she could learn about the man who attracted her as no other man ever had.

The condo was a beautiful space, open and airy, with twelve-foot ceilings and huge plate-glass windows. The view over Dallas was spectacular, and there was a lovely terrace that opened off the living room and master bedroom. Impressionist versions of Western art hung on the walls, bringing in bright warm colors.

Dark wood gleamed throughout, but the upholstery was light, a nubby cream fabric in the living and dining rooms. The overall effect was masculine but classy, just like Chase.

She wandered into the modern kitchen with its stainless appliances and granite countertops, sat down in a cozy little window seat, curled up and took out her phone. Which, amazingly, had survived the entire ordeal of the night before.

Yesterday's clouds were gone. The sun shining through the window warmed her as she checked her messages and made the necessary replies. She texted Shana but got no answer, figured her friend was probably still shopping. Shana loved any excuse to shop.

She was about to call Michael to tell him about the fire, when Chase walked into the kitchen. Though he hadn't shaved and his hair was mussed, he was still the sexiest man she had ever seen. Harper felt an unexpected stab of longing.

"You shouldn't be up yet," she said. "You've got to rest if you're going to heal."

"We need to talk, baby. It's about your brother."

Alarm shot through her. Dear God, she'd been abducted, her town house set on fire. Chase had been shot. She didn't think she could take much more. "What's happened? Is Michael… Is he okay?"

"It's nothing like that, honey. Michael's with Bran. He's fine. This is something else."

She didn't like the serious note in his voice. "What is it?"

Chase sat down in the window seat. "This sun sure feels good," he said, carefully propping his back against the wall on the opposite end of the cushion.

"Yes, it does." She caught a glimpse of the bandage around his shoulder and reminded herself to check, see if it needed changing.

Chase released a slow breath. "I have no idea how to say this so I'll just spit it out. Michael is my half brother."

She frowned, unable to digest what Chase was saying. "What are you talking about?"

"Your dad isn't Michael's father. My dad is. Until a couple of days ago, Reese was the only one who knew. I was trying to find the right time to tell you, but then things went south and this is the first chance I've had."

Her insides were trembling. "Your father had an affair with my mother?"

"Not exactly. According to my father, it only happened once." Chase went on to explain what Reese had told them about their parents and how they had acted rashly one night. That it was a secret her mother was determined to keep.

Harper finally began to focus, make sense of what Chase was telling her—and why. "So…after what happened to Michael in Colombia and men coming after me, Reese decided to come forward?"

"That's about it. Michael is a Garrett. Bran, Reese and I are very happy to welcome him into the family. Bran's in Houston with Michael, making sure he's safe. By now Michael knows the truth."

Harper moistened her suddenly dry lips. "But you and I... We aren't..."

Chase grinned. "No. Absolutely not."

Relief almost made her smile. She leaned back in the window seat. "I'm glad for Michael, actually. It explains a lot. I have a feeling my father knew the truth all along. He must have seen Michael as a reminder of my mother's betrayal. That's the reason Dad treated him so badly."

"Yeah, that's kind of what I figured." They talked about it for a while, about what it meant for Michael to be a member of the Garrett family, how Chase and his brothers felt about it. Then the doorbell rang.

Maddox was already in the foyer when they arrived, standing next to the door, gun drawn.

"I think it's my friend Shana," Harper said. "She's got my clothes."

"I left word for the guard in the lobby to send her up," Chase said.

Maddox checked the peephole, opened the door and Shana walked into the condo. Exotically beautiful, with the kind of curves men fantasized about, she was dressed head to toe in EC fashion: skinny jeans and a colorful short-sleeved sweatshirt, high-heeled leather boots and a leather belt slung low around her waist.

"Thank God you're okay," Shana said, tugging a rolling suitcase in behind her. She carried several shopping bags, which she dropped on the floor. "Girl, I've been so worried about you. Are you really all right?" Shana leaned over and enfolded Harper in a long, reassuring hug.

"I'm okay...considering. Thanks for doing this."

"Are you kidding me? After everything you've done

for me, I'd have gone into your flaming town house to find you something to wear."

Harper laughed and shook her head. She'd given Shana Davis a chance to prove herself, but Shana had more than earned her half of their partnership.

She turned toward the men. "Shana, this is Jason Maddox and Chase Garrett. They saved my life."

Shana's assessing glance slid over Maddox with definite approval. "Good to meet you, Jason."

"You, too," he said, a faint smile on his lips.

Shana shifted her attention to Chase. "At last...the infamous Chase Garrett. I've heard a lot about you—not all of it good." Her smile was slightly cool. "I guess taking a bullet to save my friend's life gives you a pass on some of it."

Chase smiled. "Don't worry. I plan to make up for the rest of it—whatever it takes."

Shana's black eyebrows went up. "Well, then, I guess we'll see."

Harper felt an unwanted tug at her heart. She tried to tell herself it didn't matter what Chase did or didn't do. The problems they faced were just too much to overcome.

She grabbed her friend's hand. "Come on. I've got a lot to tell you. It's going to take a while."

Shana cast a last glance at Maddox, clearly enjoying the view, then a glance at Chase, sizing him up and maybe sending him a warning.

She turned back to Harper. "I love a good story." She smiled. "I can't wait to hear it."

Eduardo Ramos stood in front of the massive oak desk in his employer's study. The report he had given

Montoya had thrown the man into a blinding rage. His meaty hand slammed down on top of the desk.

"You said you could handle it! You told me it would only take a few more days! I want the Winston girl! I want her father to pay!" He ground his teeth together, making his lower jaw stick out. "This is my country. No one goes against Luis Montoya without paying the consequences. Not Knox Winston. No one!"

Behind his back, Eduardo clenched his hand into a fist, working hard to maintain his highly prized control. He did not appreciate being scolded like a schoolboy. If it weren't for the obscene amount of money he'd amassed through his work for Montoya, the man would have been dead long ago.

"A problem came up," Eduardo explained. "The men ran into unexpected interference. Some of them paid for their mistake with their lives."

Montoya grunted. "Good riddance. I will not tolerate incompetence. I will see the rest of them dead if they fail me again." He rose from his chair. "Since you assured me you could take care of this, I expect you to do exactly that. You will travel to Texas. You will find the girl and bring her back to me."

Eduardo had been expecting this, in a way looking forward to it. He had always enjoyed a challenge. "It will take some time and require more men."

"I don't care if it takes an army! The girl killed my cousin. Family honor alone requires retribution."

"*Sí, mi jefe.* You are right, of course."

"Do not come back without her. If you fail, do not bother to come back at all."

Eduardo made a curt bow of his head, turned and walked out of the study, closing the door softly behind him. Once he arrived in Texas, he would meet with his lieutenant, Roberto Chavez. Chavez had survived the encounter, but failed to deliver the girl.

The young man was undoubtedly fearful. He understood what failure meant to Luis Montoya. Chavez would do Eduardo's bidding. He would hire the extra men they needed and assemble the weapons they would require while Eduardo located the girl.

He would take a commercial flight to Texas, first-class, of course, but charter a jet for his return to Colombia. Easy to board with their unwilling cargo and few questions asked. Easy to get through customs after they landed in Santa Marta.

When he produced the Winston girl at the villa, he would be a hero in his employer's eyes. Montoya rewarded loyalty and success with amazing amounts of money.

In the drug business, the vast sums acquired were endless. That kind of money made up for the occasional abuse he suffered at his boss's hands. Eventually he would have enough to deal with Montoya, retire from the business and live the life of wealth and privilege he had earned after all these years.

Eduardo thought of his upcoming journey and smiled.

CHAPTER THIRTY-EIGHT

Flames licked the grate in the gas fireplace built into the wall of Chase's study. Propped against a pillow, he rested on the sofa, his mind running over the meeting he needed to have with Knox Winston.

He'd call him, try to set up a mutually agreeable location for the meet. Earlier he'd called Mindy and sent her on an errand. Sometime during the car chase and shoot-out, he had lost his iPhone. Wherever it was, it no longer worked. He had pinged it, trying to track its location, but no luck. Probably crushed into a thousand pieces on a Dallas city street.

Fortunately, he'd downloaded his contact list onto his office computer. Mindy had replaced his old iPhone with the newest model, then loaded his contacts before she brought it over. Chase smiled. The girl was becoming an essential member of the Maximum Security crew.

Sitting on the coffee table, the phone began to play

the Brad Paisley country song Mindy had set up as his ringtone, "Mud on the Tires."

Hissing at a slice of pain, he reached for it and saw Bran's name on the screen. "Everything okay?" he asked.

"Hey, bro, what the hell? You're supposed to be in the hospital. Are you okay?"

Wishing he could take another pain pill but unwilling to numb his brain along with his body, Chase just grunted. "Okay enough."

"When I couldn't reach you, I called Maddox. He's with you and Harper, right? At your condo?"

"He's here. We're all safe." *For the time being.* "What about Michael?"

"He's fine. Pia's here. She came back with him from Miami. Long story."

"Yeah? At the moment, I've got nothing but time."

Bran explained about the Feds showing up in Houston to question Michael and at Pia's place in Miami, and how worried Michael had been about her.

"He needed to see his woman. He's our brother, right? So I took him to Miami, and she came back with him."

"Since we can't be sure what's going on or who might be in danger, it's probably good she's here. Does Michael know what happened last night? About the fire and the attempt to abduct his sister?"

"I filled him in after I talked to Maddox. You think whoever did it'll make a run at Michael?"

"I don't know. Might be a good idea if you got him and Pia out of town, somewhere safe."

"I'll talk to him. Maybe I could take them to the ranch."

It wasn't a bad idea. The Garrett Ranch was off the

grid on two thousand acres of prime Texas Hill Country, and reasonably secure. If needed, they could schedule additional guards to patrol the property.

"Call Reese. Find out when the company jet is available. Have him send it to Houston to pick you up."

"Good idea. Give Harper a hug and take care of yourself. Later, bro." Brandon hung up the phone.

Chase glanced up at Harper and ignored a rush of heat he couldn't do a damn thing about. She had changed into skinny jeans and a soft peach cashmere sweater with a turtleneck collar. Long blond hair gleamed around her shoulders and teased her cheeks.

He loved her sense of style, her sleek looks and toned, feminine body. Hell, he loved a lot of things about Harper Winston. It had taken him way too long to figure that out. Or maybe he had known it all along.

"We have company," Harper said. "Detective Ford is here."

Chase blew out a breath. Looked like Ford had answered his call in person. Chase had yet to give the police his statement of events last night. Maybe he could kill two birds with one stone.

Ford walked in, a tall man, his sport coat a little wrinkled but his dark hair freshly trimmed. "I went by the hospital, but you'd already been discharged. How are you feeling?"

"I've had better days. You able to ID any of the shooters involved last night?"

"We're working on it. Two dead, one in the ICU who still hasn't woken up after surgery. Looks like gang-bangers, MS-13. Thugs for hire. We're going over the Buick that crashed at the scene. Looks like the driver got away. We're also looking at the black Suburban. No

ID on the dead guy in the passenger seat. Probably an illegal. Maddox says you took him out."

"That's right."

Ford reached into the pocket of his coat, took out a notepad and flipped it open. "You up to giving me your version of events?"

Not really, but he'd manage. "Sure. Maybe something I say will click with something you've learned."

Heath nodded. "Let's start at the beginning. The fire at Harper's town house—which, by the way, is pretty much a total loss."

Chase sighed. No surprise there.

"On the positive side, the fire department got there in time to save the other units. No damage to any of her neighbors."

"Harper'll be glad to hear it." For the next half hour, Chase went over the details of the attempted abduction, beginning with the town house being firebombed and ending with Chase passing out in the street from loss of blood.

Ford closed his notebook. "So you've got no idea who's behind this."

He had every idea, but if it involved Knox Winston, which Chase was fairly sure it did, he didn't want to do anything to screw up the DEA investigation.

And he had found out a long time ago, until you knew exactly what was going on, you didn't want to give out information that might wind up biting you on the ass.

"The shooting was obviously self-defense, so you and Maddox are in the clear."

A relief, but not unexpected.

Ford stood up from the deep leather chair he'd been

sitting in next to the sofa. "One more thing. I've got news on the Dickerson case."

His interest stirred. "Good news, I hope. I've been meaning to call you for an update. With everything that's happened, I kind of got sidetracked."

"Yeah, getting shot has a way of throwing you off your game."

"So what have you got?"

"We were able to confirm Betsy Dickerson's romantic connection to Dr. Bernard Atwood, the physician in attendance when James Dickerson died. Motel receipts showed up on a credit card in Atwood's name. His phone records showed text messages to Betsy arranging their rendezvous."

"That's a start, I guess."

"Yeah, well, once we knew we were on the right track, I got to thinking, trying to figure out how we could connect the rat poison Betsy bought online—which we confirmed—to James Dickerson's death."

"DNA would have shown it," Chase said, "but since James's body was cremated, I figured that for a dead end."

"I thought so, too. Then I remembered this case I read about. Guy named Graham Young. Medical examiner was able to extract DNA from Young's cremated remains. Showed rat poison in Young's system. His wife was arrested for murder."

"No kidding." Excited at the prospect of catching a killer, Chase started to sit up, but the pain in his chest had him lying back down. "Even so, Betsy must have spread James's ashes."

"She didn't have a chance. Errol Dickerson picked up his son's cremated remains at the funeral home, but instead of spreading them, as Betsy insisted, Errol had the urn stored in the Dickerson family vault. He was more than happy to hand them over to the police."

"How long before you get the results back?"

A satisfied grin stretched across Heath's face. "ME owed me a favor and put a rush on it. Got the call this morning. DNA test results showed traces of thallium in the victim's ashes."

In concession to the ache in his chest, Chase refrained from shooting a fist in the air. "Looks like the good guys are about to win one."

"District attorney's putting together an arrest warrant for Betsy Dickerson and Dr. Bernard Atwood. Once we bring them in, I figure we'll have Betsy and the good doctor at each other's throats in a matter of hours. Loyalty isn't generally a character trait in people like that."

"That's good work, Heath. Keep me posted, will you?"

"You bet. I'm looking forward to sharing the news with Errol Dickerson."

Chase nodded and closed his eyes as fatigue settled over him. "Tell him I won't be sending him a bill. I just made a couple of stops and a few phone calls. You did all the work."

"You're the guy who figured it out, but I'll be happy to tell him. Take care of yourself."

Heath left the study and Harper came back in. She looked tired, worried and beautiful. "Everything okay?"

"Better than okay. Maddox and I are in the clear, and you remember that case I told you about, the client's son who was murdered?"

"I remember."

"Looks like Heath was able to find DNA evidence to

prove the wife and her lover were guilty. The bastards killed him with rat poison."

Harper sat down on the sofa beside him. "You got justice for the father. You're a good man, Chase."

He took hold of her hand. "Even good people make mistakes, Harper. I hope you'll keep that in mind."

Harper glanced away.

Chase turned her hand over and kissed the palm. "We're going to make this work, honey."

Troubled blue eyes swung back to his face. "I'm the daughter of a drug lord, Chase. You're an ex-cop. Tell me how this is going to work."

Harper stood up from the sofa and walked out of the study. Chase stared after her retreating figure, the doubt he'd felt before returning full force. He didn't want to lose her.

But maybe Harper wouldn't give him any choice.

Several times, Harper went into the study to check on Chase. He'd been sleeping fitfully off and on. When she'd examined his bandage and found it needed changing, she had brought in what she needed and done it right there.

As time slipped away and the hour grew late, she convinced him to take a pain pill and go to bed.

"Jason's stretched out on the sofa in your man cave. His gun's on the table right next to him, so you don't need to worry. You have to sleep if you're going to regain your strength."

Chase didn't argue. She was right, which he seemed to accept. Yawning, he got up from the sofa, and Harper helped him down the hall into his bedroom.

Chase reached out and gently touched her cheek. "You said you'd stay."

She wanted to. She was in love with him. No matter how it all turned out, she wanted this time with him. "It's not a good idea. You need to sleep, and if I'm in bed with you, you'll be thinking about sex."

His mouth edged up. "Even if you aren't in bed with me, I'll be thinking about you, remembering what it's like to make love to you."

She flushed.

"I promise you all we'll do is sleep. That's about all I can handle right now."

He'd been shot because of her. He had risked his life and almost been killed. The thought of what might have happened made her feel ill. "All right," she said softly. "I'll stay."

Chase bent his head and brushed a soft kiss over her lips. Even that light touch brought a rush of heat. Harper helped him strip off his clothes and climb into bed, then changed into the nightgown Shana had brought her, a pretty little blue silk nightie with ecru lace on the front.

She convinced Chase to take a pain pill, though he insisted on only half, then slid into bed beside him.

Chase leaned over and brushed a last soft kiss on her lips. "Good night, baby," he said, his voice deep and sexy. "Try to get some sleep."

Harper closed her eyes, surprised at how weary she felt. It had been an exhausting day and she hadn't slept at all last night, yet worry nagged her. Time drifted past and drowsiness began to slip over her. The rustle of the wind through the trees on the terrace was the last thing she remembered.

It was close to dawn when she started to dream, a

wonderful, sweetly erotic fantasy of snuggling spoon-fashion against Chase's hard body, of touching him, feeling him stir, of moist kisses against the side of her neck and her breasts being softly caressed.

She moaned as her nightgown slid up and her legs parted to welcome Chase's attentions, the skillful play of his hands, the heat he could stir with the slightest touch. When he slid inside her, she moaned and arched her back, taking him deeper, heard his quick intake of breath.

Not a dream—not even close. The deep, saturating pleasure pouring through her was better than any fantasy she'd ever had.

She opened her eyes as his arm slid around her waist and he lifted her, urged her up on her hands and knees. Chase shifted their intimate position, staying close behind her, gripped her hips to hold her in place and began to move.

Desire burned through her. Harper moaned and took up the rhythm he set, taking even more of him, enjoying his low groan of passion.

"You're mine," he said softly, driving hard, demanding a response. "You know it and so do I. Let yourself go."

The words sent heat sliding over her skin and hunger burning through her. It was true. She belonged to him. Maybe she always had.

Giving in to the needs of her body, Harper did as Chase commanded, and pleasure, sweet and pure, washed through her. She absorbed it, sank into it, drowned in it, let it flow in and out like a tide.

Chase followed her to release, his muscles tightening, his body going rigid as he bit back the growl locked in his throat. With a deep sigh of satisfaction, he pulled her down beside him on the mattress, their bodies still entwined.

For long moments, she just lay there absorbing his warmth, the feel of his arm draped over her waist.

Then her foggy brain began to clear, and she turned so that she could see his face. "Oh, my God, did I hurt you? What about your injury? Oh, my God."

Chase chuckled and slid out of bed to dispose of protection. "I'm all right. I took the other half of that pain pill. I'm fine." He bent and kissed her lips. "You were worth it, angel. You always have been."

Harper closed her eyes. He had promised this wouldn't happen. But how could she be mad at him when she was fairly sure she was the one who had initiated the lovemaking?

Injured as Chase was, she should feel guilty. Instead, when the bed dipped under his weight, signaling his return, she snuggled against him, careful not to hurt him, and drifted back to sleep.

She didn't wake up till sunlight shone through the crack in the curtains and Jason Maddox was knocking on the bedroom door.

"You better get dressed," Jase said. "You've got company."

Chase was already gone, she realized, alarm bells ringing in her head. Harper slipped out of bed, grabbed her robe and shrugged it on.

As she started for the door, the sweet feelings of last night slipped away, replaced with a fresh shot of fear.

CHAPTER THIRTY-NINE

Chase leaned back on the overstuffed leather sofa, flames licking the grate in the gas fireplace built into the wall of his study. DEA Special Agent Zach Tanner sat in a nearby leather chair. Tanner stood as Maddox led Harper into the study.

Her gaze went from Chase to Tanner, and her spine stiffened. "Agent Tanner." Beneath her yellow cashmere sweater, her shoulders subtly straightened. "I wish I could say it's good to see you, but we both know it wouldn't be true."

"Why don't you have a seat, Ms. Winston?"

Chase rose, offering her the place next to him on the sofa. He was almost surprised when Harper sat down beside him. As he returned to his seat, he caught her hand, which felt icy cold.

"What's going on?" she asked.

Tanner leaned forward. Beneath his leather jacket, Chase caught a glimpse of the pistol in his shoulder holster.

"I came here to let you know that your father was arrested early this morning. It's going to be a big news story. I wanted to let you know before the media picks it up."

The color drained from her face, and the hand Chase was holding began to tremble. He tightened his hold. She wasn't alone in this. He hoped she knew that.

"What are the charges?" she asked.

"Money laundering, extortion, wire fraud, sex trafficking—"

"Sex trafficking? What exactly does that mean?"

"We found evidence that at one time your father was part of a smuggling ring that brought women in from South America to commit sex acts for money."

"Prostitution," she said.

"That's right. His involvement ended a few years back when he began to consolidate and legitimize some of his business interests."

She moistened her lips. "What else?"

"One of the most serious charges he's facing involves cocaine trafficking and distribution. For the large amount of drugs that were being brought into the country and distributed, the penalty is ten years to life."

Harper closed her eyes and leaned against the back of the sofa. Chase eased her against him and settled an arm around her shoulders.

Harper took a deep breath. He could see she was working to summon her courage, force herself to face the truth.

"It's hard to believe," she said. "I've been praying you wouldn't find anything, that it was all some kind of mistake." She looked at Tanner. "You got all this from the bug Chase put in my father's study?"

"No. We've been aware of your father's criminal activities for years. Eventually our investigation became official. We finally got the proof we needed from the warrant we obtained, which allowed us to search his residence and warehouse locations. What we found gave us enough to make an arrest."

"What about—"

"I'm sorry, Harper, that's all I can say. This is an ongoing investigation. I shouldn't even be telling you this much. By tonight it won't matter. The details will be picked up by the media and be all over the news."

Harper didn't say more. Chase wondered what she was thinking, whether she blamed her father's arrest on him and if so, what it would mean to their already shaky relationship.

Tanner rose from his chair. "I need to get going. For your sake, Harper, I'm sorry it turned out this way."

She swallowed but made no reply.

Maddox walked Tanner out of the study, leaving Chase alone with Harper.

"I'm sorry, honey. I really am."

She turned, pierced him with a cool blue stare. "I don't think you're sorry. I think you're glad the police finally arrested him."

"I'm sorry for you, Harper. I can't imagine what you're going through right now. But your father chose the life he's been living. He sold his soul years ago in exchange for money and power. Now it's time for him to pay. Justice has a way of catching up with a person. Knox Winston is no exception."

Harper rose from the sofa. "If you'll excuse me, I need some time to myself. I need to think things through, figure things out and decide what I'm going to do. I'll be in the guest room I should have slept in last night."

So much for their relationship. Clearly in Harper's opinion he was the bad guy. In a way, he was. Even so, he didn't regret it. Knox Winston belonged in jail.

As Harper walked away, Chase rose from the sofa. "Whatever you're thinking of doing, Harper, remember that someone just tried to kidnap you. After hearing the charges against your father, you must realize what's happening to you and Michael is very likely connected to Knox Winston's criminal activities."

Her pretty lips trembled, and Chase felt a stab of guilt. He refused to back down. Keeping Harper safe meant she had to accept the truth.

She gripped the back of the sofa and released a shuddering breath. "I don't know what to do, how to handle this. What should I do, Chase? How do I make this go away?"

Chase walked toward her. He wasn't sure what would happen when he reached for her, but instead of pulling away, she went into his arms and rested her head on his shoulder.

Chase drew her closer. "We'll figure it out, baby. You aren't alone in this. You aren't going to get rid of me until you're safe." She wasn't getting rid of him at all if he had his way.

"Okay?" he asked, inhaling the scent of her sweet-smelling hair. A long moment passed before he felt her nod of agreement. "Good. Why don't you lie down for a while? You still haven't caught up on your sleep."

She swallowed and eased away. "I have work to do. Shana brought my laptop from the office. I'll set it up in the guest room."

"All right. I've got things to do myself." Like figure out how the hell he was going to track the men who had attacked them. He needed a lead, something to help him connect the dots. Heath Ford had said one of the shooters was in the hospital. Maybe he was awake by now. Maybe he could tell them something.

Harper's footsteps receded on the hardwood floors as she walked down the hall.

Dammit, he'd been hoping to talk to Knox Winston. Now Winston was in jail.

He used his iPhone to call Detective Ford for an update on the shooter in the hospital. "I need something, Heath. Anything you come up with might help."

"Guy's awake," Heath said. "Name's Rico Gonzales. MS-13 gangbanger. He's in rough shape. Caught a bullet in the lung. So far he isn't talking. Seems more afraid of the guy he works for than going to jail."

"He didn't give you any idea who that might be?"

"Like I said. He isn't talking."

"Keep me posted, will you?"

"You know I will," Heath said.

Frustrated, Chase ended the call. His shoulder was throbbing so he stretched out on the sofa to rest for a while. He must have fallen asleep. When he awoke, Maddox had the noon news on TV.

"Check it out," Jase said, turning up the volume.

Chase sat up and focused on the broadcast. As Zach Tanner had predicted, Knox Winston's arrest was the lead story of the day.

Harper had been working in the guest bedroom all morning. She'd started by calling her insurance company to file a claim on her town house. She had no idea how long it would take to settle the claim or where she'd end up living until things got back to normal, but she had even bigger problems right now.

Preferring to immerse herself in work rather than think about the trouble surrounding her, she opened her laptop and started going over some of the new designs Shana had sent via email. She gave her friend some feedback, then took a look at invoices that hadn't been paid.

Her stomach growled. She'd only had a bagel all day, eaten at noon as she'd watched the news on her laptop. As Agent Tanner predicted, it gave all the lurid details of her father's arrest.

Afterward, she was so depressed she crawled into bed, pulled a pillow over her head and slept for a couple of hours. When she awoke, she pushed her worry aside and worked for a while.

It was six o'clock now. She was hungry, and she couldn't hide out in the bedroom any longer. And she was fairly sure if she didn't come out soon, Chase would come in and get her.

She was making her way to the door when her cell phone began to ring. She pulled it out of her jeans pocket but didn't recognize the caller ID.

"Ms. Winston?" An older man, she thought, the voice slightly familiar.

"This is Harper Winston."

"I'm Miller Bernstein, your father's attorney. We've met at the house a few times."

"Yes, I remember." Distinguished older man with silver hair, always impeccably dressed.

"Your father asked me to call you. Fill you in on what's been happening."

Her hand tightened around the phone. "I know what's been happening, Mr. Bernstein. I saw news of the arrest on TV."

"I wanted to let you know your father is out on bail. He'd like to see you, explain a few things."

She almost hung up the phone. She didn't want to see her father. He was a criminal who had lied to her all of her life. He was the reason she was in danger—or at least Chase believed he was to blame.

She looked up as a faint knock sounded, watched the door swing open and Chase walk into the room.

"I'll have to call you back," she said, ending the call without waiting for his reply. She looked up at Chase. "That was Miller Bernstein, my father's attorney. My father wants to see me."

Something shifted in Chase's features. "That's good. We need to talk to him, find out what's going on. That's the only way we're going to make this end."

"You really think he knows?"

"Yeah, I do. Call Bernstein back and put the phone on speaker."

She nodded, pulled up the number in the recent calls, and the attorney picked up right away. Harper pushed the speaker button. "When can we meet?" she asked.

Bernstein must have heard the echo on the other end of the line. "Who's listening to this call?"

"Chase Garrett," she said. "If we meet, he'll be coming with me."

Bernstein said something to someone in the background, then came back on the line. "Your father will see you tomorrow morning at the house."

She looked at Chase, her stomach knotting as she thought of the bug in the study.

His eyes remained on her face. "Not the house," Chase said to Bernstein. "Tell Winston she'll meet him at your office. Tell him his daughter's life is in danger, and we need his help."

Silence fell. She could hear the attorney talking to whoever was in the room. "Tomorrow morning," Bernstein said. "My office. Ten o'clock."

"We'll be there," Chase said and ended the call.

Harper looked up at him, into the handsome face that had turned stone cold. "Why did you do that? You could have met him in his study. Everything he said would have been recorded."

Chase reached out and gently cupped her cheek. "You've done enough, Harper. I know how hard this has been for you. Whatever happens now is in the hands of the justice system."

Her eyes welled. Whatever Knox Winston had done, she didn't want to make things worse. "Thank you."

"Let's just hope your father knows something that will help us."

But Harper wasn't sure that even if her father knew who was behind the attacks, he would be willing to tell them.

Eduardo Ramos prowled his elegant suite on the fifth floor of the luxurious Four Seasons Las Colinas on the outskirts of Dallas. Beyond the paned windows in the French doors leading onto the balcony, the lush green grasses of two eighteen-hole golf courses surrounded him.

Eduardo refused to stay in less than five-star luxury when he traveled, and the hotel was the closest suitable accommodation to the Love Field Airport, where the private jet he had chartered would be waiting to fly him and his reluctant traveling companion back home.

In the meantime, he had work to do. Eduardo checked the time on his cell phone. His lieutenant, Roberto Chavez, should be arriving any moment. Chavez had been sent to Dallas to bring the girl back to Colombia, where she would do Luis Montoya's bidding for as long as it pleased him.

Unfortunately, Chavez had failed. Which meant in his boss's eyes Eduardo had also failed. It was a problem that needed to be resolved, and quickly.

A soft knock sounded at the door. Eduardo walked over and pulled it open, allowing Chavez to walk into the beautifully furnished living room of the suite. Over-stuffed cream sofas were arranged in front of a manteled hearth, and brass lamps perched on walnut end tables.

Eduardo didn't bother to offer Chavez a handshake or invite the man to sit down. "What have you done to resolve the situation you have managed to embroil us in?" he asked.

"Please, Senor Ramos, let me begin by explaining what happened, how things went—"

"I do not wish to hear how you failed. I wish to hear what you are doing to succeed."

Roberto swallowed. A handsome young man with his olive skin and jet-black hair. In his late twenties, he was smart or he would not be working for Eduardo. He had been educated in the States, preferred to call himself Bobby, but he had learned quickly that he could earn far more money working in Colombia.

"I have hired more men as you instructed," Roberto said. "Members of the same group, Mara Salvatrucha. Here they are known as MS-13. The men are angry at the deaths of their brothers and determined to extract revenge from those responsible. Which works in our favor. Still, they demanded to be paid more. They say the risks are now greater, which is true. I agreed to pay what they asked. I assumed that would be your wish."

Eduardo nodded. The pittance more it would cost meant nothing to a man like Luis Montoya. "If they bring me the girl, the cost will be worth it."

"Of those who were involved in the failed attempt, several were killed, but only one apprehended. He will not talk to the police. He knows his family will pay the price if he does."

Eduardo nodded. "Good. That is good. We need to locate the girl and make plans."

"*Sí*, Senor Ramos." For the next few minutes, Roberto filled him in, telling Eduardo everything he had learned about the Winston girl and her lover, Chase Garrett, the man who had traveled with her to Colombia to find her brother, the same man who protected her in Dallas and had rescued her from his men the night of the fire.

When Chavez finished, he reached into his pocket and pulled out a cracked cell phone with a broken screen. "This belonged to Garrett. He dropped it after he was shot. It no longer works, but perhaps it will help you in some way."

Eduardo reached out and took the phone. "I will find the girl. Tell the men to be ready. Once we have her location, they must be prepared to move." He looked at Roberto hard. "There cannot be another failure."

"No, Senor Ramos. I understand."

Eduardo's gaze darkened. "Do you? Senor Montoya will not be so forgiving a second time."

Roberto's face paled beneath his dark skin. *"Si, senor."*

"I will call when I have the necessary information," Eduardo said. "You may go."

Chavez made a curt bow of his head, turned and walked out of the suite.

Eduardo glanced down at the phone in his hand. He opened the back and removed the SIM card. Walking over to the laptop he had set up on the desk against the wall, he dug into the briefcase beside it and took out the tools he needed.

In minutes he had a card reader plugged into a USB port, the SIM card in the slot at the back of the reader. The data began to flow into the computer. Emails, text messages, phone contacts, a treasure trove of information about the man who owned the phone.

Chase Garrett, Harper Winston's lover and devoted protector, would lead him to the girl. Eduardo smiled. It was almost too easy.

CHAPTER FORTY

A harsh wind blew over the Dallas streets. Cars dodged leaves and blowing papers while pedestrians pulled up the collars of their coats and huddled into the folds. The usual sixty-five-degree late-October days had fallen into the low fifties, and a storm hovered on the horizon.

"You ready for this?" Chase stopped Harper just outside the Bernstein Law Office on the sixth floor of a ten-story high-rise on North Central Parkway.

"No. I'm never going to be ready for my father to explain why he's a criminal. Unfortunately, I don't have any choice."

Chase opened the door, and they walked into an opulent office with deep burgundy carpet and dark wood paneling. French Impressionist art hung on the walls, and Rodin-inspired sculptures sat on pedestals and on the table in front of a tailored burgundy sofa and chairs.

Chase let Harper precede him up to the receptionist desk, where a svelte brunette in a gray skirt suit sat behind a computer.

"May I help you?" the woman asked.

"Harper Winston and Chase Garrett, here to see Mr. Bernstein."

"Of course." The brunette rose from her chair. "Please follow me." As she led them down a hall into the interior of the office, the woman tossed Chase a glance he ignored. He wasn't interested in other women. Hadn't been since the day he and Harper had flown off to the Caribbean to find her brother.

When Harper picked up on the exchange and cast him a look down the length of her pretty nose, he found his mouth edging up. He liked that she cared. He liked it a lot. But before he could do anything about it, he had to find a way to keep her safe.

The receptionist held the door open, and Chase followed Harper into a conference room dominated by a polished mahogany table surrounded by eight round-backed rolling chairs. The door closed behind them, giving them privacy.

Seated at the far end of the table, Knox Winston's gaze zeroed in on Chase as he walked into the room, and though the man knew Chase would be accompanying his daughter, his silver-threaded eyebrows knit in anger.

He shot a hard glare at Harper. "I thought you said you were through with him."

"Take it easy, Knox," his attorney soothed before she had time to answer. Bernstein rested a hand on his client's thick shoulder, then walked over to Chase and extended a hand.

"I'm Miller Bernstein. I've seen you and your brothers at various social functions, but I don't believe we've ever been introduced."

Chase shook the man's hand, ignoring the twinge of pain the motion caused. "Chase Garrett." Knowing the effort would be futile, he didn't extend the gesture to Winston.

Harper smoothed the front of the brown plaid, calf-length wool skirt she wore with a pair of brown boots. "You wanted to see me, Dad, so I'm here."

"Thank you for coming, Harper. I wanted you to understand what's going on."

She tucked shiny blond strands into the tight knot of hair at the nape of her neck as she sat down at the table.

Her gaze went to her father. "Before you start, I want you to know I've seen the news. I know you've been arrested for cocaine smuggling—among numerous other charges. I can't imagine what you could possibly have to say, but I'm listening."

Winston leaned back in his chair, a big man, still imposing though he was somewhere close to sixty. "I'm innocent, Harper. All those charges are nothing but a pack of lies. The government will do anything to bring down a successful man like me. I'm innocent." He flicked a glance at his attorney. "It's Miller's job to prove it."

Harper shook her head as if she couldn't believe what he was saying, what he expected her to believe.

When she made no reply, Chase spoke up. He hadn't bothered to take a seat. "I realize you're having your own set of problems, Winston, but the police must have told you about the attack on your daughter. Harper was abducted during a fire that destroyed her town house. There was a shoot-out and a car chase—where, fortunately, she managed to escape."

"Chase and Jason Maddox ran the car I was being held in off the road," Harper said. "If it hadn't been for them, I might be dead by now—or worse."

"I heard you had some trouble," Knox said, as if they were talking about a flat tire. "I was told you came out of it all right." Like Bass Garrett had been, Knox Winston was a powerful man. Not much happened in Dallas that Knox didn't know about. Especially if it involved his daughter.

"Chase believes the men who came after me are connected to the men who kidnapped Michael in Colombia. They think whoever did it came to Dallas to kidnap me."

Winston pushed up from his chair, anger riding hard on his thick shoulders. He drilled Bernstein with a glare. "You understand what I'm going to say is attorney-client privilege."

"Of course, Knox, but Mr. Garrett isn't bound by—"

"Whatever you say in this room goes no further," Chase said. "You have my word on that."

"Why should I believe you?" Knox asked.

"You knew my father. His word was gold. So is mine. More important, I want your daughter safe." *I love her.* But he had only just figured that out and it wasn't the time or place. "I can't protect her unless you help me find a way to deal with the men who are after her."

Winston sat back down, and Harper laid her hand over his where it rested on the table. "Can you help me, Dad?"

Winston's face flushed with angry heat and his jaw hardened. "Luis Montoya." He spit out the name like a curse. "Montoya wants revenge. We had a…business arrangement. There were problems. Montoya went after Michael as retribution—the penalty for my going against him. We talked while you were in Colombia. I explained what happened, and we agreed to continue working together. I thought I had things straightened out."

He looked up at Chase. "I knew you were down there with Harper searching for Michael. I figured if anyone could bring the boy back, it was you. You found him and brought him home, and I thought the problem was solved."

"Apparently not," Chase said dryly, barely able to keep the disgust out of his voice. "The question is what do we do to stop him before Harper gets hurt?"

"Fucking Montoya. The bastard goes after something, he doesn't quit until he gets it." Winston rose and paced over to the window, turned back. "I'll call him, see if there's some kind of deal, something I can give him in exchange for my daughter."

Chase clamped down on his temper. He wanted to tell Knox Winston that Luis Montoya didn't own his daughter and never would. But he needed Winston's help.

"You have to take care of this as soon as possible. Harper's life is in danger every second you delay."

"Give me your number," Winston said. Chase rattled off his cell number, and Winston punched it into his phone. Then Chase plugged in Winston's personal number. It felt odd exchanging information with his father's lifelong enemy, a criminal he was helping bring to justice.

"You ready to go?" Chase asked Harper.

She rose from her seat at the table. "I'm ready." She turned to her father. "Goodbye, Dad." There was a note of finality in her voice Chase hadn't expected. He settled a hand at her waist and urged her toward the door. His chest still ached, but gaining Winston's cooperation made him feel better.

They rode the elevator to the lobby in silence, crossed the polished marble floor and walked out of the building. They didn't talk on the way back to his condo. As he pulled into his parking space in the garage and turned off the engine, Harper's cell phone started to ring.

"This is Harper." As the conversation progressed, her face went sheet white, and Chase softly cursed.

Whoever it was, it meant trouble.

The conversation was brief and one-sided. She set the phone limply in her lap. "It's Shana," Harper said, her eyes big and her hands shaking. "Montoya's men have Shana."

Harper felt a crushing weight on her chest. Her best friend was in trouble. And it was all her fault.

"Let me guess," Chase said, turning in the driver's seat to face her. "Montoya's men are willing to make an exchange. You for her."

Harper swallowed and nodded.

"Not gonna happen, sweetheart." Chase cranked the key, and the powerful Mercedes engine rumbled back to life.

"They said not to tell anyone. They said if I go to the police, Shana is dead."

Chase's jaw looked hard. "They really think you're just going to hand yourself over? That isn't even a remote possibility."

Harper didn't bother to argue. It wasn't open to discussion, not with Chase or anyone else. Shana was in trouble because of her. This was something she had to do. But she wasn't a fool. She needed Chase's help.

"They know about you. I'm supposed to find a way to get away from you. They said they would call again with more instructions." ·

"When's the exchange?" Chase asked, pulling the car back out of the garage.

"They're calling back."

"Good. Maybe that'll buy us some time." As he drove onto the street, he punched a number into the hands-free, and Harper recognized Jason's voice on the other end of the line.

"Maddox."

"Hawk, I need your help."

"What's going on?"

"Guy behind all this is a Colombian drug lord named Luis Montoya. Montoya wants Harper as payback for some beef he's got against Knox Winston. His men took Harper's business partner, Shana Davis. You met her at my place."

"Yeah, beautiful girl."

"They want to trade Shana for Harper."

Jase swore foully. "Well, that ain't gonna happen. How are you planning to get the girl back?"

"Who else is in the office?"

"Ryker's here. That's it. Wolfe's out with a client. Nobody else around. Bran's with Michael and Pia out at the ranch."

"Yeah, I talked to Bran this morning. We can't pull him away, but we're going to need more men and we don't have much time."

"The cops?"

"We could call in the Feds. I trust Zach Tanner—

he's a straight shooter, and he knows what he's doing. But Tanner's DEA. That means he'll be bringing in his superiors. Once that happens, we lose control and a thousand things could go wrong."

"Shana Davis's life is at stake," Maddox said. "Bringing in the Feds? I don't like the feel of it."

"Neither do I. No cops. Not unless we have to. Stay at the office. I'm coming to you."

Harper felt a jolt of surprise when Chase voice-dialed her father.

"Winston, it's Garrett."

"I haven't reached the bastard yet. What do you want?"

"Montoya's goons have Harper's friend Shana. They want an exchange—Harper for her friend." Her father swore crudely. "Don't worry, that isn't going to happen," Chase said. "I've got a couple of men I can count on, but from the way things went down last time, the three of us won't be enough. I'd rather not involve the police. I'm hoping you can help."

"No cops. How much time we got?"

"Not much."

"I got a couple of guys I can call. Give me the address, and I'll have my men there."

"I'll be in touch." Chase ended the call, his foot hard on the gas all the way to Blackburn Street.

"What are you planning to do?" Harper asked as he roared through a yellow light without looking back.

"We need enough men to keep Montoya's thugs busy while we go in and get Shana out."

A chill went through her. She couldn't help thinking of the shoot-out and how close Chase had come to dying.

"You're going to need my help," she said. "That's the only way it's going to work."

Chase just shook his head. "No way. You aren't getting anywhere near these guys."

Harper didn't argue. Chase wasn't a fool, either. Sooner or later he'd figure out she was right. Montoya's men wouldn't let Shana go unless they believed they'd get Harper in exchange.

Chase parked in the lot behind The Max, and they went in through the back door.

"Hey, lady." Maddox walked toward her, concern stamped into his handsome face. "How you holding up?"

She kissed his cheek. He always seemed to be there when they needed him. "I'm okay. Shana's in trouble."

"Yeah, I know. We're going get her out of trouble, okay?"

She swallowed and nodded.

Maddox introduced her to the man beside him. "This ugly SOB is Jaxon Ryker." Around six feet tall, Jax was all solid muscle, dark-haired, dark-eyed and handsome as sin. "Jax is going to help us. He's an ex-SEAL, so he knows a thing or two about hostage rescues."

Harper managed to smile. "Thank you, Jax. My friend Shana's in trouble because of me. I'll do whatever it takes to get her back safely."

"That's good to hear," Jax said, "because if these guys are planning to trade you for her, they're going to expect you to be there."

"Harper isn't getting anywhere near these guys," Chase said as he walked up. "That's not open for discussion."

Harper pinned him with a glare. "It isn't your decision, Chase. It's mine. If you'll stop being so bull-headed, you'll see there's no other way it's going to work."

"You aren't going."

"I'm going."

Ryker rested a hand on Chase's shoulder. "If you want the girl out alive, you're going to need Harper's help. You know it and so does she. Now, let's stop wasting time and figure out how to make this happen and keep Harper safe."

CHAPTER FORTY-ONE

Chase softly cursed. Jax, Harper and Maddox were all looking at him as if he needed to get a grip. Apparently, he did because he knew they were right.

"Fine, we do it your way. Jax, you're the snatch-and-grab expert. Let me lay out what I've got in mind and you can punch holes in it, find any weak spots."

"Sounds good."

"As I see it," Chase continued, "our biggest obstacle at the moment is not knowing the location of the meet. Once we have that, we can figure the best approach, set things up."

"Montoya's in business with Winston," Maddox said. "There's a chance whoever's in charge of this operation is someone familiar with Winston's properties, warehouse locations, distribution centers, that kind of thing. Could even be someone who works with Winston's people."

"You're thinking they could choose someplace they're familiar with," Jax said.

"My dad owns a number of warehouses out in West

Dallas," Harper said. "I considered renting space from him when I first moved back to the city, but I didn't want him keeping tabs on me. Or interfering in my business."

"It makes a certain amount of sense," Jason said. "Given the payback angle. What could be better than kidnapping Harper right under her father's nose?"

Harper's phone signaled just then, and Chase caught the panic in her eyes. It was gone in a heartbeat, replaced by the same courage he had seen in Colombia. She'd been determined to save her brother then. She'd do everything in her power to save her best friend now.

Emotion rolled through him, feelings for Harper he didn't dare think about now.

"Stall for time," he said. "And demand proof of life." When the color drained from her face, he softened his tone. "Tell them you need to talk to her, make sure she's okay."

Harper nodded, accepted the call. Since they couldn't risk putting the call on speaker, she held it away from her ear so Chase could listen.

"There is an empty warehouse on Singleton Boulevard." Harper recognized the man's voice, laced with a Spanish accent. "Your father owns it. Do you know where it is?"

"I know the area. But nothing happens until I talk to Shana. I need to be sure she's okay."

"You will do as I say. You will come to the warehouse on Singleton. Number 3841. If you do not, the girl will die."

Her hands tightened around the phone. "I'm not coming unless I talk to her. Put her on the line."

The man swore a string of Spanish curses, which the blush seeping into Harper's cheeks said she understood. The caller spoke to one of his men, told him to bring the girl.

Chase could hear scuffling in the background. "Go to hell," Shana said. He heard a slap, a whimper, then Shana's shaky voice. "Harper?"

"It's me." Harper's hands were trembling. "Shana, are you all right?"

Her breath shuddered, came over the line. "These guys are a bunch of low-life dicks, but I'm okay."

"I'm coming to get you. Just stay strong."

"Don't do it, Harper. They won't let either of us go. They're taking you back to—" The phone jerked out of Shana's hand. Chase clenched his jaw at the sound of another ringing slap.

"Don't hurt her!" Harper shouted. "I'll do whatever you want! Just don't hurt her."

"Are you still with Garrett?"

She glanced up at him with those beautiful, trusting blue eyes, and pressure expanded in his chest. "No," she lied. "I sneaked out of his condo. He's still not recovered from the shooting. I left him sleeping and took his car. He doesn't even know I'm gone."

"You have thirty minutes. If you are not here—"

"I can't get there in thirty minutes! I need at least an hour! There's a ton of traffic, and I'm on the other side of town. And the car needs gas. If I don't fill the tank, I won't get there at all. Please!"

The caller scoffed. "One hour. When you reach the address, you will turn onto the property and drive to the back. You will pull up to the gate, and we will let you in. The exchange will take place inside the warehouse. If you do not come, the girl dies. If you bring the police or your boyfriend, the girl dies." The phone went dead.

Chase took out his cell and hit Knox Winston's number. "I need to coordinate with your men. How many have you got lined up?"

"Two so far. I can get more. I just need a little more time."

"Two will have to do," Chase said. "Hold on." Maddox set his laptop on the desk and turned it around to show Chase the Google Maps screen. He pointed to the warehouse property and what looked like a vacant lot around the corner not far away.

"There's an empty lot on Leland Street. It's around the corner and down a block from the warehouse you own on Singleton Boulevard. How fast can your men get there?"

"Tell me that bastard doesn't think he can steal my daughter right off my own property."

"Lie down with dogs, you're bound to get fleas."

Winston cursed foully. "He won't get away with this. Not even close."

"Whatever you do to Montoya, don't do it until we have Shana Davis and your daughter out of danger. Your word on that." Not that Chase gave it much credence.

"I won't make a move until the women are safe."

"Good. I need one more thing. Any chance you've got a floor plan of that warehouse you can send me?"

"I'll make a call, have my people text an image to your phone."

"That'll work." Chase ended the call. He turned to Harper. "All right, angel. You've managed to get yourself smack in the middle of this. Now, unless you want me to tie you up and leave you locked in the back room, you're going to do exactly what I say."

Shana hunkered in the corner on the cold concrete floor. She moved, trying to get more comfortable, and pain shot into her legs. With her wrists bound behind her with nylon ties, her ankles also bound, she was almost completely immobile.

She still couldn't remember all the details of how she'd gotten here. She'd worked late, then met Tony and Debbie for a margarita at La Paloma, not far from the office. She'd wound up staying for something to eat.

It was after eleven when she'd left the restaurant and headed home, drove into the covered parking space in the lot behind her apartment and climbed out of her red Mazda CX. One of the overhead lights had been out, she recalled. She didn't see the three men who stepped out of the shadows until it was too late.

She squeezed her eyes shut at the memory. Hard-looking men, midtwenties, Hispanic, black hair shaved close, shirtless, inked-up sinewy torsos, bandannas tied over the lower halves of their faces.

The fourth man, their leader, was different, his eyes sharp above his bandanna, black hair neatly combed, dressed in chinos and a long-sleeved knit pullover. Nice clothes, she remembered thinking in some terrified corner of her brain.

She remembered struggling as the men held her immobile while their leader pressed a damp cloth over her nose and mouth, muffling her screams, shutting her mind down and plunging her into unconsciousness.

When she awoke hours later, she sat where she was now, leaning against the wall of a big empty building on a cold concrete floor. Steel girders held up the metal roof, and there were a number of roll-up doors. More men with the same group who had taken her last night were there. Gang members covered in tattoos and armed with knives and pistols prowled restlessly around the interior of the warehouse.

The cloth had been replaced with duct tape. Instead of chemicals, she inhaled the tang of motor oil and the subtle smell of hemp. She still wore the brown leggings

and dark red cowl-necked sweater she had been wearing last night, but her high-heeled boots were gone, her
feet freezing in the icy space.

Aside from the slaps she had received when she had
been forced to talk to Harper, so far the men hadn't hurt
her. But their intentions were clear. She had heard them
mention Colombia, where they were taking Harper, but
Shana belonged to the men who had abducted her, a re-
ward for their efforts.

She shuddered as fresh fear rolled down her spine.
Tears threatened. Since she had already cried enough,
she blinked them away. She needed to stay strong.
Harper was coming. She knew that without doubt.

She thought of her friend, of the kidnapping Harper
had managed to escape—thanks to Chase Garrett. She
thought of how Chase had been shot trying to save her.
The man was insane for her. No way was he letting
Harper give herself up to a gang of cutthroats.

Injured or not, Garrett would be coming with her,
perhaps with the big, powerful man, Jason Maddox,
who she'd met at Chase's condo, the man who had
helped him the night of the fire.

No police. Chase wouldn't take the chance.

Garrett and Maddox. Both smart, strong, determined
men.

Shana said a silent prayer as she glanced toward the
door. There were men everywhere, too many to count.
It seemed hopeless but she refused to give up. If they
all worked together, maybe they would stand a chance.

CHAPTER FORTY-TWO

From The Max, Harper drove Chase's shiny silver Mercedes onto 75 South toward her father's warehouse on Singleton Boulevard. Chase had shown her the property location on Google Maps. She remembered her dad owned several large steel warehouse buildings in the heavily industrialized zone. This property sat on five acres, well off the road in a fenced compound.

She wondered if her father had used the buildings to house illegal drugs, or as a distribution center of some kind. She wondered what other criminal activities had gone on inside and a shiver ran through her.

It was a twenty-minute drive to the location. Maddox and Jax Ryker had gone ahead of her to recon the property and then meet up with her father's men. Once they saw the layout, they would make adjustments and finalize the plan Chase had laid out.

Chase rode next to her. Like Maddox and Ryker, he and Harper both wore tactical vests and earbuds,

Harper's hidden beneath her hair, so they could remain in constant communication. Winston's men had also been outfitted. Chase carried his backup Nighthawk .45, his .380 strapped to his ankle. The revolver Harper had taken from The Max rested on the center console.

Nerves jangled through her, and her stomach knotted.

"All right, let's hear it again," Chase said. Though she knew the plan by heart, Chase had made her repeat it over and over.

"Once I reach the location, I turn onto the property and drive toward the gate in front of the warehouse, which is the big metal building in back. Even if the gate is open, I don't pull in."

"That's right."

"I just sit there, idling the car. When I don't drive through the gate, the men will either call my cell or come out to get me. If they call, I don't answer."

"The object is draw them out of the warehouse," Chase reminded her.

Harper nodded. "I need to get as many men outside as I can so Jax and Maddox can go in through the back and get Shana out with as little resistance as possible."

"Exactly."

She swallowed against the nausea swirling in her stomach. She couldn't mess this up. If she did, Shana would die. Maybe Jax and Maddox, too. And Chase. Dear God, she didn't want to think about him getting shot again. The timing had to be perfect.

She took a calming breath and checked her watch. She needed to pull up outside the gate at exactly 1400 hours. That, she had learned in Colombia, was military speak for 2:00 p.m.

"What's next?" Chase asked, forcing her to continue repeating the plan.

"I put the car in Reverse and wait outside the gate as long as I can. Just before Montoya's men reach the Mercedes, I hit the gas." And as the car shot backward, her father's men, one located on each side of the warehouse, would open fire on the men who came out of the building into the area in front of the gate.

"I'll be close by. I plan to have you in my sights every minute." He would be getting out of the car before she made the turn, making his way back to the warehouse, positioning himself outside the gate to handle any threat to her that might come up.

"Whatever happens," Chase said, "once you start backing up, you don't stop. You get the hell out of there. Head for your father's. The place is a fortress. You'll be safe there."

Her gaze shot to his side of the car. "What about you?"

"I'll have men there. They may need my help. Whatever happens, you don't hesitate. You get out of there as fast as you can. If you wait, you become a liability instead of an asset. Understood?"

She swallowed. She didn't like it, but she understood. "Yes."

"There's way too much room for error in this plan, but it was the best we could come up with in so short a time."

The men were doing everything in their power to save Shana. Risking their lives. It was all anyone could ask.

"The turn is just up ahead," Harper said, checking the addresses.

"You ready?" Chase asked.

"I'm ready." Shana and the men were counting on her. She wasn't going to let them down.

"Pull over," Chase said, checking their location against the time on his watch. "Two minutes till you make the turn onto the property."

The car pulled to the curb to wait, allowing the clock to run down, giving Maddox, Ryker and Winston's men time to get into position. Chase checked the area for scouts as he had been doing for the last few miles, but saw no sign of anyone.

Sliding a hand around the nape of Harper's neck, he leaned over and kissed her, quick and hard, then opened the door and slid out of the vehicle. He disappeared into the trees, cutting diagonally back toward the warehouse. Once he got there, he would take up a forward position, out of sight behind a low concrete-block wall across from the tall iron gate at the entrance.

Chase's earbud crackled to life. "Two exterior guards down," Maddox said, referring to lookouts behind the warehouse. "Winston's men are moving into position along the sides. We're ready to retrieve the package."

"Copy that." Through the trees, he could just make out a flash of silver as the Mercedes turned onto the narrow road leading to the back of the property. "Harper just made the turn."

Exactly on time, the Mercedes continued slowly down the road toward the gate. It had already been rolled open, Chase saw as he crouched behind the block wall, preparing for Harper's arrival.

The warehouse itself stood two stories high, a big metal structure with a large open interior, a loading dock just off to the right of the front office door. He could see two armed men standing guard next to the dock while another stood beside the office door, armed with an AR-15.

Harper slowed the Mercedes to a stop just outside the gate. Chase saw the faint rock of the car as the transmission slipped into Reverse. Long seconds passed. When the car didn't drive through the gate, Chase heard Harper's cell phone ring. She ignored it. It continued to ring but she didn't pick up.

Men began to pour out the front door of the warehouse: one, two, four, six, eight. Rough-looking men, gangbangers, heavily tattooed, probably more MS-13. The two in front of the loading dock started toward the car, as well. The plan was working.

Adrenaline coursed through him as the men began crossing the asphalt in front of the warehouse, heading for the gate. Heading for Harper. Neither Ryker nor Maddox had confirmed securing Shana—and time was running out.

Inside the warehouse, Shana watched the guard pacing a few feet away. Though most of the men had filed out of the main building, two of them remained. A third man walked to the front to look out the window.

Shana's stomach knotted. She prayed her friend wouldn't do something foolish, didn't believe she would drive right through the gate and give herself up to them. Surely not.

"Hey, *chica*." One of the guards smiled evilly as he looked down at her. "You know what I got for you?" He grabbed his crotched and lewdly humped his hand, then laughed maniacally. Shana glanced away, the bile rising in her throat.

She clamped down on a surge of fear and tried to shift away from him on the concrete floor. Her eyes widened at the sight of a man behind him in the shadows. He was dressed in camouflage gear, brawny and hard muscled, his face streaked with black paint the color of his hair.

He raised a finger to his lips as he swiftly closed the distance between him and the other man. A hard arm wrapped around the guard's neck, and though the man struggled and squirmed, his cry for help never escaped and in seconds he lay unconscious on the floor.

Her gaze shot to another man, moving silently toward the second guard, a man she recognized even through the black greasepaint as Jason Maddox. The second guard opened his mouth to shout a warning, but the flash of silver as a knife sliced through his windpipe and silenced his cry for help.

Shana closed her eyes to block the gristly image as Maddox wiped the bloody blade on his camo pants, then used it to cut through the nylon ties on her wrists and legs. He grabbed her arm to help her up from the floor, and she caught a glimpse of the man he had come with, who seemed to have magically appeared behind the guard at the window.

There was a brief struggle before the guard slumped silently onto the floor.

"Can you walk?" Maddox asked.

Shana nodded but when she started forward, her knees buckled. Before she hit the floor, she was hoisted up on Maddox's powerful shoulder and he was striding across the warehouse toward a narrow back door.

"Three interior guards down," Maddox said. Shana

noticed a device in his ear. "Package secure. Exiting building now."

As they stepped outside, Shana took a deep breath of the clean, unfettered air. She was safe. But a deep fear surfaced for Harper.

Chase kept his eye on the silver Mercedes idling just outside the gate, ready to make its escape. Montoya's men slowly approached, eight from the warehouse, two from the loading dock, one standing guard beside the front door. Three men were armed with assault rifles, the rest carried handguns, two with bandoliers of bullets strapped across their chests.

Sixteen men in total. Montoya had sent a virtual army to capture his prey.

But five had already been dealt with. That made the odds, counting Winston's men, a little more than two to one. With Hawk and Ryker on his side, Chase would take those odds any day of the week.

Crouching out of sight behind the concrete-block wall, he watched Montoya's men spread out to surround the car as it idled at the gate to the warehouse. It was time for Harper to move, and as more seconds ticked past, tension settled deep inside him.

The men were closing in on the Mercedes when someone shouted a warning.

"¡Es una trampa! ¡Una trampa! It's a trap!"

"Go, Harper!" Chase's shouted into Harper's earbud, but the Mercedes was already reversing, engine racing, Harper looking over her shoulder as she steered the car at breakneck speed.

Gunfire erupted. Winston's man on each side of the warehouse started firing, a barrage of bullets pounding into the sea of gangbangers. The bangers returned fire, dispersing like a cluster of ants madly running for cover. Chase caught a glimpse of Ryker firing from behind a parked truck, while Maddox protected Shana somewhere out of sight.

Chase fired off a string of bullets, taking out a man at the front of the Mercedes, bullets pinging off the grille, one drilling into the hood, one smashing through the passenger side of the windshield.

"Keep your head down, Harper!" Chase shouted, hoping she could hear him over the roar of gunfire. She ducked but kept her foot on the gas and the car racing backward. She hit the brakes when a black pickup burst out of nowhere and roared up behind the car, blocking her escape.

Chase ran toward the Mercedes as both pickup doors flew open and two men leaped out, one firing an automatic rifle, the other firing a pistol. Chase aimed at the bigger threat, taking out the man with the assault rifle, then swinging the Nighthawk toward the second man, firing a center shot double tap that sent the guy flying backward across the asphalt, clutching the wounds in his chest.

Chase kept running toward the Mercedes, both hands wrapped around the pistol, holding the two men at gunpoint, kicking their pistols out of reach. Neither man moved. Chase's chest throbbed, but the adrenaline rush dulled the pain.

The gunfire in front of the warehouse grew more and more sporadic, until there was nothing but silence.

Maddox's voice came over the earbuds. "Situation under control."

"Copy that," Chase said.

One of Winston's men spoke up, and Chase pressed on his earbud to hear him. "One of us is wounded. We're leaving."

"Copy," Chase said. "Thanks for the help." The deal was Winston's men would not be involved in any way. They would exit the scene as soon as the mission was complete, leaving Chase, Maddox and Ryker to deal with the police.

Which was just about to happen. *Right on time*, he thought, hearing sirens screaming toward them in the distance. Red and blue lights flashed as a dozen patrol cars and unmarked vehicles roared up to the warehouse from every direction.

Wishing he had time to speak to Harper, Chase set his pistol on the ground and raised his hands. Harper got out of the Mercedes and lifted her hands into the air. Chase felt a sweep of relief as Special Agent Zach Tanner emerged from one of the unmarked vehicles and strode toward him.

With any luck, aside from a helluva lot of paperwork, the immediate threat was over. Unfortunately, before Harper was truly safe, they still had to find a way to deal with Luis Montoya.

CHAPTER FORTY-THREE

Chase sat behind his desk at The Max. A week had passed since the shoot-out at the warehouse. A plan that, aside from the unexpected arrival of the black pickup truck and the bullets that had come way too close to where Harper sat behind the wheel of the Mercedes, had worked almost perfectly.

Which was good, since there had been no plan B.

Even the arrival of the police and DEA had gone according to schedule. At Chase's instruction, Mindy had phoned Agent Tanner precisely ten minutes after Harper's two o'clock arrival at the warehouse. By then, Maddox and Ryker should have had Shana secured, Winston's men would have had time to leave, and the warehouse would be under their control.

Or not.

DEA and police had arrived within minutes of the call. They'd taken over the scene, called for ambulances and begun demanding answers.

"Looks like we missed out on all the fun," Agent Tanner had said, far from pleased with the way things had gone down.

His dark gaze ran over the bloody battle zone in front of the warehouse, where EMTs worked over the wounded men. "Might have been a good idea if you'd given us a heads-up before you took on half the drug dealers in Dallas."

"We knew you were on the way, but as it turned out, we didn't have time to wait for you to get here."

It was a total crock, but Tanner seemed willing to accept it. Though a number of gang members had escaped, clearly he figured the rest of the vicious gang got exactly what they deserved.

Zach seemed especially delighted to arrest a guy named Bobby Chavez. Chavez was the leader, he said, a Hispanic American who worked in Colombia for Luis Montoya.

"We'd had our suspicions Winston was involved with Montoya," Tanner had said. "With any luck, Bobby Chavez will turn state's evidence, and we'll be able to move forward."

Clearly self-defense. No charges filed. All in all, a very successful mission. The bad news was Harper and Shana had both been taken into protective custody. Tanner and his superiors were adamant that the women were still in danger. Chase couldn't argue with that.

He hadn't seen or heard from Harper since Tanner and a female agent had driven off with them in the back of an unmarked car.

Chase was worried sick. His appetite was gone and he hadn't had much sleep, and though Zach had phoned several times to assure him the women were safe, Chase couldn't rest until he'd talked to Harper and assured himself she was all right.

Add to that, there were things he wanted to say, conversations he wanted to have about the possibility of a future with her.

His intercom buzzed. "Agent Tanner is here to see you, boss."

Relief swept through him. "Thank God. Send him in." Maybe Tanner was ready to release the women into his care. He could put a protection detail in place—one he completely trusted.

Chase rounded the desk as Tanner walked in, his leather jacket flapping over the shoulder holster underneath. "I figured you were due for an update in person," Tanner said.

"Hell, yes." The men shook hands. "Where's Harper? I want to see her."

"First let me tell you where we are with the investigation."

"Fine, go ahead. Just tell me the women are safe."

"They're fine." Tanner sat down, and Chase returned to the chair behind his desk. "Since I saw you last, a lot has happened," Tanner said. "Most important, Knox Winston and his attorney requested a meeting with the district attorney. In exchange for a reduced sentence— the best he could negotiate with all the evidence against him—Winston rolled on Luis Montoya."

Chase was only mildly surprised. Knox wanted revenge on Montoya. Cutting a deal to get it was actually a pretty smart move. No one ever said the man was a fool.

"Winston provided names, dates of upcoming shipments and where they would arrive. Enough evidence against Montoya for the attorney general of Colombia to issue a warrant for his arrest. Unfortunately—or maybe fortunately, depending on the way you look at it—Montoya resisted and was killed outside his villa in Santa Marta when his men fired on authorities."

"Montoya is dead?"

"That's right. With the indecent amounts of money involved in the drug trade, the business will eventually resume with a new man at the helm. We assume Eduardo Ramos, Montoya's second in command. Ramos has gone to ground, so it's hard to know for sure. Whatever happens, it's a major setback for the cocaine industry. Without Montoya and Winston, the amount of drugs on the street will drop considerably. It's a big win for all of us."

"Congratulations," Chase said. "Now, what about Harper?"

"She and her friend have been released from DEA custody. According to her father, Montoya was the only real threat to her. Apparently his obsession with Harper was a personal vendetta."

"So where is she?"

"She and Shana took a hiatus. Even I don't know where they are. A beach somewhere, I'm guessing." Reaching into his inside coat pocket, Tanner pulled out a white envelope. "She asked me to give this to you." Chase accepted the letter and Tanner rose from his chair.

"Good luck," Zach said, heading for the door. "And thanks for your help."

Tanner walked out, and Chase sat back down at his desk. As he opened the letter, the paper seemed to burn his hands.

* * *

Wearing a bright orange-striped bikini, a big straw hat and a pair of white oversize sunglasses, Harper lay on a lounge chair beneath an umbrella on the pool deck.

A few feet away on the opposite side of the umbrella in a white bikini that showed off her perfect figure, Shana read a sexy romantic suspense novel. The beautiful couple entwined on the cover made Harper's throat tighten.

She hadn't seen Chase since the shoot-out at her father's warehouse. In the days that followed, Agent Tanner had kept her informed. He'd told her that her father had turned state's evidence against Luis Montoya, knew Montoya was dead, knew she and Shana were no longer in danger.

Still, after Shana's kidnapping and the bloody scene at the warehouse, Harper figured they both needed time to recover.

She looked across the blue water of the swimming pool to the beach beyond and the white surf washing up onshore. They were staying in a two-bedroom ocean-front suite at the Four Seasons Resort in Palm Beach, a room that cost a small fortune. After what Shana had suffered because of Harper and her father, her friend deserved at least a brief luxury vacation.

They both did.

But for Harper, the sad truth was, she would rather be back in Dallas with Chase.

Her eyes stung behind her dark glasses. Just thinking about him, remembering her painful decision, made her heart hurt.

Instead of going to Chase when she had been released from protective custody, she and Shana had each packed a bag and the two of them had flown down to Florida, leaving the business in Tony's and Debbie's capable hands for the few days they planned to be gone.

Before she'd left town, she had asked Zach Tanner to deliver a letter to Chase. Harper still remembered every painful word.

Dear Chase,

I will never be able to thank you enough for what you have done. You saved not only my life, but the lives of my brother and Shana, people who mean the most to me in the world. For that, I will always be grateful.

I know you have feelings for me, and you must know I have deep feelings for you. But the truth is you're a Garrett. You and your brothers are Dallas royalty. Your family is respected and revered. My father is a criminal, a man who will spend years in prison.

I'm his daughter. That is never going to change. It would always be a cloud hanging over your head.

I'm saying goodbye with no regrets for the time we spent together. I will always treasure those memories and keep them close to my heart. I hope you have a wonderful life, and know that I will never forget you.

With warmest gratitude,

Harper

PS Please don't call. I'm asking you as a favor. It's better to end things this way.

In the safe house, she hadn't been allowed to take calls. Honoring the request in her letter, Chase hadn't phoned since he had received her note.

She lifted her sunglasses and wiped the wetness from her eyes. She missed him so much. She hadn't put into the letter what she really wanted to say. That she was desperately in love with him, that she ached for him every minute of the day, that for her there would never be another man who could replace him.

But telling him she loved him would only make him feel obligated in some way. He cared for her, yes, but loved her? He had never said those words, and even if he had, no way could they ever marry—it wouldn't be fair to Chase.

For the rest of her life, her father's sins would stand between them. Like a member of the Gambino family or the Luccheses, people would stare at her and whisper as she passed. That wasn't the kind of life a man like Chase deserved.

A shadow moved over her. She glanced up to see Shana smiling down from beneath the wide brim of her hat. "I'm going in. You probably should, too. We've both been out for quite a while."

"Thank God for sunscreen," Harper said.

"True." Shana checked her oversize wristwatch. "It's almost five o'clock. Why don't we shower, go down to the bar and have a drink?"

Maybe a drink would numb her a little, ease some of the pain that wouldn't leave her. Harper nodded. "One of those fruity cocktails with the little paper umbrellas sounds good. I've been thinking about it all afternoon."

Rising from the lounge, she grabbed her towel and her beach bag and followed Shana through the door into the elegant hotel, down the hallway leading to the elevators.

As she walked into the suite, her cell phone rang. For an instant, she thought of Chase, imagined hearing him call her angel. Instead she recognized her brother's number and ignored the disappointment she had no right to feel.

"Hey, sis, it's me."

"Michael...it's great to hear from you." She knew Michael and Pia had returned to Houston, knew her brother had been updated on everything that had happened. "How are you doing? Is everything okay?"

"Everything's great. I've...umm...got wonderful news, sis. Pia and I... We're getting married."

Her heart squeezed. She tried not to think of Chase. "That's wonderful, Mikey! I'm so glad for you. For both of you."

"We don't want to wait. If you can make it, we're getting married a week from Saturday. I know it's short notice, and we wouldn't think of doing it unless you can be there, but—"

"Are you kidding? Of course I can be there! My big brother is getting married. I wouldn't miss it for the world."

She could feel his smile over the phone. "Okay, then. I'll text you all the info."

"Michael, I'm really happy for you. Let me know if there's anything I can do to help."

"Thanks, sis, I'll do that. I'll see you soon." The call ended, and she turned to see Shana watching her.

"Michael's getting married next weekend."

"Wow, that's great!"

Able to see through her happiness to the pain underneath, Shana walked over and hugged her. "I know you're hurting right now, but in time things will get better."

Harper nodded. In time, she'd accept the way things were and get on with her life. It didn't make losing Chase any easier. It didn't make her miss him any less.

Her stomach knotted. *The wedding.* Michael was a Garrett now. Surely his brothers would be invited to the wedding, including Chase. It was hard enough when she didn't have to see him.

Dear God, how would she manage to get through it with him right there?

CHAPTER FORTY-FOUR

Wearing a white dinner jacket that matched the one worn by the groom, Chase stood next to Michael, acting as his best man. Above the altar in the small chapel where the marriage ceremony was being held, Madonna and child watched over them through a brilliant stained-glass window.

In a long white lace gown, Pia held on to Michael's hand while her maid of honor, Christy Riggs, held a bridal bouquet of white and pink roses.

Chase did his best to concentrate on the minister's words, but his gaze kept straying to the beautiful woman sitting in the front pew of the chapel. She was wearing a pale blue dress that hugged her curves and stopped just above her knees. A pair of sky-high heels showed off her gorgeous legs.

He hadn't seen Harper since the shoot-out. Honoring her request not to call, he hadn't spoken to her, though he had finally given in and left her a message at the front desk of the Houston St. Regis, where the out-of-town guests were staying.

He had asked Harper to call him, but after rereading her note for what seemed the hundredth time, he hadn't really expected to hear from her. She didn't want to see him because she was Knox Winston's daughter. Because her father was a criminal.

Chase didn't give a flying fuck.

She couldn't avoid him forever. She would be at the wedding and later at the reception. Considering the plans he'd made, Chase thought her avoidance might actually work in his favor.

Or maybe not.

The gray-haired minister droned on, bringing him back to the moment. As his brother and Pia repeated their vows, Chase couldn't keep his eyes off Harper. She sat like a pale marble statue, her hands folded tensely in her lap. She hadn't looked his way—not once—and for the first time his confidence wavered.

What if he was wrong and Harper didn't love him?

What if he asked her to marry him and she said no?

He had talked to Michael, told him his plan and asked his permission. He and Pia had both been wildly enthusiastic. Both were convinced Harper loved him.

Still, he was taking a risk. If things went wrong… If Harper turned him down…

Chase battled the heaviness in his chest and managed to hand his brother the beautiful diamond wedding band right on cue. Michael slid it solemnly onto Pia's small finger.

"Let this ring be a symbol of the value, purity and constancy of true wedded love and a seal of the vows you have made." When the minister pronounced the couple man and wife, Harper wiped tears from her cheeks.

"Whom God hath joined together let no man put asunder." The minister smiled. "Michael, you may kiss your bride."

Michael pulled Pia into his arms and very thoroughly kissed her, not stopping until Brandon finally whistled and everyone applauded. The wedding party filed out of the chapel, followed by family and friends.

Chase caught a glimpse of Harper as Michael rounded everyone up for photos, including his sister and newly acquired brothers.

When the photographer was finally satisfied and they walked outside, it took all Chase's willpower to keep his distance from Harper, but he had bigger plans for his angel tonight.

Still, he couldn't resist stopping her, speaking to her just to hear her voice. "You look beautiful, angel. I've missed you."

She glanced up at him, but stayed a few feet away. "It's good to see you, Chase."

"We need to talk."

"I know," she softly agreed. "When we get back to Dallas—"

"Harper! Wasn't it a beautiful ceremony?" Christy gushed over the vows, and Chase didn't miss the relief that swept over Harper's lovely face. She wanted to escape him. She had said her goodbyes in the letter.

His chest clamped down. Did she really think he would let her go that easily?

All of them moved out of the foyer onto the sidewalk in front of the church, where a string of white limousines waited to transport the wedding party to the hotel.

Delayed by more photos, the reception was underway when they arrived. In a private room at the elegant St. Regis, a lacy three-tier wedding cake rested on a pedestal next to the linen-draped table where the bride and groom sat beside the best man and maid of honor.

Harper sat at a table of eight that included Reese, Brandon and Pia's mother and father. As a wedding gift, the Garrett jet had flown to Florida to pick up Pia's parents, along with some of her cousins and several of her closest friends.

Nerves churned in Chase's stomach. He could handle the embarrassment of being rejected in front of a roomful of people. Living without Harper for the rest of his life was something different altogether.

The evening progressed: a gourmet dinner, champagne toasts, cutting the cake, the bride and groom laughing as they fed each other. It was amazing how quickly a wedding could be arranged if the motivation was strong enough and the couple had friends willing to help.

Though there were only forty guests, a three-piece orchestra played in the corner. Michael had his first dance with Pia, then the bride danced with her father. Reese and Brandon danced with guests, including Harper. Chase ignored a twinge of jealousy, and reminded himself if things went well she'd been dancing with him for the rest of his life.

An hour slipped past. Chase glanced over at Michael, and a look passed between them. Michael smiled. It was time.

Chase rose from his place at the table just as Harper walked up to speak to her brother. She extended her best wishes to the newlyweds and gave them some lame excuse for leaving early.

Chase wasn't having it. He flicked a glance at the orchestra, signaling them to begin the special song he had chosen. Repeating a silent prayer that his plan would succeed, he strode forward, blocking Harper's escape.

Harper looked up as Chase appeared at her side. "You can't be leaving yet," he said. "Not before you dance with me."

Her stomach churned. All evening she had carefully avoided any interaction with Chase. She had forced herself not to glance in his direction, not to notice how gorgeous he looked in his white dinner jacket, to ignore the heat that slipped through her whenever she remembered how good they were together. To ignore the women who did their best to capture his attention.

She had no choice but to look at him now, battled down the yearning that surged through her. "I'm sorry, Chase. I'm not really feeling all that well." She swallowed. "Maybe another time."

"I chose this song especially for you. One dance. I asked them to play it just for us. If you still want to leave when it's over, I won't ask you to stay."

The music softly swelled. She knew the song, recognized the beautiful Beatles melody sung by John Lennon, "Something in the Way She Moves," knew that the man in the song was attracted to the woman like no other lover. For him she was the only one.

Her heart hurt. She told herself it didn't mean anything. It was just a pretty song. She told herself she had to walk away. She didn't want to cry in front of Chase.

Instead, she looked into his handsome, beloved face and stepped into his arms.

Chase swept her into the music, and her throat closed up. She remembered the solid strength of his body, the way they fit so perfectly together. She remembered the way he had protected her, saved her, always been there for her. She loved him so much. Ached for him every day that he had been gone.

Chase drew her closer, pressed his cheek to hers. She could feel the roughness of the dark gold beard along his jaw.

"I've missed you, angel," he said softly. "I need you, honey. I need you so much."

He looked down at her, and there was something in his eyes, a hint of vulnerability she had rarely seen. He needed her, he had said. Could it be true?

She let him sweep her around the floor, along with the other couples who danced to the beautiful love song.

Chase didn't say more as the song played out and slowly came to an end. Couples left the floor, but Chase held on to Harper's hand.

"I love you, angel," he said. "I've known it for a while. I wanted to tell you. I hope it's not too late." Pulling a small blue velvet box out of the pocket of his dinner jacket, he dropped to one knee on the floor in front of her. "I love you, Harper. Will you marry me?"

Her heart constricted. *Oh, dear God.* Her eyes filled with tears that spilled onto her cheeks. "Chase…"

"I don't care about your father. He has nothing to do with us. He never has. Marry me. Will you, angel?"

He loved her. "Are you… Are you sure?"

He rose to his feet. "I love you. I'd be the proudest man in Dallas to have you as my wife."

More tears slipped down her cheeks. "I love you so much. I don't want to live without you, Chase." She went into his arms. "I'd be proud to be your wife."

A shudder rippled through his hard body, relief, she realized. How could he think she'd say no?

He stepped back to slip the ring on her finger, and the room erupted in cheers, whistles and applause. Chase kissed her, and love for him washed through her.

She had thought this part of her life was over. Told herself she would learn to live without him. Instead, tonight her life had just begun.

EPILOGUE

Three months later

Chase sat behind the desk in his Maximum Security office. It was Saturday, the office mostly empty. He'd taken some extra time off, so the quiet day gave him a chance to catch up.

A lot had happened in the months after his brother's wedding. He thought of Michael that way now—as his brother, not just a friend. In a way, he always had.

Michael was happily married. So was Chase. He smiled to remember the wedding ceremony a month after Harper had accepted his proposal. No way was he taking a chance his angel would change her mind.

They'd been married in a small, private ceremony at the ranch, followed by a quiet, intimate week alone, just the two of them. Harper had fallen in love with the ranch, which pleased him because he loved it, too. Eventually, he would take her on a real honeymoon wherever she wanted to go, but for now, both of them were content just being together.

Harper had moved in with him as soon as they returned to Dallas. In a way, her town house burning down had worked in his favor. He had given her carte blanche to make the condo a place for both of them, and she had changed a few things. He liked what she had done, the little feminine touches that made the place feel like a home.

Things had been good. Even the endless media reports about Knox Winston's criminal activities hadn't interfered with their happiness. Winston was in jail and would be for the next ten years. With all the charges against him, it was the best deal Knox could cut. Chase figured he deserved a helluva lot more, but for Harper's sake he was satisfied with the way things turned out.

Roberto Chavez, the man who had led the kidnap attempts, had been wounded in the warehouse shooting, but survived. Chavez had refused to give any information on Montoya, members of the MS-13 gang, or anyone else—probably wise, considering his connection to the Colombian drug cartel. Bobby was currently in prison and would be for a very long time.

Harper had worried that all the media about being Knox Winston's daughter would hurt her business, but the opposite had happened. Maybe the old P. T. Barnum adage was true and there was no such thing as bad publicity. Chase figured it was because his wife and Shana were producing good quality products that people wanted to buy.

On a different but extremely satisfying note, Betsy Dickerson and her lover, Dr. Bernard Atwood, had been arrested and charged with premeditated murder. They were currently awaiting trial, facing the possibility of a death sentence in Texas.

Couldn't happen to a nicer couple, Chase thought.

Aside from now being happily married, he was back to his usual routine, running the Dallas branch of Maximum Security while loosely keeping tabs on the offices in San Diego and Phoenix, and occasionally taking an interesting case. All in all, things had been pretty mellow lately.

He glanced up at the sound of his door swinging open. A shot of adrenaline hit his bloodstream as Raymond Martinez, the man he'd sent to prison for pimping underage girls, walked through the door.

"I thought you were in jail." Chase quietly eased the bottom desk drawer open. His Glock waited inside.

Martinez continued toward the desk, a hard smile on his face. He looked leaner, tougher, his head shaved, tattoos ringing his neck. "Food was rotten. I decided it was time to leave. I owed you a visit for putting me in there—so I came here first."

Martinez stopped right in front the desk. Reaching behind his back, he pulled a big semiauto from the waistband of his pants. "You should have minded your own business, Garrett. The little whore—she wasn't worth your life."

Everything happened at once: Chase grabbed his Glock, caught the edge of the desk, hoisted and flipped the desk into Martinez and dropped to cover behind the heavy wooden top.

Martinez fired and so did Chase. Martinez's bullet slammed into the desk. Chase's bullet slammed into Martinez, spinning him around. Before his adversary could fire again, two quick shots rang out. Jason Maddox stood in the doorway, his Kimber .40 cal gripped in his two big hands.

Martinez didn't get up.

"Good to see you, Hawk." Chase climbed to his feet.

"Good to be back," Jason said. He'd been tracking a skip for the last two weeks. He kicked Martinez's gun aside and crouched to check the wounds in the escaped convict's chest. Since Martinez was still breathing, Maddox pulled out his cell and hit 9-1-1.

"Looks like business as usual," Hawk said as Chase headed for the door to retrieve the first-aid kit.

Yeah, business as usual, Chase thought. *Never a dull moment when you work at The Max.*

* * * * *

AUTHOR NOTE

I hope you enjoyed Chase and Harper in *The Conspiracy*, the first book in my new Maximum Security series. You met some of the hunky guys at The Max, including Jason "Hawk" Maddox, the hero of my next book.

I'll also be writing about Chase's brothers, Brandon and Reese, as well as novellas about some of the other detectives, bodyguards and bounty hunters who work at The Max, and, of course, the strong, smart women who tame them.

I hope you'll watch for more Maximum Security novels in the future and that you enjoy them. Till then, all the best and happy reading.

Kat

WAIT UNTIL DARK

A Maximum Security novella

CHAPTER ONE

Dallas, Texas

The sound of voices cut through the pounding in her head, dragging her from a deep, dark void into the light of day.

As the door swung open and uniformed policemen streamed into the bedroom, April Vale looked down at her naked body and saw a sea of blood soaking the mattress beside her. A naked man lay next to her, a bullet hole in the center of his chest.

A scream tore from her throat as she recognized David Dean, Mayor Rydell's campaign manager. Then strong arms hauled her upright and a wave of dizziness hit her, making her stomach roll. One of the officers draped a blanket around her bare shoulders, covering her nudity, and then hustled her over to a chair by the window.

Fighting a fresh wave of nausea, April sat down on

the chair, gripping the blanket, her body shaking head to foot.

"What…what's happening?" She didn't realize her hands were being cuffed together in front of her until she heard metal clanking and cold bands of steel wrapped around her wrists.

"What's your name?" The room swarmed with policemen. The one in front of her was stocky and balding, in his early forties. A pair of EMTs rushed into the room and began working over the bloody man on the bed, but his eyes were open and staring at nothing and she knew he was already dead.

April swallowed the bile rising in her throat and fought to clear her head, but when she tried to remember where she was or how she got there, all she came up with was a splitting headache.

"I don't understand what's happening," she said, trying to keep the blanket around her.

"This will all go smoother if you cooperate," the stocky policeman said. "Tell us your name."

"I'm… I'm April. April Vale." She glanced over at David. The hole in his chest seemed even bigger and bloodier than before.

"Can you tell us the name of the victim?"

Victim. A thick lump rose in her throat, threatening to choke her. "That…that's David Dean. We work for Mayor Rydell."

A young officer with black hair slicked straight back from his forehead walked up. "Looks like we've got the murder weapon, Sarge. It was right there on the floor next to the lady's purse."

April frowned, her mind foggy again. "Wait…wait a minute. What's going on? I don't understand." Her fingers tightened on the blanket. "I don't know how I got here. I don't remember what happened."

A gray-haired man in a navy-blue suit brought the gun over in a plastic bag. She recognized the little .380 handgun she carried for protection.

"I'm Detective Sullivan. Does this belong to you, Ms. Vale?"

She took a deep breath. "I think it's mine. I have one like that. I have a legal permit to carry."

The EMTs began checking her over, her blood pressure, her vision, whether or not she had a concussion.

"We need to get her to the hospital," one of them said, "have her checked out, get a blood sample."

"Hospital? I don't want to go to the hospital."

A female police officer walked up just then. "We've cuffed your hands in front of you so you can hold on to the blanket. If you cooperate, we'll leave them that way. If not, we'll have to cuff them behind your back."

She closed her eyes. This couldn't be happening. "You think I shot him? I don't even know how I got here."

The woman's expression never changed. "You need to go to the hospital. We need to make sure you're okay. If you were drugged, it'll show up in your tox screen."

Tox screen. Drugs. Her pistol and a dead man.

That's when it began to sink in how much trouble she was in. That's when April's brain finally started working and she began to figure out what she needed to do—before things got a whole lot worse.

CHAPTER TWO

At the sound of the glass front door swinging open, Jonah Wolfe looked up to see a tall, leggy redhead walk into the office.

"I hope she's looking for me." Jason Maddox, one of the country's top bail enforcement agents and one of Jonah's best friends, had an eye for beautiful women. This one definitely met Jase's exacting standards.

But being a former undercover police officer, Jonah noticed more than her stunning face and figure. Her hands were shaking as she approached the receptionist desk and her face was pale. He wondered what kind of trouble the lady was in.

"May I help you?" The receptionist, Mindy Stewart, removed the half reading glasses perched on the end of a pert nose and smiled. She was petite and cute, and smart enough not to date any of the confirmed bachelors who worked at Maximum Security.

"My name is April Vale. I'm looking for Jonah Wolfe."

When Maddox groaned his disappointment, Jonah's focus sharpened on the redhead.

"Do you have an appointment, Ms. Vale?" Mindy asked politely.

"I'm sorry, I'm afraid I don't, but it's extremely urgent. If Mr. Wolfe is in, please… I really need to speak to him."

The redhead glanced his way as Jonah rose from behind his desk and started walking toward the front of the office.

A waiting area with a dark red tufted leather sofa and matching chairs, oak coffee and end tables, gave the place a Western feel that perfectly suited the misfit Texans who worked there.

The men and women, all independent contractors, were an assortment of private investigators, bail enforcement agents and personal security specialists. Only the best of the best were good enough to work for Chase Garrett at the Max.

"I'm Wolfe," he said when he reached her. "What can I do for you?" His gaze ran over her, taking in her spectacular curves. He couldn't help hoping she needed him for something far more intriguing than his skills as a private detective.

He might have smiled, would have if TROUBLE wasn't stamped in the middle of the pretty lady's forehead.

"My name is April Vale. Thank you for seeing me."

"No need to thank me, Ms. Vale. I haven't done anything yet."

"I'm hoping you will." She had the face of an angel and legs that went on forever. But she was a redhead and all that fiery hair just ramped up the warning signs flashing in her big blue eyes.

She glanced around the office. Nine oak desks set in lines of three filled the open area they called the Bull Pen. Antique farming tools hung on the walls, along with framed photos taken at the ranch Chase owned with his two brothers, Reese and Brandon, out in the Texas Hill Country.

"Is there somewhere we can speak in private?" April asked.

"Conference room. Follow me." As he led her down the hall, she caught an appreciative glance from Jax Ryker and Dante Romero, the only other guys currently in the office, but she didn't seem to notice.

"This way." Jonah held open the door into a glass-enclosed chamber with a long oak table seating twenty, and April walked inside.

He closed the door, pulled out a brown leather chair near the end of the table, waited for her to take a seat, then sat down at the end of the table next to her, giving himself a little more leg room.

April smoothed the navy-blue pencil skirt she was wearing with a pair of sky-high heels and a short-sleeve peach blouse dotted with tiny blue sailboats. She looked good. Classy but not completely untouchable.

"As I said, I appreciate your seeing me."

Jonah leaned back in his chair. "How did you get my name?"

"A friend recommended you. Madeleine Townsend. She said the two of you went out a couple of times but just didn't click. She said you introduced her to her husband, Ross."

"Ross is a friend." He was also a private investigator. "I'm glad they got together. Now, April, tell me why you're here."

She took a deep breath, drawing his attention to the full breasts he'd been doing his best to ignore. Since he never mixed business with pleasure, he shoved the buzz of attraction he was feeling to the back corner of his brain.

"I work for Mayor Rydell," April said. "As you probably know, he's up for reelection. I'm his marketing manager. Or I was. Currently I'm… I was just released from police custody a short time ago, Mr. Wolfe. That's why I'm here."

Jonah straightened in his chair. "You were under arrest?"

"Officially, I haven't been charged yet. But the charge could be murder."

Jesus. He hadn't seen that one coming. Now she really had his attention. "Who have you been accused of killing, Ms. Vale?"

For a moment, her eyes glistened with tears. One spilled onto her cheek but she quickly wiped it away.

"The police say I killed a man named David Dean. He was Mayor Rydell's campaign manager. If I did, I don't remember. I was found unconscious in the master bedroom of David's condo. David was in the bed next to me. He was…he was dead."

Silence fell as he digested the information. "How did he die?"

"He was shot in the chest."

"Have they found the murder weapon?"

She nodded, softly curling dark red hair sliding around her shoulders. "The gun belongs to me. I carry a Smith and Wesson .380 handgun in my purse for self-defense. There have been a couple of muggings in the neighborhood around the office, so I've been taking it with me to work. I have a legal carry permit."

This was Texas. Half the women in the state were licensed to carry.

"So you had the gun with you last night."

"Yes. The police found it in the bedroom. My purse was open, lying on the floor next to the bed. The gun was lying beside it."

Jonah released a slow breath. "I presume you have a good attorney."

Her bottom lip trembled. It was plump and perfectly curved. Desire slipped through him and his blood heated, pooled low in his groin. He liked women in general, but this one appealed to him more than most. He wished he'd met her under different circumstances.

"Ross recommended a lawyer named Nathan Temple," she said. "He was at the station while the police questioned me."

"Temple's good. One of the best."

She swallowed and her spine went a little straighter. "I don't think I killed David, Mr. Wolfe. We weren't dating. I'm not the type of woman who enjoys one-night stands. I need to know what happened last night. How I ended up in David's bedroom, in his bed. I need to know who killed David Dean. And I pray to God it wasn't me."

Wolfe excused himself to get them some coffee, and April used the time to collect herself. The man was not what she had expected. Not at all.

Her best friend, a woman with discerning tastes, had gone out with him a couple of times so she figured he'd be attractive. She hadn't imagined he would be at least six feet two inches of handsome-as-sin, black-haired, lean-muscled male. With his perfectly symmetrical features, slashing black eyebrows and brooding dark eyes, Jonah Wolfe was beyond good-looking.

Though in a way she was surprised she'd noticed.

With the election bearing down on them, she had no interest in men, hadn't dated in nearly a year. More importantly, her thoughts were consumed by the murder of a man she worked with and the terror of what might happen to her.

Murder was a dangerous business. She needed help, and Jonah Wolfe appeared to be exactly the kind of help she needed. Wolfe's wide shoulders stretched the seams of the button-down shirt he was wearing. The short sleeves revealed impressive biceps and corded forearms. His shrewd brown eyes assessed her every move and seemed to miss nothing.

The private investigators who worked for Chase Garrett were reputed to be the best in Dallas. Wolfe wouldn't be there if he weren't extremely good.

He returned to the conference room with a yellow pad tucked under one arm and two foam cups filled to the brim with freshly brewed coffee. He set a cup down on the table in front of her, black, as she had requested, and returned to his seat, stretching his long legs out in front of him.

"Ross told me the amount of your fee," she said, toying with the rim of the cup. "I know you don't work cheap, Mr. Wolfe, but I can afford to pay you."

"Good to know. If we're going to be working together, let's stick with first names, all right, April?"

"All right."

"Start at the beginning. Give me a quick run-through of your day, into the evening as far as you can remember."

She took a fortifying drink of coffee, then set the cup down on the oak conference table. "It started off as usual. I got up, got dressed and went into the mayor's campaign office. I had a meeting scheduled with members of my staff to work on poster designs. Mark is up for reelection in November so we have plenty of work to do."

"I'll need a list of everyone in the office. Separate the ones on your personal staff."

"All right."

"What happened after the meeting?"

"I took the designs down to the printer to get things started."

"And afterward?"

"I went back to the office. We had a working lunch and kept going. We didn't finish till about six p.m."

"So you left around six?"

"Some people left, some of us stayed. It's not unusual for me to work till seven or eight."

"What about Dean? Was he there?"

She nodded. It made her chest feel tight to think those were David's last hours. "We both stayed. There were five others besides David and me."

He pulled a pen out of the pocket of his jeans. "I need the names."

She rattled off the two volunteers: Timothy Mahoney and Susan Buchanan, and three staff members: Collin Rutherford, Brad Schweitzer and Peggy Watt. Wolfe clicked the pen and wrote down the names without asking her to repeat them. She had a feeling he could recount everything she had told him from memory.

"We all walked out at the same time. Since it was Friday night, we decided to stop at the Derby and have a beer. It's just a few doors down from the office. It's got kind of a British atmosphere. Dark wood and racehorse pictures on the walls. If we're going somewhere after work, that's usually the place we go."

"You and Dean went there together?"

"And Susan and Timothy, Collin, Brad and Peggy. Collin sprang for pizza."

"What happened after that?"

"David drank too much. He's been known to over-indulge on occasion. He needed a ride home and I was the only one with a vehicle parked close by. The others all left. David stopped by the restroom on his way out. My car was in the lot behind the office so he and I went out the back door and walked directly there."

"So you and Dean left the bar together. The police will be looking at camera surveillance in the area. They've probably already found that out."

"I told them that. It wasn't a secret." She took a sip of coffee, her hand trembling when she picked up the cup. She took a moment to compose herself. Wolfe didn't rush her, for which she was grateful.

"Okay, so the two of you were out in the parking lot."

"That's right. I remember feeling a little dizzy as I reached my car. I was thinking maybe I shouldn't be driving either. I considered sharing a cab, but David's condo was only a few blocks away. I knew I hadn't had that much beer, and I'd eaten plenty of pizza, so there was no way I could be drunk."

"Go on."

She touched her forehead, straining to recall more of what had happened. She'd had a headache all morning. The harder she tried to remember, the more her head throbbed.

"I got in my car and David got into the passenger seat. He was really drunk—or at least that's the way he seemed. I remember reaching for my seat belt, but I was beginning to feel sluggish and I had trouble clicking the belt into place."

She looked up at Wolfe. "I don't remember starting the car. In fact, trying to fasten my seat belt is the last thing I recall before the police burst into David's bedroom this morning."

CHAPTER THREE

Jonah took a drink of his coffee, lukewarm now. He studied his newest client over the rim of the cup. "Who called the police?"

"David's housekeeper found us and called 9-1-1. We were both...umm...naked."

He was careful not to let his mind wander where that image led. He'd always been a sucker for redheads. Those big blue eyes combined with that pretty face really did a job on him. Just his luck she could be a killer.

"The police hauled me out of bed," she said. "The sheets were...were covered with blood." She swallowed and took a shaky breath. "I remember screaming when I saw David. There was a bullet hole in the middle of his chest. I thought I must be dreaming. I couldn't make myself believe it was real."

"What happened then?"

"One of the officers brought a blanket in from the hall closet and wrapped it around me. They asked me some questions and took me to the hospital to be checked out. From there they took me to the police station. I probably should have asked for an attorney back at the house, but my mind was still fuzzy. I told them what I just told you, but that was all I knew."

"All right, that'll do for now. We'll need to talk again soon, but I've got some preliminary work I need to do first. Anything else you want to tell me?"

Her eyes slid closed for a moment. "God, I wish there were more I could remember."

Jonah stood up from his chair. "Like I said, I'll have more questions. In the meantime, where can I find you?"

April rose beside him. "I'm going back home. I just... need to be home."

"Give me your address and phone number."

"Of course." She pulled a business card out of her purse, turned it over and wrote her personal information on the back.

She handed him the card. "Thank you for helping me, Mr....Jonah."

"We'll figure this out, April." *One way or another.* He didn't tell her that if she was guilty, he'd figure that out, too. So far the story didn't make any sense. If she shot David Dean, why was she still in the house, lying in bed next to him?

Turning, April walked out of the conference room. Jonah watched her long legs in those five-inch heels and the sexy sway of her hips, and an image of her naked in bed popped into his head.

If Dean was a straight red-blooded male, there was no question he'd want her.

Jonah wondered how much of what she'd just told

him was the truth, how much she'd left out. How much more she would eventually recall.

How much the police knew about the incident that April didn't.

On the surface, drugs or alcohol had to be part of the equation. Someone could have roofied the beer she was drinking at the Derby. It would explain the lengthy blackout. The cops would have tested her. He needed to know the results, and he needed to know if Dean had been drugged, as well.

For a number of reasons, he wanted to believe she was telling the truth—at least as far as she remembered. Foremost being she was a friend of Maddie and Ross, who were two of his closest friends.

Jonah sighed as he returned to his desk. If he wanted to find out what had happened, he had plenty to do. As a PI, he knew his way around the Internet. In the age of information, you could find anything if you looked hard enough.

Add to that, Maximum Security had its own secret weapon. Chase's computer guru, Tabitha Love—her real name—was twenty-seven years old, near genius IQ and about half crazy. She'd never gone to college, never had a steady job and never wanted one. She wasn't your average employee, but if you needed information, Tabby was the one who could find it.

Jonah didn't need Tabby's skills to get the basics on April Vale. It was amazing what a simple Google search could tell you. Taking a seat at his desk, he typed in her name, pulled up several articles about her.

April Marie Vale was twenty-nine years old, born and raised in Dallas. No siblings. Mother and father divorced, father deceased, mother living in California.

April had put herself through college, graduated from the University of Texas with a bachelor's degree. Never been married.

Jonah went into Facebook, found her page and a photo of her smiling face, a few freckles on the bridge of her nose. There were photos of her as a kid, and pictures of her as the young woman she had grown into. He had always been attracted to redheads. April's gorgeous curls had him craving her even more.

There were pictures of April with Maddie Townsend and one with Maddie and Ross and their new baby. Pictures of her with other friends in Dallas. There were photos of her with Mayor Mark Rydell and a string of local politicians.

He searched Twitter, LinkedIn, Pinterest, all the social media sites, picked up bits and pieces here and there.

Once he had the basics on April, he did a thorough search of the murder victim. David Dean was a single man, thirty-nine years old, from an upper-class Dallas family, attractive in the photo on his profile. Sterling reputation, no ex-wives, no current girlfriends. Earned a larger than average campaign manager's salary working for Rydell.

No photos of Dean with April Vale. No former relationship with her that he could find. Which didn't mean she hadn't gone home with him to have sex that night. They were two adults. If April wanted to screw the guy, there was no law against it.

Killing the guy was an altogether different matter.

He spent the rest of the day digging up information. By this time tomorrow, he intended to know everything there was to know about April Vale and David Dean.

He tried to make sense of her story but so far the puzzle pieces didn't fit. The cops had to have a working theory. If they knew something April didn't, he needed to know what it was.

Late in the afternoon, he called Detective Heath Ford, a friend on the Dallas PD. Jonah had been an undercover cop before he went private. He and Heath had a history and it was a good one, but Heath wasn't in. Jonah left a message knowing Heath would call him back.

In the meantime he went to work trying to find a motive for April to kill David Dean.

Unfortunately, as he worked from his apartment that night, Jonah found one.

Sitting at the kitchen table sipping a cup of Cozy Chamomile tea she hoped would help her sleep, April jerked upright at the pounding on her door.

A memory arose of the police rushing into David's bedroom, of the man lying dead beside her. Her pulse raced, began to thunder. She pulled her white terry-cloth robe a little tighter and cinched the belt.

Hurrying across the deep gray carpet in the living room, she peered through the peephole and relaxed at the sight of Jonah Wolfe in worn jeans, a black T-shirt and a pair of black motorcycle boots standing on her porch.

Her fear receded and she opened the door, but the grim look on his face had a fresh jolt of worry pouring through her.

"What is it?"

Wolfe stepped into the house, forcing her backward a couple of paces. He closed the door a little too firmly behind him. "Why didn't you mention you and Dean were seriously at odds at work?"

His anger shot up her nerves. She fought not to answer with the same kind of heat. "We disagreed on occasion, mostly about the way we thought the campaign should be run, but it certainly wasn't anything that would make me want to kill him."

"No? That's not what the tabloids say." Though she was five foot eight, Jonah towered above her. Few men intimidated her these days but Wolfe was one of them.

"According to what I read, Dean wanted to fire you and you were furious about it. The papers said you'd do anything to keep that from happening. The implication was you'd trade sex to keep your job—or already had."

Fury swept away caution. "That's complete and utter bull! I never slept with David. And I sure as hell wouldn't do it to keep my job." She opened her mouth to say more, but paused. "I mean...unless something happened last night that I can't recall."

Her hand was shaking. She clenched it into a fist to make it stop. "I don't think I slept with David last night. I wasn't attracted to him and I would never sleep with a man I didn't want."

Some of the tension drained out of those wide shoulders. In the overhead track lighting in her modern apartment, Jonah's wavy raven-black hair gleamed. She might not have been attracted to David Dean, but just looking at the man in front of her sent her blood pressure up a notch.

"You want something to drink?" April asked. "I entertain people here, hold meetings on occasion. I've got just about anything you could want."

"I don't drink on the job."

"Neither do I." She glanced at the clock at the end of the breakfast bar in the kitchen. "It's almost eleven p.m. Surely you're off work by now."

He relaxed even more and the corner of his mouth edged up. The late evening shadow along his jaw and his long hair made him look dangerous, and even more attractive. "Got any scotch?"

"Of course. It's in the bar." He followed her into the living room, over to the wet bar built into the wall. She could feel him behind her, at least six-two, all lean muscle nicely packed together.

"I like your place," he said as she took down the bottle of Dewar's and two cut-crystal glasses.

"Thank you. Neat?"

"Please."

She filled one of the glasses and handed it over, poured some into a glass for herself. "I was drinking chamomile tea, hoping it would help me sleep, but maybe this is a better idea."

Those intriguing chocolate-brown eyes ran over her. As sure as she was standing in her living room he was thinking of a far better way to help her sleep.

As heat slipped through her body, April didn't doubt it would work. She hadn't been to bed with a man in a year. She had simply been too busy, or perhaps she just hadn't met a man she was attracted to.

If she weren't trying to prove herself innocent of murder, maybe she would pursue her attraction to Jonah Wolfe.

On the other hand, a man like Jonah probably ran through women at the speed of light. She'd had trouble like that before. She didn't need it again, no matter how attractive the package.

She led him across the living room and they sat down on the sofa and chairs, dove-gray with black cording, and bright red accent pillows.

Done in a modern décor, contemporary artwork hung on the walls of her Oaklawn town house, nothing expensive, mostly reproductions of paintings done by famous artists. Miros and Picassos, a Chagall, some lithographs and serigraphs she had picked up at boutique galleries over the years.

Jonah sipped his drink. "You've had some time to think," he said. "Any idea why you were passed out naked in Dean's bed?"

She swallowed as her mind returned to the murder. "Since I can't remember what happened and assuming I'm not the one who killed him—someone must have drugged me. They must have driven both of us to David's house, probably in my car, and staged the murder scene. Whoever did it must have taken my gun out of my purse and shot him."

"The police will be canvassing the neighborhood, trying to find someone who heard something."

"I hope they do."

"Who would have known the gun was in your purse?" Those dark eyes searched her face, looking for any indication she was lying. In a way she was glad he wasn't just taking her word. She wanted the truth and she was beginning to trust that Jonah Wolfe would find it.

"The gun wasn't a secret," she said. "In fact, I let it be known I regularly carried a weapon for protection. I figured the more people who knew, the safer I was."

"I can see the logic."

She glanced away, took a sip of scotch, felt the alcohol slide relaxingly through her limbs. "Didn't exactly work out the way I thought it would."

Jonah sipped his drink. "I talked to a friend of mine this afternoon, a detective with the Dallas PD. They found your fingerprints on the gun. They expect ballistics to confirm it was the murder weapon."

"I was expecting that. If someone were trying to set me up, they would have made sure my fingerprints were on the pistol that killed him."

"That's what you think? Someone set you up?"

She sighed. "To tell you the truth, I have no idea what to think. I'm hoping you're going to help me figure it out."

His dark gaze never wavered. "The CSIs found something interesting at the crime scene."

He was watching, gauging her reaction. Worry made her pulse speed up. "What…what was it?"

"There were two glasses on the bar in Dean's apartment. One had his prints on it, the other had yours. The one with your prints tested positive for Rohypnol. That's a date-rape drug. They're waiting for the tox screen of your blood to come back, but they're pretty sure it's going to show traces of Rohypnol."

"So I was right—I was drugged. What about David?"

"No sign of it in his glass. Looks like Dean was just drunk. His blood alcohol was two and a half times the legal limit."

She frowned. "Wait a minute. The police think I was drugged at David's house instead of at the bar? That can't be right. I don't remember anything after I got into my car. I had to have been drugged at the Derby."

"The cops have a working theory. They think you and Dean left the bar together. You drove Dean to his condo, which is only a few blocks away. The two of you went inside together. Maybe you were helping him into the house because he was so drunk."

"And?"

"And he offered you a nightcap and you accepted. They think Dean roofied you. Once you were drugged, he managed to get you into the bedroom. You must have had your purse with you. He got you undressed, but you hadn't completely passed out. You managed to get your gun out of your purse and you shot him. Then you passed out on the bed."

A memory of David's lifeless body rose in her mind and nausea rolled in her stomach. Her hand started shaking. She set the glass down on the glass-topped coffee table.

"If that's what happened, that would mean David was trying to rape me. Wouldn't…wouldn't killing him be self-defense?"

"It could be. You haven't been officially charged with anything. Your attorney might be able to make a case for self-defense and get the police to close the investigation."

She rested her head on the back of the sofa and stared up at the ceiling. Had David drugged her to get her in bed? She tried to wrap her head around the notion. He had never really shown that kind of interest in her. In fact, as Jonah had said, they didn't really get along.

She started shaking her head, sat up and looked him in the eye. "I don't believe it. I think someone murdered him. I have no idea why, but whoever did it must have had it planned ahead of time. They were waiting for the right opportunity and they found it that night. They killed David and now they're trying to make it look like I'm the one who murdered him—but it wasn't me."

Jonah finished the last of his scotch. "Might be easier if you just accepted the theory and let Temple handle it. The sooner the case is dropped, the less chance something might turn up that could incriminate you."

"Are you kidding me? No way am I taking the blame for a murder I didn't commit."

"You're that sure you didn't do it? You were drugged. You admit you don't remember what happened."

"David was raving drunk. He could barely get in the car, let alone manage to drug me and try to rape me. And I don't believe for a minute I'd have had a friendly little drink with him in his condo. We didn't even like each other. If I accept that version of the story, the real killer is going to get away with murder."

CHAPTER FOUR

It was a hot, mid-August day in Dallas. Heat radiated up off the sidewalk and the pavement was soft beneath the wheels of the cars on the street.

Jonah hadn't slept well last night. He'd lain awake thinking of April Vale and her stubborn insistence that she was innocent of the murder of David Dean.

Still tired when he got up the next morning, he drank enough coffee to give him a badly needed jolt of energy, then started making phone calls, beginning with a call to Heath Ford for an update on the investigation.

"Anything new you can tell me?" Jonah asked.

"Nothing you're going to want to hear, I'm afraid. To start with, there was no sign of forced entry."

"Which means no one broke into Dean's apartment and shot him. No surprise there."

"Ballistics confirmed the bullet that killed Dean matched the S&W .380 found at the crime scene. The gun is registered to April Vale. Her fingerprints were on it."

"I figured. Anything on the cameras in the parking lot?"

"Unfortunately, no cameras out there."

"Cell phone calls?"

"Nothing after Dean left the Derby. Earlier he talked to some of the people in his office, nothing that seemed out of the ordinary."

"What about the tox screen?"

"Came back this morning. Confirmed Rohypnol in April's blood. Nothing in Dean's blood but alcohol, which we already knew."

"So she was drugged, just like she said. You think the department would support a self-defense claim?"

"The way it looks they probably would. There's not much doubt about what happened. Dean drugged her, tried to rape her, and she shot him. The guy took on the wrong woman and got what he deserved."

If the cops accepted what the facts supported so far, the matter could be easily resolved and April would be off the hook.

"Thanks, Heath. Keep me posted."

"As much as I can."

Jonah ended the call and phoned Nate Temple. He had worked with Temple before and respected him. Nate said he had spoken to the police then phoned April and reported the status of the investigation so far. He had explained the working theory that she'd acted in self-defense.

Jonah was only mildly surprised to find out April had refused to accept the explanation and take the easy out.

"She's convinced David Dean was murdered," Tem-

ple said, "and not by her. She wants you to keep working the investigation."

"No problem." Jonah found himself admiring the
lady. She could save herself a lot of money and a helluva
lot of trouble if she just went along with the flow.

According to Temple, after what had happened, the
mayor had insisted April take a few days off. Which
was good. Jonah needed more information, and April
was one of his best resources.

He set up a meeting Monday morning in a little café
called Burgers and More, which was close to his office
on Blackburn Street and not too far from April's town
house on Bowser. He figured she would relax, be more
at ease in a more casual environment.

Seated at a booth in the back, he spotted her through
the window, hurrying along the sidewalk toward the
front door. She was dressed in a pair of skinny jeans
that showed off her long legs and a world-class ass. All
that fiery hair made him itch to grab a fistful and hold
on while he devoured those plump red lips.

Fortunately, he was a professional. He reminded himself to act like one.

He was waiting for her up front when she walked into
the café. High heels pushed her up to eye level with him.

"I've got a booth for us in the back," he said.

"Great." She turned and walked in front of him toward the rear of the café, giving him a chance to admire
her lovely behind. They reached the empty red vinyl
booth and she slid in across from him.

"You want coffee or something else?" he asked.
"Maybe something to eat?"

"Coffee's great."

He motioned to Molly, a longtime waitress, silver-haired and slightly stoop-shouldered but as hardworking as a twenty-year-old. He'd been coming to the café for years. The employees all knew him and he knew them.

"Two coffees, Molly. Black."

"Right away, Jonah." She hustled off, then hurried back with two heavy china mugs. Setting them down on the table, she filled them to the brim, turned and rushed off to another table.

"How you holding up?" Jonah asked, lifting his mug and taking a drink. It was scalding hot, just the way he liked.

She raked a hand through her heavy dark red hair, shoving it away from her face. "I'm not sure. Every time I close my eyes I see David lying there in all that blood."

"It'll get better in time."

"I suppose so. You've dealt with that kind of thing a lot, I imagine. Maddie told me you were a cop before you became a private detective."

"That's right. Undercover work mostly."

"Why'd you quit?"

He usually dodged the question. For reasons he didn't quite get, he found himself answering instead. "I got my partner killed."

"Oh, Jonah, I'm sorry. What happened?"

He didn't like to think about it, wished he could erase the whole episode from his mind. It didn't work that way and it never would.

"She was young, still green. We were working a drug bust. I shouldn't have let her go in with me, but she was gung-ho, eager to bust some chops, and having been there when I was a rookie, I gave in. I let her come along and Jenny took a bullet. Shot just missed her vest. She died on the way to the hospital."

"I'm so sorry."

He took a drink of the thick black coffee. "I was exonerated, but it didn't matter. If I hadn't let her go, she'd still be alive today." He released a slow breath. "After that, I needed a break so I took a leave of absence. Three months later, instead of going back, I started working for myself. No more green kids to worry about."

"No, just your clients."

Unfortunately, that was true. Some he worried about more than others. "Yeah," he admitted. "Except for my clients."

April sipped her coffee. "Why did you ask me to come today?"

Jonah leaned against the back of the booth. "I talked to Temple about the investigation. He says you turned down a chance to make this end, which would have been the easy way out."

"That's right. I'm not going to plead guilty to something I didn't do—even if it was supposedly in self-defense. Would you?"

"Probably not. So what we need to find out is, besides you, who wanted David Dean dead?"

She bristled. "I didn't want David dead. He could be a royal pain in the ass, but I didn't want him dead."

His mouth edged up. April was a beautiful woman, particularly when she unleashed that redheaded temper. "I'll buy that. So who did?"

She sighed. "I don't know. I've tried to think of anyone he might have had as an enemy, but so far I've come up with zilch. David was dedicated to the mayor. He didn't date much. Gave to local charities. I can't think of anyone who'd want to kill him."

"You make him sound like a paragon."

"He was a jerk. If he didn't get his way, he got pissy. He could go days barely speaking."

"Until you agreed to do what he wanted?"

"Sometimes I agreed, but not always. Which is why he'd pressed Mark to fire me. As far as I know, Mark had no intention of letting me go and David had accepted that."

"I talked to the campaign volunteers who were with you that night at the Derby, Susan Buchanan and Timothy Mahoney. They confirmed that Dean drank too much and that you offered to drive him the few blocks back to his condo."

"That's right."

"Susan said you seemed okay when you left. That supports the theory that Dean drugged you at his house."

"I started feeling dizzy when I got to my car. I don't even remember driving him home. In fact, I don't believe I did."

"According to your attorney, they released your car this morning. The only prints they found were yours and Dean's."

"I don't think I could have driven that car out of the parking lot, let alone all the way to David's condo."

"There aren't any cameras in the lot so there's no way to know for sure."

She slumped back in her seat. "I was hoping the cameras would show what happened."

"You're convinced you were drugged at the Derby?"

"Yes."

"You think it was someone at your table? I haven't talked to Watt, Schweitzer or Rutherford yet."

She sighed. "I don't know. Sometimes we order a pitcher of beer, but we were all drinking microbrews that night. The drinks came in mugs. It could have been the bartender. It could have been someone walking past the table. It could have been anyone."

Jonah finished his coffee. "Would you be interested in paying a little visit to the Derby tonight? I'd like to get a read on the staff, see if anyone behaves differently around you."

"That's a great idea. Maybe whoever did it will act guilty or nervous or something. What time?"

"Let's make it the same time you were there that night."

"Seven o'clock. I'll meet you there."

He'd planned to pick her up, but she didn't know him that well and after what had happened with Dean, he didn't blame her for being cautious. "All right."

They talked a while longer, going back over things she had said. Jonah watched for inconsistencies but didn't find any. He needed to find out why Dean was killed. He had talked to the volunteers who had been there that night, but they were just kids helping with the mayor's campaign, doing what they saw as their civic duty. He was pretty sure they had no part in Dean's murder.

That left Watt, Rutherford and Schweitzer. Jonah needed more information about them and he knew where to get it.

He didn't realize April was conducting her own investigation until things went south that night.

CHAPTER FIVE

As April drove away from the little café, she thought about Jonah Wolfe. There was more to Jonah than she had first thought, more than a hot male body and a darkly beautiful face. More than compelling masculinity and amazing sex appeal.

Jonah felt things deeply. She read the pain of losing his partner in every line of his face. Though the police department had cleared him, Jonah still blamed himself. She thought maybe he always would.

April liked that he cared so much. Deep down, Jonah would always be a cop, and he would always believe in justice. April thought that if anyone could help her find the man who murdered David, it was Jonah Wolfe.

Thinking of David and the murder, April made a quick change of plans, deciding to drop by her office before she went back to her town house. No matter what anyone thought, she hadn't killed David Dean. She had nothing to feel guilty about and she was determined to find the real killer.

The campaign office was humming with activity when she walked in. Volunteers manned the phones, trying to stir up votes. There was a strategy meeting going on in one corner. Dallas was a huge metropolitan city. The mayor was a powerful figure and the job of getting him reelected was all-consuming.

As April crossed the office, Peggy Watt broke away from the group and walked toward her. In her late thirties, always on a diet to keep her figure, Peggy was a wealthy widow too young to retire. Instead, she believed in Mayor Rydell and she worked tirelessly organizing his busy schedule.

Peggy reached out and caught her hand. "Good Lord, April, are you okay?"

"As good as can be expected, I guess."

"I feel terrible about what happened. We all thought it was a good idea for you to drive David home. None of us could have imagined him doing something like that."

"I don't remember what happened, Peg. I know I was drugged, but I'm not sure David is the one who drugged me."

Peggy's blond eyebrows arched up. "What do you mean? It was on TV. They said he gave you some kind of a date-rape drug."

"I think it happened before I got there. I think someone drugged me at the Derby."

Peggy's hand came up to her heart. "Surely that isn't possible."

"As I said, I don't remember. I'm trying to figure it out."

From just a few feet away, Collin Rutherford walked

over to join them. As finance director, Collin's job was to meet the financial goals of the campaign and keep the candidate on track with fund-raising. At thirty-nine, he was a handsome man with light brown hair and plenty of charm, which helped in his position.

"I'm sorry, April. If I'd had any idea David was that kind of guy—"

"The police are still investigating, Collin. They don't know for sure what happened. I'd appreciate if you didn't jump to conclusions until we know more."

"But I thought—"

"I can't remember what happened. I'm not willing to indict David without more proof."

He glanced over her head and drew in a deep breath. He worked hard and was dedicated to winning the mayor's reelection. Like everyone else, he had done a good job of spinning what had happened so that the mayor wasn't at fault.

"Whatever you think, April." He glanced around. "I need to get moving. I've got a lot to do before the fund-raiser. Are you still going?"

The fund-raiser was a major event. It was part of her job to be there in support of the candidate. "Of course."

"Great. Mark needs all the help we can give him." Collin waved to someone across the room and walked away.

"Listen, I've got to get going, too," Peggy said. "If you need anything, just let me know." She hurried away and April started walking. She didn't get far before Brad Schweitzer spotted her, excused himself from the woman he was talking to and intercepted her.

"April. I meant to call you." Brad was black-haired, good-looking and smart. He was married, with two grown kids, but he and his wife were estranged. "How are you holding up?"

"I'm okay, Brad."

"I can't believe David's dead."

The conversation was a repeat of what the other two had said. Brad was shocked and appalled. April was still uncertain.

"If you remember anything about that night you think would help…" she said.

"Don't worry. I'll be sure to let the police know." Brad went back to work and April continued toward the mayor's satellite office.

On Mondays, the mayor stopped by after lunch to strategize about the campaign and since his personal assistant, Marge Lamb, sat at the desk out front, April knew he was there.

Marge, a heavyset woman with a cap of silver hair and a winning smile, was the person who ran interference between the mayor and his legion of supporters.

"April, I'm so terribly sorry. Is there anything I can do?"

"Thank you, Marge. I'm doing fine, considering, but I appreciate your concern." She looked at the closed office door. "I see the mayor's in. I really need to speak to him."

"His schedule's packed, but I'm sure he'll find a moment for you." Instead of using the intercom, Marge rose from her chair, knocked briefly on the door and went into the mayor's office.

She was smiling when she came back out. "You can go right on in."

"Thanks, Marge." The mayor was sitting behind his

desk, an attractive man, fit and trim, with threads of silver in his thick brown hair.

The moment she entered the room, he came out from behind his desk and walked toward her. "April." Reaching out, he caught hold of her hands and leaned in for a brief kiss on the cheek before he let go.

"I didn't expect to see you for a while," Mark said. "I'm so sorry about what happened. I had no idea David was capable of something like that."

"I appreciate your concern, Mark. I realize this isn't a good time for a thing like that to happen…not with the election just a few months away."

"I'll survive. We'll replace David and move on. When it comes time to vote, I don't think people will hold something my campaign manager did against me."

"The thing is no one really knows what happened. The police think David drugged me. They think he must have been trying to rape me and I killed him in self-defense."

"Isn't that what happened?"

"I don't remember what happened. But I'm not completely convinced it happened the way the police think it did."

His eyes glinted as he frowned. "You need to consider this carefully, April. The sooner you put this behind you, the better off you'll be. This can't be good for your career any more than it's good for mine."

"I'm going to find out the truth, Mark. If David was murdered and I was set up to take the blame, the real killer is going to get away with it."

"I don't know." Mark shook his head. "This seems like something you should let the police handle." He walked over to the window and paused to stare out at the people walking past on the sidewalk.

Mark turned to face her. "I don't want you to take this the wrong way, April, but I need this to be over. I'd appreciate it if you would help me make that happen."

It wasn't an outrageous request. The man was running for reelection. Still, her instincts went on alert. "You want me to say I killed David?"

"From what I've seen on the news, there's every chance you did."

"I don't think that's what happened. What if I can't just go along with the story people want to believe?"

His mouth thinned, disapproval clear on his face. "Then you might find yourself looking for a job. I wouldn't want that to happen. I have a great deal of respect for you. But I have a lot of people depending on me. This sort of thing could jeopardize the outcome of the election. It could jeopardize their futures as well as mine."

She clenched her back teeth together to keep from arguing. Mark was her employer. She would be working for him after he was reelected. She liked her job. Perhaps she could find a way to keep it.

She pasted on a smile. "Maybe you're right. I'll give it some time, think things over. I'll see you at the fundraiser."

"All right. In the meantime, why don't you take a few more days off. After what you've been through, you deserve a little time to yourself."

Maybe she did. Or maybe Mark just didn't want her nosing around the office, looking for clues as to who might have wanted David dead.

"Thanks, Mark. Have a good day."

April left the office and headed for home, her mind going over the conversation she'd just had. No way was she letting Mark Rydell threaten her. Why had he? Was he really just worried about his campaign? Or was his motive more sinister? Was there a chance he was involved in David's murder?

As soon as she got home, she was going to get on the computer and do some digging. See if she could find a connection between David Dean and Mark Rydell that went beyond mayor and campaign manager.

When she saw Jonah tonight, she would tell him about the encounter, see what he had to say.

As she walked into the living room of her town house, she felt a thrill of anticipation at the thought of seeing him at the Derby.

Jonah was smart and, from what she could tell, extremely capable. Beyond that, he was the sexiest man she had met in years.

Until now, her taste had never run toward a guy who looked more like a biker than a businessman, but she couldn't deny the attraction. When Jonah walked into a room and looked at her with those dark, brooding eyes, she could almost feel the heat sparking between them.

She wasn't a fool. She knew when a man was interested. Unfortunately, a guy who looked like Wolfe attracted legions of women. She had no interest in a man who probably slept with a different woman every night. If she gave in to the attraction she felt for him, she could be letting herself in for trouble.

Fortunately, Jonah was a professional. Until the case was resolved, nothing was going to happen. She was off-limits—at least for the time being.

April sighed as she sat down at her computer to start

her research. She had work to do, but the anticipation remained. She was meeting Jonah tonight at the Derby. She couldn't act on the attraction she felt for him, but there was no reason she couldn't enjoy herself.

After he left the café, Jonah returned to the Max for a while. He spent an hour digging around on his computer but came up with nothing new.

It was time to bring in the big guns so he phoned ahead, then climbed into his black Range Rover and headed for Tabitha Love's old brick house in Richardson not far from the university.

As he walked up the cement path to the porch, the door swung wide and a tall young woman stood in the opening. She had very short black hair, shaved on the sides and moussed on top, a little silver hoop in one of her sleek black eyebrows and a row of hoops down the side of each ear.

She also had a tongue stud and a nose ring. She looked like a woman who should have an unusual name like Tabitha Love.

"Wolfe! Come on in."

As he walked past her into the living room, he bent and brushed a light kiss on her cheek. "How's it going, Tab?" She was pretty but far from his type. Lucky for him, she had no interest in him, either.

Tabby had a geeky boyfriend named Lester Lewis she was crazy about, plus she wasn't that fond of cops— even the *ex*-variety.

Still, they were friends.

She led him through a living room cobbled together in a sort of dark wood shabby chic, with bookshelves and end tables she had purchased from a thrift store. Brown shag carpet covered the floor.

"When you called to say you were coming out, you mentioned this had something to do with the murder of the mayor's campaign manager," she said, leading him down the hall into a bedroom converted to an office that was wall-to-wall, floor-to-ceiling computers and high-tech equipment.

This was Tabby's world and she thrived in it.

"His name was David Dean." As succinctly as possible, he filled her in on the case, her eyebrows going up at the rape/self-defense theory of Dean's murder and April's certainty the story wasn't true.

"I've got three names. I need to find out if any of those names are connected to David Dean other than as campaign staffers who worked for him." He rattled off Peggy Watt, Brad Schweitzer and Collin Rutherford's names. "You may need to go deep, Tab."

"No worries, I can handle it. It may take a while, but if there's smoke, I'll find the fire."

"I know you will. Thanks, kiddo. I'll let myself out." Which he hadn't needed to say since Tab's attention was already focused on the computer screen.

Jonah closed her front door, climbed into the Rover and drove back to the office.

Maybe his trip to the Derby that night would turn up something or at least eliminate possibilities. In the meantime, he hoped Tabby would uncover the one thing he couldn't seem to find—a motive for David Dean's murder.

CHAPTER SIX

The Derby was quiet when April walked in a little before seven that evening. With all the smooth dark wood, the long, ornate bar and forest-green accents, the place felt slightly old-fashioned. The racehorse pictures on the walls were a favorite of everyone, and the staff was always friendly.

April recognized the bartender, Ian Van Horne, as she approached. Ian was a good-looking, sandy-haired guy close to her age. He'd asked her out a couple of times, but she was always too busy. The truth was she could never work up any interest.

Ian spotted her and waved. Since she didn't see Jonah, she headed for the bar and climbed up on one of the green vinyl stools, the skirt of her sleeveless black sheath dress riding up as she settled herself. She pulled the skirt back down as Ian walked over.

He wiped off the bar in front of her. "I heard what happened the other night. Man, that sucks."

"Yeah, it does."

"You ask me, the bastard deserved a bullet in the chest. Or maybe you should have aimed lower—shot him in the nuts instead."

Her mind flashed back to the bedroom, the sheet soaked in bright red blood, and suddenly she felt dizzy. She swayed a little on the bar stool, caught the shadow of a man beside her, felt Jonah's hand at her waist, steadying her.

"It's all right. Just take it easy." He looked over at Ian. "Cut the crap. She doesn't need that tonight."

Ian took one look at Wolfe's dark expression and took a step back. "Sorry." He turned to April. "I wasn't thinking, April. I'm sorry."

She released a shaky breath. "It's okay. Something like that doesn't happen every day."

"What are you drinking?" Ian asked. "It's on the house for both of you."

"Thanks, I'll have a glass of Chardonnay."

"What about you?" he asked Jonah. "House is buying."

"Johnnie Walker on the rocks."

"Coming right up."

The place was starting to fill, as it usually did this time of night. They moved to a table in the back and Lou, a friendly blonde waitress, came over with Jonah's drink.

"I heard about the other night," Lou said to April. "I'm real sorry, hun."

"Me, too."

She set the drink on the square oak table. "You know, I always thought that Dean guy was a pretty straight shooter. I wouldn't have pegged him for one of those scumbags who has to drug a woman to get her in bed."

"The police aren't exactly sure what happened."

Lou glanced at Wolfe, who had definitely snagged her attention. He was wearing black jeans, a navy T-shirt and a lightweight black leather jacket. A shadow of beard darkened his jaw. The man was a walking ad for sex, which Lou didn't miss.

The woman might be older than Jonah, but she wasn't dead yet.

"You ever have a problem here with women being drugged?" Jonah asked her.

"Nothin' like that's ever happened here before," Lou said. "The owner's real strict. Anybody caught with drugs is out of a job."

"Good to know."

Lou left to wait on another customer, leaving Jonah to enjoy his drink.

"Were Lou and the bartender both here the night Dean was killed?" Jonah asked.

"They were both here. They work the early shift so they're usually here when we come in after work."

"Any other employees here that night?"

"There was another cocktail waitress working. Her name's Vicky. But now that I think about it, Lou was the one who waited on us that night."

Jonah leaned back in his chair, stretching those long legs out in front of him, his eyes roaming over the customers scattered around the room, missing nothing.

April shifted in her seat. "Something happened today that I wanted to mention."

His gaze sliced to hers, dark and disturbing, making her heart beat faster. Just looking at him made her think of sex. Was she really that needy? Or was it Jonah Wolfe?

"What happened?" he asked.

"I stopped at the office and talked to my boss. He thinks I should accept the blame for the murder, just say it was self-defense and make it all go away. He insinuated I'd lose my job if I didn't. I understand that would be best for his political ambitions, but…"

"But…?"

"But I'm not sure he didn't have a different motive, something more than just winning the election."

"You think Rydell could have been involved in Dean's murder?"

"When I got home, I did a little digging. So far I haven't found anything that would connect the two of them outside of work." She crossed her legs and the skirt of her black sheath rode up again, attracting Jonah's attention.

For an instant before he shuttered the look, a hot gleam flashed in his eyes. April's stomach contracted and desire unfolded like butterfly wings in her stomach.

She couldn't remember the last time a man had attracted her so strongly. Maybe no man ever had.

Jonah took a drink of his scotch. "You're in over your head, April. Murder's a dangerous game. You'd be wise to let me do the digging. You never know where something like this could lead."

"I need to know what happened. I can't get on with my life until I find out the truth."

"Then we'd better get going." Jonah shoved back his chair and stood up, reached a hand down to help her to her feet. A tingle moved up her arm. "I'll walk you to your car," he said, and began guiding her toward the door.

Walking beside him as they made their way through

the bar, April felt feminine in a way that rarely happened. She reminded herself how dangerous it was to let her attraction grow and pulled her hand away.

The air outside was warm and humid, only a sliver of moon overhead. Not wanting to retrace her steps the night of the murder, she had parked her car in front.

"So what do you think?" she asked as they paused for a moment on the sidewalk. "Did you learn anything useful in there?"

"Maybe. I think we may have narrowed down the list of who might have drugged you. I don't think it was one of the Derby employees."

"You don't?"

"I didn't see any indication. The owner runs a clean operation and none of the staff showed any signs of nerves when they talked to you. That leaves the five people from your office who were sitting at your table. Which one encouraged you to take Dean home?"

She tried to think back. Her memories were clear until the moment she had climbed into her car. "I don't know. Everyone seemed to think it was a good idea. I don't remember who suggested it first."

Jonah's cell phone rang as they crossed the sidewalk to the curb where her vehicle was parked, a three-year-old BMW 320 sedan. Good for work yet small enough to feel sporty.

He stopped to take the call but April kept walking, making her way behind the car, pausing just past the rear fender to dig out her keys.

She didn't see the dark sedan speeding toward her until headlights appeared at the edge of her vision. She screamed the instant before Jonah slammed into her from behind, sending both of them flying toward the opposite side of the street, knocking her out of the path of the oncoming vehicle.

At the last second, Jonah must have turned midair, using his body as a shield, taking her weight on top of him as they landed, skidding across the rough black asphalt, her dress riding up, the bodice tearing, the front gaping open.

The car shot past, its engine revving, tires squealing as it disappeared into the darkness. April fought to battle down her fear and catch her breath. Her mind was spinning, her heart racing. It took a moment to realize she was still lying on top of Jonah, probably crushing him, his arms wrapped tightly around her.

Thank God he was wearing his leather jacket, she thought in some far corner of her mind. "My God, Jonah, you saved my life."

For an instant, Jonah tightened his hold, grateful he'd been able to reach April in time. Grateful she wasn't dead.

Cars coming down the lane slowed to a stop. Headlights illuminated the two of them lying on the pavement. April was shaking as she lifted herself away from him and Jonah followed, coming to his feet. Ignoring the scrapes on his hands, the dirt and cuts in his leather jacket and the rip in his jeans, he led her back to safety on the curb in front of the Derby.

He could hear voices inside but apparently no one had heard the commotion out in the street. April's high heels were gone, the bodice of her sexy black dress ripped and hanging open, exposing the tops of her pretty breasts above a lacy black bra.

Without the shoes, she was inches shorter than he

was. Her eyes were big and blue and filled with the remnants of fear.

"Jonah..." she said softly.

At the plea in her voice, the last of his control vanished and he pulled her into his arms. "It's all right, honey. You're safe. Everything's okay."

She was shaking all over. A shudder rippled through her body as she buried her face in the curve of his neck and just hung on. He thought she would start crying but only a sob escaped. Then her shoulders straightened, she pulled in a shaky breath and eased away.

April looked up at him. "The car didn't stop."

"No."

"Were they...were they trying to kill me?"

"It looks that way. Come on. I'll take you home." Where he planned to spend the night. She was his client. She was right. He felt responsible for her. He wasn't going to let her end up like David Dean.

"Should we call the police?"

He would—if he had a plate number or a decent description of the hit-and-run vehicle beyond a dirty white four-door sedan—one of thousands in the city. Unfortunately, he'd only had seconds, barely enough time to keep April from getting killed.

"We don't have a plate number or anything else. We'll call Detective Ford when we get you home and settled. Let him know what's going on."

She didn't object when he led her to his black Land Rover and helped her climb in, let him fasten her seat belt across what he now knew to be soft, very feminine breasts. She was shaken up and he didn't blame her.

He drove out of the parking lot and headed for her town house on Bowser, where he had been before.

"What about my car?" she finally asked, as if the thought had just occurred.

"We'll pick it up tomorrow." He drove along in silence, giving her time for the adrenaline to wear off. An occasional tremor still slipped through her.

"Who do you think it was?"

"I'd say whoever killed Dean or someone the killer hired."

April fell quiet, digesting the situation in which she suddenly found herself. They had almost reached her town house when she asked the question that had been on his mind since the incident.

"How did they know where to find me?"

Jonah flicked her a sideways glance. "Did you tell anyone where you were going tonight?"

"No."

"Then they were probably watching your house. You drove to the Derby from home, right?"

"That's right." Her eyes widened as the implication sank in and she sat up straighter in the seat. "What if they come after me at home, Jonah? What if they try to kill me again?"

A shot of fury rolled through him, a warning his job had become far too personal. It was followed by a rush of dark anticipation.

"If they come after you they're going to be very sorry." He pulled open his scratched and battered black leather jacket, showing her the Glock 19 in his shoulder holster. "Because I'll be there waiting to say hello."

CHAPTER SEVEN

April brought pillows and sheets out to the living room to make up the sofa. Jonah was spending the night. He was there to keep her safe and she wasn't about to argue. She still saw David Dean's lifeless, bloody body every time she closed her eyes.

Or the car careening toward her at breakneck speed.

She told herself it was probably standard operating procedure for a private detective to provide protection for one of his clients if they were in danger. It was nothing more than that, she was sure, though she found herself hoping it was.

Considering the bad luck she'd had with men, she knew her attraction for Jonah was dangerous, but it didn't stop her from hoping he was there because he was beginning to care for her, at least a little.

The thought dredged a memory of her last serious relationship. She had fallen hard for Roger Kosky, a professional baseball player. She had stupidly believed

Roger loved her, believed him when he'd said his legion of female fans meant nothing.

Stupid. Stupid. Stupid.

When she'd found out he was cheating just days after he'd bought her an engagement ring, she felt like a fool. She had vowed then and there to choose the men she dated a lot more carefully.

Which was probably the reason she rarely dated at all and hadn't had sex in over a year.

Now there was Jonah. Exactly the kind of man she should run away from screaming. Instead, she fantasized about what he would be like in bed.

Stupid. Stupid. Stupid.

For the moment, she needed Jonah's protection. She trusted him to keep her safe and tonight he had proven her instincts were right. She thought of the scene in front of the Derby and shivered, thinking how close she had come to death.

If Jonah hadn't been there…

Forcing the thought away, April spread open the sheet, bent over the sofa and started tucking it in. A few feet away, she could hear Jonah's deep voice on his cell phone, talking to his friend, Detective Ford.

"I'd appreciate it, Heath. There's no way to prove it was more than a drunk driver, but in my book, it looks like April was right about Dean. Whoever killed him wanted her to cop to the murder, say it was self-defense. When she wouldn't do it, they got worried. Maybe they figured if she had some kind of accident, all of it would go away."

He nodded at whatever the police detective said. "This afternoon she went to see Mayor Rydell. Clearly he didn't want her digging around."

She couldn't hear what was being said on the other end of the line, but Jonah finally ended the call and walked toward her.

"There's no way to prove it was more than a careless drunk who didn't want to wind up in jail, but the police are putting an extra patrol in your neighborhood."

"That's good."

Jonah took the sheet from her hand. "Why don't you go to bed? You've had one helluva night."

She nodded, but didn't move. She kept thinking that Jonah had risked his life to save her. That she would be dead if it hadn't been for him. She thought how safe she had felt when Jonah had his arms around her.

"Thank you for what you did," she said softly.

"You're my client. It's part of my job."

She looked up at him, into those dark, intriguing eyes. "Is that all it is? Your job?"

His jaw subtly tightened. Reaching out, he gently touched her cheek. "I won't let anyone hurt you." He was staring at her mouth. He looked like he wanted to devour her.

Against every instinct for emotional survival, it was exactly what she wanted him to do.

He must have read her thoughts because he started shaking his head. "We can't do this, April. Not tonight. I need to keep you safe."

Her cheeks flushed with embarrassment. She felt like a fool. *Again.* "You're right. I don't know what I was thinking. I'm sorry. I'm just…after what happened, I'm not…not myself." She started to turn away, but Jonah caught her shoulders. His eyes locked with hers and she couldn't look away.

"Don't be sorry," he said. "You're more than a job

to me. I tried not to let it get personal, but it is. When this is over…" He drew her against him, his hand sliding into her hair, tipping her head back to hold her in place while his mouth came down over hers.

Everything inside her went still. Jonah deepened the kiss and heat surged through her, floated out through her limbs. April clutched his shoulders. Bands of muscle tightened in response, and dampness settled in her core. April moaned and Jonah growled low in his throat.

The kiss went on and on, wet and hot and so intense her knees nearly buckled beneath her. His chest felt like steel where the hard muscles rubbed against the peaks of her breasts through her lacy black bra. She could feel his erection against her belly.

It was Jonah who broke the kiss—long before she wanted him to.

"I want you, April," he said gruffly. "When this is over, we'll start where we left off, explore this thing between us." His hand came up to her cheek. He brushed a last soft kiss on her lips. "In the meantime, you need to get some sleep."

Gently, he pushed her toward the hall. "I'll see you in the morning."

Her lips tingled. She forced herself to back away. She knew better than to get involved with a dangerous man like Jonah Wolfe. Knew the consequences, the heartache. And yet part of her was willing to risk the danger, eager to fan the fire that burned in his eyes.

"Good night." Turning, April headed down the hall to her bedroom. Though her body still tingled with arousal, she was exhausted. And still frightened. Someone had tried to kill her.

Still, as she pulled on a short nylon nightgown and

slid beneath the covers, she wasn't thinking of speeding cars and her close brush with death. She was thinking of the hottest kiss she had ever tasted.

She was thinking of Jonah Wolfe.

Jonah heard the knock at the front door the next morning. He walked over and checked the peephole, saw Chase Garrett, his boss and one of his closest friends, standing outside on the porch. Jonah opened the door.

"I got your message," Chase said as he stepped into the condo. "I'd already heard about the hit-and-run."

"Word travels fast."

"Maddox always has an ear to the pavement. What can I do to help?" Chase was as tall as Jonah, at thirty-five, three years older, with dark blond hair and whiskey-brown eyes. A short-cropped beard ran along his jaw. Chase was good-looking—and rich as Croesus. And he didn't give a damn about either of those things.

All Chase had ever cared about was law enforcement, first as a cop, then a detective, now as the owner of the top private security firm in Dallas.

"I could use a little feedback. Thought maybe we could brainstorm, figure out where this might be headed." He hadn't wanted to leave April alone or he would have just gone down to the office. "You want some coffee? I just made a pot."

"Sounds good."

Jonah led Chase into April's sparkling white kitchen and poured each of them a mug of the French roast he had found in the cupboard and brewed. They filled their mugs and carried them over to the high, round white Formica-topped table and each sat down on a stool.

"Your client still asleep?" Chased asked.

Client. Sometime during the seconds between life and death, April had become more to him than just a client. Maybe that was the reason he had kissed her. Or maybe he just couldn't resist temptation any longer. Whatever the reason, he meant to keep her safe.

"She's asleep. She didn't get much rest last night. I heard her moving around pretty late."

Chase sipped his coffee. "Nothing new on the hit-and-run?"

"No, and I don't think there will be. No plate number, not even a decent vehicle description."

"No way to prove what happened had anything to do with the murder."

"No."

"But you're convinced it's connected. What's the motivation?"

"Whoever killed Dean wanted April to roll over, just let things play out. Dean would be dead and the case would be closed."

"But April wouldn't go along with it."

"That's right. I have a hunch they figured if she was out of the picture, the whole thing would just go away."

"If they'd managed to make it look like an accident, they might have just been right. With April gone, there's no one to keep stirring the pot."

"She never believed she killed David Dean and last night makes me pretty sure she's right."

Feminine footfalls sounded, padding down the hall in their direction. "Good morning," April said, walking into the kitchen in jeans and a Dallas Cowboys' T-shirt, all that luscious red hair curling around her shoulders. "I didn't realize you had company."

Jonah flashed back to the taste he'd had of her last night, the way her curves fit him so perfectly, and fought to control the tightening in his jeans.

"April, this is Chase Garrett. He's the owner of Maximum Security and also a friend. Chase, meet April Vale."

"Pleasure," Chase said.

"Nice to meet you, Chase."

"You want some coffee?" Jonah asked.

"Love some," April said.

Jonah rose and poured her a cup and they joined Chase at the table.

"You've got a problem," Chase said, sipping from his mug.

Jonah grunted. "Which one?"

"Unless you force these guys out in the open, they could just lie in wait until they're ready to create another 'accident.'"

"That's what I've been thinking," April said. "They want to be rid of me, but if they just shoot me, the cops will immediately link my murder to David's and start digging deeper—exactly what the killers don't want."

"Depends on how much is at stake," Jonah said. "If the problem is big enough, they'll do whatever it takes to protect themselves."

April sipped her coffee. "Aside from killing me, there's another way they could get my cooperation."

"What's that?" Jonah asked.

"If they want me to take the blame for killing David, they could pay me."

Chase looked impressed. "Blackmail? Interesting idea."

"We can be pretty sure one of the people I was with

at the Derby drugged me. Jonah doesn't think it was either of the campaign volunteers or the employees at the bar. That leaves the mayor's staff. I could talk to them, hint that I can be bought and see who takes the bait."

"Wait a minute." Jonah set his cup down on the table. "You aren't thinking of setting some kind of trap?"

Chase shifted on his stool. "Until whoever killed Dean is caught, she's a target, Jonah. You have to face that."

Jonah shook his head. "If she tries to blackmail these people, instead of agreeing to pay her, they might just kill her."

"They've already tried to kill her," Chase reminded him.

"We have to do something," April argued. "I can't keep looking over my shoulder, checking my drinks for drugs or waiting for another car to run me down."

"You need to be patient," Jonah said. "Sooner or later something will break and I'll get a lead. I just need a little more time."

April gently touched his arm. "I'm going to a fundraiser Thursday night. Being there is part of my job. The people who were with me at the Derby will also be there. I'll talk to them, let them know I've had time to think things over. I'll tell them I'm ready to cooperate, accept the story that David tried to rape me and I killed him in self-defense—if enough money is involved."

"No," Jonah said flatly. "It's too dangerous."

"It's not a bad idea," Chase argued. "I supported Rydell in the last election. I've got an invitation on my desk. I wasn't planning to go, but plans change."

Jonah shook his head. "I don't like it. Not even a little."

"If both of you are there, I'll be safe," April said. "I spread the word I can be bought and we see who offers to pay me."

Jonah thought of his dead partner, Jenny Stevens. She'd thought she would be safe with him, too.

"We've got to do something, Jonah," April said. "This could work."

He clenched his jaw. He didn't like it. But they needed to take the fight to whoever was involved in this before something else happened. Something that might prove fatal.

He blew out a long breath, raked back his hair. "Fine, but you and I go together and you stay close to me every second."

"So you'd be my date?"

The ex-cop and the college girl. It seemed such a stretch something grim shifted inside him. "I know I'm not what you're used to, but—"

April flashed him a brilliant white smile. "I'd love for you to be my date."

Jonah blinked, tried to wrap his head around it. He shouldn't have jumped to conclusions. No way could that smile be anything but sincere. He wished he wasn't so relieved.

He returned his attention to Chase. "Looks like I'm taking April into the wolf's den—so to speak. Long as I can count on you for backup."

"Not a problem."

"You fit in with that crowd. No one will spot you as personal protection."

Dealing with wealthy clients was Chase's specialty. He was comfortable moving in upper-class circles. And it paid big money. His connections were part of the reason he was so successful.

"I'll call Reggie Porter," Chase said. "Ask him to drive you. He doubles as a bodyguard."

"Reggie's good. I've worked with him before."

Jonah felt April's gaze on his face. "You don't think they'd actually try to kill me at the fund-raiser?"

"They're more likely to agree to pay you," he conceded, since the idea was, in fact, a good one. "Killing you would only make the cops more suspicious about what happened to Dean. But blackmail is dangerous. And anytime you're setting a trap for a killer, things can go wrong."

"Which," Chase said, "considering what's happened so far, is way more than a remote possibility."

CHAPTER EIGHT

April dressed with care for the mayor's black-tie fund-raiser. Choosing a long, off-the-shoulder chiffon gown in blush tones, she stood in front of the mirror admiring the way the fabric flowed over her curves, showing off her figure while still looking elegant and sophisticated.

As she walked, a split in the skirt allowed a glimpse of her legs. Strappy silver high heels peeped from beneath the hem.

If she managed to forget the task ahead of her, she was excited to be going. The posters she'd helped design would be plastered all over the ballroom. Her staff had been responsible for the decorations—with only a few frantic phone calls to her.

As the time for Jonah's arrival drew near, her nerves crept up. He hadn't spent any more nights in her town house. He was working the case, trying to dig up information, but he'd insisted a security guard be parked in front of the house round the clock.

Since she knew how to handle a pistol, he'd brought

her a Colt .38 revolver for protection. April didn't tell him David's bloody murder was enough to last a life-time—there was no way she was pulling the trigger.

At least not unless she had absolutely no choice.

Instead of a knock, the doorbell rang, setting the formal mood. April checked the peephole, saw Jonah on the porch and pulled the door open.

Oh, dear God.

Black leather suited him, but the man looked entirely edible in a gleaming black tuxedo. Her mouth went dry. Her attraction to this man was way over the top.

"You look gorgeous," he said, sweeping her with those long-lashed, hot dark eyes. "You ready for this?"

"I'm ready. And you look pretty gorgeous yourself."

His mouth edged up and his eyes smoldered.

She took a deep breath. "Let me get my purse."

Grabbing the silver clutch that matched her shoes, she walked in front of him out to a black stretch limo waiting in front.

The driver, a big muscular African-American with impressively-sized biceps, opened the door. "This is Reggie," Jonah said. "He's a friend and a colleague. Reggie, meet April."

The introduction surprised her since she wasn't used to chauffeurs being introduced as friends. She liked it.

April smiled. "Nice to meet you, Reggie."

"You, too, April." He grinned. "Don't you worry about a thing. I'm gonna take real good care of you."

April believed him. She slid across the red leather seat and Jonah followed her in.

Reggie drove sanely to the Westin Dallas Downtown, and the limo pulled up at the entrance. Reggie walked around and opened the car door. Jonah slid out and helped April out, and she walked into the building on his arm.

Jonah paused a moment to speak to hotel security. He showed his ID and the weapon in his shoulder holster, and they continued on, heading down the hall into the ballroom.

The place looked spectacular, sophisticated yet welcoming. Organized and supervised by April and her staff, a small army of volunteers had done the decorations. Wispy lengths of white chiffon draped from the ceilings. Tiny lights glittered overhead and along the walls, and bouquets of white chrysanthemums marched down the center of the linen-draped tables.

Along the hall leading into the ballroom, campaign posters in the red, blue, white and gold colors of the Dallas City flag read, *Keep Dallas Moving. Reelect Mayor Mark Rydell.*

The event was already in full swing when they got there. Chase, who had arrived ahead of them, spotted them and started striding in their direction.

"You look stunning," Chase said, leaning in to brush a light kiss on her cheek.

"Thank you."

In a white dinner jacket, with his thick dark blond hair, the short-cropped beard along the edge of his jaw, and broad-shouldered, solid build, the man was an eyeful. But it was Jonah's hard masculinity and brooding dark looks that appealed to her.

She caught him watching her, his sexy mouth faintly curved, and desire washed through her. She thought of the heated kiss they had shared and wondered if they would be as good together as she imagined in her fantasies.

"I want you to introduce me around," Jonah said. "I want to get a read on the people you work with, especially the ones who were with you at the Derby."

"The cocktail hour is the best time for that to happen. We'll wander. Then I'll go back and talk to Peggy, Brad and Collin later. Mark, too, if I get the chance."

A muscle tightened in Jonah's cheek. He wasn't happy with this whole blackmail idea but that was just too bad.

They made the rounds, April introducing him as a friend of a friend, namely to Maddie and Ross Townsend, but said nothing about him being a private investigator. Jonah conversed more easily than she would have guessed. He was especially interested in Peggy, Brad and Collin.

With time slipping away, she needed to execute her plan. "I have to go," she said, picking up a glass of champagne off a passing waiter's tray.

"I'll be close by if you need me," Jonah said. "So will Chase. You may not see us, but we'll be able to see you."

"Good to know." April wandered off in search of her quarry. She had already worked out what she planned to say, at least the general drift, and gone over it with Jonah.

She spotted Collin near the bar. He had just finished talking to an older woman April recognized as a big contributor to Mark's campaign. April walked up and stopped right in front of him.

"I know you're busy," she said. "Have you got a minute?"

"Of course." Collin looked good in a tuxedo. He was an attractive man who wore clothes well and he knew it.

"I've been doing some thinking," she said. "Mark wants me to go along with the theory the police have come up with and maybe he's right. David's dead. There's no need for this to drag out any longer."

Collin's interest sharpened. "If you're serious, I think you're making a very wise decision. I'm sure Mark will be glad to hear it."

"There's only one thing."

"What's that?"

"I feel like I should be compensated. I'm doing this to help Mark get reelected. I deserve something for my trouble. You're the finance director. You can make it happen."

Collin's features shifted and turned to granite. "You want money?"

She shrugged as if it were no big deal. "It only seems fair."

"I can talk to Mark, see what he says."

"Maybe you don't need to go to that much trouble." She took a sip of champagne. "I bet you could make the decision yourself."

Collin glanced off into the distance. She could almost see the wheels turning in his head. "Maybe we can work something out."

"All right. If you're interested, I'll expect a call no later than noon tomorrow."

"Fine, I'll be in touch." Collin emptied his glass of champagne and blended into the crowd. April made her way back to Jonah. She could feel his eyes on her though he seemed to be conversing with an older couple.

Jonah ended the conversation and broke away. "How did it go?"

"Too easy. Collin seems to think it would be worth paying me off to help Mark get reelected."

"Interesting. From what the polls are showing, it doesn't appear the murder of the mayor's campaign manager for attempted rape has caused him that much political trouble."

"I don't think it has. Which is why I can't believe Collin is actually considering the idea. He's supposed to let me know tomorrow."

They moved through the crowd together, April continuing to introduce Jonah, who had a surprising knack for handling people. Not far away, Chase mingled. He was a charming man and women clearly loved him, but no matter where he was, she could always feel him watching her. As if he had eyes in the back of his head.

"Peggy is over there. I'm going to see what she has to say. I won't be long."

Jonah nodded. He was drinking a scotch rocks. So far the volume in the glass had barely gone down. He was staying alert just in case.

She made her way up to Peggy Watt. "Got a minute?"

"Sure." The little blonde glanced around. "Everything seems to be running smoothly."

"Yes. Mark's campaign is definitely moving in the right direction—which got me to thinking. Maybe I should go along with the results of the police investigation. It would certainly be a benefit to Mark."

"Yes, it would."

"If I do, it seems to me he should compensate me for the trauma I've suffered. After all, David was his campaign manager."

Peggy looked intrigued. "You're saying money would convince you to let the matter go?"

"That's right. I'd have to know by noon tomorrow."

Peggy sipped her drink. "Maybe there's a way it could work."

Interesting. April spotted Jonah in the crowd. "I'd better go before my date gets bored."

Peggy's pale eyebrows arched up. "I don't think you have to worry about that. I saw him when you walked in." She winked. "Yummy." Peggy took off, and April returned to Jonah.

"This isn't going to work."

"Why not?"

"Because Collin and Peggy both think blackmailing Mark into paying me is a good idea. I have a hunch if I ask Mark, he won't hesitate to find the money to keep me quiet, either."

"What about Brad Schweitzer?"

"He's over there. Cocktail hour is almost over. I'll go talk to him."

She headed in that direction, felt a little better when Brad became indignant at her suggestion.

"I can't believe you'd be willing to lie about something like that. You don't even remember what happened. You realize that's blackmail."

"I don't see it that way."

"If David was murdered, his real killer needs to be brought to justice."

She gave him a smile. "I think you're right, Brad."

"You do?"

"Yes, I do. Moment of weakness. Have a good night."

As she headed toward Jonah, Brad's assessing gaze followed her. She wondered what he was thinking.

"How'd it go?" Jonah asked.

"He wasn't happy with me. He isn't sure David drugged me and he wants the real murderer found."

"So we're left with Collin and Peggy."

"I can talk to Mark but I don't think he'll balk at whatever figure I come up with." She sighed. "I can't believe people can be so low. Don't they care about getting justice for David?"

"Not enough, apparently. Since they don't seem to care, maybe you shouldn't either."

"Unfortunately, my conscience doesn't work that way." She glanced around. They were calling everyone in to dinner.

As she took Jonah's arm, she couldn't help noticing the glances he was receiving from the women. She told herself it was a warning she needed to heed. Instead she walked beside him to their table, her heart beating a little faster than it usually did.

As the campaign speeches started, she caught a glimpse of Chase sitting next to a beautiful blonde not far away. Collin sat next to Peggy, and April wondered if they were discussing her proposal.

They were both attractive people. She wondered if they could be having an affair. If they were, they kept it under wraps. She noticed Collin excusing himself and heading out of the ballroom toward the men's room, but he wasn't gone long.

The speeches droned on. Or maybe it was just that she had heard them so many times. Her eyelids felt heavy by the time Jonah helped her up from her chair an hour later.

"Thank God it's over," she said, stifling a yawn.

"Come on. I'll tell Chase we're leaving."

They were going home. As a condition of setting the trap, Jonah would be going with her.

It occurred to April that the most dangerous thing that was likely to happen to her was Jonah spending the night in her living room.

CHAPTER NINE

Jonah texted Chase and Reggie, letting them know he and April were on their way out of the ballroom. The limo was waiting when they arrived out front, Reggie holding open the rear door.

"No problems?" the big man asked.

"Not so far." Jonah settled April inside the plush interior and Reggie slid in behind the wheel. He cranked the engine, put the car in gear and pulled into the street.

He was rolling through an intersection three blocks away when an old black SUV shot out of nowhere, roaring up beside them. Bullets smashed into the passenger window on April's side of the car. Glass flew and April screamed.

"Get down!" Jonah shoved her down on the floor, jerked out his weapon and started firing out through the broken window. "Hang on!" he shouted as Reggie punched down on the gas and raced ahead of the SUV, jerking the vehicle from side to side to throw off the shooter's aim.

Two more bullets smashed through the rear window, shards of glass flying. Jonah returned fire, shooting out the front windshield of the black SUV bearing down on them.

April made a sound in her throat, but she was smart enough to stay out of the line of fire. Halfway down the block, Reggie cranked the wheel, sending the limo into a sidespin. He straightened the wheel, steering out of the slide, and the car barreled into an alley.

The black SUV made the turn, but lost precious time. The limo rolled through the alley like a cannonball and out the other side, took a sharp turn and shot down the street.

A silver Mercedes 550S coupe raced up beside them, Chase behind the wheel. He cut in behind the limo, putting the Mercedes in front of the SUV. Chase leaned out and fired off a couple of rounds, shooting out one of the SUV's tires.

The pursuing car hit the brakes, swerved then hit the gas, racing forward once more, but the vehicle was losing ground. Reggie drove through a parking garage and came out the entrance on the opposite side.

Jonah lost sight of Chase and the black SUV, but Reggie kept making defensive moves, blowing through a red light, then a yellow, making one turn after another. Finally, the SUV was gone.

April eased back up into the seat. She was trembling. Jonah ignored the urge to pull her against him, let her know she was safe.

"What...what about Chase?" she asked. "Do you think he's all right?"

Jonah holstered his Glock. "He only has himself to worry about. He'll be fine." Proof of that came in a text message a few seconds later.

OK here. Bad guys got away.

Jonah texted back. Going off the grid. Talk tomorrow.

10-4

What he had in mind was safer than returning to April's apartment where would-be assassins might be waiting.

"You need to take the battery out of your phone. We don't know what level of sophistication we're dealing with. We don't want them tracking you."

She pulled her phone out of her purse with a shaky hand and took out the battery. Jonah did the same.

He spoke to Reggie. "Head for my house." He rattled off the address. "I need to get my car."

"On my way."

April leaned back against the seat. In the soft interior lighting inside the limo, her face looked pale. "Well... I guess you could say our trap worked," she said.

"Yeah, I guess you could say that." But the last thing he wanted was for April to be in more danger.

"At least we know how far whoever is involved is willing to go to keep their secret."

Jonah sliced her a glance. "That's right. They've stopped playing games. You threatened them. You know the whole rape/self-defense story was a ruse and that makes you dangerous. They figure they're better off taking you out and dealing with the consequences later."

"There were two people in the SUV. Who were they? Where do you find someone you can hire to kill someone?"

"These guys aren't pros. If they were, you'd be dead. They're scumbags willing to do just about anything for money. They're not that hard to find if you know where to look."

Her eyes found his, big and blue and worried. "What are we going to do?"

"We're going to figure a way to keep you alive while we find out exactly why David Dean was killed, exactly who was behind the murder, and get the evidence we need to prove it."

Jonah lived in a decent apartment on Belmont Street. As a PI, he made good money, but living alone, he didn't need fancy.

He checked the area to make sure the place wasn't being watched, then went inside to strip off his tux and grab his go bag while April waited in the limo with Reggie.

Just to be safe, he checked the Land Rover for any sort of explosives, retrieved it from the single-car garage that came with the apartment, drove around and pulled up next to the limo.

"Thanks for the help," he said to Reggie as he assisted April into the Rover. "You really came through out there."

"Not a problem. You got my number. Let me know if you need me."

"Will do." Jonah surveyed the area again, saw no sign of anyone, but still took precautions to make sure he wasn't being tailed.

"I have to go by my house," April said as he drove out of the neighborhood. "I need something to wear besides a long formal gown."

"Not a good idea. There's a Walmart near where we're headed. I'll get you something there."

"Where are we going?"

"I keep a safe house, share it with a couple of guys from my office. One of us runs into trouble, he's got a safe place to go."

He made his way up onto I-30 and headed east out of town. In Rockwall, he pulled into a Super Walmart, found a space in the lot and turned off the engine.

Since the gun he'd loaned April was still at her house, he raised his pant leg, pulled his ankle gun—a lightweight .38 snub-nose revolver—and handed it over. "I'll be right back."

"You think I'll need this?"

"No. Nobody followed us." His mouth edged up. "The gun's just to make you feel better."

April relaxed, smiled slightly. She rattled off her clothes sizes but he didn't really need them for the generic jeans and T-shirts he meant to buy her. Her shoe size would be a help.

He took off at a lope across the parking lot, dashed through the women's department, grabbed what he needed, found her a pair of sneakers, and returned to the car with an armload of merchandise. He handed April the bag as he slid into the driver's seat.

"I'd rather you kept this." She handed him back the pistol, which he returned to his ankle holster.

He didn't have to be a shrink to know what was going on. April hadn't killed Dean, but she felt responsible.

Finding yourself in bed with a dead guy had a way of messing with your head.

"Jeans and T-shirts," he said as she started prowling through the plastic bag. He drove back onto the highway. "There's also a pair of sneakers."

April began pulling clothes out of the bag. She cast him a sideways glance. "How much of a gentleman are you?"

Just thinking about the sexy redhead stripping off her clothes sent a shot of lust straight through him.

His gaze slid to hers. "Depends on my motivation. I'd prefer you in nothing at all, but I'm trying to keep you alive. Which means I can't afford to drive distracted, and you, lady, are a major distraction."

Her cheeks warmed and a soft sound slipped from her throat. She turned away and he heard her zipper buzzing down. She peeled out of the evening dress and slipped the yellow T-shirt on over her head.

Jonah caught a glimpse of smooth bare skin and realized how little she must have had on under the gown. No bra for sure. Probably just a pair of thong panties.

His mouth went dry. "We can go back to the store tomorrow if you need something else."

"I'll be fine."

Fine she most definitely was.

He drove another three miles, heading into a rural area, pulling down a single-lane road, then a long dirt driveway, up to a small, white wood-framed farmhouse.

"Home sweet home." Shoving the car into Park, he turned off the engine. "Let me check the place out before we go in. I'll be right back."

He exited the Rover, pulled his Glock, climbed the front steps to a screened-in porch and went inside.

When he came back out, April joined him at the bottom of the stairs and they went into the house.

The place was simple but clean, a bedroom and bath, a living room furnished with a basic brown tweed sofa and chair, and an eat-in kitchen. There was a fireplace with an insert for heat but he'd never used it. He hadn't been there in the winter and this time of year it was way too hot.

He turned on the air-conditioning, the single modern convenience, and cold air began to circulate through the rooms.

"You must be exhausted," he said. "There's a queen-size bed in the bedroom. I'll sleep out here on the sofa."

She looked at him with those big blue eyes and his blood heated. April walked over to where he stood, leaned up and gave him a soft kiss on the lips. "Thank you for being there tonight."

"Just doing my—"

She pressed a finger over his mouth to stop the words. "Don't say it. Let me believe it was more than that." She started to walk away, but Jonah caught her arm.

"It is more than that, April." Then he broke his cardinal rule—never get involved with a client—hauled her into his arms, slid his hands into her heavy red hair and very thoroughly kissed her.

It's only a kiss, April told herself. They both knew it couldn't go any further. She was a client. He was her hired detective. Men were out to kill her and Jonah was there to find and stop them.

But as his mouth moved hotly over hers, as she felt the rush of heat and the streak of longing, she opened to him, inviting him in. Hard bands of muscle pressed into her unfettered breasts and hot need burned through her. Liquid heat slid into the place between her legs and her nipples peaked beneath the T-shirt.

Jonah's big hands cupped the back of her head, holding her in place as he ravaged her mouth, and she molded her body full-length against his. She could feel his erection, thick and hard, feel his hunger.

"We can't do this," he whispered between scorching kisses, but he didn't stop, just kept kissing her, first one way and then another.

"We're safe here," she pointed out. "No one knows about this place."

Jonah kissed the side of her neck. "No," he softly conceded. "No one knows." For a moment she was sure he would stop. Instead, he pulled the T-shirt off over her head and his dark gaze roamed over her, the hunger in his eyes making her tremble.

"Beautiful," he said, cupping a plump breast, scraping his fingertip across her stiff nipple. Lowering his head, he took the fullness into his mouth and her knees went weak.

"Jonah…"

Hot, wet kisses trailed over her throat and shoulders. "I want you so damn much." He took her mouth again, tasting and sampling, his tongue sliding over hers, making her burn.

"Tell me to stop," he said. "Remind me who you are and why this can't happen."

She slid her fingers into the silky black hair curling at the nape of his neck and leaned into him. "I don't want you to stop. We don't know what might happen tomorrow. We both want this. We deserve tonight."

He groaned low in his throat. April dragged his black

T-shirt off over his head and took a moment to admire his hard, perfectly sculpted body, the muscles across his chest and the ladder of muscle down his stomach.

She pressed her mouth against a flat copper nipple and Jonah hissed in a breath. When April leaned up and kissed him, Jonah allowed her a moment of control before he took over, deepening the kiss, turning it hotter and even more fierce.

Scooping her into his arms, he carried her down the hall into the bedroom and set her on her feet beside the bed. It didn't take long before both of them were naked, Jonah's heavy weight pressing her down on the mattress.

He kissed her, long and deep. "You sure about this?"

Was she sure? Not at all. She wondered if she should stop before it was too late for her heart. But she wanted this, couldn't remember ever wanting a man the way she wanted Jonah. She wasn't sure she would ever feel this way again.

"Very sure," she said.

Jonah started kissing her and this time he didn't stop. She was moaning his name, arching beneath him, when he tore open a condom and sheathed himself, kissed her again and drove himself deep inside. Pleasure, sweet and sharp, burned through her and she couldn't stop a moan.

Jonah kissed the side of her neck. "I won't let anyone hurt you," he said softly.

Her throat tightened and her eyes stung. "I know." She trusted Jonah to keep her safe. He was sure to break her heart, but she had a feeling it was already too late to avoid it.

Seating himself even more deeply, he started to move, slowly at first, drawing out the moment, the incredible sensations, then faster, deeper, harder, exactly the way she wanted him to. She wrapped herself around him and felt the wildness pouring through her, felt the building heat. She had never been so hot, so needy.

She dug her fingers into his powerful shoulders and cried his name as she reached her peak, biting her bottom lip as pleasure washed through her and her body trembled with bliss. Seconds later, Jonah's muscles went rigid as he reached his own release, his fierce need and driving passion sending her over once more.

They lay quiet for a while, letting their heartbeats slow. Jonah kissed her softly one last time, eased away and disappeared into the bathroom to take care of the condom.

She was growing drowsy when he returned, his hard body stretching out on the mattress beside her. Leaning over, he kissed her and April opened to him, deepening the kiss, turning it hotter, wilder, arousing him fully again.

"I knew once wouldn't be enough," he whispered, nibbling an earlobe, then taking her mouth once more.

April's sleepiness was gone.

Once with Jonah Wolfe wasn't enough for her, either.

CHAPTER TEN

The hours slipped past and with them came the cold light of day. Jonah had never been good at morning-afters. He preferred to leave after sex rather than wake up in bed with a woman he barely knew. It was the reason he almost never took a woman home with him.

And yet, when April walked into the tiny kitchen wearing nothing but the T-shirt she'd had on the night before, all he felt was a shot of lust that made him instantly hard, and a fierce urge to protect her.

She cast a glance his way, probably feeling the kind of nerves he usually felt, poured herself a cup of coffee, wandered over and sat down across from him.

"Hi," she said.

His mouth edged up. "That the best you can do?" Leaning across the table, he kissed her. "Good morning."

April relaxed and her lips curved into a smile. "I wasn't sure about…things."

"This wasn't a one-night stand for me, April. I hope it wasn't for you."

Her smile slowly faded. "Last night was wonderful, Jonah, beyond wonderful, but…"

One black eyebrow went up. "But…?"

"I don't have good luck with relationships. I always seem to pick the wrong men."

He leaned back in his chair, stretched his legs out in front of him. "Maybe your luck has finally changed."

"I don't know…maybe."

"You don't trust me? Or men in general?"

"I see the way women look at you. I've been in that situation before."

"I see the way men look at you, April. And I think, if someone cared about me enough, other men wouldn't matter."

"And you'd be right. I've never cheated on a man in my life. I never would."

Since he had no idea where their relationship—or lack of one—was headed, and April clearly wasn't ready to think about it either, he let the subject drop. He got up and refilled his mug, brought the pot over and re-filled her cup.

"Last night was truly spectacular," she said. "But someone still wants to kill me. What are we going to do?"

He sat back down and took a drink of coffee. "The trap we set went sideways, but we can be pretty sure one of the people who you talked to last night called in the hit. Probably Rutherford or Watt. Which means one or both of them were involved in Dean's murder."

"How do we prove it?"

"We find out why he was killed. That should tell us

what makes them desperate enough to want you dead. Once we know that, we'll be able to find the evidence we need to stop them."

"Where do we start?"

"I talked to a friend the day we met at the café, someone who works for Chase. Her name's Tabitha Love."

"Tabitha Love? Seriously?"

His mouth edged into a smile. "I called Tabby earlier this morning. Looks like she's got something for me."

"Did she say what it was?"

"I'll find out when I get there." He set his mug down on the table. "There's a catch to this, April. The kind of stuff Tabby digs up falls into a gray area. She doesn't tell us how she gets her info and we don't ask. Can you live with that?"

April's pretty mouth thinned. "These people are trying to kill me, Jonah. I'll do whatever it takes to protect myself."

He relaxed back in his chair. The lady had grit. He had seen it from the start and admired her for it. "I was hoping you'd say something like that. Since I don't want to leave you here, you're coming with me."

April flashed him a smile, apparently glad to be taking some sort of action. She rose from the table. "I need to finish getting dressed."

Jonah's gaze went to her soft breasts beneath the cotton T-shirt and the long, shapely legs showing beneath the hem. An image flashed in his head of sliding up her T-shirt, bending her over the table and easing the lust he'd felt since she walked into the kitchen.

"If I had my way," he said, "I'd haul you straight back to bed, but unfortunately, we're expected."

A pink blush crept into her face, but there was interest in those big blue eyes.

Jonah forced himself to think of murder, which always cooled his ardor. "As soon as you're dressed, we'll go."

April drained her mug and headed for the bedroom. She came out a few minutes later in her Walmart jeans and sneakers, holding the little silver clutch she'd had with her at the fund-raiser last night.

It didn't take long to reach Tabby's house. Jonah parked in front and the two of them walked up the concrete path to the door.

Jonah rang the bell and waited. It took a couple more tries before the door finally swung wide and Tabby stood in the opening.

"Hey, Wolfe. Good to see you." Her straight black hair and the Maltese cross hanging around her slender neck gleamed in the sunlight. "Come on in."

They walked into the living room. "Tabby, this is April Vale. April, meet Tabby Love."

April smiled. "Hi, Tabby."

"Hi, April. Nice to meet you. Jonah told me about the murder. The news said it was self-defense."

"That's what the police are saying. But David didn't try to rape me and I didn't kill him."

Jonah began filling Tabby in on recent events, including the blackmail trap they had laid at the fund-raiser last night.

"Unfortunately, it worked a little too well. A couple of thugs in a black SUV shot up the limo as we were leaving the hotel. Reggie Porter was driving or one of us might have ended up dead."

"You think someone called them from the party?"

"That would be a good guess."

"Well then, you'll be happy to know I found your motive—the reason David Dean was killed. Come on, I'll show you." Tabby led them down the hall into her crowded bedroom/office and sat down in front of a row of computers and high-tech monitors. A dozen lights of various colors and sizes blinked around the room.

Tabby worked the keyboard and a series of columns popped up on one of the screens.

"What are we looking at?" Jonah asked.

"Bank account transactions."

Jonah wasn't surprised. "Follow the money. Always a good place to start." He'd wanted Tabby to keep an open mind, take a look from every possible angle, but it usually came down to money, sex or revenge.

Tabitha tipped her head toward the monitor. "That's a Cayman Island offshore account. It's in the name of Action Advertising." She tapped the screen with a dark red fingernail. "The deposits came from an account at the Alamo Bank in Houston."

"I'm trying to connect the dots," April said, frowning. "Is Action Advertising somehow involved in the mayor's campaign?"

"Oh, yeah," Tabby said. "It's involved, all right."

"I'm the mayor's marketing manager. I work with a lot of advertising firms, but I've never heard of Action. Of course they could be doing work for the social media people or something."

Tabby looked up from her chair in front of the keyboard, the silver studs in her nose and eyebrows glowing in the light of the computer screen. "You've never heard of Action, because it doesn't actually exist. The account is owned by Collin Rutherford."

Jonah could almost see April's mind working. "Collin's in charge of fund-raising," she said, putting the pieces together. "A huge amount of money passes through the account into the campaign treasury. If he's writing checks to himself—"

"How much money are we talking about?" Jonah asked.

"To date, four hundred forty thousand dollars."

"That bastard!" April's eyes blazed and her cheeks turned red.

"How much is the mayor's reelection budget?" Jonah asked.

"Six million dollars. Mark's raised almost five million so far."

"Of which, good ol' Collin has siphoned off nearly half a mil."

"David must have somehow found out what Collin was doing," April said. "Collin murdered him to keep him quiet, and set me up to take the blame."

"Damn near worked, too," Jonah said. "Would have if it weren't for your stubborn sense of justice." The admiration he felt for her kept growing. He had never met a woman like April Vale. Probably never would again. As a man who went out of his way to avoid entanglements, it was a disturbing thought.

"Collin was at the Derby the night you were drugged," Jonah said. "According to you, he left early. Probably waited for you out in the parking lot. The problem is, the setup required two people."

April nodded. "One to drive my car with David and me passed out inside. One to help him unload us, stage the murder, and drive him away from the crime scene."

"Collin's a good-looking man and Peggy's a widow,"

Jonah said. "Peggy was also at the Derby the night of the murder. Rutherford and Watt both believe paying you blackmail money to get you to take the blame is a good idea. I'd put my money on Peggy Watt as the second player."

"Me, too," April said.

Jonah looked over at the bone-thin girl with the short black buzz cut. There was a new tattoo—a rose with thorns—on the top of her arm. "Good work, Tab."

"Thanks." She walked them back out to the living room.

"You know where to send the bill."

Tabitha smiled. "Always a pleasure doing business with you, Wolfe." She opened the front door. "Nice meeting you, April. Good luck."

"Thanks."

Jonah walked April out to the Rover. They climbed inside and strapped themselves into their seats.

April shot him a look. "That was amazing, but I'm guessing it isn't information we can actually take to the police."

"'Fraid not." He started the engine.

"So how do we prove it?"

Jonah could almost smell the scent of his soon-to-be cornered prey. "I think it's time we talked to Mayor Rydell."

CHAPTER ELEVEN

April put the battery back in her cell phone and called Marge Lamb, the mayor's personal assistant. The mayor of Dallas was an extremely busy man, usually hard at work in his downtown City Hall office.

Luck was on their side. Today he was working on his election strategy at his campaign headquarters. April told Marge it was urgent she speak to him, and asked her to set up a meeting.

"He's got appointments all afternoon, love, but if it's really that important, I'll find a way to fit you in. How soon can you be here?"

"I'm en route. I can be there in twenty minutes."

"All right. You might have to wait a bit, but I'll make it happen."

With Jonah behind the wheel, they arrived a little early. It was work as usual when April walked into the office, a swarm of activity that would go on until the election was over.

As she crossed the room in front of Jonah, she glanced around in search of Peggy Watt but didn't see her. Interesting that Collin Rutherford didn't seem to be there, either.

In her loose jeans, T-shirt and sneakers instead of her usual suit and heels, she caught several speculative glances from fellow employees. Jonah caught the eye of half the women working the phones, but April pretended not to notice.

She headed straight for the mayor's office at the rear of the building. Marge sat at her desk out front, snacking on a cream cheese bagel.

"Marge, this is Jonah Wolfe. As I said on the phone, we have some very important information we need to discuss with the mayor."

"I talked to him. I told him you said it was urgent and he told me to send you in as soon as you arrived."

"Thanks, Marge. You're the best."

Jonah opened the door and April walked into the room in front of him. Mark stood up as Jonah closed the door.

"You're Wolfe," the mayor said, surprising her. "I remember meeting you. You're a private investigator. We met through Chase Garrett. He recommended you to a friend of mine."

"That's right."

Mark walked over and extended a hand, and the men shook. "Why don't you two have a seat and tell me what this is about."

April sat down on a chair next to Jonah on the opposite side of the mayor's big oak desk.

"I might as well get right to the point," Jonah said. "We've come across reliable information that one of your employees is embezzling—siphoning campaign finances into his personal account."

Mark's features tightened. He never liked to hear bad news. "That's ridiculous. My people are all extremely loyal. I don't believe it."

"We think David found out what was going on," April explained. "He was murdered to keep him from going to you or the police."

The mayor leaned back in his chair. "I find that hard to believe. Are you sure?"

"As sure as we can be without looking deeper," Jonah said. "To do that we'll need your help."

"Who are you suggesting took the money?" Mark asked.

"Collin Rutherford."

The color drained from the mayor's face.

Rydell braced his hands on the table. "Let me get this straight. You're saying Collin Rutherford murdered David Dean."

"Him or someone he hired," Jonah said. "It looks like there was at least one other person involved."

"These are wild accusations, Mr. Wolfe. Do you have any proof?"

"Not that I can provide at this time. But you have the means of getting all the proof you need. All you have to do is audit Rutherford's fund-raising account. Look for expenditures to a company called Action Advertising."

"Action Advertising. I don't think I've heard of it."

"Because it doesn't exist," April said.

For several moments, the mayor just sat there. "Exactly how certain of this are you?"

"I'm a private investigator," Jonah said. "My sources

are confidential and extremely reliable. In this case, I believe what we've uncovered is the truth."

Mark exhaled a deep breath. Clearly he was beginning to believe there might be some truth to the story. "How much money is involved?"

April shifted forward in her chair. "It's nearly half a million dollars, Mark."

The color rushed back into the mayor's face, staining his cheeks an angry red. "Half a million dollars! Good lord! You may be sure I'll get to the bottom of this—and soon."

"In the meantime," Jonah said, "I'd like you to invite Collin Rutherford into your office. I'd like to hear what he has to say when he's confronted."

The mayor's bodyguards stood just outside the office door. Inside the room, Jonah's Glock rested in the shoulder holster beneath his lightweight leather jacket. April sat next to him on the sofa against the wall. Wishing she would wait outside, Jonah swore a silent curse. There was always a chance of trouble when you confronted a killer. That said, leaving her out of this wasn't going to happen. Not after what Rutherford had put her through. She wanted to be there when the shit came down and Jonah didn't blame her.

The mayor was seated at his desk when Rutherford walked unsuspectingly into the office. Nattily dressed in a linen sport coat and slacks, he jerked to a halt just inside the door, his gaze swinging from Rydell to Jonah and April.

"What's going on, Mark?"

"Close the door, Collin."

He did so slowly, as if he needed every second to

prepare for what might lay ahead. Jonah knew people. From the moment he had met Collin Rutherford at the fund-raiser, he had known Collin would be the weak link if he was involved in the murder scheme.

"The man next to April is Jonah Wolfe. He's a private detective."

"We've met," Collin said. "What's this about, Mark?"

Jonah lounged against the back of the sofa. "It's about the money you stole from the mayor's campaign fund, Collin. It's about killing David Dean to cover it up."

Rutherford blanched. "I don't...don't know what you're talking about."

Jonah rose from the sofa. "I'm pretty sure you do. Does the name Action Advertising mean anything to you?"

When Rutherford didn't answer, April stood up, too. "How about the Alamo Bank in Houston?"

Rutherford swallowed and started shaking, his eyes darting back and forth between Jonah, April and the mayor—the instant before he bolted.

He was out the door and racing through the office at breakneck speed, shoving people out of the way, knocking over chairs, stumbling, righting himself, determined to reach the glass front door and escape.

Jonah tackled him just before he got there, the two of them crashing into a table, sending campaign brochures flying. Jonah swung a punch that sent Rutherford careening backward, sprawling on the floor.

Grabbing the front of Rutherford's shirt, Jonah hauled him to his feet and hit him again, snapping his head back, a blossom of blood appearing at the corner of his mouth. He groaned as he teetered back and forth, still standing. The fight had gone out of him, and his brief struggle was over.

The mayor's two bodyguards ran up and dragged Collin's hands behind his back, slid on a plastic cable tie and cinched it tight, slamming him down on a chair.

"Cops are on the way," one of them said.

"You'd be smart to cooperate," Jonah said. "It'll go easier on you. That includes giving the police the names of the other people involved in David Dean's murder."

Collin whimpered and started crying, fat tears rolling down his cheeks.

April ran up beside him, took in Jonah's skinned knuckles and the pulse thrumming in the side of his neck. "Are you okay?"

Jonah drew her against him, an arm around her waist. "I'm good. We're almost there, baby."

She looked up at him but didn't pull away. "You think he'll tell them the truth about what happened?"

"Rydell is going to call for an audit and it's going to prove Rutherford embezzled funds. He knows that. He also knows the longer he waits to come clean, the worse it's going to be. Rutherford's going to roll over on whoever helped him and he's going to do it soon."

The police arrived within minutes. The call had come from the mayor of Dallas, after all. Rutherford was settled in the back of a patrol car and hauled off to the police station with twenty people in the office watching.

Jonah wondered how long it would take him to incriminate Peggy Watt.

CHAPTER TWELVE

You had to be smart to be a good private detective. That didn't mean you were always right. It took less than twenty-four hours for Collin Rutherford to confess to embezzling money from Mayor Rydell's reelection campaign fund.

The surprise came when he copped to the murder, but refused to give the name of whoever helped him. If there actually was one.

"I did it," Rutherford said. "No one else was involved. I made sure I didn't leave any DNA or fingerprints in the car or anywhere else. I muffled the shot with a pillow then walked back to Jacobsen Street. I tossed the pillow into a dumpster and hailed a cab to take me home. No one else was involved but me."

"What about the men who tried to kill Ms. Vale?" one of the detectives asked. "Two attempts were made on her life. We need their names."

"I found them in a bar in Old East Dallas." It was

one of the meanest areas in town. "I paid them cash. I don't know their names."

No amount of questioning was able to shake him.

Hell, maybe he was telling the truth.

The good news was, the threat to April's life was over. With the embezzlement and murder out in the open, there was no reason to kill her. At best, it had been a last-ditch, desperate effort to keep her from pushing the investigation, and it had failed.

April was back in her town house and Jonah was back in his apartment. He missed her. He hadn't expected his feelings could grow so strong so fast. He wanted to see her. The bad news was, she hadn't returned any of his phone calls.

You win some, you lose some, he'd learned.

Recently, he'd learned he really hated losing April Vale.

April replayed Jonah's latest phone message for the third time that night. "I want to see you, April. I don't want us to be over. If you don't call me back, I'm coming to your house. One way or another, we're going to talk."

The message ended and April felt the same hollow ache in the pit of her stomach she'd felt the first time he had phoned. She had convinced herself to play it safe, stay away from Jonah.

But she didn't want to. Being with him felt right. He made her hungry for life, hungry to experience the feelings he stirred, see where the future might lead. He made her start thinking it might be worth taking a risk on another man.

She had just picked up her cell phone to return his

call—at least listen to what he had to say—when an odd sound came from the kitchen.

April frowned. Had she locked the back door? She usually did, but not always. Her little .380 was evidence in a homicide, so it was still in police custody. She had returned Jonah's pistol. When the sound came again, she wished she'd kept it.

She still held her phone in her hand. She brought up 9-1-1 in her contacts and carried the phone into the kitchen, her finger on the Call button just in case. She'd only taken a couple of steps into the room when a man's thick arm locked around her neck, sending fear sliding through her and freezing her in place. He knocked the phone from her hand and it landed with a clatter on the floor.

She managed to drag in a lungful of air, but it was hard to breathe. She tried to pry the man's arm loose, tried to scream, but only a muffled cry escaped. She couldn't see him behind her, but when he spoke, she recognized the voice.

"Do you have any idea how much trouble you've caused?"

Confusion slipped through her, followed by a shot of anger. Brad Schweitzer. What the hell?

She tugged on the arm that held her immobile and it loosened enough for her to catch her breath. "What do you think you're doing? Let go of me, Brad."

He released his hold and spun her around to face him. Her heart jerked at the sight of the big semiautomatic pistol he pointed at the center of her chest. April fought not to cringe at the look of hatred on Brad's handsome face.

"You managed to put Collin in jail for murder," he

said. "But all he did was steal a little money. He never would have had the guts to kill David."

Her pulse was throbbing, her heart thumping wildly. "You did it? You were the one who killed him?"

"That's right. Collin means everything to me. He's the only person who ever gave a damn about me. And you destroyed him. You destroyed both of us."

Her mind was spinning, trying to connect the dots and at the same time figure out a way to get control of the gun.

"So you and Collin...you're together? Not Collin and Peggy?"

He grunted. "People are so easy to dupe. 'If David was murdered, his real killer needs to be brought to justice,'" he mimicked, repeating the words he had said at the fund-raiser. "What a load of drivel. Collin always had a weakness for the finer things. I didn't know he was stealing until it was too late. When David found out, I knew it was him or Collin. I chose Collin."

She stared at the gun and tried to stay calm. "Why did you come here, Brad? Collin confessed to the murder. He told the police he did it alone. You were safe."

"Thanks to you, he'll be in jail for years and I'll be alone. I want you to pay for what you've done." He lifted the pistol, pointed it at her head. It was now or never.

When a noise outside drew Brad's attention for an instant, April sprang forward, knocking his hand into the air, the pistol discharging with a roar, the bullet smashing through the window above the kitchen sink. The blast echoed in her ears as she and Brad crashed to the floor.

April gripped his wrist with both hands and fought for control of the weapon, but he was bigger and stronger and she could feel him gaining the edge. She gritted her teeth and held on with all of her strength, but he was winning, forcing the gun around, pushing the barrel toward her heart. She had seconds to live.

She clamped down on her fear and continued to fight, heard the back door crashing open and saw Jonah rushing into the kitchen. He grabbed Brad by the back of the neck and jerked him off of her, kicked the weapon out of his hand with a big black motorcycle boot, and smashed a fist into Brad's handsome face.

Brad went down hard, blood spurting from his nose and mouth. He managed to roll to his feet, lowered his head and charged, his shoulder hitting Jonah in the stomach, carrying him backward into the refrigerator. Jonah jerked him up and threw a punch that sent Brad flying. He slid down the wall, slumped on the kitchen floor, and his eyes rolled back in his head. Unconscious, he didn't get up.

April's heart hammered as Jonah knelt beside him. Turning him onto his stomach, Jonah cuffed Brad's hands behind his back with a plastic cable tie Jonah took out of his jeans pocket. Brad groaned but didn't move.

Rising, Jonah strode the distance between them and pulled her into his arms. "You okay?"

She clutched his shoulders and managed to nod.

"You scared me to death," he said, burying his face in her hair. "I heard the gunshot. As I ran around back, I saw him through the window." A shudder ran through his tall frame. "I was afraid I'd be too late."

April clung to him, fighting to hold back tears.

His hold subtly tightened. "It's okay, baby. Everything's going to be all right." Pulling out his cell, he dialed 9-1-1 and gave the dispatcher the address of the town house.

April couldn't stop trembling. She felt like crying, but swallowed her tears instead. She looked up at Jonah. "It was Brad, not Collin. Collin is a thief but not a killer. Brad murdered David to protect him."

Jonah nodded but didn't let go. Police sirens wailed in the distance. Jonah kissed her softly on the lips. "I've missed you, baby. I can't tell you how much."

"I've missed you, too, Jonah. So much."

He caught her chin and tipped it up, forcing her to look into his face. "I've never cheated on a woman I was involved with. I wouldn't cheat on you, April. Give me a chance to prove it."

She looked at him and a tear rolled down her cheek. "I want to be with you, Jonah. I'm miserable without you."

"Yeah, baby. Me, too." Jonah wiped away a drop of wetness with the edge of his thumb, then he leaned down and very softly kissed her.

With Jonah's solid frame around her, protecting her, everything inside her seemed to settle and fall into place. They were right together. She should have seen it before.

Instead of being afraid she was making the wrong decision, April had never felt so safe.

* * * * *

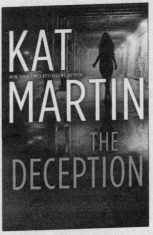